P9-DHK-730

The Treasure
of the
Celtic Triangle

MICHAEL PHILLIPS

Print ISBN 978-1-61626-586-1 (Paperback)
Print ISBN 978-1-61626-715-5 (Hardback)

eBook Editions:
Adobe Digital Edition (.epub) 978-1-60742-041-5
Kindle and MobiPocket Edition (.prc) 978-1-60742-031-6

This book is a work of fiction. Names, characters, places, and incidents are either products of the author's imagination or used fictitiously. Any similarity to actual people, organizations, and/or events is purely coincidental.

Cover photography by Brandon Hill Photos

Published by Barbour Publishing, Inc., P.O. Box 719, Uhrichsville, Ohio 44683, www.barbourbooks.com

Our mission is to publish and distribute inspirational products offering exceptional value and biblical encouragement to the masses.

ecpa Member of the Evangelical Christian Publishers Association

Printed in the United States of America.

Dedication

To the memory and legacy of
George MacDonald,
whose books and characters and spiritual vision still contain a power
undiminished by the passage of more than a century to inspire hearts,
change lives, and fill the soul with the wonders
of God's expansive fatherhood.

[My purpose in my novels is] to make them true to the real and not the spoilt humanity. Why should I spend my labor on what one can have too much of without any labor! I will try to show what we might be, may be, must be, shall be—and something of the struggle to gain it.

—George MacDonald, in a letter to William Mount-Temple,
January 23, 1879, The National Library of Scotland

A little attention. . .to the nature of the human mind evinces that the entertainments of fiction are useful as well as pleasant. That they are pleasant when well written, every person feels who reads. But wherein is its utility, asks the reverend sage, big with the notion that nothing can be useful but the learned lumber of Greek and Roman reading with which his head is stored? I answer, everything is useful which contributes to fix us in the principles and practice of virtue. When any single act of charity or of gratitude, for instance, is presented either to our sight or imagination, we are deeply impressed with its beauty and feel a strong desire in ourselves of doing charitable and grateful acts also.

—Thomas Jefferson, in a letter to Robert Skipwith,
August 3, 1771, explaining his inclusion of works of fiction
in a list of books compiled for purchase from England
after his library of books and papers was destroyed by fire

The Region of Gwynedd, North Wales
at the Northern Expanse of the Cambrian Mountains

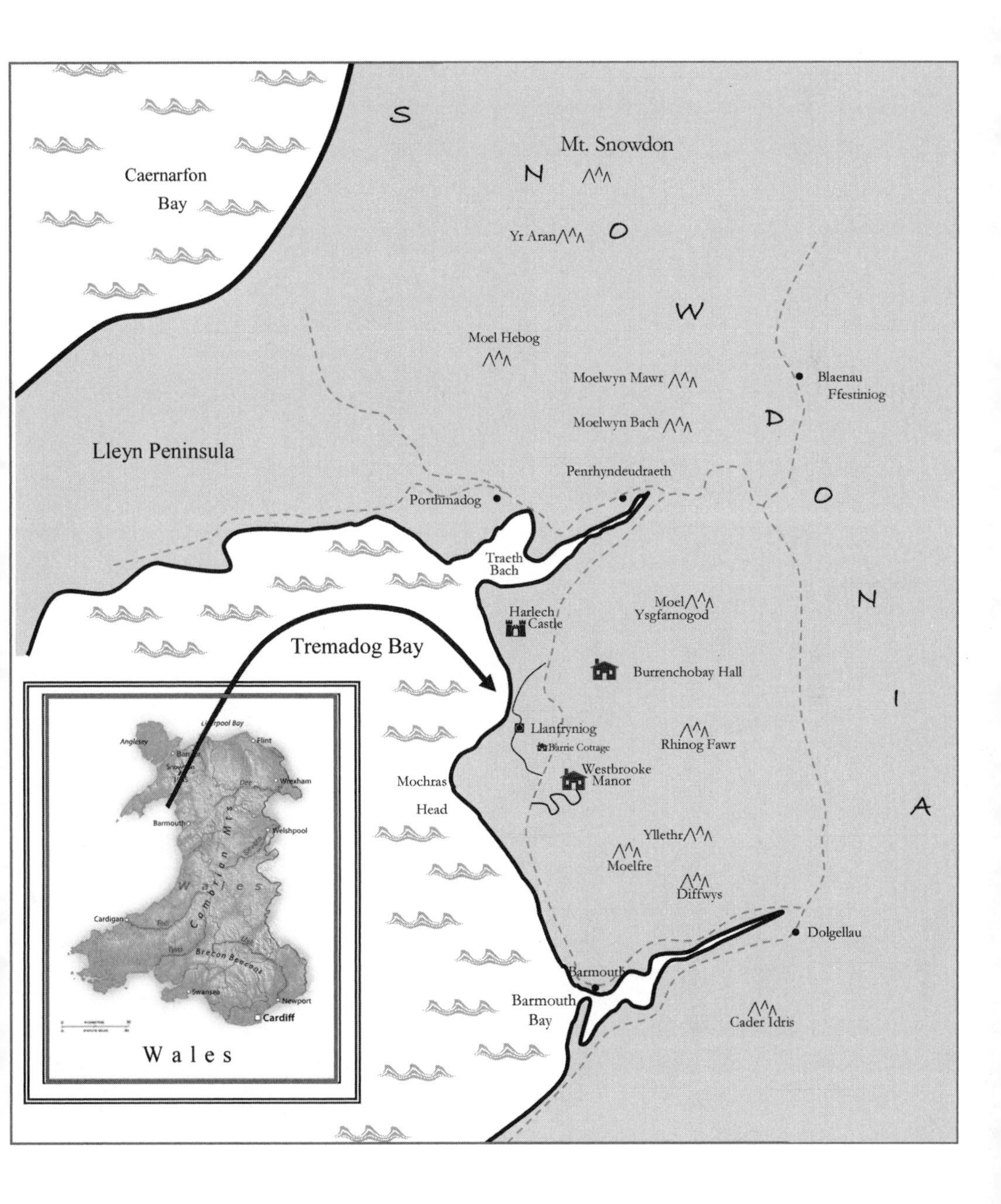

Part One

Changes at Westbrooke Manor

Late 1872

One

Factor and Heir

A clock of ancient date overlooking a stone-paved stable yard—originally rimmed with gold, fitted with brass ornamentation and shiny black hands, all now tarnished with the passage not merely of its circling minutes and hours but of centuries—had just struck the hour of one o'clock.

It was a chilly day in the second week of October. The sun was bravely doing its best to counter the effects of a biting wind blowing down through the Celtic triangle onto the coast of north Wales. Alas, it rose a little lower in the sky every day. Thus, with every successive revolution of the earth into darkness and back again into its light, the great glowing orb had less warmth to shed abroad in the land. Those offshore winds pierced to the bone. They originated far to the north in regions where glaciers and icebergs made their homes, birthplace of the winter, which even now had begun its inexorable yearly march southward into the lands of men.

Whatever happy memories remained of July and August had gone briefly into hiding. The sunlight seemed thin and not altogether up for the task. There would yet appear more exquisite reminders of the splendorous summer recently past. Autumn's delicious warmth and the fragrances of earth's slow, pleasant death into its yearly recreative slumber would return by tomorrow, perhaps the day after. It would hold winter at bay as long as it could.

But as today's chill breeze portended, it would eventually be forced to lay down the struggle and die a peaceful and quiet death. Beneath the ground its life must lie, while winter roared and blustered above, until such time as cousin spring rescued earth's life again from the grave.

A young man of twenty-two, stocky, strong, of medium height, shoulders broad and muscular, with light hair and a chiseled face, skin tough, leathery, and tan from exposure to the weather from the time he could walk emerged from the building. He was leading a gorgeous white stallion of three years, whose coat was gracefully highlighted by a few lines of gray, from its stall and through the back door of the stables. There a flat, grassy area suited his purpose more than the hard stones in front between stables and house. He was used to weather of any kind and laughed at cold and wind and rain. What were they to him when there was a world to enjoy?

The beautiful creature following him had only been wearing the bridle a week. The young man thought him ready for a saddle today. He planned to move slowly, however, and continue to wait if he displayed the slightest resistance.

He was one who knew animals *almost* as well as his diminutive cousin, who had mysteriously disappeared from Snowdonia with her father a year before. *No one* could communicate with the creatures of the animal kingdom like she did. But after a life with sheep in the nearby hills where he had made his home until recently, he found the intuitive connection between man and horse a wonder and joy. In the month since his mistress had purchased this Anglo-Arabian from Padrig Gwlwlwyd in the village, he had been talking to him and walking him daily, allowing the animal to know him and trust him before attempting to ride him.

Within a few weeks of her husband's funeral, Lady Snowdon had asked him to be on the lookout for a horse of equal or greater potential than the one they had recently lost. It would, she explained, be a way to remember her husband and perhaps in some small way mitigate her son's inevitable disappointment at finding the wild black gone. Nor could it be denied that Lady Snowdon herself loved horses no less than the two men of the family. During these recent months of loss, the solitary green hills of Snowdonia had been her frequent solace in companionship with one or another of the mounts in her well-stocked stables.

One look at the Anglo-Arabian and she had fallen in love instantly. There was no haggling about the price. She had settled the financial arrangements, and he was in his new home in the manor's stables the day after that. Surely there would be no lamenting the loss of the black now. Perhaps she would make the Anglo a homecoming gift for her son. . .whenever that might be.

Meanwhile, in spite of the brightness of the day, an autumn chill had begun. Fires had been lit throughout Westbrooke Manor, the proud and ancient house that stood at the center of the estate of the late Viscount Lord Snowdon some two miles inland from Cardigan Bay. Hours later, they were still doing their best to warm the living quarters of Lady Snowdon, Katherine Westbrooke, widowed three and a half months earlier by the sudden death of her husband, and her twenty-year-old daughter, Florilyn.

Lord and Lady Snowdon's eldest son and presumptive heir to title and property, twenty-three-year-old Courtenay, had unexpectedly returned without notice the night before, about dusk, from three months abroad. He had not appeared at breakfast and had made a mere token luncheon, with surprisingly little to say to either mother or sister after so long away.

In truth, his father's death from a riding accident the previous June had shaken Courtenay more than he wanted to admit. He had needed to get away from Wales. And he had done so.

Thinking himself recovered at last and prepared to confidently take up his mantle as the future viscount in his father's stead, he found his homecoming—forced upon him sooner than he had planned—plagued by uncertainty. After spending what money he had, he was confronted with the painful realization that he was not exactly certain how the finances were supposed to work during this awkward interim before the Westbrooke estate became legally his. He was in possession of his own bank account, of course, and had been since the age of sixteen. But where the money came from that appeared in it each month, he didn't know. He had had some vague idea that his father was responsible. He knew furthermore that his father and mother sometimes argued about money. He knew no details other than that his mother was rich and his father was less so. He had never given the matter much thought. The mechanics of finances in marital relationships lay miles outside his ken. As long as he was well provided for, that was all he cared about.

But his resources had dwindled during his sojourn on the continent, an eventuality he had neither anticipated nor made much effort to forestall. Finally the sobering reality began to hit him that his account was running dry and was not being replenished in its customary fashion. This unpleasant fact ultimately left him no alternative but to return home, irritably disposed toward the world in general for this inconvenience to himself. He assumed the matter due to a procedural glitch or legal delay in the affairs of the estate occasioned by his father's death and whatever stipulations superintended the months between now and his twenty-fifth birthday. Gnawing suspicions were at work, however, that made him uneasy.

His first order of business was to see the family lawyer and get his account beefed up. He planned to ride to Porthmadog this afternoon for that very purpose. After that, whether he would return to the continent for another month or two or perhaps spend the winter season in London, always a diverting prospect, he hadn't yet made up his mind.

After lunch, Courtenay wandered outside. He shivered and glanced about. Though not overly fond of riding as a means to interact with nature and the animal kingdom, he was enamored of it as sport. His father's dream of racing the black stallion Demon, possibly with Courtenay himself in the saddle, had remained with him, and even gone to his head. He was at least three stone too heavy to jockey a winning horse even at a backwater racetrack for the most miserly of purses. But he fancied himself an accomplished rider. In fact, his self-assessment was not far wrong. He was probably the fastest rider in Gwynedd.

That Demon had been responsible for his father's death caused him little concern. Courtenay attributed the accident as much to his father's recklessness and his Scottish cousin's presence on that fateful day as he did to the uncontrollable stallion.

But though Courtenay Westbrooke was aware that he must wait until his twenty-fifth birthday to inherit his father's title, he knew nothing of the trusteeship his father had set in motion on his deathbed giving his wife, Katherine, control of the estate for the next eighteen months. Neither was he aware of the retirement of his father's factor, Tilman Heygate, or that in his absence his mother had hired a replacement.

Ever since losing the majority of what remained of his assets two weeks before in a horse race in France, Courtenay had been revolving in his mind how he might put his father's plan into action and quickly raise some badly needed cash for himself in the event the legalities took time to sort out. He would enter Demon in a few races, possibly at Chester. He intended to begin immediately. With a few wins under his belt, and with his father's funds eventually transferred to his account, he would be able to afford to enter larger races and compete for more sizeable purses in some of the major handicap events in England.

He wandered into the old stables, seeing evidence neither of his father's groom, Hollin Radnor, nor of the black stallion whom he fancied to ride into Porthmadog. The place was virtually empty except for the old nags his mother and sister rode. He continued through to the back of the darkened building and toward the new stables where he assumed the powerful black thoroughbred now made its home.

On the grassy flat between the two stables, he saw the young man about his own age leading a graceful, almost elegant beast of white and light gray in a slow, wide circle. He stopped and watched a minute as the trainer now removed a lump of sugar from his pocket and held it toward the horse's big fleshy lips.

At length he approached, prepared to assert the rights of his position, especially over one whom he took for nothing more than a clodhopping herdsman of a ragamuffin flock of sheep. The two young men had grown up in close proximity to one another, and the scion of the region's aristocratic family looked down upon the other as contemptibly beneath him in every way. "You'll spoil that stallion, Muir," he said in a tone of command.

Steven Muir turned, though gently. The sound had startled the horse, and he sought by his demeanor to keep him calm at the intrusion of a stranger. "Master Courtenay!" he said with a wide smile. "I did not know you were back. Welcome home!"

"I arrived last night. I must admit I am surprised to find you still here."

"Your mother has been very kind."

"Yes, well. . .now that I have returned there will be a few changes. What are you trying to do with that horse?"

"He has never been ridden, Master Courtenay. I am preparing him for the saddle. I hope to ride him in another two weeks."

"Then it's the whip and spur he'll need, Muir, not sugar."

"That is not my preferred method."

"We shall see about that. In the future, you may address me as *my lord,* or *Mr. Westbrooke*. The *Lord Snowdon* will have to wait a year."

"Yes, sir. . .*my lord,*" nodded Steven.

"Where is Radnor?" asked Courtenay.

"I could not say, my lord."

"I take it you are still helping him out around the place?"

"When I can, yes."

"Well then, you can help out now by saddling the black stallion for me. I take it he is being kept in the new stables?"

"Not exactly, my lord."

"Never mind, then. Wherever he is, saddle him. I will be taking him out."

"I fear that will not be possible, my lord."

"What the devil are you talking about?"

"I assume you were referring to the stallion Demon?"

"Of course that's who I'm talking about! Either tell me where he is or why you refuse to saddle him for me."

"Demon is no longer with us, my lord. Your mother instructed me to give him to Padrig Gwlwlwyd. . .or to get rid—"

"You let that fool sell him! Why *you*?"

"Lady Snowdon trusted my judgment. She left the matter in my hands."

"I can't imagine what she was thinking!"

"You will have to take that up with her, my lord."

"So you took the horse to Gwlwlwyd?"

Steven nodded.

"I hope you got a good price."

"Your mother did not want a good price."

"That's absurd. Why not?"

"She considered the animal dangerous. After what happened to your father, she simply wanted rid of him. She was fearful of endangering a new owner."

Courtenay burst out in a derisive laugh. "That's hardly sound policy in horse selling. 'Let the buyer beware' is the foundation of that business."

"Your mother did not want the breaking of the sixth commandment on her head."

"Good enough policy in the church but heresy in the horse market. A man buys a horse as he takes a wife—for better or worse."

"That is not the way a Christian ought to look at it."

"And what would be?" asked Courtenay sarcastically.

"If one knows the dangers of a horse, failing to reveal them to a new owner would also break the ninth commandment. We are told not to bear false witness against our neighbor."

A snort sounded from Courtenay's mouth. "There is one commandment you seem to find especially difficult, Muir, and that is to mind your own business. So what did you do?"

"Your mother instructed me, if he felt he could reform him, to give Demon to Mr. Gwlwlwyd at no charge."

"That is ridiculous! The horse was worth five hundred pounds!"

"Those were your mother's instructions."

"What did the man say?"

"He declined to take the animal. He said there was the curse of death on him."

"So what did you do?"

"I put him down, my lord."

Courtenay stared back as if he had not heard him correctly.

"You *what*?"

"I put him down," answered Steven calmly.

Stunned into speechless fury, Courtenay turned on his heels and stormed angrily back toward the house.

Two

Mother and Son

Courtenay found his mother still in the luncheon room with a book.

Katherine Westbrooke glanced up. The thundercloud on Courtenay's brow was impossible to mistake.

He approached and glowered down at her. "I have just learned from that lout Stevie Muir that you instructed him to put Demon down!" he said angrily.

"That is true," replied Katherine calmly.

"You had no right."

"It seemed the best course of action under the circumstances."

"But you had no right."

"Why would I not? I am the one who bought him."

"He was my horse!"

"I believe he was your father's horse."

"Yes, and with Father dead, he was mine. How dare you presume—"

"You were gone," rejoined Katherine in a slightly peremptory tone. "I thought it best," she repeated.

"On what basis, if I may ask?"

"The beast was a murderer. He had already taken one life. I had no intention of his endangering another."

"That is ridiculous. He was only dangerous to one who did not know how to handle him. I had plans for that animal. I will never forgive you for interfering in my plans."

The words hit Katherine as if they had been shot from a gun. She tried not to allow the pain to show. She knew what he perceived as her emotional weakness would only anger her son the more. "I am sorry, Courtenay," she said softly. "As I said, I thought it best. Perhaps I was wrong. Your father's death weighed heavily upon me. But while you were away, I bought another stallion, an Anglo-Arabian. I thought you might like—"

"Yes, I saw it," snapped Courtenay. "He's nothing like what I had with Demon, what I would have been able to do with him! And what is that simpleton Muir still doing around here? He says he is training the thing. He knows nothing about horses."

"Actually, he knows horses very well. He has a compelling way with them."

"I want to know what he is doing here."

"I decided to keep him. He is a big help."

"He is an idiot. I don't like him. I want him gone before the day is out."

Katherine drew in a deep breath, struggling between tears and rising indignation of her own. "And if I choose to keep him?" she said. Her tone contained a slight edge such as Courtenay had never heard from her before. It was the hint of a challenge.

"Then he will be working for you not me," he replied curtly. "Just tell him to keep out of my way. Make sure he knows that his duties here will not last one minute past the day I am in charge. I can't stand the sight of the ridiculous fellow. What is that solicitor's name. . .Father's man in Porthmadog?"

"Mr. Murray. . .Hamilton Murray," replied Katherine.

Courtenay turned to leave the room.

"Where are you going?" asked his mother behind him.

"To see Murray and get some money in the bank and get the problem with my account sorted out."

"Courtenay," said Katherine after him as he again moved toward the door, "before you see him, you ought to know—"

"All I need to know is where to find him. What's done with Demon is done. Now that I am here and prepared to take up my position, Mother, I will thank you not to interfere further in my affairs. I would not want things to become unpleasant for you. I will not be home for dinner."

Three

Rude Awakening

During the long afternoon ride up the coast and around the Traeth Bach inlet, Courtenay's mood alternated between anger and a growing disquiet. His mother was different. It had unnerved him. She was more self-assured, confident, her manner calm but uncomfortably firm. She seemed altogether unruffled by what he said. He wasn't sure he liked the change.

All along he had assumed, though the estate was in legal limbo until he came of age, that he was de facto in charge. He tried to convince himself that all it would take was a visit to his father's solicitor to straighten out the confusion. He certainly had no intention of letting his mother throw her weight around.

Though concerned, Courtenay was still not yet cognizant of the painful reality of his position. As an indulgent father, the viscount had given him whatever he wanted and kept him well supplied with cash. Courtenay had not anticipated the least straitening of his financial security after his father's death. If anything, he assumed, notwithstanding the twenty-fifth birthday stipulation of the inheritance, that financially he would have the full benefit of his father's resources immediately at his command. Though confident the matter would quickly be resolved, an undefined angst whispered in his ear that his mother was up to something that did not bode well. In actual fact, he was about to reap the fruit of his father's financial status more speedily than he might have wished. He had no idea that without his wife's generosity, his father would have been what nearly amounted to a landed and titled pauper.

Three hours after setting out, the Gelderlander, his favorite mount before Demon, in a hot lather at the livery, Courtenay Westbrooke sat in a chair opposite the desk of Hamilton Murray in the solicitor's offices of Murray, Sidcup, and Murray. The jaw of the would-be heir hung open at what he had just heard. "A *trusteeship*. . ." he repeated in disbelief. "And it makes no mention whatever of *my* role as the future viscount?"

"I am afraid that is the situation as it stands. . .yes," replied Murray.

The office fell quiet as Courtenay sat shaking his head in annoyance. He was doing his best to keep from exploding. But only with difficulty. "At whose behest was this so-called trusteeship drawn up?" Courtenay asked at length.

"Your father's, Mr. Westbrooke," replied Murray. "It was several days before his death. I took it down myself."

"Where was I?"

"I really couldn't say, Mr. Westbrooke."

"My father did not ask for me?"

"No, sir."

"And my mother was there?"

"That is correct."

"You are positive there was no coercion?"

"Of course not. Your father may have been weak, but he had all his mental faculties. This was how he wanted it."

"And you, as the family solicitor, did not intercede on my behalf?"

"That would not have been my place, Mr. Westbrooke. I represented your father, not you."

"Well you represent me now. It might have behooved you to think of that sooner. From where I sit, it appears that you have betrayed my interests."

"I am sorry you should see it like that."

Courtenay thought a moment. "I could contest it in court," he said at length.

"You would not prevail," replied Murray. "I fail to see what advantage you would hope to gain."

"To invalidate the trusteeship of my mother over me."

"It is not a trusteeship over *you*, Mr. Westbrooke. It is over the estate. Your father simply felt—"

"Don't split hairs with me, Murray," Courtenay shot back. "This effectively puts me under my mother's thumb for the next year and a half. I have no intention of allowing such a state of affairs to persist."

"Even if the trusteeship were somehow invalidated, you would still not inherit until your twenty-fifth birthday. The terms of inheritance of the viscountcy and estate are clear and irrevocable—the eldest child of the viscount or viscountess, or their issue, regardless of gender, succeeds to the title and inherits the property on his or her twenty-fifth birthday."

"Provision would yet be made for my financial needs."

"That is true. In that case the court would act as trustee. However, you would not have unfettered access to estate funds. Perhaps there would be a stipend, but other than that—"

"That would be an improvement upon my current predicament," rejoined Courtenay testily. "So what recourse do I have? How do I access my own funds?"

"As I say, Mr. Westbrooke, those funds are not yet yours. At present your mother controls everything. Have you spoken with her about it?"

A snort sounded from Courtenay's mouth. "My mother is a woman. Do you really expect her to be reasonable about it? I am sure she is enjoying her little power grab."

"I have found Lady Snowdon to be an intelligent and thoughtful woman."

"Yes, well you are entitled to your opinion. But unless you can come up with some way around it, once I do become viscount, I will be engaging a new solicitor to handle my affairs. I doubt the Westbrooke retainer is one you would be eager to lose, Mr. Murray, so I suggest you think of something."

"I am sorry, Mr. Westbrooke, but legally my hands are tied. I must abide by the terms of the trusteeship. At this point, I represent your mother."

Courtenay's long ride back to Llanfryniog was filled with smoldering anger and venomous thoughts.

The stark reality began to dawn on him that he was dependent upon his mother for everything. The same eye-opening reality had long been a thorn in the side of the marriage between Roderick and Katherine Westbrooke. The late viscount had been a man of dreams and schemes. But his wife, who with her brother Edward Drummond of Glasgow had inherited half a small fortune from Courtenay's grandfather, was of a more prudent temperament. With what little cash remained to accompany the title and property beyond what meager rents the homes and cottages of the nearby village of Llanfryniog provided, the viscount found himself in the humiliating position of having to rely on his wife for anything that might be considered of a speculative nature.

Now the viscount's son, still some months away from his twenty-fourth birthday, realized that he had no job, no prospects, no money. Having failed to complete his studies at Oxford, he found himself at loose ends. What was he to do until he was twenty-five?

It was a good thing Courtenay saw no one, and that the manor had mostly retired for the night before he left Mistress Chattan's pub, where he had moodily partaken of what passed for a supper and far more ale than was good for him.

The only conclusion the stringy beef, hard potatoes, and brussels sprouts that resembled rocks had left him with was that he had no intention of going cap in hand to his mother to beg for money. What a humiliating prospect!

Four

Letter to Aberdeen

In the two rooms he occupied on the top floor of the Aberdeen boarding house, Percival Drummond, in his fourth year at the university in the great northern city of Scotland, eased into the comfortable overstuffed chair in his room with a cup of tea. His day's studies were done. In his hand he held a sealed letter that had been waiting for him when he arrived home.

He took a satisfying swallow, then set the cup down on the table beside him, slit open the envelope, and removed two blue handwritten sheets from inside it.

Dear Percy, he read in the familiar feminine hand.

At last it has happened. Mother and I were surprised two days ago when Courtenay appeared without warning. He has hardly said a word to either of us since returning home. We don't know where he has been. I thought he was distant and aloof before. But, goodness! It is terrible now. I can't imagine that he and I used to be close. But like you and I have talked about so many times, we have all changed since your first summer with us in Wales five years ago.

What I cannot understand about Courtenay is why he is so irritable. He's twenty-three. Shouldn't he be acting more like a man? He seems angry at the whole world. Whatever he had hoped to accomplish during his three months away after Daddy's death, it certainly has not improved his disposition.

But on to more cheerful topics! I'm sorry for beginning this letter with my dreary news!

I hope all is well and that your studies are not too demanding. I think of you constantly and cannot wait until we see one another again. But I know it is wise for you to graduate before we think of the future. Only I miss you so dreadfully!

Percy set the letter aside a moment with a smile. He missed her, too. He could almost hear her voice as if she were speaking rather than writing to him. He picked up his cup of tea with his free hand and resumed.

I told you, I think, about the gorgeous new horse Mother bought, an Anglo-Arabian stallion we have named Snowdonia. He is the most exquisite blend of white and gray. The instant we saw him, mother and I immediately thought of the snow on the gray mountains of Gwynedd. He almost seemed to name himself. Steven has been training him and thinks he will soon be comfortable with a saddle. He hopes to ride him in another few weeks. Steven has a way with horses that reminds me of Gwyneth. Maybe it runs in families! There is still no word of her. Her disappearance remains a mystery.

Steven is such a dear. He is the most gracious and considerate young man I have ever met—except for you, of course! He is so nice to everyone, and everyone loves him—other than Courtenay. Mother has not once regretted her decision to make him factor when Mr. Heygate left. Everything is running as smoothly as before, even with Daddy and Mr. Heygate gone. I can tell that Mother misses Daddy terribly. She doesn't talk about it, but I can tell. I miss him, too. Daddy was gruff and distant sometimes. But he loved us and we knew it.

Speaking of Steven—I can't think of him as Stevie anymore. Mother calls him Steven, and now that he walks about so confidently and in charge of the estate for Mother, he seems so different. Mother and Mrs. Muir have become such good friends, especially with them both losing their husbands. And with Steven now living and working at the manor, Mother asked Mrs. Muir if she would like to work for her, too, as sort of a second housekeeper. Mrs. Llewellyn is not a young woman, and she had confessed to my mother that going up and down the stairs was becoming more difficult for her. She is relieved and happy to have Mrs. Muir's help. So now both Steven and Mrs. Muir are living at the manor and working for us. Steven is selling his flock and all their animals, though it's been difficult for him to arrange everything. Some of them he is giving to the poor families of the region. Mother says she will make up any losses. I don't know what is going to happen to their cottage in the hills. But his mother seems very happy here.

I have been trying to follow in your father's and mother's footsteps, and my mother's, too, and read some of Mr. MacDonald's books. I have to admit, they are very long and sometimes difficult. The Scottish dialect is hard to understand. Maybe not for you because you are Scottish. I could read them more easily if someone translated the Scots for me. But I am going slow and trying to absorb what I read. I am reading one of his novels called David Elginbrod, *which Mother says is his first realistic novel. She says before that he wrote poetry and fantasies and short stories. It is a story about three young people called Hugh and Margaret and Euphra. (What a funny name!) I am not too far into it yet.*

Rhawn Lorimer and I had a nice visit a few days ago, just before Courtenay came home. Her little son is spunky and full of energy. Poor Rhawn, she seems sad. But I think she is growing. She is thinking about God and life and about what kind of person she wants to be. We all have to think about those kinds of things eventually. You helped me think about them, just like Gwyneth helped you do so. Now perhaps it is Rhawn's turn. It is very humbling to realize that in some small way I am helping her, too. It makes me quiet and happy inside to realize that I am actually helping another person. We talk about many things, and she asks me questions about God and life and why I changed. It is an extraordinary thing to have someone you grew up with ask you those kinds of questions. I would rather you were here to talk to her. But maybe God will be able to help Rhawn find peace regardless. I hope so. I pray for her.

I pray for you, too, and think of you, as I said, every day. I am lonely for you, but I am not really lonely at all. Steven is a wonderful friend, as is Mother of course, and now Steven's mother, too. Even Mr. MacDonald is becoming a friend in his own way, though I do not know him. I think he lives in London. Can you imagine what it would be like to meet him! So I am not really lonely, but I do miss you. I so hope that you and your family will be able to come to Wales and spend Christmas with us.

I know you are busy with your studies. But when you have time, please write me back. I long for any word from you.

Yours,
Florilyn

Percy sat back in his chair and drew in a thoughtful breath, then exhaled slowly. He glanced at his watch. It would be forty minutes before Mrs. Treadway had his supper ready. If he didn't answer Florilyn's letter now, the way things usually went, it might be days before he got around to it. He rose with letter in hand, picked up his cup of tea, and walked across the room to his desk.

Five

Brother and Sister

D*ear Florilyn,* Florilyn read.

I read your recent letter, as always, with great joy in the midst of my busy life here at the university. It is always such a happy event to find an envelope with your hand on it waiting for me after a day of classes and meetings with professors and library research and all the rest with which my life is consumed. I wait until I have a hot cup of tea beside me and can sit down and relax, sharing the peaceful moments with you and imagining that we are enjoying tea together at the end of a long day.

Hearing you talk about the manor. . .it sounds like such life is there. How could you possibly be lonely? Now I feel homesick for you all—if one can feel homesick about a place that has never been his home. . .though Llanfryniog and the manor and all the surrounding region will always feel like home to me!

After receiving your letter, I decided to find a copy of the book by MacDonald you mentioned. I know my parents have it—they have all his books. But I will buy a copy and read it with you. It will be a way to share together even though so many miles separate us—knowing that we are reading the same book, getting to know the same characters. There are any number of bookshops in Aberdeen, and MacDonald is a great favorite. Everyone at the university is very proud of him, and many professors still remember his student days here.

My parents and I are talking about our Christmas plans. Weather is always a factor to consider so far north. As long as snowdrifts are not blocking the tracks, I will take the train from Aberdeen to Glasgow. Then my parents and I will travel together by train down to Wales. It will not be like one of my former summer visits—I will only have a week to spend with you. But it will be a joy!

Florilyn continued to read of Percy's studies, about his friends and acquaintances and humorous incidents involving one or two of his professors. She relished every word, laughed more than once, and was near tears when she finally set the pages aside, remembering again how Percy could always make her laugh.

She wiped her eyes, stood, and walked to the window of her room. There she gazed out on the scene spread out before her. The sea in the distance to the west, but partially visible through the trees surrounding most of the house, stretched north and south along Tremadog Bay. Sails of a few fishing boats could be seen off the coast in the direction of the peninsula of Lleyn, faintly visible on the clearest of days stretching far west until it faded from sight.

Sheep and cattle were plentiful in the surrounding fields and pastures. As the terrain rose inland toward the mountainous slopes of Snowdonia's peaks, the population of cattle dwindled noticeably, except for here and there a family cow whose provision of milk kept many of the poor crofters alive. Mostly what remained, as grassy pastures and meadows increasingly gave way to the rocks and boulders of the higher elevations, were woolly dots of white. Sheep could survive almost anywhere.

West of her vantage point, the promontory known as Mochras Head rose above the sea. From it a wide plateau, bordered by the abrupt cliff-edge of the headland, descended to the village and harbor of Llanfryniog, a small but bustling center of activity. Many of the region's men were employed in the nearby slate mine, while others eked out a meager living from the sea or the land itself.

A single main street ran through the center of Llanfryniog. From it smaller streets, lanes, walkways, and cottages spread out in both directions in random disorder toward the sea to the west, and inland and up the plateau in the other.

Several shops along the town's main street were supplemented by homes whose windows offered an assorted miscellany of goods. Most of their offerings cost no more than a penny or two, certainly not more than a few shillings. There were also a variety of services available from a blacksmith, a cobbler, and a doctor from their homes on the outskirts of the village.

Llanfryniog boasted three churches, one school, a harbor, and an inn and pub that served the best ale for miles and in front of which a north-south coach stopped daily, connecting the coastal villages of the region with the larger towns of north Wales, where train service might take them throughout all Britain.

Near the top of the Mochras slope, a private avenue led off the main road east and inland. An imposing iron gate across it, with gatehouse beside, stood fifty yards off the main road. From this impressive entryway, the approach led for half a mile along a winding tree-lined course up a continuing incline to Westbrooke Manor, at the second-floor window of which the late viscount's daughter, Florilyn Westbrooke, still stood. It was the largest mansion for fifty miles and was situated in the foothills of the Cambrian range, which led further inland to the southern peaks of Snowdonia.

At length Florilyn drew in a long sigh, melancholy but with a heart of contentment, and left her room. She glanced down the corridor toward what they still called "Percy's room" with a fond smile then turned in the opposite direction for the main staircase and continued downstairs. The letter from Percy put her in the mood for a ride. The cold front had passed, and glorious golden autumn again reigned in Wales.

She reached the ground floor and heard voices engaged in heated exchange. One was raised in argument. The answering voice, however, was soft. She turned toward them. She had about lost her patience with Courtenay. She wasn't about to stand by and let him berate their mother without coming to her defense.

She walked through the door of the sitting room and saw Courtenay standing with his back turned. He was facing his mother who was seated.

"Why didn't you tell me about the trusteeship?" he had just said. His tone was demanding. Florilyn could hardly believe the change that had come over him.

"I tried to, Courtenay," said Katherine calmly. "You weren't listening. You interrupted me and stormed off in a huff."

"You should have tried harder. You put me in an awkward position with Murray."

"What would you have me do, restrain you forcibly as if you were a child?"

"All this begs the question why you cut off deposits into my bank account," said Courtenay, ignoring his mother's question.

"I did not cut off deposits into your account."

"Someone did. Nothing has gone into it since Father's death."

"I did not know the status of your account," said Katherine. "I still know nothing about it. I have done nothing at all about your account. For all I knew, you might have had ten thousand pounds. Your father never shared with me what his accommodations were with you."

"He made no arrangement in the trusteeship for my financial well being?"

"There was no mention of finances whatever. It was simply a matter of legal administration of the affairs of the estate."

"Be that as it may, now that you know that I have no money, what do you intend to do about it?"

"I shall have to think about it," answered Katherine. "I would be glad to provide you and your sister an allowance for your personal needs. I will be fair."

"Like you gave us when we were children?"

"That is not what I meant. Perhaps you and I could sit down and look at your plans and what you consider a reasonable—"

"I have no intention of discussing my *plans* with you," interrupted Courtenay. "I am telling you that I have financial needs. I have a right to what is mine. I intend to return to the continent."

"That is, of course, up to you. But I do not intend to finance with *my* money travels that have no purpose."

"It is my money, not yours."

"I was speaking of my own funds," rejoined Katherine. "The income from estate properties will indeed be yours soon enough. But I will not see you squander it now. It would be a different matter if you were to return to the university—"

"You actually intend to dictate my future!"

Katherine let out a lengthy sigh. "I have tried to be patient and understanding, Courtenay," she said after a moment. "I know this all must be a shock to you. But until you are twenty-five, the estate is mine to manage as I feel is best. I am doing so for you. . .for *your* best. . . maybe to protect you from yourself, from doing something hastily and foolishly."

"It is nice to hear what trust you have in me," said Courtenay in a mocking tone.

"You are young, that is all. It will take time for you to grow into your role. Believe me, I am doing what I consider best for you and for the estate. I believe you will thank me one day. And during this time when I am in charge, Steven Muir is helping me."

"You trust him above me?"

"I did not say that. It would really make this easier if you did not misinterpret and overreact to my words. You were gone. I heard nothing from you. I had no idea when you would be back or what your plans were. Steven has shown himself to be reliable and trustworthy and capable of handling my business affairs."

"What do you mean, handling your *business* affairs?" asked Courtenay almost mockingly. "I knew he was helping out Radnor as an assistant groom. But how could a groom know anything about business?"

"He is more than my groom, Courtenay. Tilman Heygate is gone. I am depending on Steven Muir now."

"He's nothing but a shepherd."

"He *is* more than that, Courtenay. Not that there is anything demeaning about being a shepherd. I believe kings occasionally come from shepherd stock. Steven is more educated and knowledgeable than you realize. He has proved himself capable even beyond what I anticipated. The people love him. That is good for everyone. When your father was gone, and after you left, I had to make a decision. You asked me if I trust him above you—during these past three months, the answer is *yes*. Where were you if I needed you? You left almost without a word. How was I to know if and when I would see you again? There was much to do in your father's absence. Therefore, I made the decision not only to keep Steven on at the manor but to hire him as my factor."

"Your *factor*!" exclaimed Courtenay, incredulous at the very idea. "That is the most preposterous thing I have heard in my life. He's a complete nincompoop!"

"Nevertheless, I have no intention of changing my mind."

"Well, unless you do change your mind, things will not go well with you, Mother, once I am in control—no, and not well for the fool, Stevie Muir, either. Don't forget, in a year and a half, I will be sitting where you are sitting now. I will be in control, and you will have nothing to say about any of it. My first order of business will be to evict Muir from that cottage of his."

"He and his mother are living at the manor now."

"Good! That will make them the easier to evict! You will pay for your interference in my affairs, Mother."

Courtenay spun around, his face red, and strode toward the door. He saw Florilyn standing just inside it. "And *you*!" he spat. "You knew all about this and said nothing to me? I thought you were my friend!"

"I thought so, too, Courtenay," Florilyn shot back. Her face, too, was red, though from a much different kind of anger. "It has been a great grief to me to see how changed you are. No friend of mine would speak so rudely to my mother," she added heatedly. "Only a bounder would speak so to his *own* mother."

A suppressed oath escaped Courtenay's lips of such nature as the mother and sister of a gentleman should never hear. He continued on his way, brushed past Florilyn with a look of contempt and scorn, and left the house with his temper at the boiling point.

Florilyn walked to her mother, who was by now in tears, and sat down beside her. "I'm sorry, Mother," she said softly.

Katherine forced a smile as she wiped at her eyes then sighed again. "He is right, you know," she said. "Courtenay could make our lives miserable. A dowager viscountess and her unmarried daughter do not command a great deal of status in this world. I can hardly imagine how changed everything will be around here when Courtenay, as he so pointedly put it, is in control. If I refuse to give him whatever he wants, he would have no qualms about doubling the rents on everyone for miles. Your father had compassion and cared for the people, though he often did not have money to do everything he might have wished. Beneath his impersonal exterior, he was a good man. I doubt Courtenay will think twice about his tenants."

"Don't forget, Mother," said Florilyn, "by the time Courtenay accedes to the title, Percy and I will be married. If Courtenay is troublesome, you will come live with us."

Katherine smiled.

"You would have me leave Westbrooke Manor, my dear?"

"Rather than have Courtenay make your life miserable. You and Percy and I, and all the grandchildren we will give you. . .we will find a cottage in the hills, and we will raise horses and we will ride and all be happy together. Let Courtenay have his old title and this house. Don't get me wrong, Mother—I love it here. I would bring Percy here to live if I could. But Courtenay *will* inherit. There is nothing we can do to change that. So we will make the best of it and all be happy somewhere else."

"And what will become of Adela and Steven? Perhaps we should not be too anxious to let their cottage to new tenants. They may need it again."

"We shall take *two* cottages in the hills," said Florilyn gaily. "We shall build a second one to go with it. Steven shall continue as factor for our small little peasant community in the hills, with the dowager viscountess as our honored mistress."

Katherine laughed to hear her daughter talk so. She had a way of making the simplest things sound so wonderful.

Six

Discussions in London

Lord Coloraine Litchfield rarely read obituaries in *The Times*. They were for the elderly, worried that they might find their *own* names among those who had departed the earth for better places. Death columns did not make up the regular reading program for mining magnates and captains of industry in the prime of their rush to expand their bank accounts and conquer the world for capitalism and commerce.

He had stumbled on the small notice quite by accident in an announcement concerning a vacancy in the House of Lords owing to the death of Gwynedd viscount Lord Snowdon, whose seat in the Lords would not be filled for eighteen months. Litchfield's eyes shot open.

Moments later he was seated in consultation with his private secretary, Palmer Sutcliffe.

"What we need to find out," Litchfield said once Sutcliffe had perused the announcement, "is who is now in control of Snowdon's affairs and his land."

"I assume, under the circumstances," said Sutcliffe thoughtfully, "that there would be a trusteeship in effect. The thing's probably in the hands of solicitors."

"But why this vacancy in the Lords? As I recall, the fellow had a son."

"Do you know when the peerage was created?" asked Sutcliffe.

"No, nothing. It is of ancient date, I believe."

"The inheritance stipulations can be unbelievably complex in some instances. Though perhaps this is straightforward enough. It may be no more than a case of the son coming of age."

"Find out what you can. This may move our Wales project back to the top of the list."

"I will make inquiries immediately—discreetly of course."

"What about the old rascal who claimed to know the exact location—that thieving Cardi who said he possessed chunks he had taken out of the ground?"

"What he showed me was real enough," nodded Sutcliffe. "Of course he might have taken it from anywhere. The question will be whether he is even still alive and whether we can locate him again. It's been, what. . .five years?"

Litchfield nodded. "I had all but given up on the thing," he said. "There was no way around Lord Snowdon's intractability after he called our bluff. I must admit, I underestimated the fellow. He was sharper than I gave him credit for. He would have owned half interest in the project before agreeing to sell. That was more than I was prepared to give. I would far rather simply purchase the land outright. Then one hundred percent of the proceeds would be ours."

"What makes you think the son is not cut from the same cloth?" asked Sutcliffe.

"I have no idea. Perhaps he is. But the thing is certainly worth exploring again," replied Litchfield. "Deaths these days often have unforeseen consequences on a man's heirs—financial difficulties, tax burdens, past debts that suddenly change the financial landscape. One never knows what might be possible. Perhaps we might find the wife or the son more amenable, shall we say, to an attractive offer to purchase a small portion of out-of-the-way acreage than we did the viscount. Find out what you can, and how we could most likely make a successful approach."

Seven

A Reflective Ride

Florilyn rode into Llanfryniog still upset at her brother. She passed between the Catholic and Church of England houses of worship at the south end of town, continued along the main street past the post, the inn, and several shops.

The familiar ubiquitous clanking of hammer against anvil from the smithy where Kyvwlch and Chandos Gwarthegydd now worked together unconsciously drew her glance to the right. Between an irregular row of cottages and buildings, through a narrow lane, she caught a brief glimpse of a steeply slanted purple roof. She shuddered briefly at the reminder of the day she and her cousin had visited the creepy home of the fortune-teller of dubious reputation. Florilyn had never forgotten Madame Fleming's spooky words.

"A great change will come to you," the mysterious woman had said. *"An inheritance that is yours will be taken away. But you will find love, and one will be faithful to you, though he is the least in your eyes. He will be your protector, and you will gain a greater inheritance in the end."*

As repulsive as was the old hag, Florilyn reflected, had her weird prediction already come true? Perhaps the inheritance she said would be taken away was her father. Now he *was* gone. He had been taken away from them all. And she had indeed found love. She didn't believe in Madame Fleming's hocus-pocus, but she had to admit that her words seemed eerily prophetic.

She continued to the far end of town, past the white Methodist chapel and school, following the road left and down to the shore and the harbor, where she arrived at length on the long stretch of sandy beach south of the harbor. There she let her favorite mare, Red Rhud, go for a good gallop the full length of the flat, sandy expanse at the water's edge.

For over a year after her race here with Percy, she had not been able to come to this beach at all. Finally she had come to terms with the past, with what she had been, and with what she was now becoming. This beach would always fill her with sad thoughts, especially with Gwyneth now gone from Llanfryniog, nobody knew where. At last she was able to let that melancholy turn her heart toward prayer for the tiny enigmatic angel, as Percy sometimes called her, rather than inward with self-recrimination for how cruel she had once been to the girl who had later become her friend.

Though today's ride was prompted by Percy's letter and her brother's insufferable behavior, she found her thoughts turning toward dear Gwyneth Barrie, the mysterious nymph of Llanfryniog.

Gwyneth's diminutive stature, kind and soft-spoken nature, and unruly head of white hair would have been enough in themselves to invite taunts from other children. Along with these visible peculiarities, however, was the fact that she had no mother—at least no one knew who her mother was—and that her father, hard-working slate miner Codnor Barrie, was himself so short as to be considered by many a dwarf. To these was added the affiliation of father and daughter with Codnor Barrie's great-aunt, christened Branwenn Myfanawy but simply known as "Grannie" to those few who claimed acquaintance with her. Though as kindhearted a woman as any in the region, she had been considered a witch by many in the village for what were considered her eccentric ways. There was not a grain of truth to the rumors. But that did not prevent them. The final and perhaps most serious charge against poor little Gwyneth was a serious impediment of speech. She stuttered, all the more so when nervous or agitated. It was all the excuse the cruel-minded children of the village had needed to torment her endlessly in her younger years. It was also the only justification the gossipmongers and old women needed to brand her a witch-child along with her great-great-aunt.

But Gwyneth and Grannie had tried to return the evil of the community with good, often in the form of anonymous floral bouquets left on one door or another about town after an offense or rude word. The general antipathy toward Gwyneth and Grannie was all the more illogical in light of the general esteem in which Gwyneth's cousin, Steven Muir, now factor at the manor, and his mother, Barrie's sister, were held. But prejudice and suspicion are rarely guided by logic.

Gwyneth's fortunes had begun to change five years before. It was then that Florilyn's Scottish cousin Percival Drummond, after a string of reckless incidents threatened to land him in a Glasgow jail, had been sent to Wales for the purpose of passing the summer with aunt and uncle and family.

She and Percy had not hit it off at first, Florilyn remembered with a smile. But Percy made little Gwyneth's acquaintance almost his first day in Wales. Knowing nothing of how she was viewed by others in the community, assuming her an odd but delightful child, and having no idea that a mere three years in age separated them, Percy was immediately enchanted. His friendship with the little blond nymph had changed Percy from a rebellious teen into a sensitive young man, newly awakened to God's presence in the world and more importantly within himself. A new relationship with his father had followed subsequent to his return home to Glasgow at summer's end.

To her own great surprise, Florilyn reflected, the change in Percy had also wrought changes in her. She, too, had begun to look up and ask how God fit into her life. . .and how she fit into His. Indeed, little Gwyneth Barrie's innocent, trusting, loving, forgiving outlook on life had influenced many—she and Percy perhaps most of all. Remarkably, Gwyneth's stuttering had ceased abruptly after the accident at the end of that same summer.

Percy, son of Florilyn's mother's brother Edward, a vicar of the Church of Scotland in Glasgow, and wife Mary, had eventually passed a good portion of three summers of his youth with them in Wales. Now he was in his fourth and final year at Aberdeen University, planning to continue his studies toward a future in law.

When she first began to love Percy, Florilyn had asked herself many times. It had come upon her slowly. Had it begun as long ago as his first summer in Wales when he was sixteen and she fifteen?

There was no doubt that she had missed him after he was gone and thought about him far more than she would have admitted either to herself or to him. By the time he returned for a second visit, she was eighteen and in grave danger of falling in love with the tall, dashing nineteen-year-old. The moment she saw him step off the coach, her heart had leaped within her. But *his* feelings remained a mystery. Even though nothing had been said, their friendship had deepened into what seemed like more. How much more she had been afraid to ask herself even then. She knew, too, that Percy remained captivated with Gwyneth, who was also growing rapidly into a young woman.

By then she and Gwyneth had become the best of friends. Gwyneth was working at the manor as a lady's maid to Florilyn and her mother. Nothing, not even a man, not even Percy, would come between them. But it was no secret that they both cherished more than a passing affection for the good-looking and chivalrous young Scot.

Then suddenly without warning, about a year ago, the enigmatic little family of outcasts had disappeared from Llanfryniog without a trace—Codnor and Gwyneth Barrie and Grannie "Bryn" Myfanawy. Not a word had been heard from them since. No one knew a thing, not even Adela Muir, Codnor's sister and Gwyneth's aunt.

Florilyn halfway expected her father to have more information concerning the mysterious affair than he let on. But he had revealed nothing, and now he was dead. Whatever secrets he may have possessed he had taken with him to his grave.

Percy had returned to Wales last summer knowing nothing of the strange turn of events. The shock of finding Gwyneth gone had unsettled him more than anything Florilyn had ever seen. But out of the suddenly altered circumstances had come the decision that would change both their lives forever. She and Percy had been engaged since the final days of the previous June.

There was still no word, no trace, no hint of Gwyneth Barrie's whereabouts. Florilyn wondered if the mystery would ever be solved.

Eight

Schemes

A week after their initial discussion about the Wales situation, as they were now calling it, Palmer Sutcliffe found his employer in his office. "I have learned a few details concerning the Westbrooke affair," he said when he was seated. "I have a contact in Porthmadog who is acquainted with the solicitor for the late viscount's estate. He was able to learn that Lord Snowdon established a trusteeship for the estate in which he named his wife trustee. That is where it stands at present. The solicitor is involved of course, but effectively the man's widow is in complete control."

"And the son?" asked Lord Litchfield.

"He will not inherit until he is twenty-five."

"How old is he now?"

"Twenty-three."

"What do we know about the woman, Lady Snowdon?"

"She is the daughter of a Scottish earl—of good family, well respected, quite wealthy. Though apparently the earl, her father, has very peculiar notions."

"What kind of notions?"

"Religious. A fanatic, they say."

"Religious fanaticism is nothing unusual in Scotland. They breed preachers there like rabbits. What's so unusual about this earl? Do I know him? Does he sit in the House?"

"I don't think he has ever occupied his seat. He is known to completely eschew politics."

"What does he do then?"

"As I said, he is a man of substantial wealth. However, over the years he has given half his fortune away to various Christian mission organizations, particularly one in China. And then—get this—at sixty-four the man went off with his wife and joined the mission himself. They have been in China as some kind of missionaries ever since."

"That's the most absurd thing I've ever heard," laughed Litchfield. "What kind of missionaries could a doddering old earl and his wife make? What in the world are they doing, preaching to the natives, for God's sake! The thing's preposterous."

"I don't know. But that is the way things apparently stand."

"They gave all their money to this missions outfit?"

"About half as I understand it, to a number of missions and charities. They split what remained of their fortune between a son and the daughter in question. Lady Snowdon's brother is a vicar in Glasgow. Both are apparently as fanatical about religion as their parents."

"A family of fools."

"Perhaps, but wealthy fools," remarked Sutcliffe. "Money apparently means nothing to them. Lord Snowdon, whatever our difficulties with him, seems to have been the only sane one in the entire brood."

"In other words, he didn't marry the woman for her religion?"

"Very unlikely, I would say. More likely for her money. He had been strapped for years."

"Then money will be no inducement to his widow."

"Again, most unlikely."

"How do we approach them then? How will we induce the woman to sell if she is independently wealthy?"

"There may be no alternative but to await the son's ascension to the title."

"How long will that be, did you say?"

"A year and a half."

"We've already waited five years! Why not approach the son now?"

"He would have no legal authority to sell any of the estate."

"What would we have to lose? It may be that he has influence with the mother."

"Or it could be that we might make the preliminary arrangements with letters of intent. It could take us eighteen months to be ready to begin blasting as it is—with all the legalities required to draw up the papers, getting the equipment there, and so on. It is not too soon to begin."

"You're right. With an agreement in place, we could be ready to begin the day the sale is consummated."

"Let me see what more I can learn about the young man. If like his father he is financially straitened, we might attempt exactly the same line of approach with him. Youth is not always wise in the ways of the world. We may be able to use that to our advantage."

"Do you suppose he knows of our previous communications?"

"There is no way to know. We must simply choose our words with care."

"Then find out what you can."

"Would you like me again to draft a preliminary letter?" asked Sutcliffe.

Litchfield thought a moment. "Yes," he nodded slowly. "But in my own name, I think. We don't want to make the same mistake twice. We will have to hope the son is not so shrewd as his father. Word it to imply that Snowdon had already agreed and that all he must do to pocket a sizeable sum of cash is to agree to what his father had already set in motion."

Nine

A Different View in the Hills

It had rained incessantly for three days. Florilyn walked out the front door of Westbrooke Manor just after lunch. She was weary of the dreary atmosphere. She had had her nose buried in the MacDonald novel she was reading for as long she could tolerate for one morning. She had never been a great reader. Though she was enjoying it, she was still, and always would be, an outdoor person. When the rain finally began to let up about eleven o'clock, she determined that one way or another she *would* spend the afternoon outside.

The clouds seemed at last to have emptied of their waterlogged floodgates and called a temporary halt to the deluge upon west Britain. The sun, however, gave no indication that it intended to battle the thick cloud cover for supremacy. A gray-white sky overspread the earth with a canopy of gloomy monotony. But it was relatively warm, pleasantly humid, refreshing in its own way with just enough bite in the moist air to keep it from being muggy. All in all it was a perfect autumn afternoon of late October.

As Florilyn meandered away from the house, she breathed in deeply of the liquid fragrant air. Three days of rain had made everything clean. The ground was wet beneath her feet. Puddles were scattered everywhere about the entryway. Drops still fell from the eaves of the house, from every branch of every tree, from fading flowers and rosebushes and shrubs. Droplets clung to every blade of grass. Water was everywhere. But at least the rain had stopped.

The air smelled *good*! It was the aroma of autumn, so different from that of its cousin spring. It was the smell of dirt, of peat, of wetness, of decay. . .of brown not green. Though it spoke of winter's approach, it was yet sweet and pleasant.

She had no plans in mind for the afternoon. It seemed too wet for a ride. She just wanted to be outside. Perhaps she would bundle up, bring out a warm cup of chocolate, and read in the summerhouse. Then let the rain come back and do its worst!

She wandered toward the stables. It was dark inside as she entered. It took a good while for her eyes to accustom themselves to the dim light, for it was not bright enough outside to help much. She heard sounds and squinted. She had not seen Courtenay all day. Perhaps he, too, planned to take advantage of the lapse in the rain and was preparing for a ride. She soon realized, however, that the sounds were coming not from her brother but from Steven Muir at the far end of the great barn. He was occupied with one of the horses. "Steven, is that you?" she called into the semidarkness.

"Miss Florilyn—yes," came the familiar voice in reply. "I am checking on Grey Tide."

"How is she?" asked Florilyn, approaching slowly.

"I would guess that she is perhaps two weeks away," replied Steven. "I am not sure she will be ready for Mr. Percy to ride if he comes for Christmas."

"He has ridden Red Rhud many times," said Florilyn. "I am not so worried about which horse he will ride as I am about snow and whether he and his parents will be able to get here at all."

"He will find a way. I am sure he is anxious to see you again." Steven turned and walked toward the back of the barn.

Florilyn followed him outside. There she saw Red Rhud saddled and apparently waiting for him. "Are you going out?" Florilyn asked.

"I am. I've been waiting for the rain to break."

"Where are you going?"

"Out to the Cnychwr croft. Their rent is due, but I haven't had the chance to get out there. I haven't seen them since Mr. Heygate left. Would you like to join me?"

"Oh. . .yes—I think I would. This rain has been making me crazy. A ride would be nice, but I didn't want to go out alone."

"Then I will saddle Black Flame. You may take your pick of mounts. But I should warn you," added Steven, "it is six miles at least. We will not be back until late. The rain may resume."

"As long as you promise to take care of me, I won't be worried."

Steven laughed. "You have my promise! It is not cold. Even if we should get wet, I don't think it will do us any harm."

"I will go change into my riding clothes and get my raincoat while you saddle Black Flame."

Twenty minutes later, Florilyn Westbrooke set out through the eastern gate beside her mother's young factor, who was only two years older than she. Accustomed to being in command and usually leading the way even when she rode with Percy, she found herself following, even occasionally along a few routes into the mountainous east she was not familiar with. Steven led the way almost due east toward the southern flank of Rhinog Fawr then veered south around the base of the mountain.

At length they came around its far slope, where he again took a northerly bearing toward their destination, which sat nearly under the shadow of the peak to its northwest. It was a strange place for a croft. But the stone cottage had been there as long as anyone could remember. One family after another had somehow managed to scrape together an existence on the five acres that surrounded it, with cows and sheep and chickens and potatoes and what vegetables they were able to grow during the summer and autumn months.

"Do you miss your father?" asked Florilyn as they rode.

"Of course," replied Steven. "But he was so unlike himself the last few years of his life, in another way it is a relief to have him released from all that. My mother misses him terribly. They spent their whole adult lives together. How about you?"

"I do miss my father," replied Florilyn. "He and I never really talked much together, though he was different the last few years. I suppose I miss his presence about the manor more than anything."

"In what way was he different?"

"He seemed to pay more attention to little things. We began to talk more often."

"What about your mother?"

"She doesn't talk about him. But I can tell she is sad. Did you and your father talk?" asked Florilyn.

"My papa wasn't a talkative man," replied Steven. "I loved him dearly, and he was a good man to one and all. But no, we didn't talk much. Sometimes we worked together for hours without saying a word. We simply enjoyed being together. But he was a quiet man."

"Percy says he and his father discuss whatever he is thinking about. He says he asks his father's advice about everything. When I listen to him, I find myself wishing I had enjoyed something like that with my father, even wondering if I could have if I had been less self-absorbed."

"I don't know whether that is true," said Steven. "People are different. Not all men are capable of that kind of thing. Percy is fortunate, but he might not have been able to talk in the same way to your father either. We take the fathers we are given. We have to find God in them as it expresses itself in their own individual ways. I learned to see God's fatherhood in my father, though I do not believe he once spoke a word about God to me in my life."

"It's amazing to hear you say that," rejoined Florilyn. "That's exactly like something Percy would say."

Steven laughed. "I take that as a great compliment. But look, there is the Cnychwr cottage ahead. We seem to have made it without rain."

As they approached the stone house, Steven looked over the flock of sheep in the field next to it with a curious expression. They were full of wool and ragged looking. They should have been shorn long before now.

Two dogs came bounding and barking out to greet them. Steven jumped down and let them get used to him before allowing Florilyn to dismount. "Wait for me just a minute," said Steven. "I'll go tell them we're here. Then I'll hold the dogs away for you."

He ran toward the cottage as a girl of eleven or twelve came outside to see what the barking was about. Steven spoke with her a minute then returned to Florilyn. "The girl says both her parents are sick in bed. I'm going in to talk to them. Do you want to wait here?"

"No, I'll go with you," said Florilyn. She dismounted, and the two walked to the cottage and inside.

They made their way through a large open kitchen into a dim sitting room. From there the girl led into the single small bedroom off the sitting room, which they all shared. There a man and woman lay in a large bed.

"Stevie Muir, so it's you, is it?" said a voice weakly from the darkness. "Arial said it was you."

"It's me, Kynwal," answered Steven. "She says you've been sick."

"It's laid us both on our backs," added a woman's voice in barely more than a whisper.

"Hello, Lilybet," said Steven. "I'm sorry to see you after so long under these circumstances."

"We heard you and your mum's gone to the manor now," said Mr. Cnychwr. "We hear that you've been made factor. I always said you was meant for bigger things. So it's Lady Snowdon's rent you'll be wanting, I'm thinking."

"That is why I came," said Steven. "And to tell you of the change. I wasn't sure you'd heard."

"We knew all about it, Stevie. But I'm afraid I've nothing to give you. I've been down near a month. Then Lilybet come down with the evil thing after me."

"He's just got weaker and weaker," said the woman. "I took care of him as best I could. But then came a day when I couldn't stand up myself. My legs just wouldn't hold me. We'd have surely died if Arial hadn't been here."

"I didn't have the strength to shear the sheep," said Kynwal. "Even if I had, I couldn't have got the fleece in to market."

"Don't you worry about it, Kynwal," said Steven. "Lady Snowdon will be more concerned for yourselves than your rent. We will see what we can do. What about food—do you have what you need?"

"Isn't much either of us can eat. No appetite, you see. No strength even to eat. But Arial's keeping the two cows milked, and there's always plenty of eggs. This time of year we've got apples and a few vegetables."

"Good. Well then, we will be on our way. We have a long ride back ahead of us. But I will send Dr. Rotherham out to see you as soon as possible."

"Don't bother the doctor, Stevie. We've got no money to—"

"We need to get you two back on your feet. Don't you worry about the doctor."

Seemingly for the first time, Mrs. Cnychwr noticed the figure standing behind Steven in the shadows. She was hardly able to lift her head off the pillow for a better look. "Who's that you brought with you, Steven?" she asked.

"It's Lady Florilyn from the manor, Lilybet—Lord and Lady Snowdon's daughter."

A gasp of astonishment left the woman's lips. "The saints preserve us!" she exclaimed. "My Lady Florilyn. . . I'm sorry for you to see us like this—but welcome to you. If only I could offer you something. You honor our poor cottage."

"Thank you, Mrs. Cnychwr," said Florilyn, stepping forward to the bedside. She reached out and laid a hand gently on the woman's arm. "I am sorry you are ill. But Steven is right. We will send the doctor out immediately."

"You are very kind, my lady."

"My mother will see to it, and anything else you need."

Ten minutes later, Florilyn and Steven began the ride back around the mountain and down to the coast.

"What would my father and Mr. Heygate do when someone could not pay the rent?" Florilyn asked.

"I don't know," replied Steven. "I'm sure under the circumstances they would have been lenient, as they were with us when my father was ill."

"Did my father ever evict people for not paying?"

"He did, yes—I knew of a few cases. But your father was an understanding man. In most cases, the people deserved to be evicted, and the town is better off without them."

"But you knew my mother would not be concerned that the Cnychwrs were unable to pay?"

"Oh, yes. . .of course. I know your mother's heart. Besides, there is money and to spare for their rent walking around on the backs of his flock of sheep."

"But if he cannot shear them. . ."

Steven chuckled as if her worry was absurd. "His sheep will all be shorn within the week," he said, "though not quite to the skin as winter is approaching."

"Who will shear them?"

"Me, of course!" laughed Steven.

They reached the manor, wet but laughing, for one brief dousing from above had nearly drenched them. They separated and went to their respective quarters for dry clothes. Then Steven sought Katherine to apprise her of the situation at the Cnychwr croft.

Ten

A Tempting Offer

The letter that arrived at Westbrooke Manor for Courtenay bore no return address or indication who the sender might be. It therefore aroused no curiosity in Lady Katherine's mind as her eyes fell upon it along with the rest of the morning's mail.

Courtenay, however, immediately noticed the London postmark and slit open the envelope with a certain mild interest. Intrigued he withdrew the single sheet.

Mr. Westbrooke, he read,

My deepest condolences at the death of your father. He and I were colleagues in the House of Lords. However, I only recently learned of his passing. I look forward to meeting you as my colleague as well when you become eligible to sit with the Lords, which I understand will be in approximately a year and a half.

Your father and I were involved in discussions involving a business transaction, which I had every reason to believe would have been mutually beneficial to us both, and especially lucrative for your father. Unfortunately the thing did not reach fruition. Our correspondence lagged as other priorities consumed our attentions. Now sadly, just as I was about to contact him again, your father's untimely death came before we could resume our plans.

I am writing now in hopes that perhaps you might be able to carry forward what your father and I were not able to complete.

My discussions with your father were quite simple: It has been my hope to purchase a small portion of acreage from your father's estate—your estate now—far on the eastern boundary of the Westbrooke property. The reason is purely a sentimental one. I spent some of the happiest years of my life as a boy romping the walking trails and footpaths of those hills. It has been my desire at the later stages of my life to build a small cottage on a site I was especially fond of that is situated on the slopes of one of Gwynedd's smaller peaks. The property lies at the boundary of your estate. Your father felt that its remote location among his holdings would represent no great sacrifice to the overall Westbrooke estate and had in principle agreed to the sale.

I can assure you that my plans would in no way encroach on your future privacy as Viscount Lord Snowdon. My access would be gained by a right of way eastward through public lands from the road between Blaenau Ffestiniog and Dolgellau.

I would purchase whatever amount of land you would graciously consent to part with up to a thousand or more acres. However, if a transaction of such size is impossible, I could carry out the plans for my small cottage with as little as twenty. Your father and I had not yet settled on the number of acres of my purchase or a price per acre, though I am prepared to be as generous in an offer to you as I would have been to him.

As you and I will be colleagues and will enjoy a long future together, it strikes me as best under the circumstances if I conduct these arrangements with yourself in confidentiality without involving your mother, whom I understand is at present trustee over your father's estate. I am hoping you and I might come to some arrangement relatively soon, even perhaps before you officially inherit your father's title. If we could come to a mutually beneficial agreement, being a wealthy man, I can assure you that I would make it worth your while. I would be in a position to forward you a sizeable advance payment as an earnest pledge toward the final purchase price.

If you feel you would be interested in pursuing this matter in your father's stead, I will put an offer together for your consideration, which, as I say, would include a cash advance to yourself.

I am, Mr. Westbrooke,
Faithfully yours,
Lord Coleraine Litchfield

Courtenay set the letter aside with a sigh filled with emotions it would have been difficult to identify. His first impulse was to set pen to paper immediately. His hand quivered to do so. But he realized it would be foolish. He was no businessman, but he was certainly knowledgeable enough in the ways of the world to know that one could not appear *too* eager.

He tried to pretend he was spending the following days thinking through the pros and cons of the thing before arriving at a well-reasoned decision. In truth, he was simply waiting for enough time to pass to make the fellow Litchfield, whoever he was, squirm just enough anticipating a reply.

His mother and sister noted the difference in his countenance instantly, the subtle smirk, as if he knew something he was not telling. Katherine suspected him of having something up his sleeve, which he did. But she was the last one to whom he would divulge what he was thinking.

After six days, Courtenay judged that enough time had gone by. He sat down at the writing table in his room and began to write the letter he had been composing in his mind since the moment his eyes had fallen on Litchfield's words, "cash advance to yourself."

Lord Coleraine Litchfield, he wrote.
My Lord,

I am in receipt of your letter and have been giving the matter a great deal of thought. Though as you note, I will not be in control of the estate's affairs for another year and a half, I would be amenable to the idea of setting in motion before that time the preliminaries for a transaction such as you have outlined.

I will entertain any reasonable offer you would make. The size of the acreage I would be willing to sell would entirely depend on the price per acre offered. The total sum would weigh most heavily in the balance as there have been inevitable strains placed upon my finances as a result of my father's death and my eventual assumption of his title and estate.

I will of course need to know the exact location in question. With that information and some idea of the specifics of the offer you are prepared to make, we will be in a position to speak more definitely about a timetable. Be assured that our discussions and negotiations will remain confidential.

I am,
Yours sincerely,
Courtenay Westbrooke

Five days later, Courtenay received his reply.

Mr. Westbrooke,

I was delighted to receive your letter and hope that this may be the beginning of a rewarding business relationship that will benefit us both.

Enclosed you will see site drawings showing the northeastern portions of your estate boundaries, indicating the area of my interest. I have outlined four potential scenarios, any of which I would be willing to consider—a twenty-acre sale, another of one hundred acres, a third of five hundred, and a fourth of one thousand acres. The price offered per acre would of course be larger for the smaller plots.

My research tells me that such land in Gwynedd has been selling in recent years for approximately five pounds an acre. As a preliminary offer, I would commit to paying you eight pounds an acre for twenty acres, six for one hundred acres, five for five hundred, and four for one thousand acres. Furthermore, I will pay one-fourth immediately upon our signing a binding sales agreement, with the balance forthcoming at the consummation of the sale once you hold legal title to the land.

If you find these terms agreeable, perhaps it might be appropriate for me to plan a trip to North Wales for us to meet in person and finalize the arrangements. We will, of course, devise some plausible explanation for my visit.

I am,
Faithfully yours,
Lord Coleraine Litchfield

ELEVEN

Nugget

Within a week of Florilyn's and Steven's visit to the croft at the base of Rhinog Fawr, not only had Katherine and Adela Muir paid the two invalids a visit, so, too, had Dr. Rotherham. He prescribed a medication he was confident would help them begin eating again and get the husband and wife on their way to returning strength.

For several days thereafter, Adela and Steven Muir stayed at the Cnychwr cottage. They nursed the two patients, prepared food, saw to the animals, and gave young Arial a badly needed rest. When they left, mother and son clattered back to town behind the croft's single horse atop a wagonload of fresh wool, which, it being late in the season and no other wool being sold, Steven was confident would bring Kynwal Cnychwr a good price.

"Do you ever miss living out here, Mother?" Steven asked as they bounced along.

Adela thought a moment. "Being out in the hills like this brings back many memories," she said at length. "I miss your father, I miss the life we enjoyed, the animals, being so close to nature all the time. But living at the manor is more like I remember from my childhood. Of course, we lived in nothing so lavish—it was a simple home by manor standards. What I mean is. . . I don't know how to describe it—the way of life, I suppose. . .having people about, servants, stables, books, gardens. My mother only had one servant, and she only came to the house three days a week. Still, reading MacDonald's books brings it all back to me now."

"In what way?"

"His stories mostly have to do with gentle folk, people of means. It's just the way he writes about them. We were certainly not wealthy by any standards. But my father and grandfather had roots among the gentility."

"You didn't miss that when you married Father?"

"Aspects of it, of course. But there were many children, and times were hard. Even from such a background, one isn't always able to dictate the future. And love doesn't always fall according to station in life. I loved your father and wanted to be his wife. And we had a good life together. I regret not a minute of it. However, I do enjoy being at the manor now, especially having access to a library again. My grandfather had a marvelous library. I've often wondered what became of all his books. To answer your question, I have no regrets about the past, nor about the present."

A wonderful warm day dawned toward the end of the first week of November, several days after Steven's return to the manor. Most of the trees, like the sheep on the surrounding fields, had lost their summer adornment. Their leaves of yellow and red and orange were strewn on the ground everywhere and rapidly turning brown.

The moment Florilyn saw the sun streaming through her bedroom window, she knew it was a day for a long ride. One could never depend on the weather after November. This might be the last such day in North Wales for months.

After breakfast, she dressed in her riding clothes and left the house for the stables. Their aging groom, Hollin Radnor, was nowhere to be seen. From the depths of the darkness, however, Florilyn heard peculiar sounds, scuffling and low snorting, as from a horse in distress. She hurried inside the great barn.

The sounds were coming from Grey Tide's stall. She was walking about, obviously restless. Her tail was high and her hips distended. As Florilyn approached, she moved about in a circular motion and awkwardly slumped to her side on the floor. Her hind portions were quivering. Snorts and whines of discomfort continued.

She was ready to foal!

Florilyn hurried from the barn. She called out as she ran to the new stables. There was no sign of Radnor or Stuart Wyckham anywhere. At length she bolted for the house. She ran straight to the factor's office at the end of the ground floor of the west wing then ran inside without knocking.

Steven sat across the room, an open ledger on the desk in front of him. He looked up at the sound of his door crashing open.

"Steven!" cried Florilyn. "It's Grey Tide. I think she's ready! More than ready—I think it's started! But I couldn't find Hollin."

Already Steven was on his feet, sprinting from the room with Florilyn on his heels. By the time she followed him into the barn, Steven was kneeling behind Grey Tide in the stall.

"You're right," he said, glancing up as she tentatively entered. "Labor is well under way. But she is in pain. It may be a difficult birth. Something seems wrong."

Florilyn stood watching wide-eyed with a grimace of mingled disgust and awe as Steven plunged his hand inside Grey Tide and felt for the position of the foal.

"Just as I thought," he said. "I can't feel the legs."

"What does that mean?" asked Florilyn.

"The forelegs and head have to come out together. Otherwise we'll have real problems. . .uh, oh, look out—stand back!"

Steven withdrew his hand and leaped back as Grey Tide struggled again to her feet and began shuffling about the stall. She was obviously agitated.

"Easy, Grey Tide. . .easy, girl," said Steven softly, walking slowly to her head where he tried to stroke her nose and neck to calm her down. "Don't be afraid, girl. . . You're having a baby. Just relax, Grey Tide."

"Oh no, ugh...Steven!" exclaimed Florilyn. "Something is happening back here. Oh, ick...Steven!"

"What is it?" said Steven, calmly leaving Grey Tide's head and returning to where Florilyn stood behind her.

"What's all that white?"

"Nothing to worry about. That's the birth sack. It's called the amnion. The foal is inside...but...yes, it's as I thought—the head is coming without the legs. The bag's already broken. Oops—she's trying to lay down again. Easy, Grey Tide...gently, big girl," he said, leaning against the mare's rump as she began to settle again to the floor. "Lady Florilyn!" he cried. "Come over here. We can't let her crush the foal's head. Here...push with me!"

Cautiously Florilyn stepped to Steven's side and shoved, though how much help she was under the circumstances was questionable. She had never witnessed anything like this in her life.

As Grey Tide struggled to ease herself to the ground, Steven pushed with all his might to make sure she came down on her side. Even as she did, the head of the foal was fully visible. The mare's contractions were coming steady and strong.

"I'll have to go inside to find the legs," said Steven when Grey Tide was lying comfortably on the ground. "Lady Florilyn, I'll need your help. I know this may be unpleasant—but can you be brave and help me?"

"I'll try, Steven."

"Kneel down here. Do you see—the head is out. Grasp the little torso just below the head with both your hands. Come—I'll help you." Steven took Florilyn's two hands and set them gently around the white mass. "Here, Lady Florilyn—we must move quickly. You can see the head and neck, can you not?"

"Yes...oh, ugh!"

"Now with your hand like this... Good—now very gently apply a little pressure and try to prevent the foal coming further until I have the legs out...very gently. Can you do that?"

"I think so... Oh, it's all wet and sticky...ick!"

"Be brave, Lady Florilyn. We have to try to save Grey Tide's foal.

Now I have to go back inside. I must get the forelegs out before the foal tries to get up. The minute she is breathing her instinct will be to stand. If her legs are still inside, she could damage Grey Tide's insides."

Again Steven reached inside. He felt along the length of the foal's slender body, now about half exposed. Gradually he managed to extricate first one tiny hoof and leg, then the other.

"The forelegs are out—good," he said at length. "Now, Lady Florilyn, very gently. . .pull. We can let her come the rest of the way."

Still grimacing but clutching firmly around the tiny form, Florilyn did as Steven said. Almost instantly the foal slid the rest of the way until only her back legs still rested inside.

Kneeling beside Florilyn, Steven set his hands atop Florilyn's. "Pull again. We must get the other two legs out."

Within seconds the tiny form lay motionless on the ground before them. The birth was over, but the foal was not breathing.

"Is. . .is it dead?" asked Florilyn as she gazed down at the wet, bloody mass in front of her.

"I don't know," said Steven, jumping to his feet. He grabbed several handfuls of clean straw from across the stall and tossed it in front of Florilyn. "Here, wipe it down with dry straw. Try to get the mouth open if you can."

"Where are you going?" she asked in sudden panic.

"Just over here," said Steven as he walked around the large form of the mother lying on her side recovering from the birth. "I need to get Grey Tide on her feet. We'll need her help to save her foal. While I'm doing that, tickle the foal's nose with a piece of straw and blow into its mouth and nose."

Tentatively Florilyn took some of the straw and began wiping at the wet, limp form.

"Oh. . .Steven—something's happening. Oh, ick. . . There's a lot of blood and icky-looking stuff coming out—ugh. I think Grey Tide's bleeding!"

"It's the afterbirth. Nothing to worry about. . .though it usually takes twenty minutes to an hour. This is fast. Come, Grey Tide. . .up!

Come, girl, you need to help us get your little foal breathing." Steven pushed and cajoled, but the poor mare was obviously spent. "Any sign of life?" he called out to Florilyn.

"No. I think he's dead."

"*Is* it a colt?"

"Oh, I. . .I don't know. I didn't actually. . .*look*." Florilyn was now stroking the lifeless little head gently with one hand. With two fingers inside its mouth, she blew at its nose and mouth and tried to coax life into being.

With a swaying and wriggling, Grey Tide struggled to her forelegs then up to her feet. Steven was careful to lead her a few steps forward before allowing her to turn around. As she turned, she gave a low snort then bent her long nose toward the newborn, nudged its head a time or two, but then turned toward the messy mass on the ground.

"Oh, no. . .ick. Goodness, Steven!" cried Florilyn. "She's trying to eat it! How disgusting!"

"She's just doing what instinct tells her. Come, Grey Tide," he said, trying to pull her back. "Time for all that later. Your little baby needs you. I'll get rid of it so you won't be distracted." He grabbed a shovel and scooped up the afterbirth and removed it from the stall.

Soon Grey Tide was bent down toward her little son, as confirmed by Steven, licking its head and nose where they lay on Florilyn's lap.

Steven bent down and began rubbing vigorously and gently squeezing the foal's ribs. Still there was no response. He lifted one of the tiny feet off the ground and dropped it. Then again.

Suddenly, the colt's head jerked on the side of Florilyn's leg. The same instant she felt a fierce sucking on her fingers. As if jolted by a bolt of lightning, suddenly the whole tiny body trembled.

"Steven. . .what should I do?" exclaimed Florilyn. "It's going to pull my fingers off."

"Nothing, just relax. You've done what you needed to do—you brought him back to life. Let his head rest on your lap another minute. He's got to get used to all this. Give him a minute."

Steven knelt beside her. "He seems to be breathing normally. That's good. I think he'll be fine. Good work, Grey Tide," he said, patting the mother's nose as she continued to lick the tiny face. "Remove your fingers from its mouth when you can," said Steven. "He needs to smell Grey Tide."

Slowly Florilyn did so.

"Now, very gently. . .ease yourself back and set the little head on the floor. We need to leave mother and foal together. He needs to get used to her smell."

Gradually Florilyn scooted away.

"Good," said Steven, smiling at her. "Now we wait."

"What will happen next?" asked Florilyn.

"He's only been breathing about a minute," replied Steven. "He'll get used to that, and then he'll lift his head. You see how he's just lying flat on his side? He'll be upright in a matter of minutes. Right from birth, horses have remarkably strong necks. After that, though he is still weak, instinct will make him try to get up."

Steven rose and glanced about the stall. "It looks like. . .yes, the cord has broken. That's good. I need to apply iodine to the stump so it will dry. Do you mind being alone a minute?"

"Where are you going?"

"Just over to the cabinet where Hollin keeps his supplies." Steven hurried away and returned quickly with the bottle of iodine. Florilyn watched in amazement as he checked the stump where the cord had broken and carefully doused it with iodine.

"How do you know how to do all this?" asked Florilyn.

"When you're a shepherd you grow up taking care of animals. It's part of the shepherd's life."

"You're not a shepherd anymore, Steven."

"I will always think of myself as one." When the procedure was complete, he knelt back.

"When will he be able to stand?" asked Florilyn.

"It will be soon," replied Steven. "Half an hour after he stands, we'll lead Grey Tide to the grass outside. The little foal will follow, somewhat wobbly. He will be walking and running before you know it. As soon as he's on his feet, he will try to suckle."

"How does he know. . .where to suck?" asked Florilyn.

"It takes some time. It's random at first. But Grey Tide will help him find the right place. It is instinctive. Both know what to do. By the way, what is his name?"

"What do you mean?"

"He's got to have a name. Grey Tide is your mare. You should be the one who names her foal."

"Oh. . . I suppose you're right. How exciting. Let me think."

It was quiet a few moments. Both sat watching mare and foal with their noses together. Grey Tide continued to lick and sniff at the tiny face and head.

"Oh look, Steven. . .it's just like you said!" exclaimed Florilyn. "Look—he's lifting his head and squirming about. Is he trying to stand?"

"Mostly just now to get his legs beneath his body. But he is feeling his legs, feeling their strength. He will try to stand up any minute now."

"I love his color. It's such a light golden hue. Will the color stay as it is?"

"Probably. It may darken in time, but it will always be tan or, as you say, golden."

"Then I think I have decided on a name. He shall be called Nugget."

"A brilliant name. I like it. Well done! And thank you for your help. You did very well. Was this your first birthing?"

"Couldn't you tell?" laughed Florilyn. "I was in a panic."

"I suppose I could," chuckled Steven. "You weren't exactly calm and collected."

"I was terrified!"

"I'm sorry to say it, but your riding clothes are a mess," said Steven. "I don't ever think I've seen you look quite so. . .earthy."

Suddenly Florilyn realized what she must look like. She glanced down at her hands and dress—covered with dirt and blood. "You're right—what a sight I must be!" she exclaimed. "I will definitely not be going for a ride in these clothes," she added, laughing.

"You look lovely—just like a farm girl! And I am glad you were here. You probably saved little Nugget's life."

"How could that be?"

"If you hadn't come for me when you did, there is no telling what might have happened. In just those first few seconds before Grey Tide got to him, touching him, stroking his head, making sure his mouth was open—those seconds may have made the difference between life and death."

Steven rose to his feet and extended his hand to Florilyn where she still knelt on the floor of the stall. "I think we can leave mother and son alone for a while now," he said.

Florilyn reached up. She took his hand, and he pulled her to her feet. "Then I think I will go inside and change my clothes," she said. "I'm afraid these may now be fit only for the rubbish bin."

"Well done again, Lady Florilyn," said Steven as Florilyn left the stall and walked toward the door of the barn.

She paused and turned back. "It sounds funny to have you call me that," she said with an odd smile. "I mean, after sharing something like this, why should I call you just Steven and you have to call me Lady Florilyn? I would rather you simply called me by name."

"But you are a lady," said Steven.

"That's not how I think of myself. If you can still think of yourself as a shepherd, why can't I just think of myself as an ordinary girl?"

"You're hardly a *girl.*"

"Don't confuse me with the facts," laughed Florilyn. "If you have the right to think of yourself as you want to, why don't I?"

"Your logic has the parallel between you and me backward."

"Girls don't have to be logical, don't you know."

Steven laughed at the logic even of her illogical argument.

"Besides," Florilyn added with a smile, "look at me. As you pointed out, do I *look* like a lady?"

Again Steven chuckled. "You have a point. But you always will be a lady to me. However, I will address you any way you like."

"Then please call me Florilyn. If something like this doesn't make us equals, I don't know what does."

"All right. . .*Florilyn*," nodded Steven. "As you wish. I consider myself honored to be allowed the privilege."

Florilyn smiled then continued out of the barn and to the house.

By the time she returned twenty minutes later, along with her mother to see the new colt, Nugget had begun struggling to stand on his four slender, frail legs. She and Katherine and Steven watched, laughing a good deal at the humorous attempt.

"He's such a little dear!" said Florilyn. "There is nothing so cute as a baby animal. Just look at him, Steven!"

An hour later, mother and son were outside on the enclosed grass between the stables. By then Nugget had found his feet and had begun to scamper about, alternating between suckling from beneath Grey Tide and exploring his new environment. Seemingly uninterested in her foal's antics, Grey Tide munched away on the grass at her feet and from a bale of hay Steven had provided.

Florilyn spent most of the day sitting on a low bench on one side of the enclosure, watching every move the little foal made. Steven's words had plunged deep into her heart. If she had not actually saved the little colt's life, that she may have helped in a small way to do so gave her a feeling that she had never had before. She would always feel a special bond with this little horse. She imagined that perhaps Nugget felt it, too.

Many times throughout the day, as he became used to her sight and smell where she sat calmly watching, he wandered over for brief sniffing visits. He took one of several naps of the afternoon at Florilyn's side, sleeping peacefully as Florilyn gently stroked his neck and back.

Twelve

Over His Head

Courtenay pondered Litchfield's offer for several days. The thought that with a mere signature on a piece of paper he could raise a sum of badly needed cash sent him into a near frenzy of anticipation to move the thing forward with all possible haste. Realistically, however, how much good would a paltry hundred and sixty pounds do him? It would only bring him forty pounds immediately, with the remainder not coming until he was twenty-five. Selling the man twenty acres was hardly the solution he needed.

Forty pounds! Courtenay thought. It was a laughable amount. He had burned through more than that in a week on the continent! It would do nothing to resolve his financial predicament.

Perhaps the man was making a fair offer. For all he knew, five pounds might be the going rate for acreage. But the language in the man's letters sounded as if money was the least of his problems. If he was a wealthy man, as he said, why not call his bluff and push him to the limit? There was no reason to part with a portion of the estate unless it put him in a significantly stronger financial position. He might be able to get double, perhaps triple, what Litchfield had put forward.

When he began his next letter to London, Courtenay knew he was running a risk. He might shove the man away. But in his gut, he doubted it. The fellow obviously wanted the land. Well then, let him jolly well pay for it. He could play the game, too. He would show the Londoner that he wasn't dealing with some country bumpkin.

Lord Litchfield, he began,

While I appreciate the offer set out in your last letter, I really could not possibly entertain the thought of selling land that has been in our family for centuries for less than ten pounds an acre for one thousand acres. I would not want you to interpret this as a commitment to that figure. But that is certainly the minimum I would look at.

If you are interested in submitting a more realistic offer, I will entertain it. Otherwise, I will consult my financial advisors with the aim of presenting you a counter proposal.

Should you choose to submit an alternative offer, I would also want to receive no less than one-third in payment up front, with two-thirds to be paid at the finalization of the sale.

Yours faithfully,
Courtenay Westbrooke

Litchfield read the communication and smiled. His ploy had worked to perfection. He doubted the boy even had any financial advisors. He was in over his head and had no idea who he was dealing with.

Litchfield knew he would probably have gone as high as fifty pounds an acre to the boy's father. Now here they were quibbling about price in the vicinity of ten!

The five-year wait appeared to have been well spent. It looked like he might get his land for a fraction of what he might have laid out for the project earlier.

Mr. Westbrooke,

I see that your father raised his son to be as shrewd as he was himself. You are an able negotiator and, as the saying goes, drive a hard bargain. As you have me at a disadvantage, since it is your land I desire to purchase and no other, it would seem that I have no alternative but to yield to your terms.

The amount you speak of is admittedly very high. It would take me some time to raise such capital. I assume, as you mention a minimum figure of ten pounds for a thousand acres that your acceptable terms for lesser acreage would be correspondingly higher.

Let me propose the following: sixteen pounds an acre for five hundred acres, a total of £8,000; or thirteen pounds an acre for one thousand acres, or £13,000.

If those terms are acceptable to you, I will have the preliminary papers drawn up. That will take some time, and winter will soon be upon us. But if you find my offer satisfactory, I will set the process in motion. Then we can arrange a time that is mutually acceptable for me to visit you in Wales, perhaps in the spring. At that time we can formalize our intentions. I will also agree to your stipulation of one-third down. When I come, upon receipt of your signature on the documents, I will place a check for either £2,700 or £4,400 into your hands.

I am,
Sincerely yours,
Lord Coleraine Litchfield

Courtenay's eyes nearly popped out of his head as he read Litchfield's letter. He had done it! He had successfully extracted from Litchfield a commitment for more than *triple* his original offer. This would definitely get him out of his financial straits and keep him flush until his twenty-fifth birthday.

He wouldn't need his mother's money now. Let her eat cake!

Thirteen

Reflections

Percy Drummond had not forgotten his uncle Roderick's mysterious deathbed commission of the previous June that had enjoined him to secrecy on an assignment he little understood.

The viscount had been fond of Percy. The lad's engagement to his daughter had put the viscount in an exuberant, even reckless mood. He and Percy had gone riding the next day. For their ride he took out the dangerous black stallion Demon. It was a decision that cost him his life. The tempestuous horse had thrown him while leaping an uneven and rocky stream. The viscount's fall proved mortal. He had broken several bones and badly injured his neck. Both paralysis and gangrene soon became apparent.

As he lay on his deathbed, after consulting with his solicitor and after a probing talk with Percy about eternal matters and the destiny of his own soul, Lord Snowdon had requested his nephew to go through his files and put in order what he could, take care of anything it might be best that Katherine not see, and then to take down the private affidavit that now occupied Percy's thoughts.

He withdrew the document from where he kept it among his personal papers. No one, not even his Aunt Katherine nor his father or mother, knew of it. No one else in the world knew of the secrets this affidavit divulged concerning the viscount's past.

Slowly Percy unfolded the paper and began reading again the words, written in his own hand, that stunned him as much now as they had that day the previous June when he first heard them from his uncle's mouth.

To whom it may concern, especially to my dear wife, Katherine, my family, and to Hamilton Murray, our faithful solicitor of many years:

I make this affidavit on the 27th day of June, in the year 1872, in the presence of my nephew, Percival Drummond, son of Edward and Mary Drummond of Glasgow. I am of sound mind, but failing body. Those matters I here disclose, I have kept to myself more than thirty years for the sake of you whom I love so dearly. It was never my intention to speak of them. But conscience now compels me to make a clean breast of it. I earnestly pray that doing so will not cause undo pain, especially to you, my dear Katherine. I pray the truth, though painful, will be its own reward. I do not want to die with secrets on my conscience. May God forgive me if it is wrong to divulge what I could never tell another soul. But if truth matters, then may God heal whatever wounds it may cause. He knows better than anyone that I have not always lived by the dictates and demands of truth. It is admittedly a late time to start. But as my nephew reminds me, it is never too late to make a beginning. I hope therefore that I can die having taken a few faltering steps in the direction of becoming a man of truth.

At sixteen years of age, as a spoiled son of what I thought was wealth, I left Wales on a youthful grand tour, as we called it in those days—to see the world and spend money and generally squander my youth on the altar of irresponsibility. It turned out that my father was not the wealthy man I took him for. Before my travels were over, I was nearly out of money. I found myself in Ireland chasing the fleeting dream of riches in the rivers of Wicklow, though what remained to be found was doubtful. There my heart was smitten with a young Irish lass of working, though not peasant stalk. Her name was Avonmara O'Sullivan.

Several months later we were married in a small parish church in County Wicklow. We were both children, she a mere eighteen years of age and myself nineteen. Whether it was wise or ill fated from the beginning, who can say. But it was done, though our brief happiness would not last...

Percy continued on to the conclusion of the sad tale that had been meant for his ears alone.

Not a moment went by that he was not keenly aware of the burden his uncle had placed upon him. On his shoulders alone rested the decision whether Katherine and Courtenay and Florilyn, or anyone else for that matter, would ever know of Roderick Westbrooke's first marriage. If he judged it best that they never know, then the secret of his past would go to the grave with the former viscount.

His uncle's words had never left him. *"No one must see it unless your search is successful. Otherwise, Katherine need never know."*

Percy had not exactly given his promise. But if he kept it to himself, even out of respect for his uncle, what kind of man of truth did that make *him*? Would he be justified in keeping the matter secret in order to protect the feelings of his aunt? The demand of truth had borne heavily upon his uncle's heart at the end of his life. But what was now the demand of truth that *he* must heed? If a full revelation did no one any discernable *good*, what would be its purpose? Even truth could injure. Was it right to injure for some abstract commitment to truth, if there was no good to anyone to be gained? Thus far, Percy had arrived at no resolution to the complex conundrum.

After talking the matter over in vague terms with his father, without divulging specifics, Percy's conclusion had been that the investigation demanded no serious urgency on his part. It could wait until his graduation from the university the following May. Then he would devote the summer to seeing what he could learn. Perhaps by then more clarity might present itself about how to balance the scales between full disclosure and faithfulness to his uncle's wish that Katherine be protected from pain if his search proved unsuccessful.

Even so, his uncle's dying words gnawed at him. Percy could not escape the feeling that perhaps the matter of the affidavit was more urgent than he might realize. Yet what could he do. . .so far away. . .in Aberdeen? For that matter, what could he do even in Wales? He had no idea how to carry out his uncle's request. To make any beginning at all would require being at Westbrooke Manor.

Obviously that would have to wait. But the more time that passed, the more uneasy he became.

Even as Percy was reading her father's words, in Wales Florilyn was engrossed in the novel by Percy's fellow Scot, George MacDonald.

As she neared the end of the book, she was reminded of its opening where the characters Hugh Sutherland and Margaret Elginbrod first met. She flipped back to the beginning of the volume and read it again.

> *"It was, of course, quite by accident that Sutherland had met Margaret in the fir-wood. The wind had changed during the night, and swept all the clouds from the face of the sky; and when he looked out in the morning, he saw the fir-tops waving in the sunlight, and heard the sound of a south-west wind sweeping through them with the tune of running waters in its course. Sutherland's heart began to be joyful at the sight of the genial motions of Nature, telling of warmth and blessedness at hand. He dressed in haste, and went out to meet the Spring. He wandered into the heart of the wood. The wind blew cool, but not cold; and was filled with a delicious odour from the earth, which Sutherland took as a sign that she was coming alive at last. And the Spring he went out to meet, met him. For, first, at the foot of a tree, he spied a tiny primrose, peeping out of its rough, careful leaves. As he passed on with the primrose in his hand, thinking it was almost cruel to pluck it, the Spring met him, as if in her own shape, in the person of Margaret, whom he spied a little way off, leaning against the stem*

of a Scotch fir. He went up to her with some shyness; for the presence of even a child-maiden was enough to make Sutherland shy. But she, when she heard his footsteps, dropped her eyes slowly from the tree-top, and waited his approach. He said nothing at first, but offered her, instead of speech, the primrose he had just plucked, which she received with a smile of the eyes only, and the sweetest 'thank you, sir,' he had ever heard. . .a lovely girl, with the woman waking in her eyes."

Florilyn had not been present when Percy and Gwyneth first met on the slopes of the Snowdonian hills, though she had heard about it from both of them. As she read again of this fictional meeting between MacDonald's two characters, she was suddenly struck with the similarity between the two. Percy's meeting of Gwyneth that day had also been accidental, prompted, Florilyn hardly needed to be reminded, by her own deceit toward her cousin on their first ride together. Even then, as Percy had described her, he had begun "to be joyful at the sight of the genial motions of Nature." His meeting with Gwyneth that day had also involved an exchange of flowers, though in their case from the girl to the young man. And could more apt words than MacDonald's of Margaret be chosen to describe Gwyneth during those years when everyone thought her still a "child-maiden," but when in fact womanhood was slowly "waking in her eyes"? The similarities between the fictional characters of the novel and Percy's first summer in Wales were remarkable.

Florilyn set the book aside and drew in a long, reflective sigh. So much had changed since then. Percy had indeed become nature's friend. Gwyneth had grown from the child-maiden into a woman. She had become their maid for a season at the manor but was now gone from their lives. In Gwyneth's absence, Florilyn herself had become engaged to Percy. Who could have foreseen any of it five years ago?

With a deep breath, Florilyn returned to her place toward the end of the book and resumed her reading.

Fourteen

Contingency Plans

Ever since her daughter's lighthearted banter about what they would do if Courtenay proved troublesome after acceding to the title, Katherine Westbrooke had been revolving an idea in her mind. The notion of living in a cottage in the hills may have sounded romantic to Florilyn, but it was not Katherine's idea of an attractive prospect. She needed no luxury—she could be happy even in a humble cottage. But she did not relish the idea of being so isolated and remote as they would be at the former Muir cottage. Especially with Roderick now gone, she needed to stay in contact with people, not only locally but with her brother and Mary in Glasgow. She needed the daily post and the option of easy travel that being near the coach and rail lines afforded.

On a day when she was certain that Courtenay would not learn of her movements, neither mentioning her plans to Florilyn or Steven or Adela, she requested of Steven a ride into the village to meet the northbound coach. She would be back the following day, she explained, when he could meet her again. She only told them that she must pay a visit to someone on the peninsula. She divulged nothing more.

Later that afternoon, she was seated in the office of Hamilton Murray, of Murray, Sidcup, and Murray. She came straight to the point. "I realize that you and I do not know one another extremely well, Mr. Murray," she began. "You were faithful to my husband, and I know he considered you a friend as well. However, as our son will himself be viscount in eighteen months, I realize that you are in a somewhat delicate position. Technically, for the present you represent me according to the terms of the trusteeship my husband established. In less than two years, however, you will be my son's solicitor. It may be that my son's interests and mine are not in harmony. He has, I believe, been to see you about finances."

"He has," nodded Murray.

"My question, then," Katherine went on, "is a simple one. How far may I trust you, Mr. Murray? If my present wishes were at odds with what might be considered my son's future best interest—or let me say, his most *lucrative* future interest—where would your loyalties lie?"

"I am the estate's solicitor," replied Murray. "At present I represent you. I will be faithful to carry out your wishes in whatever—"

"Please, Mr. Murray," interrupted Katherine. "I know a little at least about legal obfuscation. I need advice, and I need to know which side of the fence you are standing on. I need to know if I can trust you to give me advice that is in my best interest, despite the fact that doing so may prove awkward for you in the future when you find yourself representing my son. If not, I will seek that advice from an objective third party. I am asking you, as a man of integrity, to tell me candidly if you would be looking to your future professional relations with my son and the estate when he is viscount in how you advised *me* during this interim."

Murray took in her statement thoughtfully. The hint of a smile creased his lips. "Your husband knew what he was doing in making you trustee," he said at length. "You are very plain spoken, and I admire that. So I will be as well. I do not mean to offend you, Lady Snowdon, and please forgive my bluntness. . .but the fact is, I do not like your son. He may turn out to be wonderfully gracious and selfless, but at present I do not see such qualities manifesting themselves. It would grieve me to see him take actions that would hurt the estate or the people of the surrounding region. It thus behooves me to remain the solicitor for the Westbrooke estate if possible so that I might exert what influence lies open to me to keep that from happening. On the other hand, if I should offend him and should he choose to retain other counsel, I would not grieve overmuch. Though such is not always possible, I prefer to represent individuals whom I respect. I will not intentionally cross your son, but neither will I attempt to curry his favor. I hope my meaning is clear. My loyalties at present are entirely and unequivocally to yourself and your late husband. I would not give a second's thought to whether your son would approve or disapprove of either your actions or my own."

"Very well," rejoined Katherine, "then I will lay out my predicament to you. I think it entirely possible that Courtenay will make life difficult for me once he inherits. It is not for myself alone that I am concerned but also for my daughter, and for my factor, the young man Steven Muir, and his mother, who also recently lost her husband. I have money, of course. Courtenay could do nothing to render me destitute, but he could make my life extremely unpleasant. It is not my desire to leave Westbrooke Manor. But I have to realize that such may become almost an inevitability once he is in control of everything. He is already angry with me at finding himself financially strapped—a condition which he lays at my feet rather than his own. He has essentially demanded money under threat of doing exactly what I said—making my life unbearable in the future. It breaks my heart to be at odds with him. He is my son, after all, and I love him. But I must also be realistic about my own future and make plans for myself should remaining at Westbrooke Manor become impossible."

"You do not seriously believe that he would throw you out?" said Murray. "I am not certain whether he even could do so legally. I shall have to look into the matter."

"I doubt he would try anything so drastic," said Katherine. "But he could make it a miserable place for me to live, especially after Florilyn is married and possibly gone. I could not remain where I was scorned and looked down upon. The awkwardness of it would be extreme."

"What do you have in mind?" asked the solicitor.

Katherine drew in a long breath. "I have been revolving in my mind a plan about which I would need your counsel and help," she went on after a moment. "I would like to secure a property, or perhaps several properties, that I could own in my own name, free and unencumbered by the estate. Would this be possible, such that they would be unassailable by Courtenay?"

"You could of course purchase any form of property you like in your own name," replied Murray.

"But all the land for miles in every direction is owned by the estate?"

"You are, I take it, planning to stay in the Llanfryniog region?"

"Such would be my intention. It is my home. Much, I suppose, would depend on Florilyn's future. If there were grandchildren, naturally I would want to be near her family. I confess it is my hope that Florilyn and her husband may remain in the area as well. As I said, I am thinking of trying to make provision for us all that will be free from Courtenay's potential interference."

"I see. So you are asking me how you might acquire land near your present home?"

Katherine nodded.

"As long as you are in control of the trusteeship, you can sell estate lands."

"Are you saying that I could sell land or a property owned by the estate. . .to myself?"

"That would be the simplest way. I see nothing legally that would stop you."

"And if I purchased a house in the village, say, or bought a parcel of acreage and built a new house upon it, with my own money, Courtenay could do nothing to evict me?"

"Provided we attend to all the proper legalities to be certain the deed is drawn up and registered to you, he would have no power over it whatever. The property would be yours."

"He would be furious, no doubt. He would see it as my having stolen a portion of his inheritance."

"There would be nothing he could do about it. And he would benefit from such a transaction. Essentially you would be buying the property from your son. As you know, the estate does not bring in a great income, a fact that was something of a trial for your late husband. Perhaps your son would be grateful."

Katherine nodded. "Somehow I doubt it," she said. "In any event, I think you have answered my question, Mr. Murray. I shall begin looking for suitable property where, if worse comes to worst, I may live out my years. You could, I assume, draw up all the necessary legal documents?"

"Certainly. The only stipulation in any such transaction is that you would have to pay the estate a fair market price so that your son could not later contest the sale in court. But that is easily managed. We would bring in an outside appraiser for just such a purpose."

"Then I will pay *more* than market price."

Katherine spent the night at a boardinghouse and returned on the southbound coach the next day. Even as she bounced through Llanfryniog beside Steven Muir on her way back to the manor, Katherine glanced about with new eyes, wondering where among the homes of the region she might make her future.

That same afternoon she went out for a long and thoughtful ride of several hours, through the streets of Llanfryniog and back along the plateau up to Mochras Head before returning inland to Westbrooke Manor. Her mind was full of many things.

Fifteen

David Elginbrod

Florilyn was about four-fifths of the way through the novel, *David Elginbrod.* The title character was now dead. As she read, reminded of the death of her own father, Florilyn felt a fleeting bond with David's daughter, Margaret Elginbrod. But they were from such different stations. Margaret was a peasant. Try as she would, Florilyn could not quite put herself in Margaret's shoes.

Suddenly as she began reading the chapter entitled "The Lady's Maid," Florilyn realized, if she was going to place herself in the story at all, she was not the character of Margaret; she was *Euphra Cameron*—the spoiled aristocratic young woman Hugh Sutherland was enchanted with.

The realization was far from pleasant. Fictional though she was, Euphra was mean, self-centered, and petty. Hugh's fascination with her was one of the mysteries of the story.

With suddenly heightened interest, Florilyn read of Euphra's treatment of Margaret upon discovery of the personal letter she had written to David Elginbrod, not yet knowing him to be Margaret's father.

> *"Margaret had sought Euphra's room, with the intention of restoring to her the letter which she had written. Hopes of ministration filled Margaret's heart; but she expected, from what she knew of her, that anger would be Miss Cameron's first feeling.*

'What do you want?' she said angrily.

'This is your letter, Miss Cameron, is it not?' said Margaret, advancing with it in her hand.

Euphra took it, glanced at the direction, started up in a passion, and let loose the whole gathered irritability of contempt, weariness, disappointment, and suffering, upon Margaret. Her dark eyes flashed with rage.

'What right have you, pray, to handle my letters? How did you get this! And open, too. I declare! I suppose you have read it?'

Margaret was afraid of exciting more wrath before she had an opportunity of explaining; but Euphra gave her no time to think of a reply.

'You have read it, you shameless woman! Impudent prying! Pray, did you hope to find a secret worth a bribe?'

She advanced on Margaret till within a foot of her.

'Why don't you answer, you hussy?'

Margaret stood quietly, waiting for an opportunity to speak. Her face was very pale, but perfectly still, and her eyes did not quail.

'You do not know my name, Miss Cameron; of course you could not.'

'Your name! What is that to me?'

'That,' said Margaret, pointing to the letter, 'is my father's name.'

Euphra looked at her own direction again, and then looked at Margaret. She was so bewildered, that if she had any thoughts, she did not know them. Margaret went on:

'My father is dead. My mother sent the letter to me.'

'What is it to you? Do you think I am going to make a confidante of you?' "

Florilyn's heart smote her, and she could read no more. She put the book aside as tears filled her eyes.

She had been just like Euphra. She had treated poor Gwyneth the same way—rudely and angrily. If parallels with the story were to be drawn, Gwyneth was the saintly Margaret, and she was the unlovely Euphra.

She had changed, thought Florilyn to herself, and she thanked God for it. But there were times when the memory of what she had once been still made her cry. She had been shameful toward Gwyneth. Maybe she *was* Euphra after all!

Once the parallels with the story were clear, Florilyn saw them everywhere. It might as well have been a story set in Westbrooke Manor! On every page as she read over the ensuing days, as Margaret became Euphra's maid, as their friendship blossomed, as Euphra began to grow and change, and as it became clear that both girls were smitten with Hugh Sutherland, Florilyn was no longer reading about Margaret and Euphra. . .she was reading about herself and Gwyneth and Percy!

She was drawn into the story so deeply that she was living in it. What intrigue the love triangle took on in her mind! Of course Margaret and Euphra shared their feelings about Hugh far more openly than she and Gwyneth ever had about Percy.

"Margaret could not proceed very far in the story of her life without making some reference to Hugh Sutherland. But she carefully avoided mentioning his name.

'Ah!' said Euphra, one day, 'your history is a little like mine there; a tutor comes into them both. Did you not fall dreadfully in love with him?'

'I loved him very much.'

'Do you never see him?'

Margaret was silent. Euphra knew her well enough not to repeat the question.

'I should have been in love with him, I know. . .Mr. Sutherland did me some good, Margaret.'

'Mr. Sutherland loved you very much, Miss Cameron.' "

It was exactly what dear Gwyneth might have said! Florilyn remembered when Gwyneth had urged Percy to go to the party at Burrenchobay Hall with her. Even as she continued her reading, the names on the page might have been Percival Drummond, Florilyn Westbrooke, and Gwyneth Barrie.

> *"'He loved me once,' said poor Euphra, with a sigh.*
>
> *'I saw he did. That was why I began to love you too.'*
>
> *Margaret had at last unwittingly opened the door of her secret. But Euphra could not understand what she meant.*
>
> *'What do you mean, Margaret?'*
>
> *Margaret both blushed and laughed outright.*
>
> *'I must confess it,' said she, at once; 'it cannot hurt him now: my tutor and yours are the same.'*
>
> *'And you never spoke all the time he was here!'*
>
> *'Not once. He never knew I was in the house.'*
>
> *'How strange! And you saw he loved me?'*
>
> *'Yes.'*
>
> *'And you were not jealous?'*
>
> *'I did not say that. But I soon found that the only way to escape from my jealousy, if the feeling I had was jealousy, was to love you too. I did.'*
>
> *'You beautiful creature! But you could not have loved him much.'*
>
> *'I loved him enough to love you for his sake.'*
>
> *It would have been unendurable to Euphra, a little while before, to find that she had a rival in a servant. Now she scarcely regarded that aspect of her position."*

Again Florilyn put the book down thoughtfully. *Had* Gwyneth been in love with Percy? If so, she would never have divulged it.

Sixteen

Surveying the Landscape

Katherine Westbrooke's brain had been busy. She knew that time passed quickly. She must not unnecessarily delay whatever planned changes she hoped to make. She would have to complete all necessary legalities before Courtenay's twenty-fifth birthday or he would move to stop her in the courts. She hoped, as Hamilton Murray had suggested, that he might be grateful for the infusion of cash into the estate's coffers. However, she knew she mustn't bank on the unpredictable responses of a self-motivated and, as things presently stood, angry young man.

She therefore made a number of visits to the village and its environs, but thus far without inspiration coming to her.

The only home within miles that might have been considered large enough and suitable for the extended household of an aristocratic dowager viscountess was that occupied by Styles Lorimer and his wife and daughter, Rhawn, and her son. There were rumors that Mr. and Mrs. Lorimer were considering a move to southern England. But nothing was known for certain. It was doubtful they would make a decision anytime soon.

There were several sizeable farms within a mile or two of Llanfryniog. All were occupied, however, and she had no intention of evicting one of her tenants for the sake of her own potential future need.

Gradually the idea floated out of the mists to the surface of Katherine's thoughts. What was to prevent her building a new home instead? Florilyn's words returned to her memory: *"We shall build a second cottage to go with it."* If they could build a cottage, they could just as well build a house sizeable enough to suit all her needs, with stables and paddocks and pastures and meadows for whatever animals she wanted to raise, as well as quarters for Adela and Steven, and perhaps, she dared only hope, also for her daughter and family. Nothing so imposing or on the grand scale of the manor itself—her funds were not unlimited, nor were her tastes of an extravagant nature—but something large enough to be functional and comfortable for two or three families.

At length Katherine realized it was time she spoke with Florilyn, divulged what was on her mind, and canvassed her thoughts on the matter. A decision could possibly affect her future as well.

She waited until Courtenay was at Burrenchobay Hall visiting Colville Burrenchobay then sought Florilyn in her room. "I would like to talk to you, dear," she said, poking her head through the open doorway.

Florilyn glanced up from her book then laid it aside. "Of course, Mother," she said. "Come in. Your expression looks serious. Is something wrong?"

Katherine sat down in one of several chairs about the expansive room and drew in a long sigh. "It shows that plainly, does it?" she said with a melancholy smile.

"I don't always know *what* you are thinking," rejoined Florilyn. "But I can tell when you are downcast."

"It's about your brother," said Katherine. "He's much changed since your father's death."

"I know it only too well. I used to think we were friends. He's too snooty and full of himself to bother with the likes of me now. I hate the way he treats you, Mother."

"It's obvious he resents not being able to lord it over us. He thinks he should have been made viscount immediately. He also blames me for his present financial straits."

"It's not your fault that Daddy's not here to indulge him."

"He thinks it is my duty to continue doing so. The anger that is stewing inside him is worrisome to me. Honestly, Florilyn, I am very concerned for our future. You, of course, will be married. But I fear Courtenay may make my life so intolerable here that I may have no alternative but to find another place to live. We spoke about it almost jokingly before. I now fear it may be more likely than we thought. Leaving the manor may become a practical necessity."

"But the manor is *yours*, Mother."

"It won't be once Courtenay turns twenty-five."

"Where would you go?"

"I have been reflecting on what you said before, about us living in a cottage in the hills."

"I was just thinking out loud, Mother!" laughed Florilyn. "I didn't *really* think you would leave the manor."

"What if I have to? What would you think if I built a new house that would not be under Courtenay's control?"

Florilyn stared back at her mother without expression. "You mean... Where, Mother...on the grounds somewhere?" she said at length.

"I don't know...somewhere near the village, yet far enough from the manor where we could live our own lives."

Florilyn rose and wandered to her window. She stood with her back to her mother, looking out toward the hills of Snowdonia to the east and the plateau overlooking the waters of Tremadog Bay to the west. "You said *we*," she said at length.

"I know you will be married," rejoined Katherine. "But that may not take place before Courtenay's twenty-fifth birthday... I don't know what your plans are. But do *you* relish the idea of being here after that?"

"We could live our own lives, Mother."

"What if he took it into his head to charge you rent?"

Florilyn spun around from the window. "He wouldn't dare!" she said.

"He might not be able to evict me because of my position, but I doubt there would be any restrictions on what he could do to you."

The two women were quiet for several moments.

"Then let's go for a ride, Mother," said Florilyn at length. "We shall look for a perfect place for your new home!"

An hour later, mother and daughter set out from Westbrooke Manor on Red Rhud and Crimson Son. They rode east, up the rising slope to the top of the inland ridge, then bore northward. From the height they had gained, the entire plateau below, stretching down to the village of Llanfryniog, and the blue waters of Tremadog Bay were visible, with their own Westbrooke Manor and its grounds and gardens below and to their left.

"What a beautiful site this would be for a home!" exclaimed Katherine as they rode, with the sea and coastline all spread out below.

"You would have to build a road all the way up here, Mother."

"A road would be more easily managed than building a house! If it were to be *your* home, Florilyn—and who is to say that it wouldn't be one day—and if you could live anywhere in the entire region, where would *you* choose?"

Florilyn reined in and gazed all about. "That is a hard question, Mother," she said. "But. . .let me see. . . I do love the mountains. But then there is snow in the winter when you get too far inland. And the sight of the sea is spectacular. Just think what it would be to have all your windows overlooking the ocean."

Florilyn's thoughts drifted back to an hour earlier when she and her mother had been talking in her room, and the view as she was standing at the window. "Probably down there, Mother," she said after a minute. She pointed from their high vantage point to the plateau of Mochras Head. "On the headland overlooking the sea."

Katherine followed her daughter's outstretched arm. Slowly she began to nod. "Yes, I see. . .it would be a spectacular site for a home. Closer to the manor," she added, "but also near to the village and main road. Shall we go have a closer look? I may like your idea."

She turned Crimson Son down the slope in the direction of the sea, and Florilyn followed.

Seventeen

The Revelation of the Fir Wood

Florilyn reached the last chapter of her book. As she began reading, her eyes grew wide.

It wasn't only that two girls both loved Hugh Sutherland. Hugh had to discover which of the two *he* really loved. . .and had loved all along.

A sudden pang seized Florilyn's heart. It was *not* the aristocratic Euphra that in the end took possession of Hugh's heart, but the peasant girl Margaret!

"She was the angel herself," she read on the page.

Percy often called Gwyneth an angel.

Hugh at length discovered that he had loved Margaret from the first day in the fir wood. Was her own fate, Florilyn mused, destined to be the same as Euphra's? Loving. . .would *she*, too, have to let him go?

> *"It was with a mingling of strange emotions that Hugh approached the scene of those not very old, and yet, to his feeling, quite early memories. The dusk was beginning to gather. The hoar-frost lay thick on the ground. The pine-trees stood up in the cold.*
>
> *Here and there amongst them, rose the Titans of the little forest—the huge, old, contorted, wizard-like, yet benevolent*

beings—the Scotch firs. Towards one of these he bent his way. It was the one under which he had seen Margaret, when he met her first in the wood. To think that the young girl to whom he had given the primrose he had just found should now be the queen of his heart! Her childish dream of the angel haunting the wood had been true, only she was the angel herself. He drew near the place. How well he knew it! He seated himself, cold as it was in the February of Scotland, at the foot of the blessed tree.

While he sat with his eyes fixed on the ground, a light rustle in the fallen leaves made him raise them suddenly. It was all winter and fallen leaves about him; but he lifted his eyes, and in his soul it was summer: Margaret stood before him. She looked just the same—at home everywhere; most at home in Nature's secret chamber.

She came nearer.

'Margaret!' he murmured.

She came close to him. He rose, trembling.

'Margaret, dare I love you?' he faltered.

She looked at him with wide-open eyes.

'Me?' exclaimed Margaret, and her eyes did not move from his. A slight rose-flush bloomed out on her motionless face.

She looked at him with parted lips.

'Do you remember this?' she said, taking from her pocket a little book, and from the book a withered flower.

Hugh saw that it was like a primrose, and hoped against hope that it was the one which he had given to her, on the spring morning in the fir-wood.

'Why did you keep that?' he said.

'Because I loved you.'

'Loved me?'

'Yes. Didn't you know?'

'Why did you say, then, that you didn't care if—if—?'

'Because love is enough, Hugh.—That was why.'"

Tears flooded Florilyn's eyes. The deepest love had not come as Hugh had expected it. He *thought* he had loved Euphra. But his heart had belonged to Margaret all along. In the same way, Percy *thought* he was in love with her.

But from the beginning. . .since his first days in Wales. . .had his heart always belonged—?

Florilyn burst into sobs. She could not complete the thought. She closed the book, rose, and went to her window. She stood for several minutes but could not stop the flow of tears.

At length she left her room and walked down the corridor away from the main staircase, seeking the back stairs and door to the outside that Percy had himself used many times. The cool air felt good on her hot face. But it could not still the turmoil in her heart.

With the weather turning increasingly cold and damp, for the next several weeks Florilyn made the approaching winter her companion in melancholy. For hours she walked along the Mochras promontory staring down at the gray sea below or along the chilly misty beach beneath the headland or in the gardens of the manor or woods nearer home. Daily she visited little Nugget, who recognized her voice and came scampering at her call.

Not having been a great reader, Florilyn had never before experienced the power of a book to move the human heart so deeply. But this story, and the interwoven lives of its two young women loving the same young man, along with the fictional fir wood, which in her mind had become the fields and hills of North Wales, pressed heavily upon her heart.

At length she knew what she had to do.

She must let Percy discover his own fir wood. . .and who was the angel awaiting him there.

EIGHTEEN

Wales Again

As Percy and his mother and father sat clattering south in the train from Glasgow, Percy could not escape the feeling that something beyond a festive Christmas celebration awaited him in Wales. It would be going too far to call it a sense of impending doom. Yet perhaps something a little like it.

"You're uncommonly quiet, Percy," said his mother on the afternoon of their first day of the journey.

"Sorry, Mother," smiled Percy. "A lot on my mind I suppose."

"School?"

"No, not really. It's going well, though I am anticipating graduating in May with more than a little eagerness."

"You still haven't said what you will do after you and Florilyn are married—go to work for Mr. Snyder or begin law school."

"That's because I haven't decided myself. Actually, I may do neither. There's something. . .I have to take care of—a personal matter. I don't know how long it will take."

"What is it?" asked Mrs. Drummond.

"I can't say, Mother," answered Percy. He glanced toward his father. "I told Dad about it last summer and said the same thing—that I couldn't tell him the specifics. It's something I promised Uncle Roderick I would look into before he died. I have no idea what will be involved or how long it will take. Beyond that, I can say nothing. I promised it would remain between him and me."

It was quiet a few minutes. Percy stared out the window at the passing countryside and at last let out a long sigh. "But it's more than that," he said, turning again toward his mother. "Something seems to have changed with Florilyn in recent weeks."

"How do you mean, Percy?" asked Mary.

"I don't know. It's hard to put my finger on. Her letters have just been. . .different—distant, detached, almost formal in a way. We were writing back and forth regularly, sharing about everything—it was like talking with each other in person. We've both been reading the same MacDonald novel—I told you about that—and discussing it in our letters. All of a sudden last month I didn't hear from her for two weeks. When at last another letter came, like I said, it was different. It's been that way ever since. She's not mentioned the book again. She says almost nothing personal. It's altogether strange."

"She is probably just nervous about getting married."

"Why would she be, Mother? I thought all young women longed to be married."

Mary laughed. "You are probably right. I was just trying to find a logical explanation."

"I know it's pointless to worry about it," said Percy. "I'm sure it will all come clear soon enough. She says she has something important to talk to me about. Whatever it is, I know she will tell me in her own way. But the change in her letters has been disconcerting."

The three Christmas travelers in the southbound coach bounded to a stop in front of Mistress Chattan's inn on the following day. The main street through Llayfryniog lay in mud from one side to the other. A chill wind swept up from the sea, bending the smoke from every chimney in the village horizontal toward the inland mountains, by now all covered with snow.

Percy's previous visits to Snowdonia had come in summer, when the land and air were rich and full of warmth and growth and life. As he stepped out of the coach onto the muddy street and glanced about, a drearier prospect could hardly be imagined. As a Scot, he knew well enough what winter could be like. He had left Aberdeen four days earlier with snowdrifts piled three feet high along the sides of the streets. He had somehow hoped, this far south, that it might be warmer. One look up and down the familiar street, however, told him instantly how wrong he had been. Even snowdrifts would be preferable to mud.

A two-seat carriage from the manor sat just up the street waiting for them. Inside, bundled in coats and hats and scarves and blankets, sat Katherine and Florilyn.

As Edward climbed down from one side of the coach, and Percy emerged out the door of the other, Steven Muir ran along the walkway beside the inn to meet them.

"Stevie!" exclaimed Percy as the two shook hands.

"Welcome back to Wales, Percy," said Steven. "And to you, Mr. Drummond," he added to Edward.

"It is good to see you once again, Steven," said Edward. "I understand congratulations are in order for your new position at the manor."

"Thank you," replied Steven. "Your sister has been very kind to me. Hello, Mrs. Drummond," he added as Edward helped Percy's mother to the ground. "Lady Katherine and Lady Florilyn are there in the carriage," he said, pointing ahead. "I told them to stay bundled up. You may go get settled with them if you like. We brought extra blankets. I will see to your bags."

The three made their way along the walkway to the waiting carriage. As they approached, the two women set aside the blankets that had been spread over their knees and stepped to the ground.

"Mary. . .Edward!" said Katherine, approaching with open arms. "I'm sorry we aren't able to welcome you with a more pleasant day."

"Winter in Britain is a universal trial to us all!" laughed Edward. "We Scots are used to it, you know as well as I do. We both grew up in worse than this."

Behind her mother, Florilyn shook hands with her aunt and uncle then glanced toward Percy where he waited at their side.

"Florilyn!" he said, bounding forward and wrapping her in his arms.

She said nothing, slowly stretching her arms around his back, though without corresponding pressure to answer his embrace. They stepped back. Florilyn smiled, though somewhat awkwardly, then turned toward the carriage. The others followed. Whether it was by design or accident, Florilyn scrambled onto the rear bench between her mother and aunt, seemingly by intent to avoid finding herself at Percy's side, while father and son took their places in front.

A moment later Steven jumped up to join them, sat down between the two men, grabbed the reins, and they were off. The ride of a mile and a half passed quickly. Before they knew it, the gray stones of Westbrooke Manor were looming through the bare trees before them.

Nineteen

A Conversation in the Library

The three Drummonds had arrived at Westbrooke Manor on the morning before Christmas Eve. Percy returned to town with Steven to retrieve their bags. By the time they returned and were safely back inside, it had begun to rain and the temperature had dropped several degrees. There was no talk of walks or rides outside for the rest of the day.

The company remained indoors and mostly together after lunch and for most of the afternoon. Courtenay, however, did not grace their Scottish guests with the honor of his presence.

Even though they were together nearly the entire rest of the day, Percy and Florilyn were never alone, and their conversation remained light. Florilyn was friendly though subdued. By day's end, Percy was more convinced than ever that something was amiss.

Florilyn made no appearance on Christmas Eve morning in the breakfast room. She had never been an early riser. Nevertheless, Percy was surprised. As much as they had anticipated seeing one another, it was almost—though how could that be—as if she were avoiding him. Her exuberance after his arrival on his previous two visits was nowhere in evidence.

Early in the afternoon, Percy wandered to the library. The familiar sights and smells greeted him with a wave of pleasant nostalgia. He smiled as he breathed in deeply then began absently wandering through the rows of tall shelves, glancing up and down and sideways at the spines of the old volumes. He was in no frame of mind at the moment to sit down and read, though he recalled fondly his first excursion into this bookish wonderland more than five years before when his aunt had first introduced him to author George MacDonald.

He turned a corner at the end of the row of shelves and saw a figure in an alcove with her back turned. She stood staring out the tall bay window. This time it was not his aunt but the young woman whose quiet behavior had been occupying his thoughts. Slowly he approached from behind. "A penny for your thoughts," said Percy softly.

Florilyn heard his step and was not startled by his voice. She remained still as a statue.

Percy came to her side and stood looking out upon the wet, dreary winter's day. It was an altogether depressing outlook. It was nothing, however, compared to the desolation at that moment in Florilyn Westbrooke's heart.

They stood for a long while in silence.

Finally Percy turned toward her. His movement at last broke the pent-up dam in Florilyn's heart. She turned to face him with the most forlorn expression he had ever seen on her face. The look in her eyes was pleading. . .fearful for what she knew she must do.

"Oh, Percy!" she said as she broke into tears.

Still with no idea what was the cause of her dismay, Percy said nothing. He merely opened his arms and received her into his embrace. Florilyn laid her head on his chest and softly wept.

They stood thus for several minutes until the initial storm passed. After some time Percy led her to a small couch in one of the library's several reading nooks. They sat down together. He waited.

"There is something I must talk to you about," said Florilyn at length. Her voice was shaky and halting.

"I know," said Percy, smiling.

"You know?"

"I knew *something* was on your mind. Your letters changed. I knew you would tell me when you were ready."

"Oh Percy, I'm sorry. I should have told you sooner. I didn't know what to say. I wanted to wait until I saw you. But once I did see you yesterday I was filled with so many doubts and fears and I didn't want to hurt you. I didn't know what to do."

"You have nothing to fear from me," he said. "Surely you know that."

"I know, Percy," rejoined Florilyn. "You are so good to me. You were always better to me than I deserved."

"Now don't let's get started on that again!" said Percy with a light laugh. "We've been over all that before."

"You know what I mean. I'm just grateful, that's all."

"So what is it you have to tell me? Let's get it out. It's Christmas Eve, you know. Big dinner planned tonight. We don't want to cast a pall over the festivities."

"It's not so easy," said Florilyn with a sad smile. She drew in a deep breath and exhaled slowly. "Oh, Percy. . . I love you so much. You know that, don't you?"

"I do," replied Percy. "The feeling is mutual."

"That's what makes it so hard. Percy. . . How much of the MacDonald novel have you read? You haven't finished it, have you?"

"I'm afraid not. I bogged down probably about halfway. There's always a big push with papers and assignments before the Christmas break. Why? What does the book have to do with it?"

"Everything. Didn't you see the similarities in it. . .you know, with us. . .between you and Hugh and everything?"

"Hmm. . .actually, no," said Percy thoughtfully. "You think I am like Hugh?"

"You aren't *like* him—but the circumstances. . .his going to university in Aberdeen just like you. . .his meeting Margaret."

"I, uh. . .I didn't think about that. And you see a parallel between you and Margaret?"

"Not me. . .Gwyneth."

He stared back at her, confused at the point she was trying to make. "In the story, Hugh. . ." Percy began. "Hugh is in love with Euphra," he said. "What does Margaret have to do with it?"

"He *thinks* he is in love with Euphra," rejoined Florilyn. "Oh Percy, this would be so much simpler if you had read the ending. It's all in the book."

"All what?"

"Oh, Percy!" Florilyn blurted out. "I think we may have made a mistake!"

Percy looked at her in disbelief.

Again Florilyn began to cry.

"You. . .don't think we should marry?"

"That's not it! I can't imagine anything more wonderful than being your wife. Who wouldn't want to be your wife? But I think maybe we rushed into it too quickly. Perhaps we *are* meant to be husband and wife. But I think we decided too fast. I suppose that. . . Well, I'm not *completely* sure I'm in love with you, Percy. I mean. . .I *do* love you, but. . .I think I may have been, I don't know, so flattered that you asked me to marry you, that maybe I was too caught up with the *idea* of being in love that I never stopped to ask myself if I was *actually* in love with you. I thought I was, all those years after your first visit. But once we were engaged, and after finishing the book. . .I just wasn't sure anymore. I'm so sorry. And then. . .I also cannot help asking. . .whether you are truly in love with me." She paused.

Percy waited, still reeling from what he had heard.

"Do you remember telling me about you and your father talking about how God uses circumstances to lead us in making decisions?"

Percy nodded. "Of course," he replied softly.

"What I have been sensing," Florilyn went on, "is that perhaps we rushed too quickly into it last July. Perhaps we misinterpreted what the changing circumstances were supposed to mean."

"What changing circumstances?" asked Percy.

"Gwyneth's leaving," answered Florilyn. "You told me then that you had to wrestle through what it meant."

"I remember. And I did wrestle through it," said Percy. "What does Gwyneth have to do with it now?"

"Percy!" said Florilyn almost in frustration. "She has everything to do with it. *She* is the reason we have to wait. I should say she is the reason *you* have to wait. I have to wait to be sure of my *own* heart. We both have to wait for different reasons. Don't you see? You *think* you wrestled it through, but it was only a week. Then the decision was made. I'm not sure that was enough time for either of us to fully know our hearts."

Percy exhaled a long sigh. "I think I see what you mean...in principle at least. The idea is going to take some getting used to. I still don't see what you mean about Gwyneth and the MacDonald book."

"Gwyneth is Margaret in the book, Percy! Hugh thought he was in love with Euphra...but all along he was meant to discover his love for *Margaret*. Don't you see? In the same way, what if part of your heart still belongs to Gwyneth? You have to find out. You have to discover what is deep in your heart, just as I have to discover what is in mine."

Percy sat staring back at Florilyn dumbfounded. Slowly he began shaking his head. "I—I don't know what to say," he said softly.

"Finish reading the book, Percy," said Florilyn. "Then you will understand."

"What do you want to do then?"

"I think you should talk it over with your father," replied Florilyn. "Then I think we should simply call off the engagement...for now at least. Please understand, this doesn't mean that my feelings for you have changed. But I have to be sure about those feelings. I have to be *certain* I am in love with you. And I want you to discover your own fir wood."

"My...fir wood?"

"Finish the book, Percy. You have to find out who is the angel waiting for you in the fir wood."

"I will talk to my father," he said, nodding. "He will probably want to talk to us both. I'm sure he will want to hear what you are thinking from your own lips." Percy rose and walked again to the window. "It looks like the rain may be letting up," he said. "Perhaps we shall get a ride in eventually."

"It's still chilly out," rejoined Florilyn. "It was so cold yesterday I was surprised to wake up this morning and not see snow on the ground. I was certain snow was in the air."

Percy turned and walked back to the couch. He extended his hand. Florilyn took it, and he pulled her to her feet. "We're still friends, right?" he said, trying to sound upbeat, though still more than a little confused by this sudden turn of events.

"Oh Percy, we will always be much more than just friends! It is only that I want to be sure that we read God's leading in the right way. Marriage is too important to rush into."

"Then we will continue to talk and pray. . .and talk to my father. In the meantime, why don't we bundle up and go outside, and you can introduce me to this new colt of Grey Tide's that you are so fond of."

Twenty

Edward Drummond

Having disclosed the burdens that were pressing upon her, Florilyn's spirits immediately lifted. She was gay and lively again. After dressing for it, they went outside to visit Percy's old friends in the stables, as well as little Nugget who was growing rapidly. It took Percy an hour or two, however, to absorb and readjust to the suddenly altered outlook on his future.

Midway through the afternoon, as the women were busy with Adela Muir and Mrs. Drenwydd and Mrs. Llewellyn in the kitchen and dining room with Christmas food preparation and decorating, Percy sought his father. "Dad," he said, "there's something important I need to talk to you about. Could we go for a walk outside? It's not raining at the minute. I need your advice."

As she had once before, Florilyn watched from one of the windows as Percy and his father, bundled up against the cold, walked away from the house in earnest conversation. A fresh wave of sadness enveloped her. A few rapid misty blinks of her eyes followed. She could not prevent a nagging fear that she had relinquished her best and only chance to be married at all. But mostly she was relieved to have at last released the anxiety that had consumed her for weeks. Whatever the future held, she knew she had done the *right* thing. She was content now to leave the matter in the hands of the two men and God.

She turned away and tried to distract herself with candles and ribbons and the Christmas tree and a few last gifts to wrap. But it was no use. She could think of nothing but the conversation taking place outside.

At length she went upstairs to her room. In her present frame of mind, she would rather be alone. Absently she picked up a book and sat down in her favorite chair and tried to read. But she could not concentrate.

She started at the sound of a knock on her door twenty minutes later. She jumped up and ran to it.

There stood Percy. "Hi," he said with an almost embarrassed expression. "My dad would like to talk to you. . .both of us, actually."

"Sure," nodded Florilyn and left the room with him.

They walked in silence together. Florilyn's spirits were subdued. She felt awkward beside Percy's somber silence. It was so unlike him. She feared for what he might be thinking. He led her into the small sitting room adjoining the guest room where his parents were staying.

Edward Drummond stood at the window, his back to them as they entered. It was a big afternoon for staring out of windows. He turned at the sound of the door and strode across the floor. Whatever Florilyn might have been expecting, an affectionate greeting from Percy's father was not it. A warm smile spread over his face, and he embraced her with genuine feeling. "My dear!" he said, holding her tightly. As he released her and stepped back, Florilyn saw tears in his eyes. He smiled again as he blinked hard. "Shall we sit down?" he said. "We have important matters to talk and pray about."

They took seats on the couch and two chairs, and Edward resumed. "Percy has told me a little of your predicament, shall we call it," he said. "Out of faithfulness to you, he did not want to divulge too much. He felt I ought to hear whatever you were comfortable telling me yourself. I realize you do not know me so intimately—I have probably always just been a distant uncle to you. But I hope you will be able to trust me. My only desire is to help the two of you discover what is God's will. I will say or do nothing stemming from any motives of my own other than to help you know what is in your hearts and know what is best for you to do. Do you think you can trust me?"

"I will try, Uncle Edward," replied Florilyn. "I believe I can. I trust Percy, and he trusts you. So how can I not trust you, also?"

"Then why don't you explain to me what you have been thinking?"

Florilyn took a deep breath. It was quiet a few moments as she composed her thoughts. "In a way," she began, casting a half-nervous, half-humorous smile toward Percy's father, "it's your fault, Uncle Edward. . .and my mother's. It all began with a George MacDonald novel I read, which I would never have done if you two weren't talking about him all the time."

"Ah, yes," smiled the vicar. "Which one of his books was it?"

"*David Elginbrod*."

The vicar nodded. "One of my favorites. MacDonald does have a way of probing the heart through his characters, does he not?"

"I've never read a book that drew me into it so completely," said Florilyn. "By the time I was finished, I wasn't reading about MacDonald's characters at all but about Percy and me." She paused and again drew in a thoughtful breath. "Percy told me about a conversation you and he had about circumstances," she began again. "He said you talked about going slow, about how God uses circumstances to make his will clear but that you have to be careful not to imbue circumstances with *too* much significance, either, because you never know for *certain* whether God is speaking through them. That's why, Percy said, you always told him that God is never in a hurry, that we must give God as much time as possible to clarify what the circumstances are supposed to mean."

"Very eloquently put, my dear," said Edward. "I doubt if I said it so clearly myself."

"It has remained with me ever since," Florilyn went on. "Then as I read the MacDonald novel, the sense grew upon me that perhaps Percy and I had been hastier than we should have been and perhaps *hadn't* given God enough time. I knew I had to talk to him, though it was one of the hardest things I have ever done." She cast Percy an apologetic smile. She then went on to tell her uncle about Gwyneth's leaving and of the similarities she had seen in the story with their own circumstances.

At length the room fell silent. Florilyn was in tears. But they were good tears.

"My first response," said Edward after a minute or two, "is to commend you for your honesty and fortitude. What you have done in voicing your reservation is not something most young people have the courage to do. I know Percy feels the same. As painful as this time may be for both of you, he admires what you have done."

Florilyn glanced with an expression of question toward Percy where he sat. "Is that really true, Percy?" she said.

"Absolutely."

"I thought you were angry with me."

"Not for a second. Like Dad says, sure it is painful. But how could I not admire you? He's right—it took courage. It shows that you were trying to listen to God's voice."

Florilyn smiled, though almost bashfully. She was not accustomed to being praised for spiritual virtue—especially by a vicar and his son!

"However God leads in the end," Edward went on, "slowing down the process is always a good thing. There is never a disadvantage to going slow if there is the slightest doubt about a course of action. It is fearfully easy to run ahead of God. But he is never in a rush. Even should it turn out that it is indeed God's will for the two of you to marry, this pause for prayerful reevaluation will only make that decision stronger in the end."

Twenty-One

Boxing Day in Llanfryniog

The three left the room a short time later. Edward told his wife and sister that he and the young people had an important matter to discuss with them. Meal preparations and decorating was suspended. When at last everything was out in the open, Florilyn's tears had passed. She was at last ready to join in the revelry of the Christmas spirit.

The reaction of the two mothers at the news that the engagement of their son and daughter had been called off, however, was one of melancholy and a good many tears. In light of Florilyn's near gaiety, and that neither did Percy seem shattered by the turn of events, they did not ask too many questions. Both secretly hoped to get more enlightenment privately from Edward later.

The afternoon progressed. The mood of Katherine Westbrooke and Mary Drummond remained subdued. But gradually the festive spirit returned to the household. By the time they sat down with their guests and members of the household for a lavish Christmas Eve dinner, all hints of the low spirits from earlier in the day were gone.

Around the table in the formal dining room sat Katherine, Courtenay, and Florilyn Westbrooke; Edward, Mary, and Percy Drummond; Adela and Steven Muir, with Hollin Radnor; Mrs. Drynwydd, Katherine's cook; Mrs. Llewellyn the housekeeper; and Jeremiah Broakes, the Westbrooke butler. The only one of the number who did not seem to be entering into the spirit of the season was Courtenay. He had finally made a belated appearance but was annoyed in the extreme to be seated at the same table with staff and servants.

The women pitched in to clean up after dinner. The assembly then retired to the formal sitting room. The remainder of Christmas Eve was spent in lively conversation, singing carols, and exchanging a few gifts. Once the dinner had time to settle, Christmas cake and warm mulled wine punch were brought in from the kitchen to cap off the pleasant evening.

After the early morning church services and celebrations of song, Christmas day for most households in Wales was a family affair. It was a quiet day to enjoy the giving of simple gifts along with good food, warm fires, hot tea, here and there a toddy, and usually an afternoon nap to make up for the sleep lost to the early morning. By the end of the day, no one was actually hungry for an evening meal, though most went through the ritual of nibbling at the platters of ham or roast turkey or pheasant, with perhaps a fresh mince pie or plum pudding added to what was left of the fruit cake from the day before.

A thoughtful mood settled over the manor as its inhabitants returned from the village in the cold shortly after daybreak. Most climbed back upstairs to their rooms, some to sleep, some to read, some to ponder what the day represented. Edward's prayer and words of the night before had given them much to consider. But mostly they were thinking of loved ones—of what was, what had been, and what never would be again. It was after a quiet, and for some a melancholy, morning that brought sad reminders of hidden heartaches to tinge the day's glories with invisible pain.

Katherine was full of the remembrance of Christmases past—with a family of four. Now that family had dwindled to three, and for all Courtenay's grumpiness it might as well be only two.

As she sat alone in her sitting room, a distant sound caused her heart to leap. She was reminded of the happy shouts of a boy's excited voice. Memories flooded her mind. . .of the Christmas morning she and Roderick had taken nine-year-old Courtenay outside and presented him his very own first pony. It was one of the happiest Christmases ever.

The sound came again. With a wistful sigh, she realized it was only a door closing somewhere. No sounds of children would enliven this day and bring joy to her mother's heart. Those days were gone. Courtenay was no longer nine. He was an angry young man of twenty-three who cherished no fond or loving thoughts toward her.

There had been many strains in their family over the years. But they had always enjoyed Christmas as a happy time. Now she was a widow. She was estranged from her son. Though surrounded by many who loved her, she could not help feeling isolated. . .even alone. She knew she should be happy. But she could not help feeling stabs of loneliness.

Florilyn had been relieved the previous afternoon after unburdening herself to Percy and his father. When she awoke on Christmas morning, however, a wave of melancholy swept into her heart like an incoming tide. Her feelings were more fragile than she realized. Percy's reaction to their talk, and his demeanor through the rest of the day and evening, had unsettled her.

What she had expected, she could not have said. Perhaps she was surprised at how quickly he had accepted her decision. Had she wanted him to protest with more vigor? Had she hoped he would try to talk her out of suspending the engagement? Had she wanted Percy to protest and say that he was desperately in love with her and that nothing would dissuade him from marrying her?

On the other hand, if he had seemed more devastated, she might have steeled herself to be strong and supportive. But now less than a day later, he was behaving as if nothing had happened. For all she had said about God's will and knowing what they were doing was right, why hadn't he fought a little harder against it? Didn't Percy know how hard this was for her? If she didn't know better, she would think that he was *glad* to have the engagement called off!

So sure of herself yesterday, suddenly her emotions were playing tricks on her, turning themselves upside down and inside out with no logic or rhyme or reason. She didn't know what she thought or what she felt.

On his part, Percy likewise woke on Christmas morning to an inrush of confusion. He had spent half the night tossing and turning and trying to come to grips with Florilyn's decision. He had done his best to hide his turmoil by acting normal. He would need to come to terms with the sudden change in his own way. He would go for rides and walks and spend time alone, thinking and praying on his own. In the meantime, having no idea that doing so only made her think he cared less than he did, he determined to put Florilyn at ease by being as cheerful as possible. He would not add to her burden by being downcast himself.

In her own room in another part of the house, Mrs. Drynwydd prepared for her own private Christmas ritual. Alone and with her door closed, she removed from her bureau a wooden box whose red paint was worn and dulled by the passage of years. She carried it to her rocking chair, sat down, and, with lips already quivering, unlatched and lifted off its top.

Her eyes began to moisten the moment they fell on the familiar contents—love letters from a time long ago, when she was young and the hopes and dreams of life all lay ahead, the envelopes containing them brittle and yellowed with age; a few trinkets of jewelry, Christmas gifts from her husband; two or three tree ornaments; a pair of baby shoes; and finally a tiny white china doll. She had labored over the dress of yellow and red for months before the Christmas when her daughter was six. Never had a girl loved a doll so much! She carried it with her nearly every moment for the next year and slept with it cuddled beside her under her blankets every night for the rest of her brief life.

Before her twelfth birthday, her daughter was dead, and her husband with her. Whether Christmas was celebrated in heaven, Elvira Drynwydd didn't know. But she tried to comfort herself with the thought that at least they were together.

Laying the doll in her lap, she reached across to the table at her right and picked up a small silver music box. It had also been a gift from her husband. Slowly she wound its key then again set it beside her. Listening to its haunting strains on Christmas morning did not make her happy. Every year the pain of memories brought fresh tears. But she had to remember. Love never forgets.

With her daughter's doll pressed to her breast, the wife and mother who now celebrated Christmas alone rocked gently back and forth. Softly she mouthed the words, *"Silent night, holy night. . .all is calm, all is bright,"* to the simple melody that for many brought joy but caused her heart to ache more deeply than at any other time of year. . .and quietly wept.

All through the great house, others of the extended manor family found themselves similarly reflecting on the hopes and disappointments the season inevitably brings—homesickness not for a place, but for the innocent world of childhood. Family sorrows and broken relationships and bittersweet reminders of lost loved ones, all intruded minor chords into the carols of Bethlehem, reminding one and all that in the midst of its celebration, Christmas brings pangs of regret. . .and yearnings for what can never be again. The great house was still. No children's voices, no happy shouts, no scampering footsteps reverberated within its rooms and corridors. Only memories echoing with silent nostalgic dissonance against the empty walls of longing hearts.

As they gathered in midafternoon for the Christmas meal, Katherine bowed her head and herself led them in prayer. "Father God," she prayed, "we come to You with hearts full of gratitude for the gift of Your Son and the gift of Yourself You have provided for us. We thank You for this day and for all it represents in our lives. Yet some of us also come to You on this day with heavy hearts for the sorrow of losses of those we love and even with uncertainties for the future. We ask that You will enable us to grow through these heartaches and allow our fears and unknowns and our silent burdens make us into the people You want us to be." She paused.

The dining room was silent.

"Make us into Your people, heavenly Father," she added softly. "Amen."

Beside her, Adela reached over and took her hand. She smiled and mouthed a silent, *Thank you.* The two women understood one another.

The loss of a husband or wife is never so difficult as on the special days of the year. Though many avoid speaking of those who are gone, those who loved them hunger to hear their names spoken aloud. Mrs. Llewellyn, too, was also thinking of her departed husband. Even Hollin Radnor and stoic Jeremiah Broakes experienced twinges of melancholy to be reminded again of life's joys and sorrows and of mothers and fathers now passed from the earth.

"I'm sorry, Edward," said Katherine. "I didn't mean to usurp your role as head of the family, not to mention as a minister. But I felt I needed to pray."

"It was a beautiful prayer, Katherine," said Edward. "It must be hard for you to celebrate Christmas with Roderick gone. And you, Adela—I'm sorry, I've forgotten how to pronounce your husband's name."

"Glythvyr," said Adela with a quiet smile.

"Ah yes," nodded Edward. "Well, God bless them both and bless their memories in your hearts."

Both housekeeper and cook were also thinking of their husbands but said nothing.

Katherine had been taught by her parents, and had learned from her own experience, that the best antidote for personal sorrow is service to others. Midway through the meal she explained her scheme for the remainder of the day, and the day that would follow—a day when those of means traditionally boxed up gifts and food to share with those less fortunate. "Tomorrow is Boxing Day," she began. "I have plans for us all. I want us to visit every home in the village, and the surrounding crofts, with gifts of good cheer. I have been ordering food and drink and gifts from purveyors throughout Wales and northern England. Regular shipments have been arriving at the manor for two months in preparation. I have also been keeping our ladies busy in the kitchen baking Christmas cakes and puddings. They probably thought I was preparing for seven years of famine!" She looked at Mrs. Llewellyn with a smile.

The housekeeper glanced toward Mrs. Drynwydd, and both ladies nodded their heads and returned her smile.

"So we will all pitch in this afternoon and tomorrow, preparing the hampers, and then tomorrow deliver them. I want someone from the manor to visit every house and cottage in Llanfryniog with a gift in remembrance of the season. We will take Christmas hampers to those most in need and a bottle of sherry or port to the rest. Hollin knows every man, woman, and child for miles around. He has been helping me with this. In addition, each household will receive ten pounds and a note personally from me."

She paused. A far-off look came into her eye, followed by the rising of a few tears. "I've not told any of you this," she said, "but several months after Roderick's death, Mr. Murray surprised me by delivering to me a check for £1,000. He said it was from a life insurance policy Roderick had taken out. I had never heard of such a thing. I asked him what life insurance meant. He told me that Roderick had paid to have his life insured, such that if anything happened to him I would receive the amount in question. I still did not entirely understand. Roderick knew that I would not be in need. Yet for whatever reason, he chose to do it. I can only believe that he would be pleased if I were to use it, not for myself, but for our people. Therefore, I determined that I would use this money in some way that would reflect the love he had come to have late in his life for our community."

Her voice became husky, and she brushed at her eyes. "Sometimes it is not until a person is gone," she went on, "that we reflect on who they really were. We come perhaps to know them better in death in some ways even than we did in life. I want to honor the good that was in Roderick by telling the people that the gifts of these ten pound notes are from him, from money he left for me to use for the village he loved."

When dinner was completed, the extended family of Westbrooke Manor, the three families of Westbrookes, Drummonds, and Muirs, along with those of the staff who lived at the manor, gathered in Katherine's sitting room. In the last month it had become a warehouse of goods and wrapping supplies, with boxes of food and cases of sherry and port stacked everywhere. There they began the happy work of assembling and filling some fifty wicker hampers with cured hams, cheeses, crackers, biscuits, Christmas cakes and puddings, and other assorted edible treats to be enjoyed on New Year's Day, a day of yet greater feasting and celebration, with many of its own unique traditions, even than Christmas itself. After she set the work in motion, Katherine sat down at a writing table on one side of the room and continued the task she had begun some days before of writing out nearly a hundred brief notes of Christmas greeting to be included with each gift along with a ten-pound note.

Conversation and laughter in the room was lively. Once Katherine had enlisted everyone, except Courtenay, in her plan, there was no more time for the intrusion of sadness. Occasionally Edward broke into song. He was immediately joined by the rest, usually in three- or four-part harmony, such that by nightfall, weary and content with their day's work, they had sung nearly every Christmas hymn or carol in the hymnary.

Early in the evening, Mrs. Drynwydd and Mrs. Llewellyn slipped away. Half an hour later the rest took a break and went downstairs to enjoy the brief repast the two faithful ladies had set out—meats, breads, pies, cakes, and cheeses. Then again they returned upstairs and went back to work.

Conversation lasted late into the evening. Gradually sleepiness overtook the company. One after another rose, said good night, and retired in anticipation of the big day ahead of them on the morrow.

Steven and Hollin were in the barn by ten on the morning of Boxing Day hitching all available means of transport, which included the large and small carriages and two buggies. Percy soon joined them. By eleven the four horse-drawn vehicles stood outside the manor's front door. Soon a processional was in progress between the upper room of preparation and the front of the house, while two or three of the men loaded the buggies. Several boxes were also loaded containing bottles of sherry and port, each tied with a ribbon. Knowing that most of the villagers would take the opportunity to sleep as long into the morning as possible, they did not begin their first excursions down the drive until just before one.

They reached town and split in four directions. With hampers or bottles in hand, each member of Katherine's immediate family—herself, Edward, Mary, Percy, and Florilyn—began knocking on the doors of the cottages to personally deliver their gifts. Within an hour, the whole village was abuzz. No longer were knocks required. Doors were thrown wide in greeting before they reached them. At each home they found themselves enthusiastically invited in for drinks, sometimes for tea, occasionally for something stronger. With every visit their progress slowed. The villagers were beside themselves with eager gratitude to reciprocate with whatever means of hospitality were available to them. Had they allowed it, every home would have kept their visitors for an hour!

Meanwhile, Hollin, who had accompanied them to town, returned to the manor with the largest carriage, where Mrs. Drynwydd, Mrs. Llewellyn, Steven, Adela, and Broakes were all ready to load it with the second round of provisions. It was a bone-chilling day of gray skies that portended snow. But never are human hearts warmed more than when engaged in service, ministry, or goodness to others of their kind.

The busy transport and delivery of hampers and drink and monetary gifts continued all afternoon. Few at the manor or in the homes of the village even noticed the cold. Those homes Katherine visited personally considered themselves as honored as if the queen herself had appeared on their doorsteps. When the last hamper was delivered, and she, Edward, Mary, Florilyn, and Percy rode back up the hill to the manor in the deepening dusk, all five were exhausted from constant visiting with exuberant villagers.

The only difficulty presented by the day was the question of whom to deliver bottles of sherry to Madame Fleming and Mistress Chattan. None of the three women felt comfortable entering either of their two establishments. Edward therefore paid a brief call on the enigmatic Fleming, while Percy, confessing a begrudging fondness for her, delivered a bottle and the best wishes of the viscountess to the proprietress of the inn.

Late that evening, the vicar and his wife retired to their own room. Edward slipped his nightshirt over his head. "A long and tiring but satisfying Boxing Day, wouldn't you say, my dear?" he said.

"Extraordinary is how I would describe it," rejoined Mary. "The humble gratitude and hospitality of the people in town was like nothing I have ever seen. It's not something one witnesses with regularity in Glasgow. They truly *love* your sister."

"It warms my heart to realize it," nodded Edward. "Especially after the loss of her husband."

"I'm certain the holidays were difficult for her. She was probably thinking of Roderick. I noticed a quiet about the place this morning on the part of others as well. I felt that there was much sadness mingled with the joy of the day."

"Christmas always brings memories and often disappointments. As blessed as we are now to be able to share the holiday one in heart with our son, I remember the pain of those Christmases when he was estranged from us. I ache for those who find Christmas a sad and lonely time. Katherine is now facing a double sorrow. Courtenay is certainly not being a true son to her in her time of need."

"On Christmas Eve, he was rolling his eyes and had a sour look on his face when you were talking about Christmas and God's fatherhood. Poor Katherine—how it must grieve her heart."

"Yet in spite of it, she was thinking of what she could do to make the season special for others."

Mary nodded thoughtfully. "I was thinking that very thing all afternoon," she said. "I admire your sister more than I can say. She did not let her own feelings keep her from reaching out to the community. She may not have *felt* the joy of Christmas in her own heart, but she *lived* what Christmas means—giving life and love to those around us. It was a memorable day. Katherine is indeed an amazing woman."

It began to snow about midnight. By the first light of the following morning, all Gwynedd lay under a blanket of white.

Twenty-Two

Farewell

Edward, Mary, and Percy Drummond prepared to depart Westbrooke Manor for their return to Scotland on the second of January of the new year, 1873.

Percy found Florilyn alone in the sitting room after breakfast.

"So you'll soon be off," she said. She tried to sound cheery, but without much success. "It will be dreary when you're gone. Of course it always seems dreary after you leave."

"You always manage to survive," rejoined Percy. "Just think of me—far north under piles of snow, with papers to write and endless lectures to sit through."

"You'll be through, when is it—in May?"

"May it is," he said, exhaling a long sigh. "It seems too good to be true that I will actually graduate from the university! Who would have imagined it back when I was running through the streets of Glasgow trying to keep from being arrested!"

"You've changed."

"As have you."

"Then what will you do?" asked Florilyn.

"My first order of business will definitely be a return to Wales."

"Really?" exclaimed Florilyn. "Oh, that's wonderful. I didn't know if you—"

"No worries. I will be back as soon as I graduate. Or possibly June. There is something I have to do for your father. . .and I'll want to see you, of course."

"For my father?" said Florilyn.

"I will tell you all about it when I can. And we have our own future to decide on, too, you know."

Florilyn looked away. The subject was still painful to her.

"I *do* admire you for your courage," he added. "What my dad said is true."

"Thank you," nodded Florilyn. Her voice was shaky.

"I am still uncertain what I am supposed to be trying to figure out," Percy went on. "Gwyneth is gone. There is no way to find her. Even if I may have had more feelings for her once than I realized, what difference does it make now?"

"Like I said before," replied Florilyn, "we both have to know what is in our hearts."

Percy nodded then took Florilyn in his arms. Neither spoke as they embraced affectionately. After several seconds they stepped back.

"Your decision has made me admire you as a godly woman," said Percy. "Whatever happens in the future, you are my dear cousin and friend."

"And we'll both keep reading MacDonald," said Florilyn, forcing a smile.

"I don't know!" laughed Percy. "I don't want him to get me into any more trouble."

He detected momentary chagrin on Florilyn's face.

"Hey, only joking!" he added quickly. "I don't have as much time to read as you do. But I shall try."

They gazed into one another's eyes. Florilyn's were misty. Percy stepped forward and kissed her lightly on the cheek, then stepped back and smiled. Though they could not see what the future held, both knew they were doing the right thing.

As Percy climbed the stairs one last time to fetch his bag from his room a few minutes later, he paused on the landing to gaze at the portraits of the Westbrooke lineage. His eyes came to rest once again, as they often did when he was here, on the compelling face of his uncle Roderick's grandmother. The penetrating expression of her eyes was so mesmerizing that Percy felt that he *knew* her, that he had actually seen her. Yet he knew that was impossible. She had been dead decades before he was even born.

He shook his head in perplexity then continued up the stairs.

Twenty-Three

Plans and Schemes

Katherine did not bring up the subject of property or a new home to Florilyn again. She did not want to risk loose talk or overheard conversations. But she did not remain idle.

She made several more visits to Hamilton Murray's office, riding to Porthmadog by buggy and keeping her destination to herself. It did not take long after her ride with Florilyn to decide on the Mochras Head plateau as the ideal site for a future home. She knew that Courtenay had no great love of the sea. She had never seen him walking or riding along the coastline. She doubted he would miss the land in question. But she had long since given up trying to anticipate his reactions to anything. Whether he would be angry at her intentions, once they became known, or grateful for the extra sum in his account when he became viscount, she would hazard no guess.

Keeping his name out of it, under Murray's supervision an engineering firm from Shrewsbury was hired. It was far enough away, both he and Katherine thought, to keep local speculation from being able to dig too deeply into the matter. When the surveyors arrived on the scene, not only would they have no idea who had hired them, in all likelihood they would never have heard of Westbrooke Manor or the Viscount Lord Snowdon or his widow.

Courtenay, meanwhile, had replied to Lord Litchfield, agreeing to the terms he had outlined for sale of one thousand acres of land on the eastern boundary on the northern quadrant of the Westbrooke estate. Now all he had to do was wait.

Thus, both mother and son kept busy on their private schemes aimed to circumvent the difficulties posed to each by the other. Neither knew what the other was up to. But both saw an expression in the other's eyes that spoke of secrets. Courtenay had instructed the postman in Llanfryniog to keep mail addressed to him separate from what came to the manor and to hold it for him until he called for it personally. Katherine thus remained unaware of the correspondence between her son and London.

The two met but infrequently. Courtenay did not take his meals with his mother or sister. He regarded his present straitened circumstances as little more than house arrest in enemy-occupied territory. But he bore it with stoicism, knowing that his ship was on the horizon and was coming closer every day.

How Courtenay occupied his time was a mystery. He rode as much as the weather would permit. Though he looked down on the villagers and miners and farmers, he was frequently seen in Mistress Chattan's pub. In view of his future position among them, the men were deferential and friendly. The pleasure Courtenay took in hearing himself addressed as "my lord" no doubt contributed its share to his increasingly regular visits to the place. When he felt his meager supply of funds could afford it, he stood everyone a round of Mistress Chattan's best ale. He thus gradually gained the approbation of men who had been accustomed for years to regard him as a spoiled wastrel. All the while they remained unaware that one of his first planned ordinances as viscount would be to double most of their rents.

The friend of Courtenay's youth, Colville Burrenchobay, eldest son of parliamentarian Armand Burrenchobay, himself a wastrel of yet greater reputation than Courtenay, had recently returned to the family seat of Burrenchobay Hall. His return was not due to financial considerations—his father kept him well supplied with funds—but simply from the boredom of travel. He had sown his wild oats in their season, but now, as he reached his middle twenties, he had begun to think of his future. How great were his political aspirations, even he could not have said. If he had thoughts of following his father's footsteps to Westminster, however, the settled life of a gentleman would provide a more suitable basis from which to do so.

When Courtenay and Colville were together now, therefore, they were no longer two rowdy youths but the eldest scions of two of North Wales' oldest families. They drank expensive brandy and went shooting for pheasants and roe, not rabbits.

Riding back from Llanfryniog to the manor one day in late February, a strange sight met Courtenay's eyes. Five or six men with surveying equipment were spread out between the main road and the promontory. His first reaction was bewilderment, his second anger. He dug his heels into the sides of his mount and galloped off the road and over the wide plateau toward the scene.

"What is the meaning of this?" he said in a demanding tone. "Who are you people? Who's in charge here?"

The man closest to him, who did not take kindly to his tone, nodded toward a group of men across the grass.

Courtenay kicked at his horse's flanks and galloped toward them. "Which one of you is in charge here?" Courtenay asked as he rode up.

"I am," one of the men replied, turning toward him.

"What's going on here? What are you doing?"

"I would think it is obvious," said the man. "We are surveying the site."

"What for?"

"I really could not say. I am a surveyor not a planner."

"Who hired you?"

"The job came through a solicitor in Shrewsbury."

"Shrewsbury!" exclaimed Courtenay. "That's impossible. There has obviously been some mistake. So I am ordering you and your men off this land."

"And who are you to be giving such an order?"

"I own this land, you fool. I am the future viscount, Lord Snowdon."

"Ah yes, we were specifically told about you, that you might be troublesome."

"What were you told?"

"That you might try to throw your weight around, but that you had no legal standing in the matter. We were told to ignore whatever you might say."

In a white fury, Courtenay stared back at the plainspoken man a moment, then wheeled his mount around and made for home. He burst in upon his mother, making no attempt to hide his anger. "Mother, what is going on down at the promontory? There are surveyors everywhere. Are you behind it?"

"I am."

"I demand to know what it is all about."

"Just a little project of mine."

"What kind of project?"

"Nothing you need worry about. I am having some of the estate boundary lines looked into."

"There are no boundaries down there. Our land extends for miles along the coast and inland to the north-south road. I demand to know what's going on."

"That tone will get nowhere with me, Courtenay."

"Do you refuse to tell me what it is about?"

"I have told you, I am having some boundary lines looked into. That is all I intend to divulge about it."

Far from satisfied, Courtenay left the room more determined than ever to accelerate his own plans. He did not like this new tone of determination he had noticed in his mother of late. She was becoming too independent for her own good.

Twenty-Four

Visitor from England

Lord Coleraine Litchfield stepped gingerly from the tipsy dinghy that had brought him from the anchored yacht out in the bay and onto the concrete pier. He glanced up the street and at the poor-looking stone buildings comprising the Welsh village of Llanfryniog. He did his best not to grimace at the thought of where he would be forced to spend the next several days. Only one thing could bring him this far away from civilization. That was the thought of making money. For that he would endure it with as much good humor as was possible under the circumstances.

Several more communications had gone back and forth between Westbrooke Manor and London, leading eventually to an invitation to the north. Commitments in London and the horrible winter's weather had delayed his meeting with the young scion of the Westbrooke estate until early March. But he was in Wales at last.

Before the Englishman could speculate further on the locale or his own personal fortunes, a lanky and well-dressed, though obviously rustic man approached. "Lord Litchfield," he said with an accent so unintelligibly thick the Englishman scarcely recognized his own name, "I am Deakin Trenchard, former footman at Westbrooke Manor. I am retired now and living in the village, but Mr. Courtenay asked me to meet you and take you to the manor, where he is awaiting you."

"Ah, yes. . .uh, Trenchard. Lead on, then," replied Litchfield.

The man turned, and the newcomer followed him from the pier to a waiting carriage. Fifteen minutes later they were winding their way up the tree-lined drive where Lord Litchfield beheld his first sight of the estate known as Westbrooke Manor.

A tolerable looking sort of place, he thought to himself—interesting mixture of brick and stone, although it was a bit severe to his taste. *It will no doubt be a dreary time of it, but—*

Further reflections were cut short. As the carriage slowed to a crunching stop on the gravel drive, his host came from the wide front doors and bounded ebulliently toward his guest.

"Lord Litchfield," he said, "I am Courtenay Westbrooke. I am happy you have been able to come."

"I am pleased to meet you at last, young Westbrooke," rejoined Litchfield, shaking the other's hand as he stepped down.

"Come in. We shall have tea," said Courtenay. "You have had a pleasant voyage I trust?"

"I am not altogether a man of the sea," replied Litchfield. "But we enjoyed calm seas and clear skies. Actually," he added, "I prefer the train, but a passing fancy of nostalgia turned my thoughts to the ancient mode of transport. It was not so bad as I expected. I may buy the yacht when I return to Bristol."

As they entered the house, Litchfield was still speaking. "Tell me," he was saying, "is the property—"

A quick glance from his host, accompanied by an imperceptible movement of finger to lips, communicated its message well enough. He fell silent as a stately lady who appeared about fifty approached.

Courtenay presented his mother. Lord Litchfield greeted Katherine with a smile and extended his hand. She returned the greeting with a hint of question in her eyes. Katherine was certain this visit was more than a mere social call. But she had not been able to discover what her son was up to.

Litchfield detected caution in the touch of her palm as she allowed him to shake it.

"Thank you for your hospitality, Lady Snowdon," he said. "And my belated condolences at the loss of your husband."

"Thank you. You knew my husband then?"

"We were acquaintances in the House of Lords."

Katherine nodded. "And now you have business with my son?"

"As he will be filling your husband's seat himself in a matter of months, I wanted to take the opportunity of seeing how I might be able to be of service to him."

"I see. Well, if there is anything you need during your stay, do not hesitate to make it known."

"Thank you, Lady Snowdon. You are most kind."

Courtenay led his guest upstairs to his room. He left him to refresh himself, adding that he would join him downstairs in the drawing room for tea at his convenience.

Descending the stairway a few minutes later, Litchfield saw an attractive girl whom he judged in her early twenties watching him from the end of the corridor. He nodded, but neither spoke. She, too, like the woman he had just met, appeared on her guard. He wondered what kind of place he had stepped into.

After stiff conversation with son and mother at tea, during which the purpose of his visit did not arise, Courtenay invited his guest for a stroll about the grounds. Alone they would be able more freely to discuss the matter that had brought the Englishman here.

"To answer the question you began to pose earlier," said Courtenay after they had left the house behind them, "yes, we shall have the opportunity to view the property. I beg your patience, however. Let us wait a day or two. Then we shall have a ride into the hills. We must be prudent and not discuss the matter around my mother or sister."

"Your sister?"

"She is younger than myself by two years. She would be no more favorably inclined toward my plans than my mother."

"I believe I saw her in the corridor a short time ago. She looked as if she were eyeing me cautiously."

"That's her."

"Your mother does not favor the sale?" said Litchfield.

"That is precisely the case. Of course, she knows nothing about it, which is why we have to be prudent in what we say."

"Why does it matter? We cannot finalize the transaction until you become viscount anyway."

"Technically, I don't suppose it does matter. And it certainly won't after I come of age. But I would rather not upset her unnecessarily. Unfortunately until that time she still controls the estate's finances, and thus my own. I have the feeling that she may be attempting to sell off a portion of estate lands behind my back. Whatever she is up to, I do not want her meddling in our agreement. There would be no telling what trouble she might cause us."

"I was led to understand—"

"I assure you," interrupted Courtenay, "there will be no problem. I simply want us to keep my mother out of it. She has strange notions about money. Her brother is a priest, you see, and the family, though wealthy, has passed down to its present scions—my mother and uncle—an inordinate fear of what they call mammon."

Two days passed. Lord Litchfield had done his best, without success, to amuse himself with cards, boring walks, even more boring conversation, and two or three visits to the village, ostensibly to see to the yacht that had brought him here but in reality merely for something to do.

On the third day, Courtenay suggested a ride. He gave orders for Radnor to saddle his two favorite mounts now that the stallion Demon was gone, a four-year-old gelding of extremely dark gray, though not dapple, with patches of pure black, and a rich chestnut stallion with white mane and tail. They were known as Night Fire and Cymru Gold.

The two men set out for the hills northeast of the estate within the hour. From the window of the second-floor library, Katherine watched them go. Their gay mood when they returned four hours later confirmed what she had been thinking since the day of Litchfield's arrival—Courtenay was definitely up to something.

Twenty-Five

High Words

Courtenay Westbrooke left Llanfryniog, riding north to meet the main road on his way to Porthmadog. He was in jubilant spirits. In the pocket of his coat was a check, signed by Lord Coleraine Litchfield, for the unbelievable sum of £4,400. It had come in this morning's post. Litchfield had not *quite* delivered it into his hands during his visit of a month earlier as promised. But that hardly mattered now! Courtenay intended to waste no time depositing it into his account. His money problems were over at last!

He could take *ten* trips to the continent between today and his twenty-fifth birthday and hardly make a dent in his suddenly acquired fortune. And double this would be waiting for him when the transaction was consummated eleven months from now. His ordeal under his mother's thumb was over! He would buy the most expensive bottle of brandy Porthmadog had to offer then stop by Burrenchobay Hall on his return and allow his friend to share in his good fortune.

As he passed the Methodist Chapel, a woman emerged from one of the fishermen's cottages alongside the road and began walking toward the center of town. When she saw who was approaching along the road, her face brightened. She stepped into the street to meet him.

"Mr. Courtenay, my lord," she said, curtseying slightly and smiling nervously.

Courtenay reined in the gray-black gelding and stared down at her.

"I want to thank you, sir," she added, "in the matter of the rent."

"What are you talking about?" said Courtenay brusquely.

"The rent, sir. . .your forgiving our rent until my man is able to work again."

"Forgiving your rent?" repeated Courtenay. "You mean to tell me you are paying no rent?"

"My man, sir—he broke his arm from a fall in the boat during that big storm back in January, sir. Dr. Rotherham fixed him up real good, but he ain't been able to work all this time."

"What's that got to do with your rent?" asked Courtenay.

"Your man, your factor, Stevie Muir, my lord," replied the woman with growing trepidation, "he said he forgave our rent till my man was back to work."

"He did not talk to me about it," rejoined Courtenay. "But he will soon enough! As for your rent, you will pay up everything you owe or you will be evicted within the month. What is your name?"

"Naughtie, my lord," said the woman, trembling from Courtenay's sudden outburst.

With a vicious yank of the reins, Courtenay wheeled his mount away from the woman and galloped out of town as she stared after him in tears. The poor horse beneath him paid a dear price for Steven Muir's gesture of kindness. The creature was in a lather of exhaustion before Courtenay was halfway to Porthmadog, its hindquarters nearly raw from the whip.

"You can't give these people too much," he said to himself as he rode. "They will get the idea you are weak. They will take advantage at every turn." They had to know he intended to rule firmly. How much more damage was that lout of a so-called factor going to do before he was able to get rid of him! He didn't know whether to be angrier at his mother or Muir.

By the time he reached the bank, his fury had receded. He was once again aglow in the knowledge that he was in possession of more money than he had ever had in his life. When his fortune was safely deposited in his account, he lunched at the Lleyn Arms while his horse was fed and watered then purchased his brandy and started for home.

Three weeks later, toward the end of April, Steven Muir was at the harbor unloading a shipment of provisions that had come for Lady Snowdon from London. When his wagon was full, he made the rounds of the harbor visiting what fishermen were present, with the result that by the time he started back for the manor he had purchased several nice cod to deliver to Mrs. Llewellyn.

He climbed up, flicked the reins, and urged the aging but faithful cob into motion. As he left the harbor behind and approached the chapel, he saw a cart in the street ahead of him being loaded with what appeared to be household possessions. He came nearer, drew rein, and jumped down.

"Let me give you a hand with that, Jamie," he said to the woman beside the cart who was attempting to hoist a chair up into it. He took hold of the chair himself and swung it high into the air and onto the flat bed of the cart. "Where are you bound with all this?"

"Just to my sister's down in Barmouth, Stevie."

"Is she so sorely in need that you must empty your own house to help furnish hers?"

"She's in no need, Stevie. 'Tis she that's taking us in. We're going to 'bide with her."

Mr. Naughtie, his arm still in a sling, now emerged from the stone cottage.

Steven looked back and forth between the man and his wife in confusion. "But why?" he asked. "You'll surely be back to the fishing in another month, Jock. If it's food you're needing, I'll have a sack of oats and a bushel of potatoes on your doorstep within an hour."

"It's no food, Stevie," said Jock Naughtie as he walked toward them. " 'Tis money we're in need of. . .for the rent, you know. We got none."

"I told you, Jock, you'll be paying no more rent till you're healthy and strong and you're back to work on McKinnon's boat."

The man looked down to the ground but said nothing.

Steven looked toward his wife.

An embarrassed expression came over her face. "Meaning no disrespect to yourself, Stevie," she said. "We know you meant well. But you're not the laird, you know."

"Of course not. But I don't know what you mean."

"The laird, the young viscount, Stevie—he said we must pay all the rent we owe or quit."

"What?" exclaimed Steven. "When did this happen?"

"About three weeks ago."

"Why didn't you tell me?"

"We ain't seen you since."

"Why didn't you come find me at the manor?"

"The likes of us couldn't well show ourselves at the big house. We didn't want to anger the young viscount."

"He's not the viscount yet," replied Steven. "And he's got no right to pretend to be. His mother still sets the rents and collects them, and I work for her not Courtenay." Steven was brimming with anger like a pot rising to a slow boil. He stood thinking for a moment. "Jock, Jamie. . . the two of you go back inside and have a cup of tea," he said. "Don't take another thing from your house until I get back. Lady Snowdon will know of this. I can promise you that she will not hear of your leaving unless that is your wish. But it will not be over money." He turned, jumped back onto his wagon, and sent old Dusty up the street in front of his burden with as much speed as the aging cob could muster.

Steven arrived at the manor twenty or twenty-five minutes later, his anger with Courtenay's presumption greater than ever. He jumped from the wagon and strode toward the front door, intending to seek an immediate interview with his mistress. Halfway across the gravel entry, a movement caught his eye.

Courtenay had just left the house by a side entrance and was striding toward the new stables.

Steven turned and hurried after him. He rounded the wall of the barn just as Courtenay, whip in hand, was leading Cymru Gold, already saddled, out onto the grass. "A moment of your time, *your lordship*," said Steven with emphasis, "if you please."

Courtenay detected challenge in the tone. He turned haughtily to face him as Steven came forward. One look at the young shepherd's face brought all the latent anger in his own soul immediately to the surface. Courtenay's eyes flashed dangerously.

Steven stopped ten feet away. He did not want to get too close, not for fear of Courtenay but in respect of his own strength and what he might do if aroused. "I have just come from town," he said. "There I was informed by Jock and Jamie Naughtie that you gave them notice to pay their back rents or quit."

"I don't keep track of the names of the village peasantry. But yes, I spoke to a woman some time back who told me you had taken the liberty of forgiving their rents. I set her straight soon enough."

"You had no right to interfere," said Steven, forcing himself to speak softly.

"I had no right to interfere!" sneered Courtenay. "Just whose tenants do you suppose those people are?"

"At present they are your mother's. She has given me responsibility over their well-being."

"*Their* well-being! What about the well-being of the estate?"

"They are one and the same."

"Perhaps in the eyes of a fool. A businessman would see it differently."

"Fortunately, I am no businessman. I am the Westbrooke Manor factor."

"Yes, and a notable farce you have made the office. But you won't be for long. You would be advised to begin making plans for your future, Muir. You will rent no cottage or house from me anywhere within miles of here. I won't have these blackguards taking their problems to you and thinking me a cad because I don't have the heart of an old woman like you."

"Only a cad would throw a man and woman out of their home at the very time fortune turns against them."

"How dare you!" cried Courtenay. His pent-up fury at last exploded. Before Steven could protect himself, a stinging blow from Courtenay's whip lashed across Steven's midsection and shoulder. Luckily for all concerned, the thong did not find skin.

Taken completely by surprise, all Steven could do as the whip was withdrawn and sent at him again was turn away and protect his head and face. He bolted for cover as several more lashes snapped across his back.

Courtenay sprinted after him, hardly aware of Florilyn's screams as she ran from the house. She had witnessed the argument from one of the library windows. Knowing what Courtenay was capable of she had dashed for the stairs. Running straight at him, she threw herself against Courtenay with the full force of her body as he coiled his arm for another blow.

"Stop it. . .stop it, Courtenay!" she shrieked.

Courtenay swore violently and spun toward her. With his free hand, he grasped her arm and shoved her from him. "This doesn't concern you!" he shouted.

He raised the whip, but Florilyn attacked again with the viciousness of a wildcat, yelling and pummeling Courtenay's face with surprisingly accurate blows from her two fists.

The blood of his rage now reached its heights. Courtenay retaliated with a whack across Florilyn's cheek. She screamed in pain. He shoved her back, and she stumbled and fell to the ground. Courtenay advanced with the coiled whip in his hand and raised it to strike her again. In fairness, he only intended to use it as a blunt instrument, not as the lethal weapon a horsewhip could be in the hand of an expert.

More fortunately for him than for her, Florilyn's attack gave Steven time to recover. As Courtenay raised the coiled leather above his ear, he felt it suddenly wrested from his hand. He spun around to find Steven holding it and standing three feet from him. "And only a scoundrel would strike a woman, Courtenay!" said Steven, loudly yet with surprising calm. "You are both a cad *and* a scoundrel. Now get away before it goes worse for you."

With marvelous speed, Courtenay's only reply was a lightning blow with his right fist in the direction of Steven's jaw. But he underestimated

Steven's dexterity. A quick step to the side and Courtney's fist found only air. He lost his balance momentarily but quickly recovered. "Stand and face me like a man, Muir!" he shouted, adding a string of imprecations. "Defend yourself or receive the beating you deserve."

"I will not defend myself," said Steven, backing slowly away. "But I assure you that you will not lay another hand on your sister. She is the finest young woman for miles, both beautiful and honorable. You shame yourself as the lowest of men by treating her with anything less than the respect she deserves, and by speaking with such a foul tongue in her presence. I will not defend myself, but I will defend her if you touch her again. And if one more vile word leaves your lips in her hearing, you will have to answer to me, Courtenay Westbrooke—and I promise you, it will not go well for you."

A tense silence filled the small courtyard. Katherine, who had heard Florilyn's screams, now ran out the front door.

Courtenay glared at Steven through clenched teeth. It did not take more than a second or two for him to realize he did not like his chances now that he had relinquished the advantage of the whip. "I'll kill you for this, Muir," he spat. "No one makes me look like a fool. You might as well pack your bags now if you know what's good for you. Your future here is finished."

Courtenay turned, strode toward his mount, who had waited patiently through the ruckus, mounted, then galloped off. It was a mercy for the horse that Steven was still holding the whip.

Twenty-Six

Threats

Steven stooped down, offered his hand, and helped Florilyn to her feet.

Katherine hurried toward them. "What is. . . Oh, Steven—your back and shoulder are bleeding! Florilyn, what's—"

"Courtenay attacked Steven with his horsewhip, Mother!" said Florilyn angrily. "It was horrible! Then he hit me and knocked me down."

"Courtenay *hit* you?" exclaimed Katherine in disbelief. Now she noticed that one of Florilyn's cheeks was bright red. "Oh, my. . .Florilyn, dear. . .how could he. . .that. . .that—"

"I am sorry, Lady Katherine," said Steven, turning toward his mistress. "I fear it was my fault."

"Steven, how can you say that!" said Florilyn. "I saw what he did. He was whipping you!"

"I should not have confronted him," rejoined Steven. "I precipitated the argument and made him angry. I should have spoken with you first, Lady Katherine. I am afraid I let my own anger get the better of me."

"*Anger*, Steven! I watched the whole thing," said Florilyn. "You were so calm I wondered what you were doing. You didn't even raise your voice when Courtenay was swearing at you. Why didn't you give him what he deserved? Anyone could see that you weren't afraid of him."

"No, I wasn't afraid."

"Why then?"

"There are those who think it is a disgrace for a man to be struck by another man. I happen to believe the opposite. I consider it a disgrace to strike another."

Florilyn stared at him, wondering if she had heard him correctly.

"I would have struck him to protect you," Steven went on, "but not to defend myself. I am twice as strong as your brother. And I was *very* angry. That's why I was trying hard to remain calm. Anger and strength—the two do not go well together. I might have hurt him very badly. That would have done him no good at all."

"Steven," now said Katherine, "you must tell me what this was all about. Courtenay is my son, and you are my factor. If there are differences so serious as this, I must know of them. Why do you say it was your fault?"

"There was a dispute about one of your tenants, Lady Katherine," replied Steven. "You remember the Naughties, from the village—Jock Naughtie is the fisherman who broke his arm rather badly in that January storm?"

"I remember."

"I found out today that Jamie, that's Jock's wife, encountered Courtenay a few weeks ago. Courtenay learned that we had forgiven their rents until Jock was back at the fishing. Courtenay told them they must pay all back rents or quit."

"He didn't!"

"I fear so, my lady," said Steven. "I learned of it when I was in the village just now. Jamie and Jock were packing their belongings to leave."

"We must stop them. I won't have Courtenay meddling while the estate remains in my hands. Especially I am not about to allow him to evict them!"

"I told them to do nothing more," said Steven.

"I will go see them myself. I want to apologize personally. Will you take me to them, Steven?"

"Of course, Lady Katherine."

"After we get you cleaned and bandaged, that is," said Katherine. "And Florilyn," she added, turning again to her daughter, "are you badly hurt?"

"No, Mother. I will be sore. But I am more furious than hurt."

"Then let us go inside and see to Steven's injuries."

With the help of Steven's mother, who seemed less concerned about a few scrapes and bruises and cuts than the two Westbrooke women, Steven's two or three bleeding wounds were cleaned and bandaged. With a fresh shirt, he was soon himself again, though he, too, would be sore for a week.

Within the hour, he and Katherine set out for the village in one of the manor's small buggies. When they knocked and were admitted to the Naughtie cottage, with the cart still sitting in the street half full of a miscellany of possessions, the humble fisherman and his wife were beside themselves to show what hospitality they were capable of to the former viscount's wife. As hospitality is a matter of the heart more than luxury of provision, Katherine felt as welcomed as she would have in any castle in Wales. Probably more so. The good man and his wife were profuse in their gratitude. Jamie cried. Steven added as a final condition that they must tell no one of the altercation with Courtenay or what he had tried to do. He *would* be viscount one day. They must all give him the chance to become a caring landlord to his people. Toward this end, they must prejudice no one against him.

Katherine, however, moved as she was by Steven's simple speech of forgiveness, returned to the manor determined to prevent any recurrence of the incident or any further interference from her son. She was waiting for him when he returned from his ride. She met him at the foot of the stairs. "I would like to talk to you, Courtenay," she said without preamble. "Would you please meet me in your father's study in five minutes?"

"Perhaps I am not inclined to talk to you, Mother," he retorted. "After the way you took that Stevie Muir's side earlier, I have nothing to say to you."

"It may be I who have something to say to you. If you will not come to the study, then I will say it here for the whole household to hear."

Courtenay returned his mother a look of daggers then continued up the stairs.

Katherine tried to compose herself. She walked calmly to her late husband's study, sat down in the chair behind his desk, and waited. This was not an interview she was looking forward to.

Courtenay walked in ten minutes later without knocking. If his behavior from earlier or his lengthy ride had subdued or shamed him in his own estimation, he displayed no sign of it. His eyes glowed with the fire of indignation. His was not a character easily humbled. It was doubtful he had ever felt the twinge of self-mortification in his life.

"Please sit down," said Katherine matter-of-factly.

"I prefer to stand," rejoined Courtenay. It was not true. But in his present frame of mind, he would have countered *any* request or command from his mother for no reason other than to set himself against her will.

"Suit yourself," she said. "What I have to say will not take long. I have been apprised of your interference in my affairs in the matter of one of our tenants in the village by the name of Naughtie. You apparently gave them notice to quit unless they paid all their back rents, directly contradicting what my factor had told them."

Courtenay burst out laughing with disdain. "Your *factor*! Ha, ha! You continue to play this ridiculous charade with the clodhopper Muir. Ha, ha, ha!"

"He *is* my factor," said Katherine firmly. "And he is in charge of my affairs at present, not you. Fortunately he and I have been able to undo the mischief you caused the poor people. But I will thank you not to interfere with my tenants again."

The laughter on Courtenay's face died out as quickly as it had come. "*Your* tenants?" he said.

"For the present, yes."

"You haven't forgotten whose tenants they will be in a year's time?"

"You are not likely to let me forget, are you? But though I cannot control what you will do then, I can prevent your interfering now. And if you again threaten or so much as lay a hand on Steven Muir—"

"The fool deserved the thrashing I gave him."

"Nevertheless, if you lay a hand on him, or on your sister, I will take steps—"

"You will take *steps*!" Courtenay spat back. "Pray, what kind of steps would you take against me, Mother!"

"A man who strikes a woman, a brother who strikes his sister, is a rogue and a villain, and I will not have such in my house. If I have to, I will take steps to have you removed to keep you from such an attack again."

"Have me *removed*!" cried Courtenay, his rage mounting. "*Your* house! You forget yourself, Mother. This is *my* house. The entire Westbrooke estate is *mine*. You are a mere temporary trustee. But none of it belongs to you or ever will. So do not threaten me. You cannot have me removed. I will not have you make me look like a weak child in the eyes of my tenants. If you persist with such threats, you will leave me no alternative but to have *you* removed."

"You would not dare evict a former viscountess in full view of all of North Wales. Your father may be dead, but I am still Lady Snowdon. Even London would be rocked by the scandal you would bring upon yourself. Do not think too highly of yourself, Courtenay. You would be despised for such arrogance."

But Courtenay was nowise cowed. He did not know what it was to recognize that he had gone too far and back down. "In that case," he said, "I give you formal notice here and now, Mother, that neither you nor your daughter will be welcome to call this your home after next March. You will receive written notification of your eviction in due course."

He turned and strode from the study, leaving Katherine staring after him in horrified silence. Slowly her eyes filled. How could her own son have come to this? Her mother's heart broke at the thought of what he had become.

Twenty-Seven

Summer Plans

No more incidents or outbursts marred the slow dawning of spring in the gardens of Westbrooke Manor. After the high words they had exchanged in her husband's study, Katherine had not so much as spoken another word to Courtenay again. Nor had she had the opportunity. She scarcely saw him. If Courtenay had kept out of the way of the household before, he was now little more than a ghost whose occasional presence was assumed but whom no one had actually *seen*.

He came and went by one of the seldom-used back stairways, and his footsteps were heard but now and then. The echo of horses' hooves from the stables also gave evidence of his movements and his daily comings and goings. The only one of the staff who maintained regular contact with the late viscount's son was Mrs. Drenwydd. Somehow Courtenay contrived to make his wishes known. For a month she had been delivering his tea and meals, on schedule, to his private apartment of two rooms. Adela kept his quarters clean, the bed made and supplied with fresh linens, but rarely saw its occupant. Sometimes, she reported, the bed was not slept in for days at a time. At such times, the cook was not notified in advance, only learning that the young master, as they still called him, had not touched his food when she came to take away the tray. But she continued to bring tea and cakes and the next meal at their appointed times, for one never knew when he might be in residence again, and she was terrified of angering him. How he occupied his time was a mystery.

He was certainly not missed. Absent though he was, however, the bitter argument between Katherine and Courtenay cast an ongoing pall over Westbrooke Manor. Though Katherine did not divulge the specifics of their exchange, the heated shouts had been heard by Florilyn in her room and Adela Muir in hers, as well as two or three of the staff.

Katherine had not been herself since. There was no doubt what was the cause of her gloom. Her own future did not concern her. She grieved for what her son had become. She did, however, accelerate her plans for Mochras Head. She wrote to solicitor Murray with the request that he discreetly retain a suitable architect and arrange a meeting at the manor to begin the process of designing what she was now confident would be her new home. It was already too late to hope to complete construction before Courtenay's birthday. But she and Florilyn could spend a month, even a year if need be, with Edward and Mary in Glasgow. She had no intention of waiting for the ignominy of being cast adrift by her son. She and Florilyn would be packed and gone the day before Courtenay acquired the title. She still had not resolved how best to care for Adela and Steven and the rest of her staff. Those who wanted to remain in Courtenay's employ, if he chose to keep them, could certainly remain. Those he did not plan to keep, she would employ at the new house. What to do in the interim, however, before construction was complete, weighed upon her as an unknown yet to be resolved.

Courtenay, meanwhile, bided his time with useless and vain distractions—traveling, eating, visiting, drinking, hunting. While Lord Litchfield in London was busily engaged in making plans for his new acquisition in Wales, the sale could not have been further from Courtenay's mind. With Litchfield's money in the bank, he felt again the exuberant freedom of wealth. The only hint that he planned to sail for the continent for the summer and possibly longer were a few words to Mrs. Drenwydd around the first of May, telling her that he would be traveling abroad and would not require meals for some time, adding that he would apprise her further when his plans became definite.

He and Colville Burrenchobay were returning from a pheasant hunt one afternoon, on their way through Llanfryniog from the north, where they intended to slack their thirst with however many tankards of Mistress Chattan's ale it took to accomplish the job. Courtenay had been trying to persuade his friend to accompany him to France in two weeks.

The figure of a woman came toward them along the walkway beside the street, a boy of two to three years at her side.

"Is that. . .by the saints—is that Rhawn Lorimer?" exclaimed Courtenay in a low voice.

"I can hardly tell," chuckled Colville. "I haven't seen her in years."

"She must have put on two stone. To think that I once fancied *that*!"

Rhawn saw them as they approached. Her eyes narrowed as she glanced from one to the other.

As they rode by, both young men nodded slightly. No words were exchanged.

"If looks could kill, eh?" said Courtenay softly.

"That expression she cast you was the look of a woman spurned, old man," said Colville. "When are you going to own up to being the father of her brat there?"

"What are you talking about?" Courtenay shot back irritably.

"Everyone knows it."

"Don't talk rubbish. They know no such thing."

"If not you, who else could the father be?"

"Some might think it was you."

"Bah. I wasn't even around at the time. I heard she met several no-goods when she was in London. You know the English! None of them would own up to it. With the reputation she had, I doubt she even knows who the father is."

Both burst out laughing. Their speculations went no further as they reined up in front of the inn, dismounted, and went inside.

Further to the north, Edward and Mary Drummond sat in a second-class coach of the Aberdeen Express, bound for the great northern seaport and the graduation of their son from Aberdeen University. Their enthusiasm for the trip had been heightened two days before by a letter from Edward's cousin Henry in Stirling with the news that he and his son of the same name, Percy's junior by six months, had decided to accept their invitation to Percy's graduation. That same afternoon, they would take the train north from Edinburgh, where young Henry was studying for the ministry of the Free Church at New College. They would meet them at their boardinghouse after their arrival.

Though the families of Edward and the elder Henry Drummond had been much together as the two had grown into adulthood, Edward's eventual settling in Glasgow had greatly reduced their contact in recent years. In spite of the reasonable proximity of Stirling to Glasgow, the two younger Drummond cousins had met but two or three times during their boyhood. As both boys had grown into fine young men with hearts for God, it seemed a shame to Edward that they were not more intimately acquainted. He was thus delighted with his cousin's acceptance of the invitation.

The five Drummonds sat together at a celebratory dinner two evenings later in the restaurant of one of Aberdeen's finer hotels. The two second cousins hit it off immediately. They would have been taken by an observer to be lifelong friends.

"So it's law next, is it, Percy?" young Henry had just asked.

"No decision yet," replied Percy. "Actually, for a time I was considering the ministry, like my father. . .and like you now, too. But after much prayer, I am sensing a leading in the direction of law. I have to tell you, though, at the moment the thought of more schooling is not especially appealing. I just want to put it behind me."

"I know what you mean," rejoined Henry. "After I graduated, I considered taking a break from my studies. But," he added, casting a glance across the table, "my father encouraged me to keep the momentum strong. If I wanted my divinity degree, he said, it would be best to continue in pursuit of the goal."

"No doubt wise advice. I have the advantage of having worked for a law firm here in Aberdeen for several summers. They will hire me full-time as an intern if I want to postpone law school."

"Is that what you're going to do?"

"Again. . .no decision yet. There is something I have to do first, before I embark on any career plans—a promise that I must fulfill."

"Sounds mysterious."

"It is mysterious!" now laughed Edward. "Neither Mary nor I know what it is. Percy has been very tight lipped."

"I promised to tell no one," said Percy. "That's part of it, too—confidentiality. The first thing I need to do is return to Wales in a few weeks to attempt to fulfill my promise."

"Wales?" asked the elder Henry.

"To visit my aunt," said Percy.

"Ah, right. . .Katherine. She's the one who married into the aristocracy, is she not?"

"The Viscount Lord Snowdon," nodded Edward. "My sister, your cousin, is none other than the Viscountess Lady Snowdon. The viscount died a year ago. Percy was there at the time and made a deathbed promise to Katherine's husband, which is the source of his perplexity and our mystery."

The eyes of the others around the table all came to rest on Percy. He drew in a long breath and sighed. "That's about it," he said. "It is indeed a perplexity because I am not sure how to carry out my uncle's dying wish. But I promised him I would try. So I will go to Wales and hope to be given direction on what to do next."

"I have an idea for you," said young Henry. "Actually, I haven't talked to you about this yet, Father," he added, glancing toward his father. "I just learned of it a few days ago. D. L. Moody and Ira Sankey are coming to Scotland on an evangelistic mission in the fall. I would like to take a leave from New College and work with them. . .with your permission, Father." He turned again to Percy. "Why don't you join me, Percy?" he said enthusiastically. "Can you imagine what an experience—to work alongside Moody! It's an opportunity that may never come again. I want to be part of it."

Percy took in the suggestion with obvious interest. "I will have to see how it goes in Wales," he said. "It sounds like an intriguing possibility. What will you do?"

"They enlist local support wherever they travel to help with organization and crowds and in counseling people after the services. I suppose it will be personal evangelism with those who have shown interest or have given their hearts to Christ."

The conversation and dinner continued late into the evening. When they finally retired for the night, the two young cousins agreed to stay in touch and keep one another apprised of their future plans.

Parting the next day, as the two Henry Drummonds prepared to board their train for Edinburgh, young Henry approached his father's cousin as they waited in the station.

"Cousin Edward," he said. "I have a request to make of you, if you don't mind."

"Certainly, Henry," replied Edward.

"My mother and father have always spoken highly of your spiritual insights—how you see things in the spiritual world differently from most Christians. I am embarrassed to ask, but would you look at some writings I am working on? My father has read most of them and offered a few ideas. I would like to hear what you think as well."

"I would be happy to, Henry," replied Edward. "What's it about?"

"It's a series of devotional talks based on First Corinthians 13. I am occasionally called on to address my fellow students at chapel. I would appreciate any thoughts you might have."

"It would be my pleasure," replied Edward.

His cousin's son handed him a small sheaf of handwritten pages.

"You don't mind if I read it, too?" asked Percy.

"Of course not, Percy," replied Henry. "I would appreciate your thoughts as well—as someone my own age."

"This is not your only copy?" asked Edward.

"No, I copied out a clean draft for you. My own is too filled with notes and scratchings from my pen. No one could possibly make sense of it!"

With final handshakes and promises to write, the two Henrys, father and son, boarded their train.

The three Glaswegians departed for Glasgow the following morning, with all Percy's belongings from four years at the university.

Twenty-Eight

Wales through New Eyes

Percival Drummond, M.A., arrived at Llanfryniog in North Wales in the last week of May, 1873. As he alighted from the coach in front of the inn, he thought to himself how the progression of his life seemed inexorably linked to his periodic sojourns in this rural seat of his aunt and uncle and cousins. Westbrooke Manor had come to feel more like his true home even than the parsonage in Glasgow in which he had been raised.

While the coachman took down his bags and set them beside the inn, he glanced up and down the familiar street. How many times had he been here, he wondered. His first visit as a rebellious sixteen-year-old in 1867 had been filled with so many discoveries about God and nature and himself. Then his return visit as a nineteen-year-old university student in 1870. . .and again two years later. That was the fateful visit of a year ago, when the accident had occurred that had taken his uncle's life. Finally the short stay last Christmas. Now here he was again, a university graduate of twenty-two, with an uncertain future ahead of him.

Almost simultaneous to the departure of the coach and four that had brought him down the coast from the train at Blaenau Ffestiniog, the Westbrooke Manor buggy appeared at the end of the street to the south of town, coming between the two churches and making good speed. As he approached, Percy saw Steven Muir at the reins.

He waited as the carriage slowed and drew alongside the inn. Steven jumped down and ran toward him with outstretched hand. He seemed to Percy's eyes to have aged two years. Being in a position of responsibility obviously agreed with him.

"Hello, Stevie!" said Percy, reverting to the nickname by which he had first known him.

"Welcome back to Wales, Percy!" said Steven. "As always, the whole manor is anxiously awaiting you."

"The *whole* manor?" laughed Percy.

"Ah, if you're meaning Mister Courtenay. . .he's away to the continent."

Behind Steven, Percy now saw Florilyn alight from the carriage. She smiled and walked toward him. The two cousins embraced affectionately, then stepped back and gazed a moment into one another's eyes. If anything since the ending of their engagement, Florilyn had grown quieter and more beautiful, reminding all who saw her of Katherine.

After the initial heartache from what she had done, the months since had been good ones for Florilyn's soul. She participated in the domestic life of the manor and spent much of her free time in the library. There her newfound love for reading blossomed into a passion. She and her mother grew closer than ever, talked often about Percy and what Florilyn had done, and had even begun to pray together. As rare as such a thing might be in the world, mother and daughter truly became the best of friends and confidantes.

In the second or two as she gazed into Percy's eyes, a strange and unexpected sensation filled Florilyn's heart. How she *loved* him! Yet in that instant, she realized that her love for Percy was the love of a sister for a brother. . .the natural love for a brother that Courtenay had never allowed to flourish within her.

"You look well, Florilyn," said Percy. "You seem at peace."

"Perhaps I am," said Florilyn. "You look good, too, Percy. I can see from your face that you are relieved that the stress of school is behind you."

Percy nodded. "It is a great relief, I will admit. If I go to law school eventually, it will probably be far more rigorous. But I'm not thinking about that now."

Steven already had Percy's bags loaded. The three climbed into the buggy.

Florilyn sat down between the two young men and slipped her hands through their two arms. "I don't know that I have ever felt so safe and secure and happy as to have two such wonderful men beside me!" she exclaimed as they set off.

Percy roared with laughter.

"Oh Percy, it is always so good when you come home, isn't it, Steven? Your laughter brings the sun out!"

"I am glad to be of service!" said Percy, laughing again. "So, Steven," he went on, "how does the life of a gentleman suit you?"

"I am hardly that, Percy!" laughed Steven. "Merely a humble factor."

"A factor is *almost* a gentleman, is it not?"

"I will always be a sheepherder at heart."

"Don't let him tell you stories, Percy," said Florilyn. "Steven knows everything about the estate. Mother says he manages it all. The business of the estate would be impossible without him, she says."

"Good for you, Steven! I am happy it has worked out well for everyone. What does Courtenay think of having you for his—" Percy stopped abruptly as they passed a young woman from behind. "Wait a minute—Hold on, Steven!" he said. "Isn't that. . . Yes, it is!" He leaped down from the carriage as Steven pulled to a stop. He ran around the horse to the side of the street. "Rhawn!" he cried. "I thought it was you!"

Before Rhawn Lorimer had a chance even to greet him, she found herself embraced by the last person she had expected to see. "Percy!" she exclaimed as he stepped back. "You're back in Wales!"

"I only just arrived. Florilyn and Steven came to collect me from the coach," he added, glancing toward the two where they sat in the buggy.

Rhawn smiled up at them.

"You're looking well. Being a mother must be a good influence on you."

"Thank you," said Rhawn a little shyly, glancing away.

"Are you still living at your parents' home?" asked Percy.

Rhawn nodded.

"And your son?"

"He is well. He's two and a half now—rambunctious and talkative."

"I can't wait to see him. I'll come visit. We'll go for a ride together!" Percy turned and walked back to the carriage and climbed up.

Steven flicked the reins and they bounded into motion as Rhawn stood a moment staring after them.

It was quiet in the carriage for a minute or two.

"Is there still no. . ." Percy began. "I mean. . .the boy still has no father, I take it?"

"No *acknowledged* father," said Florilyn.

"Do you and she still see one another?"

"We get together from time to time," nodded Florilyn. "I've actually gotten her started reading MacDonald's books."

"She's said nothing to you about who the father is?"

"She would never do that. It's never come up between us."

They left Llanfryniog behind them, joined the main road, and continued southward.

"What is happening over there?" said Percy as they rode up the plateau and he looked toward the promontory of Mochras Head.

"Actually," said Florilyn, "my mother is building a new house."

"What?"

"She and I will be leaving the manor when Courtenay becomes viscount."

"You're kidding! Voluntarily, or is he forcing you out?"

"A little of both!" laughed Florilyn. "Now that the new house is begun, Mother is excited. Just wait till you see the drawings. It will be beautiful, overlooking the sea with the most spectacular views imaginable."

"So how is my old friend and nemesis doing?" asked Percy.

"Courtenay you mean?"

"Who else? Can't wait to see me, what?"

"Actually, Courtenay's gone," replied Florilyn. "He left for France about a month ago. How he found the money for a trip has Mother baffled," she went on. "To all accounts he was basically penniless except for what Mother occasionally gave him. Then all of a sudden something seemed to change. The next thing we knew, he was gone again. We've not heard a word from him."

"But he becomes viscount. . .when?"

"He turns twenty-five next March."

~

On the continent, Courtenay's newfound wealth was in fact evaporating rather more quickly than he would have hoped, largely from unwise investments at Europe's racetracks. He seemed neither concerned nor inclined to moderate his expensive addiction. There was more waiting for him in a few months' time. Once he was viscount, he would raise rents across the board sufficient to keep from finding himself in the same boat as had his father.

His father's dream of owning a stable of thoroughbred racehorses of his own had taken possession of Courtenay. His travels also served the ostensible purpose of giving him the opportunity to make several purchases. He was not a wise judge of horseflesh, far too impetuous and given to the lure of externals. But as is often the case with such young men, his confidence in his decision-making prowess was of inverse proportion to its wisdom. The *last* thing he would think to do was seek the counsel of those older and wiser than himself. His hubris was well developed in the extreme.

The thought never now entered his mind of resuming his studies at Oxford. What did he need a degree for? By this time next year, he would be sitting in the House of Lords!

~

Steven and Florilyn continued with their Scots passenger through the gate into the precincts of Westbrooke Manor.

Katherine was watching for their arrival from the window of the study. The moment the buggy came into view, she was on her way down the stairs. The entire household staff was also aware of their honored guest's impending arrival and had contrived to be at or near the front door with their mistress to greet him.

Katherine walked outside and hurried toward the carriage. She embraced Percy almost the moment his feet touched the ground. “Welcome home, Percy!” she whispered into his ears.

Percy stepped back and looked into his aunt’s eyes. He saw a new light of assurance, poise, and calm in her countenance.

In the six months since Christmas, the viscount’s widow had added more than a few strands of gray now that the milestone of fifty had come and gone. The grief of finding herself without a husband while still a relatively young woman caused her, even now, occasional tears when alone at night. But that she had grown within herself was obvious from one look deep into her eyes. Notwithstanding the tussles with Courtenay, she was more confident and self-assured. Many decisions had been forced upon her. She had risen to meet them with a maturity and grace that would have made her late husband proud. She continued what she and her husband had begun during the final year or two of his life, visiting the homes and shops of the villagers who were, even if but temporarily, her tenants and making sure their needs were being met.

Even with the prospect looming of having to leave her home, she was looking to the future not with defeat but as a challenge to be met with zestful optimism. She had successfully concluded the purchase from the estate of one hundred sixty acres stretching inland from the promontory of Mochras Head approximately a quarter mile at its narrowest up to three-quarters of a mile at the point of the promontory, bounded to the east by the village road and main road south to Barmouth. Now that Courtenay had laid his cards on the table, she was almost looking forward to the inevitable move to the new home of her design. Nevertheless, she was greatly relieved to be able to embark on the project in his absence.

Mostly, however, Katherine Westbrooke had grown spiritually. The sensitivities of her youth, nurtured in the home of a godly mother and father, had been so thoroughly stifled during the years of her marriage as to almost have receded into dormancy. The strong roots of that spiritual legacy had now revived and sent new life throughout the entire plant of her being. Not only was she now reading every new MacDonald novel as it came off the press, she was venturing into the deep waters of his sermons as well and had begun her own inquiry through daily Bible reading into the true nature and character of God.

Truly had she allowed the tragedies that had come to her to work together for good in her life.

Twenty-Nine

Reflections Past and Future

In the warm soft-scented twilight, Percy Drummond stood at the open window of his familiar room in Westbrooke Manor. It was late. Though tired from his journey and the emotionally draining day of visiting and laughter and rekindling old friendships, his brain was too occupied for sleep.

He was here at last. The moment of truth had finally arrived when he would have to decide how to carry out his uncle's dying commission. He had put off the *how* of that mystery for almost a year. The future had arrived.

After today, learning of Courtenay's intolerable actions, the urgency of his mission was suddenly borne upon him with new force. Perhaps it had been a mistake to wait so long. With Katherine involved in the construction of a new home on the assumption that Courtenay would be viscount in nine or ten months, there wasn't a moment to lose. The perplexity, and seeming impossibility of his mission, again pressed with great weight upon Percy's mind.

Slowly the words rose unbidden from his subconscious. Yet they were words his subconscious was training itself to pray with every inward breath and exhaling of his spiritual lungs. "Lord," he whispered, "show me what to do."

This visit was unlike any previous. He was, if not quite, *almost* a grown man. Florilyn was a grown woman. He had completed his studies at the university. This was no mere summer holiday between school terms. Eventually he would have to explain himself—what he was doing here. If he disclosed that he was on a mission for his uncle, questions would immediately arise. He must keep his purpose to himself. Yet he must also have some pretext for being here.

Still without a clear picture of what he would do, Percy turned from the window and blew out the candle to end the long day.

The next morning dawned warm and bright. Percy slept till after nine and found Florilyn and Katherine in the breakfast room awaiting him. "That's as late as I have slept for a long time!" he said. "I have to say, it felt good."

After a friendly visit with his aunt and cousin, Percy found the question he had been hoping to avoid suddenly staring him in the face.

"I had been under the impression you were thinking of law school, Percy," said Katherine. "Listening to you yesterday, it sounds as though your plans are indefinite. I was actually surprised to learn that you would be visiting us again. Delighted, of course! Merely surprised. How long will you be with us? What *are* your plans?"

Katherine saw him glance down at the cup of tea in his hand with an uncertain expression. "Please," she added quickly, "you are welcome as long as you like. You are always welcome—you know that! I am simply interested."

"Actually, Aunt Katherine," replied Percy, "my future is cloudy. I honestly don't know how to answer you. Yes, law school looms on the horizon as a possibility. And of course Florilyn and I have to talk," he added, glancing toward Florilyn with a smile, "and seek what is God's will for us."

"I understand."

"This has become like a second home to me," Percy went on. "As much as I love being with my mother and father, I am more at peace here in the country. With my future uncertain, I felt that this was where I should be to ask God about it. I hope you don't mind."

"Of course not. You are family. This *is* your home! At least," she added, "for another few months. Once Courtenay turns twenty-five, the manor may no longer be home to any of us! Florilyn and I may have to spend a few months or a year in Glasgow with *your* parents while our new home is being completed."

Percy realized that he may never have a more appropriate moment to hint at the most important reason he had returned to Wales. "There is another thing," he said, choosing his words with care. "Before he died, Uncle Roderick asked me to. . .well, sort through some of his old things, papers and so on." He hesitated.

His aunt was looking at him with an expression of perplexity.

"He, uh. . ." Percy went on, "he didn't feel he could trust Courtenay to do it, he said. I'm sorry to have to say that—"

"No, I understand completely," said Katherine. "Courtenay has not shown himself to be the young man of sterling character we had hoped he might be."

"He knew his death would be devastating for you," Percy continued. "So he asked me to put his things in order, I suppose is how one might put it. I think the fact that I was hoping to study law may have influenced him as well. He was under the impression that my being a *student* of law gave me a sort of legal standing if such became necessary—that while you were trustee for the estate, I would be able to act on his behalf as well. I assured him that I had no legal standing and suggested that he speak to his own solicitor. But he was insistent that he wanted me to dig into his past. . .that is. . .to see that legalities were being followed. I have the sense that he may have been concerned about Courtenay as well, afraid that he might try to manipulate affairs to his own advantage."

"Roderick had good reason to be concerned."

"Perhaps Courtenay was his chief concern. It may be that he preferred that I be the lightning rod for Courtenay's hostility rather than you, that is if it turned out that Courtenay attempted to exploit his position prematurely or in some manner inconsistent with his rights as presumptive heir." Percy drew in a long breath. He was having great difficulty avoiding the central issue of his uncle's secret affidavit.

"What exactly. . .did he want you to *do*?" asked Katherine.

"Actually, I am uncertain about that myself," replied Percy, thankful that the wording of his aunt's question allowed him to answer with complete candor. "I think simply to go through his papers and files, put things in order for you. He didn't want you to be burdened by anything. As I understand it—though as I say, I have been in some perplexity about it myself—he simply wanted to be certain that all the affairs of the estate were properly settled and in legal order. His main thoughts were of you. He wanted to protect you from any burden his death was likely to cause. Perhaps I should have undertaken the charge sooner. It now seems that Uncle Roderick's fears about Courtenay were indeed well founded. Now that I learn what he has done, I regret waiting until now. At the time there did not seem to be great urgency. After talking with my father, we determined that I should complete my studies and then return here. It may be that decision wasn't the best."

"Whatever he had in mind, he chose you for good reason, Percy. What's done is done. None of us can go back and rewrite the past."

It was silent momentarily.

"Well, the whole thing remains a mystery to me," said Katherine at length. "I have no idea what Roderick expected you to do. The affairs of the estate seem to be in good hands with our solicitor, Mr. Murray, and with Steven managing my daily affairs. But it sounds as though you have no more idea than I do what he had in mind."

Percy did not reply. Already he feared he had said too much. But it was too late to take his words back.

"I assume that you will want to start in Roderick's study," said his aunt, interrupting his reverie. "I have been using it for my office as well, but he was right in that I had no appetite for going through any old papers or files. I have not even looked in the safe. So consider the study yours for now, Percy. I will remove my few things while you are working. If there is anything you need, or any way I can help, of course you will tell me."

"I will, Aunt Katherine," nodded Percy.

"And if you unearth any deep, dark mysteries, I will be curious to learn of them!"

Again, Percy said nothing.

Thirty

The Green Hills of Snowdonia

"It is a gorgeous day. How about a ride?" asked Percy as he and Florilyn left the breakfast room and wandered outside into the warm morning together.

"If everyone saw us riding off," said Florilyn with a smile, "there will be sure to be talk. All the servants are dying to know if we are going to resume our engagement."

"How do you know?"

"I overhear them," laughed Florilyn. "They're not so clever at hiding their curiosity as they think. Mrs. Drenwydd says that you have come to propose to me again!"

Percy chuckled. "Well then, it would be a shame for us not to keep them guessing. But we could go out as a threesome or a foursome instead."

"With whom?"

"I don't know—I thought with Stevie. . .I mean Steven. And maybe Rhawn Lorimer."

"Rhawn!" said Florilyn in surprise.

"I feel sorry for her. And I like her. She's lonely."

"She was awful to you."

"That was a long time ago. She's changed. You know that better than I do."

"How can you be so *good*, Percy?"

"I'm not. But my heart goes out to her."

"It might be fun at that. I know it would mean the world to her."

They walked toward the garden in silence. Florilyn slipped her hand through Percy's arm.

"Percy, Percy. . ." she sighed, "what does the future hold for us? Do you think there is an *us*?"

"I don't know. I'm in no hurry. And I can tell that you are content. You look *well*, Florilyn—prettier than ever and at peace with your life. The more time that passed after my Christmas visit, the more I saw the wisdom in what you did. I mean, I love you and always will. But now I am asking God if the love I have for you is the love of a brother, or a cousin I suppose I should say, or the love of a husband."

"That's exactly what I found myself thinking when I saw you yesterday!"

"It may be that what I have to do for your father will help us know what we are to do."

"How could that be?"

"I don't know. I am just taking one step at a time and seeing what comes of it."

A peculiar look of question came over Florilyn's face. "There's more to it than what you told Mother, isn't there?" she said. Percy glanced toward Florilyn to see if she was baiting him. But her expression was serious.

"Why would you say that?" he asked.

"Because I know you. I could tell that you were hemming and hawing, trying as hard to keep from saying what you wanted to avoid as to say what you did."

"Do you think your mother noticed?"

"I don't know. I doubt it."

They walked on in silence.

"So are you going to answer my question?" said Florilyn at length.

"Do I have to?"

"No. I won't coerce it out of you."

"Fair enough. Then. . .yes, there *may* be more to it. But there may not be. I was perfectly truthful in saying that your father's request is mostly a mystery to me, too. I may turn up nothing. I have no idea what to expect."

"I still think there's more to it even than that," said Florilyn with the hint of a twinkle in her eye. "But I will let that suffice. . .for now. As long as you promise to tell me if you discover anything interesting . . .especially about Courtenay. How I would love to turn the tables on him after how he has treated Mother."

"I'm sorry, I can make no promises. I will promise you this—I will tell you whatever I *can* tell you."

"Very cryptic!"

"So what do you think, shall we ask if Steven can tear himself away from his duties for a ride?"

"I will go see him right now," said Florilyn. "Why don't you ride into town and see if Rhawn can join us?"

The four young people set off from Westbrooke Manor shortly after midday with a picnic lunch packed by Mrs. Drenwydd. Rhawn Lorimer was quiet but happier than she had been in months to be on the back of a horse again with friends her own age. They rode into the hills eastward, four abreast, until they crested the first inland ridge. The trees thickened as they descended out of sight from the sea.

Florilyn and Rhawn took the lead, riding beside one another. Soon they were talking like the old friends they were as Percy and Steven lagged behind.

"It is so nice to have a break from mothering," said Rhawn. "I love little Aiden to death. . .but he is exhausting! Thank you so much for inviting me, Florilyn."

"It was Percy's idea."

"It was?"

"He is very fond of you."

"Are there any. . . I mean, have you and he—" Rhawn hesitated.

"Have we come to a decision yet? No. We are waiting to see what develops."

"Don't you. . . I mean, don't you still *want* to marry him?"

"Not if he's not the right one for me."

"How could he *not* be? Young men like Percy don't come along every day!"

"That's true. He's one in a million. But it still has to be right. Marriage is too important to rush into."

Rhawn did not reply. It was already too late for her to have a marriage that was *right.*

Their two squires rode briskly up beside them, cutting off further conversation.

"Take us to the meadow where we first raced, Florilyn," said Percy. "That will be a good place for lunch."

"I think I have heard that story," said Steven. "Didn't you come to an inglorious end?"

"I did indeed!" laughed Percy. "But I have learned a little about keeping the saddle beneath me since then. Perhaps I shall play a return engagement!"

"You and I've already done that!" laughed Florilyn. "You don't have to prove anything to me. I know you're as fast as I am now. Rhawn used to be the best horsewoman for miles," she added.

"That was a long time ago!" laughed Rhawn.

"Perhaps we should coax the men into a race, Rhawn," said Florilyn playfully.

"Steven and I are not competitive with each other," rejoined Percy. "Both of us would probably want the other one to win. If you're itching for a race, you'll have to lay down the challenge yourself, Florilyn, my dear!"

Florilyn cast Percy another smile that said, *Perhaps I will at that!*

They continued eastward down the ridge, through the valley at its back, across several streams, through woodland and meadow, and gradually up the next ridge until again they rose to its height and reached the parallel crest another two miles farther inland. There they reined in and gazed about. The regularly spaced peaks of Gwynedd running in a line north and south were clearly visible both to their right and left, their jagged peaks of granite dotted with snow.

"Look," said Steven, "you can faintly see Snowdonia there, far to the north beyond the other mountains."

"It's still covered in snow," said Percy. "I assumed it would be gone by now. This could be the Scottish Highlands."

"We had a good heavy snowfall only two weeks ago," said Steven. "It's early yet—not quite June. Snowdonia can keep its snow till July in a late spring."

"Have you ever climbed it, Steven?"

"My father took me up when I was a lad. It's not a rigorous climb. But it's certainly desolate up there—nothing but rock, gray and barren. It's a wasteland. But the view is spectacular. Personally, I prefer the green hills all around, with meadows and forests and rivers and pasturelands. A mountaintop, I have always thought, is a dead thing. A meadow with a brook running through it is a *living* thing—abundant with life. I would rather see *life* and *growth* about me, not death."

"Eloquently put, my friend." said Percy. "In people most of all."

Gradually they continued down the slope from the ridge toward the expansive meadow at its base, which was their objective.

"I have always considered green the color of growth and life and energy and hope," Steven said as they went. "It must be God's favorite color, don't you think, since so much of his creation he painted with so many interesting and varied shades of green."

"People are like mountains or meadows, too, don't you think, Steven," said Percy reflectively. "If they are not growing, then something is dead inside them. God's meadows, that's what he created us to be. We are intended to be live, growing, flourishing reflections of his creation."

"The vicar's son!" laughed Florilyn good naturedly. "Is a sermon coming on, Percy? Perhaps you are cut out for the pulpit after all."

"What's this?" said Steven.

Percy laughed. "I once asked Florilyn what she thought of my career options—law or the ministry."

"You were thinking seriously about the ministry?"

"I was," nodded Percy. "Once the Lord got hold of my life, everything changed. I wanted to be God's man in whatever vocation I was most suited. I wanted to be an effective spokesman for truth. Eventually I decided that would be law."

"But you're still not opposed to delivering the occasional short sermon, are you, Percy!" chided Florilyn in fun.

Percy laughed with delight. "One never knows when the occasion may call for it, my dear!"

"I rather like it," said Rhawn. "The others glanced at her and saw that she was serious. "I've never heard people talk about God like you three do. I always thought of God as so distant and far away. But you all bring him into everything. It's not easy to learn to grow when you've been a self-centered dead mountain of stone all your life."

Rhawn had not intended to bring an end to the conversation. But her words caused them all to become reflective. They rode on some distance in silence.

At length Florilyn urged Red Rhud ahead. A few minutes later, she led with a brief gallop into the meadow. "Here we are again, Percy!" she called out over her shoulder. "Are you sure you don't want to race me to the far end?"

"Maybe after lunch," he answered. "I'm hungry! I'm eager to see what Mrs. Drenwydd has prepared for us."

They reined in and dismounted. Soon the four horses were enjoying the grass and water from the living meadow, and the two young women and two young men were seated on the grass in the warmth of the sun enjoying the provisions provided by the Westbrooke Manor cook.

Thirty-One

Growing Human Meadows

For individuals of any age, especially young people full of thoughts and experiences, to share with equal give-and-take in conversation with their peers is one of life's rare treasures. Most are so enamored with the sound of their own voices that listening becomes a lost art.

These were four friends, however, interested equally in each *other* as they were eager to orate at length from the storehouse of their own ideas and opinions. When one spoke, the others truly *listened*. . .listened to the heart, to the soul, listened to the *person*, because they were interested and cared. There was no debate of ideas, only sharing of thoughts and feelings and impressions. They were more intent to *know* one another truly than to be known themselves. The occasional silences that arose between them were part and parcel of the fabric of human intercourse.

It is not often in life that such conversations are allowed to take place. In most discussions, individuals have some ideas to put forward or some commentaries on life from their own experiences to share. The object in the former case is to bolster their own theses while disproving their neighbors'. The object in the latter is to hold the conversational floor for as long as their breath holds out. They may have originally adopted this particular viewpoint because of some sign of truth in it. But now this method of communicating is generally to block up every cranny in their minds where more truth might enter or to keep talking long enough that no alternate perspectives are able to squeeze a word in edgewise.

In the present case, unusual as it is for as many as four earnest, humble, truth-seeking, and listening young people to come together, here were four simply set on gaining what insights the *others* were able to offer. Thus it was that after an hour, they had partaken of two meals, both physical and relational. Each of the four knew the other three more deeply than before. They were no longer mere youths, but young adults embarking on life and desirous of knowing all that life could mean and should mean.

"I don't like to be the one to break this up," said Steven at last as he stood to stretch his legs, "but it is time I thought about returning to the manor. I promised your mother, Florilyn, that she could have her first ride on Snowdonia this afternoon. She has been waiting so long, I daren't disappoint her."

"That's the new white stallion?" asked Percy, rising to his feet, also. He offered Rhawn his hand and helped her up from the grass.

Steven nodded. "I've been bringing him along very slowly. I've been riding him myself now for a few months, and he has at last settled down. Lady Katherine is a skilled horsewoman. But after what happened to the viscount, I will take no chances."

"You will accompany her, I take it?"

"For her first ride, absolutely."

Florilyn and Rhawn gathered up the lunch things and put them into the leather bag. Slowly the four walked to their waiting mounts.

"Are you ready for that race now, Percy?" said Florilyn with a twinkle in her eye.

"We shall see."

They mounted and set off slowly. Gradually Florilyn increased the pace, then broke into a gentle gallop and wheeled Red Rhud back the way they had come toward the edge of the meadow.

"Where are you going?" Percy called out.

"I'm giving you the advantage!" Florilyn called back, laughing. "You'll need all the help you can to beat me to the far end!"

Percy laughed but did not seem inclined to take the bait.

Beside him, however, a grin spread across Steven's face. He was riding one of Courtenay's favorite mounts, the Chestnut stallion Cymru Gold. He well knew what the horse was capable of. He turned to Percy. "Watch this," he said. "We'll show the little lady a thing or two." Suddenly he bolted away from them with marvelous acceleration.

Behind them they heard Florilyn shriek. "Steven!" she cried. "I offered *you* no head start!" The next instant she was after him in a mad frenzy of shouts and pounding hooves across the grass.

Looking behind him, once Steven realized that she had taken his bait, he slowed to allow her to catch up. Side by side they rode for a few seconds, glancing back and forth at one another with the gleam of fun and challenge in their eyes, Florilyn's auburn hair trailing behind her.

Steven held Florilyn's eyes for a moment then winked in fun and shouted something in Gaelic Florilyn did not understand. Suddenly, though she was at nearly a full gallop, Cymru Gold began to pull steadily away from her.

"Steven!" she shouted again.

All she heard in reply was the sound of Steven's laughter receding away from her.

Florilyn dug in her heels and urged Red Rhud on with a mighty effort. But it was little use.

Behind them Percy and Rhawn watched and laughed in delight.

"I am afraid Florilyn has at last taken on a more worthy adversary than I ever was!" said Percy.

"Steven looks like he is loving every minute of it!" said Rhawn. "And so here we are together again, Percy—just like that other time, do you remember, when I was the one who baited Courtenay and Florilyn?"

"I remember!" laughed Percy. "Then you fell back so you could get me alone. You really were devious in your day."

A look of pain came over Rhawn's face.

Percy saw that he had touched a raw nerve. "Sorry," he said. "I meant nothing by it."

"I know, Percy. You couldn't hurt a fly if you wanted to. You're the most considerate person I've ever met. That's what makes it hurt so much to remember how I used to be."

"How so?"

"I had eyes for you for all the wrong reasons. I thought you were too cute for words. And I was tired of Colville and Courtenay. You were a challenge. But I never saw the real person you were. I didn't care about all that back then. I was shallow and selfish. I thought I could turn the head of any boy in the world. Then I met you. You were different. But I still had no eyes to see it. And look where it got me," she added with a ironic laugh in which the sadness was all too evident.

"I don't know, Rhawn," said Percy. "You are *growing*, like Steven was talking about. You are becoming God's live meadow. Maybe it took some heartbreak to get you there. Don't forget—or maybe you never knew, I don't know—I was sent to my Uncle Roderick and Aunt Katherine for the first time because my parents were desperate."

"Yes," Rhawn smiled. "Florilyn told me all about you back then. She didn't like you much at first."

Percy roared with laughter. "The feeling was mutual!" he said.

"Then five years later, the two of you were engaged."

"And now are un-engaged," said Percy. "An altogether strange sequence of events. But whatever you think you were, I was probably worse. You didn't know me then. I was a petty thief. I was in trouble with the Glasgow police. I had the best parents in the world, but I despised them. It still brings tears to my eyes to remember what I put them through. When my father finally put his foot down and sent me here, I thought he had sent me to prison. I was rebellious and conceited and self-centered. Yet somehow God used all that to wake me up inside. Look. . .they've reached the opposite side of the meadow! From here, I would say Steven had her by at least two lengths."

Neither spoke for a minute as their two horses walked gently across the grass.

"How does God wake people up, as you say?" asked Rhawn at length.

"By using the circumstances of their lives," answered Percy. "At least that's what he did with me. I found myself in new and strange—and at the time unpleasant—circumstances. Those circumstances forced me to start thinking about things."

"What kind of things?"

"I suppose mostly the kind of person I wanted to be. And about who God is and whether he had something to say about the way my life went."

Again Rhawn was silent. She was obviously thinking. "May I ask you something, Percy. . .something serious, I mean?"

"Of course. You know you can."

"There's really no one else I can talk to about. . .you know, about what happened. . .about my son. Everyone around here. . .even Florilyn—I know what they think. But you, Percy. . .I *think* that you don't care about all that. I think you accept me. . .just as a person who knows she made a mistake but who wants to be better."

"That is exactly how I see you."

"I want to wake up. I'm trying to wake up. Florilyn's given me some books to read where the people are thinking about God all the time. But it's hard to wake up. I don't know what to do. Maybe I was like a mountain of rock for too long. Maybe I can never become a growing meadow." She turned away, blinking hard trying to keep away the tears.

"Anyone can grow, Rhawn. Surely you know that. If you want to grow, you will. It's just that most people don't care about being different than they are. What they *are* is good enough. But for people like you and me, who have been through some scrapes in life, what we were *isn't* good enough. We want to be *better*. At least I did. And you're telling me that you do. So you *will* be. You *are* growing, Rhawn. I can see the change in you."

"Really?"

"Of course."

Rhawn wiped at her eyes and smiled a melancholy smile. "There were people who thought you were my son's father," she said at length.

"I know."

"I'm afraid I allowed them to think so. I'm sorry, Percy. It was an awful thing for me to do."

"All is forgiven."

"I wish you were Aiden's father. I mean. . .not because of—you know. . .not because of *that.* I just mean. . .you would be a good father, Percy. You wouldn't desert me and leave me alone."

Again Rhawn was quiet. "That's what I wanted to ask you, Percy," she said after a moment. "I don't know what to do."

"About what?"

"Whether to say something. . .whether to confront him. . .whether to force him to tell what happened."

"I hope you won't take this the wrong way," said Percy. "I mean, it is an awkward question to ask, but I'm sure you knew that there was talk. You *do* know who the father is?"

Rhawn nodded. "But I don't know how long to be silent. My son needs a father, a family, grandparents and cousins. But he would hate me if I told who he was. I want him to *want* to be a father."

"You are in a difficult position. You're right—to try to force him might make him all the more antagonistic."

"But how long do I wait, Percy? I've been waiting three years."

"Have you prayed about what to do?"

"Why would God listen to someone like me? You know what I've been."

"God doesn't care what we have been. He only cares what we are becoming. The growing meadow, remember?"

Rhawn forced a smile. "It's hard to believe that God cares about me," she said.

"He doesn't just care about you—he loves you. . .as his daughter. Just think how you love your little son. That is only the tiniest measure of how God feels about us. We are really and truly His children, and He is the best Father in the world."

"Do you really think God loves me?"

"Oh, Rhawn—He loves you more than you can imagine!"

Rhawn glanced away. This time the tears came. By the time she was herself again, Steven and Florilyn were riding back to join them, laughing and talking gaily.

Thirty-Two

The Search Begins

On the morning following their ride into the hills, Percy sought his aunt after breakfast. "I think I would like to begin looking through Uncle Roderick's papers and things, Aunt Katherine," he said. "Whatever it is I am to do, it won't get done unless I make a beginning."

"Of course, Percy. What may I do to help?"

"I don't know. I suppose I should start in his study, if you don't mind."

"You may consider it your own office, for as long as you like," replied his aunt. "It's not locked. You may come and go as you please. There are a few keys on a ring. I don't even know what all of them are for. One I believe is to the safe I mentioned. Shall we go upstairs and have a look?"

Percy walked up the main staircase and followed his aunt into the late viscount's study. He glanced about fondly. It was just as he remembered it. The last time he had been in this office, his uncle had been giving him his blessing to marry his daughter.

"Here are the keys I told you about," said Katherine, taking a small ring from a hook on the wall behind the door. "There is the safe next to Roderick's gun cabinet. You will want to go through the desk, of course, and the file drawers over there in the cabinet on the far wall. I can't think what you will find. But perhaps it is as you say, just putting Roderick's papers in order."

She turned to leave, then hesitated and looked back to where Percy stood in the middle of the room. "I confess," she added with a smile, "I know this must be daunting for you, but I am relieved. I have little taste for paperwork. No one enjoys going through a loved one's personal effects after they're gone. But if you have questions or need my help, please ask."

Percy nodded, and his aunt left him.

He wandered about the small room, looking about thoughtfully, then sat down in his uncle's chair behind the large desk. What *was* he to do, he wondered.

Slowly he began to open one drawer of the desk at a time. Nothing of possible significance caught his eye—only the assorted paraphernalia of years. . .perhaps even centuries. How old was this desk? How many of these old tools, knives, fasteners, keys, pencils, pens, sealing wax, nails, screws, matches, tape, and the memorabiliac gadgetry and odds and ends that inevitably accumulate in a desk had preceded his uncle? As interesting as some of the old items might be, there was certainly nothing among this miscellany of flotsam and jetsam to offer any clues.

He opened the two larger bottom drawers. They were filled with files, folders, and envelopes, mostly yellowed with age and few displaying labels or the least hint of their contents. It would take forever to go through them all. And for what purpose? Surely his uncle had left nothing in plain view like this that would connect him to his brief former life in Ireland so long ago.

Percy rose and walked to the safe. His natural curiosity was aroused by the mere presence in the room of something that spoke so obviously of secrets. It sat on the floor to a height of approximately three feet, and in width about half that.

He knelt to one knee and tried several of the keys on the ring until he found one that turned in the lock. He grasped the handle and turned. A dull muffled clank sounded from within the mechanism. The mere sound sent a thrill of mystery through him. There was no safe in his parents' home in Glasgow. Who had safes but wealthy people for the purpose of protecting their riches? He had never actually looked inside a safe in his life.

Slowly he swung back the massive iron door. What he was expecting it would have been difficult to say. But gazing inside the small vault turned out to be a disappointment. The thing was half empty. A few large envelopes lay on the bottom. Shelves contained assorted papers. Several locked drawers were built into the lower quadrant of the right side. He tried the smaller keys of the key ring but none fit. Judging by the rest of the safe, they were probably empty. Whatever might be inside them, it would have to wait until a later time.

He had hoped perhaps to discover a stash of 100-pound notes or a silver-lined box full of diamond and pearl and ruby jewelry, or some other mysterious treasure. He cast a last look about the uninteresting contents then closed the door.

He rose, walked to the window, and stood staring out at the countryside below. From deep within the subconscious recesses of his brain, words from his grandfather drifted hazily up into his memory. He tried to remember the occasion. . .his father and grandfather had been talking seriously about spiritual things. He hadn't been interested himself. He was probably ten or eleven at the time.

Suddenly now from out of the past, as if bringing a message for this moment in his life, they returned with crystalline clarity.

"When you are uncertain of the course you are to pursue," he could hear his grandfather saying almost as if he were sitting in his uncle's chair behind him, *"get quiet before God. Center down, as our Quaker brethren like to say. Then listen. The still, small voice will speak. But you must learn to hear it. You must attune yourself to its soft and subtle rhythms within your spirit. The inner voice is never loud. You will not receive its promptings through the newspaper headlines, but as it were through some tiny printed message embedded deep in the paper. The Spirit speaks with nudges, not proclamations. These it takes years of practice to learn to hear. They emerge out of your own thoughts. . .yet they are distinct from your own thoughts. Even that distinction, however, is subtle, oh so very subtle. The enemy will seek with his wiles to ensnare you into thinking that your desires and ambitions, couched in the thoughts that come, are God's thoughts. They may be, though it takes great wisdom to know how to divine between them. Always be wary*

of justifying your own ambitions. The still, small voice most often nudges you to lay down your ambitions, not pursue them. Until the desires of your heart emerge out of the wellsprings of God's will, your own ambitions may be your enemy. It is only after they are laid on the altar of relinquishment, and there die into the will of God, that your ambitions become your strength. So lay aside your own ambitions, then listen. . .listen to the heavenly nudges. As they grow within you, move one step at a time into the light of their leading."

Percy found himself wondering how old his father was at the time. What had been the circumstances that had prompted the discussion with his grandfather? He could not imagine his father wrestling with personal ambition. Though it had taken him some years to recognize it, his father had been what seemed such a rock of spiritual wisdom. Yet some uncertainty in his life must have occasioned the conversation that he now found himself recalling.

But none of that mattered. The words had come today for *him*. Percy stepped back from the window and slipped slowly to his knees.

Spirit of God, he prayed quietly, *I am exactly at such a moment. I don't know what course to pursue. I do not even know if I have any ambition or will of my own in the matter. I simply don't know what I am to do or how I am to do it. I ask for Your help, Your guidance. Speak to me, Lord. Show me what You would have me do.*

He remained where he was, silent, listening, for perhaps five minutes. Finally he rose with a deep sigh of peace and again stood at the window. Far below in the distance, in the direction of the village, he could just make out the roof of the old Barrie cottage.

With the sight came an inner impulse to visit it again. Was this a quiet nudge in response to his prayer? What could the Barrie croft possibly have to do with his mission for his uncle?

Again his grandfather spoke from out of the past: *"Listen to the heavenly nudges and move one step at a time."*

Percy drew in a long breath then turned from the window and left the office in search of his aunt. If one step had been shown, he would take it.

Percy began to descend the main stairway, glancing about him. As he had been so many times in this house, he was again arrested by the gallery of portraits, some centuries old, of his uncle's ancestors. The compelling face of his uncle Roderick's grandmother above the landing halfway down the stairs was usually what drew the eyes and demanded attention, as if she were the matriarch presiding over the entire family legacy, past, present, and future. On this day, however, Percy found his eyes drifting to the other women, some young, some old, whose images hung between the ground and first floors. He stood staring at each, one at a time, for several seconds. Slowly began to dawn upon him a recognition of familiarity that all the women had in common. Was it the eyes. . .the nose. . .the forehead. . .the chin. . .the prominent cheekbones? He could not tell. The dresses were different, the styles of portraiture distinctive as having been painted in different eras. Yet some indescribable feature in every face was common between them.

Now rose before his mind's eye *another* face. Even as he stood staring at the wall, a voice sounded from the first-floor landing above him.

"What are you staring so intently at?"

He nearly jumped out of his skin and spun around.

"Percy. . .what!" laughed Florilyn. "You're face is white as a sheet. You look like you've seen a ghost."

"I. . .just—you startled me!" said Percy, joining her laughter. "Maybe it was a little like seeing a ghost. I had just realized how much you look like all these women."

"Those women!" exclaimed Florilyn. "Ugh—they're all ancient and dour!"

"You know what I mean—I noticed the family resemblance. Of course *you* are far more beautiful than any of them."

"That's better," smiled Florilyn gaily. She walked down to join him. "Why shouldn't I look like them? They *are* my ancestors, after all."

"I just hadn't seen it before. I was seeing your face, then suddenly you spoke, and there you were—not a ghost exactly. . .but you know what I mean."

"So have you finished your sleuthing in my father's study?" asked Florilyn as they continued down the stairs together.

"Finished!" laughed Percy. "I only started fifteen minutes ago."

"Did you find anything?"

"No. I don't even know what I expect to find."

"What are you doing now?"

"I'm looking for your mother. Then I'll probably ride in toward town."

"Would you like company?"

An awkward expression crossed Percy's face. "Actually. . .this is something I have to do alone, Florilyn," he said. "I hope you don't mind."

"No, that's fine. I shouldn't have asked."

Percy nodded and smiled, and Florilyn left him. He found Katherine in the kitchen with Mrs. Drenwydd.

"Aunt Katherine," he said, "when I was here last summer there was an Australian in the cottage where the Barries used to live—an unfriendly chap! Is he still there?"

"No, he didn't last long at the mine from what I understand. He's been gone for months. The place is vacant now."

"Would you mind if I went down there?"

"Not at all."

"I would like to see the place again. I spent some happy times there. Will I need a key?"

Katherine laughed. "I doubt if there are a half dozen cottages in all Llanfryniog that even have locks on the doors! No, you won't need a key."

Thirty-Three

The Cottage

It was with a strange feeling almost of reverence an hour later that Percy opened the door and crept into the cottage that had once been filled with such life. It was so still and quiet. Even in Gwyneth's absence, the sense of her presence remained. Slowly Percy walked about through the two rooms of the cottage. He recognized a few pieces of furniture that were left. What clue he hoped to find here about his uncle, he could not imagine. Nor to answer the mystery of why Codnor Barrie, his daughter Gwyneth, and his great-aunt had disappeared from Llanfryniog without a trace, or where they might have gone.

As he walked about, Percy reflected further on the small family's strange disappearance. He gazed at the stone walls, the fireplace, the great beams overhead, the floor of thick wood planks. He stood in front of the hearth, now cold and lifeless. The mantle was embedded in the stonework, a massive beam of oak of obvious ancient date, gnarled and pitted.

At length Percy turned away and walked outside, closing the door behind him. He wandered behind the house where Gwyneth had kept her animals. The lifelessness here was even more profound than in the cottage. Most of the large enclosing fence where her menagerie of animals had made their home was still visible, though in poor repair. But the pens and animals were gone. Only one small enclosure was left, mostly in ruins, its thin roof partially collapsed upon the decaying boards of a wall. Percy walked toward it.

On the other side of the fence, a movement caught his eye. He turned and saw a small gray rabbit hopping slowly toward him across the grass. It slowed as it came closer. It did not seem afraid.

Percy knelt down and gently extended his hand through the fence.

Tentatively the small creature took a few more steps toward him and sniffed at his fingers.

"Is that you, Bunny White Tail?" said Percy, gently stroking the furry gray back.

Still the bunny did not shy away.

"I believe it is you. You miss your mistress, too, don't you? Have you been here all this time waiting for her?"

For some moments, the young man and the bunny held a magical communion, bound together by the one who was the reason they were both there but who was now gone. At length Bunny White Tail bounced away, and again Percy stood.

Turning from the fence, he ducked low and walked under the partially collapsed roof of the dilapidated pen where once hungry animals knew to come along with those who were injured. With a fond smile, he looked about.

What was that hanging from an end of rusted wire? It looked like a clump of dried flowers!

He took two quick steps toward it and gently took hold of it. It was one of Gwyneth's friendship bouquets!

Images and memories flooded him from that first day when he had been the recipient of a fresh bouquet of wildflowers not so very different from this.

"Grannie says always greet a stranger with flowers," he recalled her saying at their first meeting.

Full of the cockiness of youth, he had replied with the air of one more pleased with himself than he had a right to be. *"So you consider me a stranger, do you?"* he had said.

"I've never seen your face before."

"Then what do you intend to do about it?"

"Give you the flowers I picked for you, of course."

Even now, so much later, Percy recalled how his sixteen-year-old rebel's heart had been suddenly touched by the kindness of the child-stranger.

"Surely you meant these for someone else?" he said.

"I picked them for you," Gwyneth had answered simply, gazing into his face with wide, innocent eyes. *"Now that I have given you flowers, I must know who you are. What is your name, so I shall know whom to ask for when I go to Glasgow?"*

Percy had laughed with delight. She was charming beyond words!

"My name is Percival. . .Percival Drummond, at your service," he had answered. *"My friends call me Percy."*

"What would you like me to call you, Mr. Drummond?"

"You must call me Percy. What is your name?"

"Gwyneth Barrie."

"Then, Gwyneth Barrie, I am happy to make your acquaintance. But why did you pick these for me?" Percy had asked about Gwyneth's simple gift of flowers on that day.

"I saw you coming," she replied.

"You didn't know me when you picked them. Surely you don't give flowers to every stranger you pass."

"Only those who are going to become my friends."

"You knew that about me?"

"Of course."

"How did you know?"

"I saw on your face the look of a friend."

Percy's thoughts returned to the present. The quietness around him deepened. It was too quiet—the stillness of desolation.

He glanced down at the flowers in his hand, held together by a small piece of yellowed paper and tied around with a bit of blue ribbon.

The blue ribbon! Of course—he remembered now. . .the very ribbon he had given her!

Slowly he untied the ribbon, so as not to damage the fragile flowers, then unfolded the crinkled paper that had held them together. There was writing inside!

Dear Percy, he read.

These flowers are for you. I hope you come here one day and find them. I will never forget you.

A stab stung Percy's heart. He remembered the day he had waited for her so long on the edge of the bluff at Mochras Head. He had never seen her again.

"Oh, Gwyneth," he whispered, "where have you gone?"

Thirty-Four

The Inn

As he left the cottage and rode toward Llanfryniog, his mind and heart quiet and full of many things, Percy recalled his return to Wales a year ago when he had stopped in at Mistress Chattan's pub before continuing on to the manor. She had dropped several cryptic comments he had hardly understood, things about his uncle along with hints that she knew more than she was saying. Maybe it was time he paid the good Mistress Chattan another visit.

Percy walked into the thin light of Mistress Chattan's establishment. It was midafternoon. He was glad to find the place empty of patrons. Mistress Chattan was nowhere to be seen. Percy sat down at one of the tables and waited.

Presently the proprietress appeared from her quarters, walking out from behind the long wooden bar. Still large, still clad in the familiar white apron spread about with stains and splotches evidencing the day's work, she appeared to have shed a few pounds since he had last seen her. She still glided across the floor with the soft, stealthy step of a cat. Her hair was nearly entirely gray now, the wrinkles in her face and neck more pronounced.

For the first time since he had made her acquaintance, a fleeting tinge of sadness swept through Percy at the sight. She was aging and alone. What did her future hold?

"Well, young Drummond," she said as she saw her lone customer, "you're back, are you?"

"Hello, Mistress Chattan," said Percy, greeting her with a smile. "You probably already knew I was here."

"I did indeed."

"You know everything that goes on in this village."

"It pays for one like me to keep abreast of happenings."

"Is your ale still the best?"

"I've no cause to think otherwise. But you shall be the judge of that yourself."

"Then pour me a pint and we shall see!" laughed Percy. "Come join me, Mistress Chattan," he added.

She returned a moment later, set a tall glass in front of Percy, then eased into a chair opposite him. "So you're not going to marry the lass after all?" she said.

"You do know everything!" laughed Percy. "Are we so much the subject of the town's talk?"

"There's nothing quite like a broken engagement to set tongues wagging."

"It's not so much a broken engagement but a *postponed* one. We are simply waiting."

"Waiting for what?"

"To see if it is right."

Whether Percy's answer conveyed in any sense of the word an *accurate* view of the situation was doubtful. But she did not press her inquiry further. A student of the human condition in her own way, which she exploited through her position, aided by the liquid inventory of her stock-in-trade, Mistress Chattan was not by any stretch of the imagination a spiritual woman. What insight she possessed into human nature had been gleaned for one purpose alone—that she might gain power over those who came her way. She had come into more than her share of secrets. By subtle art, attentive ear, and skillfully placed sympathetic comment, she had through the years obtained much information that might be useful to possess. But to understand the spiritual movements within the heart of one like Percy Drummond lay completely outside her ken.

"So what do you know of Lord Snowdon's past, then?" asked Percy abruptly.

Mistress Chattan's eyes narrowed. If the question took her by surprise, she did not reveal it. "What makes you think I know anything?" she said.

"You dropped many hints when I was here a year ago. You told me there had been another woman before my Aunt Katherine."

"I only told you what I have heard. But no one around here knows of it, for it all took place across the sea."

"You said there was a child?"

"There's children and there's children. That's why I asked you if you knew about your uncle's past."

"I may know more than I once did," said Percy with an enigmatic tone of his own.

It was not lost on Mistress Chattan. One of her dark eyebrows curled up in question.

"But it's my opinion that you know more than you've said as well," Percy added. "Now it is time for me to know what you know."

It was silent for twenty or thirty seconds. Mistress Chattan was thinking. "So the young man's about to become the new viscount, is he?" she said at length.

"You seem well up on the affairs of the manor."

"I know things, young Drummond. I know when his twenty-fifth birthday is and what might make him rue the fact that it didn't come earlier."

"What do you mean?" asked Percy.

"Just that there may be others to consider."

Percy took in the whispered words without revealing anything. Now he was thinking hard, wondering how much to reveal. He knew one like Mistress Chattan *might* be dangerous. He had to walk with care. "Others?" he repeated. "Who are you talking about?"

"I will say no more than that. There were rumors."

"What kind of rumors?"

"About what drew your uncle to Ireland in the first place."

"What was it then?"

"The lure, what else? What seduces all young men—and the lure of riches. . .the lust for gold."

Thirty-Five

The Library

Percy left Mistress Chattan's with much to think about. From the inn he went to the Lorimer home, visited with Rhawn for an hour, then began the ride back up the plateau to Westbrooke Manor. When he arrived it was nearly time for dinner.

He took his mount to the stables, unsaddled it, and then made his way around to the side entrance of the manor. He hurried up to his room with the bouquet tied with the blue ribbon in his hand, clutching it as if it were a tiny baby bird, careful over every stem and petal, but strangely shy lest Florilyn see it. Depositing it in his room, he descended by the main stairway to the dining room where his aunt and Florilyn were about to begin the evening meal without him.

Later that evening, Percy went upstairs. Instead of returning to his room, he went to the library. He had not wanted to tell Florilyn that he had not even brought the MacDonald book she had been reading with him.

He sought the shelf where he knew his aunt kept her growing supply of MacDonald books. The collection had indeed grown since he was last here. He stepped closer and examined the spines where the titles stood side by side. Some were familiar. Some he had heard his parents mention. Some were altogether new to him: *Adela Cathcart, Alec Forbes of Howglen, Guild Court, Unspoken Sermons, Annals of a Quiet*

Neighbourhood, Ranald Bannerman's Boyhood, Robert Falconer, A Seaboard Parish, At the Back of the North Wind, The Princess and the Goblin, The Vicar's Daughter...

There was the one he was looking for—*David Elginbrod.* Percy removed it from the shelf, found his favorite chair in one of the window alcoves, flipped through the pages toward the end until he found his place, and began reading.

An hour later, as Percy began to get drowsy, the words on the page suddenly arrested his attention. *"He gathered together the few memorials of the old ship gone down in the quiet ocean of time; paid one visit of sorrowful gladness to Margaret's home..."*

It was just like his visit earlier in the day to the cottage on the moor—memorials of the passage of time from his visit to Gwyneth's former home. Even with the thought, he remembered what Florilyn had said when he was here for Christmas.

"Gwyneth is Margaret in the book, Percy!" she had said. *"Hugh thought he was in love with Euphra...but all along he was meant to discover his love for Margaret. Don't you see? In the same way, what if part of your heart still belongs to Gwyneth?"*

Wide awake now, Percy continued to read, remembering again how Gwyneth, when he was a "pilgrim" in Wales, had awakened him to nature, to God, to himself. And yet, through it all, it was the face of Gwyneth herself that rose, dawning within him like a crescent moon.

> *"Perhaps the greatest benefit that resulted to Hugh from being made a pilgrim on the earth,"* Percy read, *"was, that Nature herself saw him, and took him in. She spoke to him from the depths of air, from the winds that harp upon the boughs, and from the streams that sing as they go. It is no wonder that the form of Margaret, the gathering of the thousand forms of nature into one harmony of loveliness, should rise again upon the world of his imagination.*
>
> *She had dawned on him like a sweet crescent moon, hanging far-off in a cold and low horizon. Now, lifting his eyes, he saw that same moon nearly at the full, and high overhead. He knew that he*

> *loved her now. He knew that every place he went through caught a glimmer of romance the moment he thought of her. But the growth of these feelings had been gradual—so slow and gradual, that when he recognized them, it seemed to him as if he had felt them from the first. The fact was, that as soon as he began to be capable of loving Margaret, he had begun to love her. Now that Nature revealed herself to him full of Life, it was natural that he should recognize Margaret as greater than himself. She had been one with Nature from childhood, and when he began to be one with Nature too, he must become one with her."*

Percy's hands were nearly trembling by now as he held the book. Florilyn's words were probing his brain, his heart, his whole being: *"Gwyneth is Margaret in the book, Percy! What if part of your heart still belongs to Gwyneth? You have to find out. You have to discover what is in your heart."*

He continued to read MacDonald's words about the fictional Hugh and Margaret. But he was no longer reading about Hugh Sutherland. He was reading about himself!

> *"But dared he think of loving her, a creature inspired with a presence of the Spirit of God, clothed with a garment of beauty which her spirit wove out of its own loveliness? She was a being to glorify any man. What, then, if she gave her love! She would bring with her the presence of God himself, for she walked ever in his light, and that light clung to her and radiated from her. True, many young maidens must be walking in the sunshine of God, else whence the light and loveliness and bloom, the smile and the laugh of their youth? But Margaret not only walked in this light: she knew it and whence it came. She looked up to its source, and it illuminated her face.*
>
> *The silent girl of old days, whose countenance wore the stillness of an unsunned pool, had blossomed into the calm, stately woman, upon whose face lay slumbering thought, ever ready to wake into life and motion. Dared he love her?"*

Percy drew in a deep breath, closed the book, then rose and stared out toward the sea in the distance. From the alcove he could also view the sea that Gwyneth loved so much. . .and to the east the hills where he had first met the nymph of Gwynedd when she was a mere thirteen and he was a sophisticated youth of sixteen.

How little he had known back then! All the wisdom had dwelt in *her*, not him. But he had had no eyes to see it at their first meeting.

He still stood at the window ten minutes later, absorbed in his thoughts. At length he turned. Taking the book with him, he left the library and returned to his room.

Night slowly closed in upon Westbrooke Manor. Two hours later Percy lay in his bed, awake and full of many thoughts.

Somehow he drifted to sleep. As occupied as his brain had been, he slept surprisingly sound—the gift given to youth—and awoke rested and refreshed with the sun streaming into his room.

Then rushed back upon him the torrent of thoughts from the previous night. Rather than overwhelming him, however, they poured over him as though he were standing beneath the waterfall of a bracing mountain stream, with its icy waters pounding over his head. He would meet the challenge of whatever the new day brought him with vigor.

Yes, he had loved Gwyneth. Oh, how difficult it must have been for Florilyn when she realized it—and how hard for her to tell him!

After breakfast he saddled Red Rhud and set off for the village. But again, his way led him to the Barrie cottage. Something was here, he mused as he rode up, something he was meant to find.

But where. . .but what?

He dismounted and again entered the cottage. Everything was just as it had been the day before. Yet in his mind's eye, it now glowed with the luster of the love blossoming in his heart. But alas, the bloom had flowered too late!

God, he prayed silently, *what do You have for me to see? Why have You led me here? Guide my steps, my thoughts, my eyes.*

Moving slowly through the rooms as he had the day before, a sense of anticipation, of something at hand, filled Percy's mind.

His thoughts full of Gwyneth and what he had read the night before, he left the cottage. As he prepared to mount Red Rhud, he turned back.

There, several yards to the right of the door, partially obscured by several overgrown rosebushes, stood a small stone sign or monument with words carved into it: Mor bhairne a Inbhear Dé.

What could it mean? It was clearly Gaelic, that much he knew. But the words conveyed no hint of meaning.

He remembered seeing it many times before but had never thought to ask what the Gaelic words might mean or why that particular name had been given to the cottage. He must ask Steven.

With a new mystery added to all the rest, thoughtfully he rode away from the cottage.

Thirty-Six

The Meadow

Instead of returning to the village as he had on the previous day, Percy found himself leading Red Rhud east into the hills and toward the peaks of Snowdonia. He hardly knew where he was bound at first. But gradually he knew. Would he be able to find the place without Gwyneth to guide him?

He rode up and inland for an hour, stopping many times to assess his position, often uncertain yet sure he was moving steadily closer to his destination.

At last he began to recognize the granite cliffs and the shape of several peaks. Certain of his bearings now, he led Red Rhud a short time later through the jagged opening to his left where the shoulder of a projecting ridge opened between one hill and the next, then up the rocky incline, round the large cluster of boulders, and finally to the overlook where he was again able to see the tiny lake of blue-green far below.

Its surface shone like glass. Near the water's edge, several deer were drinking from the lake and nibbling at the surrounding grasses of the meadow.

With a momentary pang of sadness, he realized that he would hear no haunting ethereal melody on this day from the lake creature of Gwynedd. He saw no sign of the wild horses. After a few moments, he urged Red Rhud on.

Soon he was descending steeply through a rocky ravine surrounded on both sides by fir and pine, with granite cliffs looming high above. When he judged he had come near the place beyond which Gwyneth would not let him go, he stopped, dismounted, tied the reins to a tree, and walked on gently and quietly.

In the clearing beyond the wood, a half dozen deer grazed upon the carpet of green while a dozen rabbits scurried among them. Behind lay the shimmering emerald surface.

He stood in silence for ten minutes. Quietness reigned in this place. Gwyneth's spirit surely hovered over it.

Suddenly a sound disturbed the hush of peace. Within seconds the deer and rabbits disappeared into the surrounding trees. Percy wondered if he had caused their flight.

Then it came again, from high above him on the other side of the valley. . .metallic noises and the sounds of horses. Then he heard voices. . . men's voices.

He looked all about. There they were, three or four men on horseback high above the lake on a projecting ledge on the far side. They were unloading equipment of some kind.

They were too far away to see clearly. But though he could not hear their words distinctly, their voices echoed off the rocks.

As he watched, one of the men now set up a surveyor's tripod and transit. Another pulled out a sketch pad and began to draw the lake and valley.

With stealthy and careful step, Percy retreated deeper into the safety of the pine and fir wood until he could retrace his steps to Red Rhud. If he had heard them, surely they would soon enough be alerted to his presence as well. He led Red Rhud back the way he had come as slowly and quietly as possible. Once on the high path again, he remounted. For several minutes he took great care to lead Red Rhud quietly, then increased his pace and made for the manor with greater speed than he had ridden up into the hills.

He tied Red Rhud in front of the house and went to find his aunt. "Aunt Katherine," he said, "do you know that small lake in the mountains to the northeast?"

"There are an abundance of small lakes in Snowdonia, Percy."

"It's between here and Burrenchobay Hall, but east and surrounded by high granite cliffs."

"It could be any of several—I really cannot say that I know for certain the one you are speaking of. Why, Percy?"

"I just came from there. It is a place I ride occasionally. I first heard about it from Florilyn and Courtenay. They said it was the home of a water kelpie."

Katherine laughed. "I have heard those stories as well. Gwberr-niog I believe he is called."

"That's him! I had forgotten the name. But after hearing about the lake, Stuart gave me directions so I could find it for myself. I rode up there again today. I saw some men there with surveying equipment—Englishmen as far as I could tell from their accents, though I couldn't make out what they were saying. I wondered if the lake was on Westbrooke property. Are you having surveying done?"

"No," answered Katherine with an expression of concern. "My surveying for the new house was completed months ago."

"They definitely had surveying equipment. I saw that much."

"I don't know that I like the sound of this," she said rising. "I will have a talk with Stuart to find out exactly where this lake is and if it is on our land."

Keenly aware that he had been neglecting Florilyn since his arrival and concerned for her feelings, Percy spent the afternoon with his cousin. They had a long ride and talk together. Percy even dared suggest a race on the beach with their two favorite mounts again, Grey Tide and Red Rhud, and was happy with Florilyn's acceptance. Her feelings of guilt over the accident involving Gwyneth seemed at last to have faded completely into the past.

The delightful afternoon reminded him why it had been easy to love her. That love had now turned to respect and admiration. He was now more certain than ever that she was right and that he must discover what might be the depths of his other love.

Thirty-Seven

The Drawer

The following morning found Percy again in his uncle's study.

On this occasion he took more care than had been possible with a mere cursory search. He spent the entire morning examining the contents of the desk drawers and cabinet and safe. Most of the papers he found were of little apparent use, many of the files predating his uncle altogether—personal correspondence, business records, journals and ledgers from the various factors who had worked for the estate dating back centuries.

He did, however, locate a brown envelope with the single word LITCHFIELD in ink on the flap. It appeared more recent than the others he had opened. The letters from one Lord Coleraine Litchfield contained no particular significance as he perused them. Yet they clearly concerned the potential sale of estate lands. He knew his aunt should be made aware of them, if she was not already.

Percy found his aunt reading in her private sitting room. "Aunt Katherine," he said, "I found an envelope containing some letters to Uncle Roderick from a few years ago. You might know all about it, but it seemed important enough to ask you about." He handed her the envelope.

Katherine removed the letters. As she read one after another, Percy saw her internal temperature beginning to rise. At length she began shaking her head. "I don't know whether to yell or cry," she said. "No. . .I had no idea Roderick was engaged in this correspondence. Apparently he was planning to sell some of the estate's land. I cannot say I am surprised," she added with a smile. "He was always short of cash, always trying to talk me into giving him money for one of his schemes. I am sorry to think that money came between us. But the sad fact of the matter is, it did."

"You don't know what came of this, then?"

Katherine shook her head. "I cannot imagine that anything did," she said. "Technically as viscount, Roderick could have sold estate lands without my permission. But surely I would have known. The fact that Hamilton Murray has never mentioned it convinces me that nothing came of it. These are all dated six years ago. However. . ." she added thoughtfully, "this man Litchfield was here visiting only a couple months ago—ostensibly because of Courtenay's eventual role in the House of Lords. I wonder. . ." Her voice faded away. She shook her head but did not complete the thought.

"Would you like me to leave the letters with you?" asked Percy after a moment.

Katherine sighed. "No, take them back to the study. I don't want them," she said. She returned the letters to the envelope and handed it to Percy. "Where did you find them?"

"In the cabinet of files."

"If I should need them, I'll know where to find them."

Percy returned upstairs to the study. Again he sat down at his uncle's desk. One at a time he opened its drawers. As he pulled out the bottom drawer, he heard a sound, as of something shifting. He stooped and peered all the way to the back but saw only the papers and envelopes he had looked through before. Puzzled, he gave the drawer a sharp jiggle. The sound came again. Examining the back of it more closely, he saw what now looked like a false back to the drawer.

He pulled it all the way out toward him. A thin block of wood had been wedged across the width of the drawer. He tried to dislodge it with his fingers, but it held fast.

The next moment he was outside and making for the workshop to find a small hammer. Five minutes later he sat down again, reached into the back of the drawer, and gave one edge of the piece of wood a light rap. Then again. The wedge of wood gave way. Percy removed it, set it aside, and reached all the way now into the true back of the drawer that had not been visible before.

His hand fell on something. He pulled it out and saw that he was holding a black lacquered box about eight inches by six inches and perhaps three inches deep. He lifted it out of the drawer and set it on the desk.

The latch for the lid had no lock. He unfastened the latch and lifted the lid back. Inside were a few five and ten pound notes—not exactly a fortune—several pens, a bottle of ink, and a few other odds and ends. Most interesting of all, however, was a key ring containing perhaps a dozen small keys.

Why had his uncle kept these keys here, nearly impossible to find unless one were looking for them, instead of with the others on the ring behind the door?

Percy looked them over. Suddenly he remembered. The drawers in the safe!

He was out of the chair and across the room in an instant. Quickly he unlocked the safe as before, threw back the door, and fumbled with the new set of small keys.

The first four accomplished nothing. The fifth, a small brass key scarcely two inches long, slid effortlessly into the lock of the bottom drawer to the right of the inside of the safe. Percy turned the key, heard a slight click, and then pulled the drawer toward him.

There sat a pile of letters, still in their envelopes. . .unopened.

He reached into the drawer and removed them. He did not immediately recognize the names to whom the letters were addressed. But he knew his uncle's hand well enough, as well as the return address: WESTBROOKE MANOR, LLANFRYNIOG, GWYNEDD, WALES. Every letter had been sent to a town in Ireland. Every one had been returned, unopened, stamped with the words, MOVED WITHOUT FORWARD.

The yellowed age of the envelopes indicated that they were old. Percy squinted and could faintly make out the postal stamps. All had been sent in 1842.

He drew in a long breath and exhaled thoughtfully. Letters in his uncle's hand that predated his 1847 marriage to Aunt Katherine.

He closed the safe and returned with the stack of envelopes to his uncle's desk. He sat down and set the letters in front of him. To read them seemed almost a sacrilege. But he could not show them to his aunt. There was no one else to read them but him.

He glanced through them all again. Folded between the envelopes was a newspaper clipping, the paper old and brittle. Carefully he unfolded it. The small headline read: GOLD FINDS ON INCREASE WEST OF WICKLOW.

He began to read the article.

> *"It has been assumed for years that the 1795 gold rush had spent itself well before 1820. But sporadic new finds continued to rekindle interest throughout the 1830s, and even more recently. Gold was first discovered in County Wicklow in what was subsequently named the Gold Mines River in 1795. The boom continued until 1830, during which time it is estimated that eight thousand ounces of gold were extracted from alluvial gravels of the region. Simultaneously, this period also witnessed the greatest coal mining and slate production episode in Ireland. All this activity also prompted a boom in shipbuilding in eastern Ireland, most notably in the seaport of Arklow, south of Wicklow. . ."*

Percy continued to peruse the article. But the letters held far more interest. He glanced through them again. All bore the destination Laragh, County Wicklow, Ireland.

Wicklow. . .where they had been mining for gold!

He scanned the newspaper clipping again. He could find no mention of the date when the article was written. Was it gold that had taken his uncle there?

Along with Mistress Chattan's words, he now remembered, on his deathbed, his uncle's words, *"I was young and foolish and had dreams of making my fortune. There were rumors of gold, and that was enough to fire my imagination."*

Percy knew he had to read the letters. But he could take no chances of his aunt discovering them. Closing all the desk drawers, locking the safe again and keeping the small ring of keys with him, then carefully taking the stack of letters and slipping them beneath his shirt, he left the study and hastened up to the privacy of his own room.

Before he lay down to sleep that night, Percy knew that fulfilling his uncle's commission must next take him to Ireland. He must attempt to accomplish, even if it were thirty years later, what his uncle had not been able to with these letters.

If he failed, no one need ever know.

Thirty-Eight

Departure

The next morning at breakfast, Percy broke the news to Florilyn and Katherine. "I am afraid I must take my departure sooner than I had planned," he said.

Mother and daughter looked at him with surprise.

"Why. . . Are you going home so soon?" asked Florilyn.

"I'm not going home. There is something I have to do."

"Where are you going, then?"

"I would rather not say."

Florilyn's face registered obvious disappointment. "But. . .you've only been here a few days," she said.

"I know. I am sorry," said Percy. "I can see that this has come out of the blue. I realize I haven't spent as much time with you as I had hoped. I will make it up to you when I return—I promise. But there is something I have to do. I don't think it can wait."

"Does this have to do with what Roderick asked you to do for him?" asked Katherine.

"It may, Aunt Katherine," replied Percy. "I can't be certain."

"Did you find something in his study?"

"I may have. Again, I cannot say for certain. I am sorry, but I just cannot say more. Actually, Uncle Roderick did not give me specifics. I am nearly as much in the dark as you. I hope you can trust me."

Again his aunt and cousin stared back with expressions of bewilderment.

"Of course we can, Percy," said Katherine after a moment. "When will you leave?"

"Tomorrow, I think."

The rest of the breakfast passed somewhat somberly. Percy knew that Florilyn was not merely disappointed. He could tell that her feelings were hurt, as much that he did not feel himself able to confide in her as that he was leaving.

He spent the rest of the morning in his room, again perusing the letters he had found as well as completing *David Elginbrod.*

After lunch, he invited Florilyn for another ride, this time into the hills. Her mood was obviously subdued.

"I was embarrassed to tell you when I came," he said after they were well away from the manor and climbing toward Rhinog Fawr, "but I hadn't yet finished the MacDonald book. I knew it was important to you, but school was just too hectic. I finally did so last night and this morning. I think I see everything you were saying to me last Christmas."

Florilyn nodded.

"It was hard to hear at the time," Percy went on, "but the wisdom of it is growing on me."

"Does your leaving have anything to do with Gwyneth?" asked Florilyn. "Mother said you went down to her cottage."

"Not really," answered Percy. "I just wanted to look around. There was nothing there."

"So you're not leaving because you have some new idea where she went to."

"Nothing like that. It has nothing to do with her."

"Does it have anything to do with *me*?"

"How do you mean?"

"Are you. . .disappointed with me?"

"No, not at all. Why would you think that?"

"I thought maybe that you. . .I don't know. . .that you found it awkward or didn't want to be with me anymore."

"Oh, Florilyn—that's not how I feel at all. I'm sorry if I—"

"It's not you, Percy," said Florilyn. "It's only that I feel. . . It is just hard sometimes. I miss you, that's all."

"I know. The feeling is mutual. I've had bouts of sadness, even depression, these last six months. . .you know. . .wondering about it all."

They rode on for several minutes in silence.

"What about the book?" asked Florilyn at length.

"I now understand about Hugh and Margaret," replied Percy. "Whether their story has to do with me. . .with *us*. . .that I still do not know." He paused a moment. "Are you. . ." he began hesitantly, "are you still at peace with what you did?"

Florilyn smiled wistfully. "I think so," she replied slowly. "It makes me sad when I think about it. Doubts creep in. I wonder what it will be like if I one day have to watch you marry someone else." Her voice quivered slightly. "Then I worry that I may never marry at all. Girls always worry about such things. The worse thing I worry about is that I do not want to be like Euphra—like she was before, you know. But if and when we do marry, or *don't*. . .we will be stronger for having waited long enough to be sure. I know that in my head, but sometimes my heart forgets."

"You would never be like Euphra. You are too wonderful for that. But you don't know how much it relieves me to hear you say what you did," said Percy. "I think you've pretty well summed up how I feel as well."

Having cleared the air, the rest of the ride proved thoroughly enjoyable. They raced several times, explored a few new places, and spent the entire afternoon and most of the evening together.

The enjoyable day brought to Percy's remembrance that he had actually made *two* promises to his uncle. One of them, after he left, he would not be in a position to keep. He had not thought of it in practical terms during his final year in Aberdeen. But with so many changes bound to come to Westbrooke Manor in the coming months, he must perhaps be more attentive to it than ever. Late in the day he found Steven Muir in his office.

"So you are leaving us, eh, Percy?" said Steven where he sat behind his desk. "We've hardly had the chance to exchange two words, and now you are off again!"

"I am sorry about that," nodded Percy, easing himself into a chair opposite him. "It is actually quite unexpected but cannot be helped. I made a promise to my uncle that I have to attend to." Percy paused then drew in a thoughtful breath. "There is something I need to ask you to do for me, Steven," he said.

"Just name it."

"Before my uncle died, he asked me to take care of my aunt and Florilyn. Of course at the time he thought that Florilyn and I would marry. With those plans now uncertain, the situation is obviously changed. Nevertheless, I told him I would do my best to protect them and see that no harm came to them."

"He could not have left them in better hands," said Steven.

"Perhaps," rejoined Percy. "But now I am leaving. And with the strain caused by Courtenay's position looming larger every day, I cannot help being concerned. I don't know how long I will be away. . .and I would like to ask you to do your best for them in my absence and make sure no hurt of any kind comes to them."

"I would do so even without your request," said Steven solemnly. "I try to do so every day. But knowing I am standing in your stead, and indeed acting on behalf of the viscount himself, I will be especially diligent."

"Thank you. That will make my leaving easier," said Percy. "I know they are in good hands."

Percy was up early, and his two bags packed the following morning. He had breakfasted an hour before the northbound coach was scheduled to pass through town.

Florilyn and Steven took him in the small carriage into the village.

One last item of business remained. "I need to say good-bye to Rhawn," said Percy as Steven led the carriage into town. "Do you mind if we stop by her house?"

They drew up in front of the Lorimer home a minute or two later.

Percy jumped down and went to the door. Two minutes later, Rhawn returned to the carriage with him.

"Room for one more?" said Percy. "I think we can all squeeze in. Rhawn's going to the inn with us." He climbed back up, gave Rhawn his hand, and helped her up beside him.

Ten minutes later, the northbound coach bounded along the street and pulled to a noisy stop in front of Mistress Chattan's inn. Percy shook Steven's hand, then embraced Florilyn and kissed her on the cheek. She did her best to smile but was wiping at her eyes. Finally Percy turned to Rhawn. He opened his arms, and she walked into his embrace.

"Thank you for believing in me, Percy," she whispered. "I am going to keep coming awake. I will become a growing meadow, Percy."

"You already are, Rhawn. The flowers of spring are bursting out all over."

She smiled. "You are too nice to me, Percy! No one has every treated me like you have. And I am going to be better. I am going to keep growing. I will make you proud of me one day."

"I am already proud of you, Rhawn. Anyone who is growing is deserving of great respect."

She was blinking hard.

"And I will ask for God's help about what I should do," she added in a quivering voice, "like you said I should."

She stepped back and smiled again. In her moist eyes was the light of hope. She had begun to know that she was truly loved, both by God and by the faithful friends he had given her.

Part Two

Ireland

Summer-Fall 1873

Thirty-Nine

Across the Ancient Waters

Twenty-two-year-old Percival Drummond, third in the generations of godly Drummond men and who now prepared to take his place in the man's work of that lineage, stood at the prow of a passenger ferry plunging through the waters of the ancient Celtic Triangle. He was on a mission whose result he could not possibly foresee.

Not divulging to his aunt and cousin that his destination was Ireland, he had taken the coach north to Blaenau Ffestiniog then to Bangor and finally Holyhead on the island of Anglesey, where he had embarked the next day for Dublin. In the Irish capital, he had dispatched a telegram to his parents informing them briefly of his plans. From Dublin, led only by the newspaper clipping and letters he had found, he took a coach south along the Irish coast to the county seat of Wicklow.

A few days ago, the only possible clues he had to guide him in what his uncle had desired of him he had derived from the deathbed affidavit he had written out for him a year before. The entire thing had been mysterious, and many of his uncle's words cryptic and puzzling. At the time, he had himself been filled with the youthful emotions of feeling partially responsible for his uncle's mortal accident. He had been too overwhelmed to absorb what was happening and his role in it.

Now that a year had passed, he realized how ill prepared he was for the task his uncle had set before him. If only he had asked more questions, probed his uncle for more details. But the events of that fateful week had rushed by him like a blistering wind of uncertainty. The death and grief and funeral had consumed all else by their intensity. Now his uncle was gone. He had taken his secrets to the grave with him.

Suddenly, Percy had the newly discovered letters to accompany the affidavit. He still had no idea where they would lead. But at least he had *something* to shed additional light on his uncle's dying disclosure—the name of the town that had apparently been his first wife's home, or that of her relatives. It was a place to begin.

The day was fair, the ocean breezes light and fragrant with sea, salt, and sunshine. Percy turned from the bow of the vessel, walked to the passenger deck, and sat down in one of several vacant chairs. From inside his coat he pulled out the affidavit and again read, in his own hand, his uncle's words.

> *To whom it may concern, especially to my dear wife Katherine, my family, and to Hamilton Murray, our faithful solicitor of many years:*
>
> *I make this affidavit on the 27th day of June in the year 1872 in the presence of my nephew, Percival Drummond, son of Edward and Mary Drummond of Glasgow, whom, for reasons that will become clear, I have asked to set my final affairs in order. I am of sound mind, but failing body. . .*

Even to read the words brought his uncle's familiar voice back into Percy's memory and tears rose in his eyes. Whatever his uncle had been, however he may have failed as a husband and father early in his life, Percy had grown to love him. The remembrance of their brief friendship would always be dear to him.

> *At sixteen years of age,* Percy continued, *as a spoiled son of what I thought was wealth, I left Wales on a youthful grand tour, as we called it in those days—to see the world and spend money*

and generally squander my youth on the altar of irresponsibility. It turned out that my father was not the wealthy man I took him for. Before my travels were over, I was nearly out of money. I found myself in Ireland chasing the fleeting dream of riches in the rivers of Wicklow, though what remained to be found was doubtful. There my heart was smitten with a young Irish lass of working, though not peasant stock. Her name was Avonmara O'Sullivan.

Several months later we were married in a small parish church in County Wicklow. We were both children, she a mere eighteen years of age and myself nineteen. Whether it was wise or ill fated from the beginning, who can say. But it was done, though our brief happiness would not last.

I can hardly recall what my plans were. The years have faded and my memory with them. I think I assumed that one day we would return to Wales as Lord and Lady Snowdon, after I inherited the title. But I was in no hurry to return after our marriage. The lure of the gold in eastern Ireland still possessed me, though most of the treasure had been unearthed decades earlier. Nor was I anxious to bring a new wife back to Llanfryniog where I would always be looked upon as a spendthrift son who had never amounted to much. Whatever I was, at least in Ireland I could be myself. People knew that I was of aristocratic stock, but they had no preconceptions formed against me. The thought even fleetingly occurred to me that I might find work—though I had never worked in my life—in the shipyards down the coast in Arklow. The husband of my sister-in-law had been involved in that trade before marrying my wife's sister.

So we remained in Ireland and the following months were some of the happiest of my life. A daughter was born to us a year later, but my dear Avonmara died in childbirth. I was devastated. I could not even think clearly enough to give her a name. I did not return to the house for days. It was Avonmara's mother who gave her the name Morvern and took charge of caring for her and saw that she was baptized in the Catholic church.

As I recovered from the shock of losing my young wife, I knew I was unfit to care for a child. I had married at nineteen and was now a mere twenty and without means. Without Avonmara, Ireland became suddenly desolate. The thought of remaining was odious to me. My life had been shattered. I decided to return at last to Wales, thinking, I suppose, to try to establish myself and prepare for my eventual role as viscount. My father was aging and not in the best of health by this time. Marriage and becoming a father had begun to sober me to my responsibilities but sadly had only begun to do so. I told Mrs. O'Sullivan that I would return for my daughter as soon as I was able and would provide a good life for her and, as my resources enabled me, to help all of the rest of them as well, for times then in Ireland were difficult not only for the poor but for everyone.

Alas, time went by more quickly than I anticipated. I became involved in two or three questionable business schemes—that was always my Achilles' heel—and before I knew it, years had passed. I was still a foolish young man. Finally I made plans to go back to Ireland after my father's death and my assumption to the title. Even then I was young, only twenty-eight, but I assumed on the strength of my new position that I would be capable of providing my daughter the life she deserved. I wrote to Mrs. O'Sullivan, telling her of my plans, but my letters were returned unopened. I wrote several times, then to her sister. But all the letters were returned. I assumed that Avonmara's family was angry with me for, as they saw it, deserting my child. So I sailed for Ireland myself. But what should I find but that they were all gone from the town where we had lived. The entire family had disappeared.

It was not perhaps altogether to be wondered at. Those were desperate times in Ireland. The worst of the potato famine was still a year or two away, but it had begun by that time. People were starving and fleeing Ireland in droves. Entire villages were sometimes abandoned. The country was in chaos, and it would get worse. I went to the home where Avonmara and I had lived, where

Mrs. O'Sullivan had lived, where her sister, Vanora Maloney, and her family had lived. Two were vacant, the third was occupied by a newcomer who had never heard of either the O'Sullivans or the Maloneys. It crossed my mind to wonder if they had left with the intent of keeping me from my daughter. They must have wondered what kind of father I would make after deserting her for so long. If that were true, I could hardly blame them.

I returned to Wales, disconsolate all over again. At last I wanted to be a father to my daughter, who would now have been eight. But I had no idea how to find her. I took to travel again, suffering great pangs of conscience and remorse. I met dear Katherine in Glasgow. At first I saw no reason to tell her of my past, but doing so became increasingly difficult with each passing year. We were married in 1847, and gradually my past faded away as a dream and I put the memory of that time behind me. Courtenay was born, then Florilyn, and I managed to convince myself, now that I was a father again, that my sin had not been so very great and tried to excuse it on the basis of youthful folly. For years, whenever I remembered, I was jealous of protecting the estate for Courtenay, my only son. But now I realize that right must be done. . .whatever it might mean. I must attempt to make my past right by my daughter Morvern. For if she can be found, she is my rightful firstborn and heir. . .

Percy set the paper down and sighed deeply. Thoughts of Courtenay made him realize again what was at stake. Even if he did find the viscount's first daughter, Courtenay would surely challenge any threat to his position in the courts. In the hands of the right barrister, he would no doubt have a strong case. Percy knew well enough that a skilled barrister could twist the law into so many knots it could say anything. Sadly, there were many in the legal profession who were motivated by money more than truth or justice.

Not a moment went by that Percy was not aware of the consequences of his uncle's secret first marriage. He could still hear his uncle's voice imploring him to help him do what he had never been able to do himself.

"God forgive me, not even Katherine knows of it. . . . You are a good boy, Percy. Be good to them. They may need you now more than ever. Promise me you will try to find her, Percy my boy. . . . Everything hinges on whether you are successful or not. I tried to find her, but she was gone, I tell you. Makes repentance dashed difficult, I dare say. Tell her I'm sorry I didn't come back. But she had disappeared, you see. . ."

He didn't like doing this behind his aunt's back. But he knew the pain such a revelation would cause her. And such had been his uncle's wish as well, that if at all possible she should be spared that pain.

"I am loath to hurt Katherine," his uncle had said. *"If you cannot find her, this need never come out. No one must know about what you have written unless you are successful."*

A year had passed since he had heard those words. Now suddenly everything was changing. His aunt was building a new home, his cousin Courtenay would be the new Lord Snowdon in less than a year, and he was on his way to Ireland to see what he could do to fulfill his uncle's dying wish to find the daughter he had never seen again.

Forty

The Westbrooke Factor

The day after Percy's departure, Florilyn walked into the kitchen. There she saw Adela Muir, Mrs. Drenwydd, Mrs. Llewellyn, Stuart Wyckham, and Hollin Radnor talking to a man who had his back turned, dressed in an impeccable black suit who was holding a top hat in his hand. She hadn't known her mother was expecting a guest. This man looked like someone important, though she almost thought she recognized the back of his head and wild shock of light hair. And what was he doing talking among the servants?

Two or three of the heads turned at the sound of her entrance.

"Oh, I'm sorry," said Florilyn, "I didn't know you had a guest. I was looking for—" Her next words died on her lips.

The man in the black suit turned toward the sound of her voice.

"Steven!" she said softly, her eyes wide in astonishment. She stared at him another moment then suddenly became aware of the heat that was creeping up the back of her neck. Rarely one at a loss for words, she was unaccountably filled with embarrassment from the eyes resting upon her. She turned and walked quickly from the room.

Steven hurried after her. He came alongside her halfway along the corridor. "Sorry," he said. "Did I do something to—"

"No," laughed Florilyn, recovering herself. "The sight of you all dressed up. . .it just took me by surprise. I didn't know what to say.

Goodness, Steven—you are an aristocratic gentleman!"

Steven laughed. "I had the same reaction when I looked in the mirror this morning," he said. "Who's *that*! I said."

"What's the occasion?"

"It's a suit of my father's. My mother thought I should wear it if I was to be in London on business for a respected woman like Lady Snowdon. She cleaned and pressed it and dressed me up like I was a boy again!"

"You're going to London?"

"I leave on the train this afternoon from Dolgellau."

"What for?"

"On business for your mother," replied Steven. "There are some papers she wants me to file with the proper agencies concerning the transfer of title on the land, as well as talk to an engineer about the window design on the west-facing walls of the house that look out to sea. She also wants me to find out what I can about a certain fellow in the House of Lords she is interested in."

"Who is that?"

"You should probably ask your mother," replied Steven. "She asked me to keep my inquiries confidential. I'm sure she wouldn't mind your knowing, but she ought to be the one to tell you. But," he added apologetically as his step slowed, "I have to be off or I will miss my train. I was just saying good-bye to the others and giving Hollin and Stuart some last-minute instructions for the days I will be gone."

"Then have a good trip, Steven," said Florilyn, turning toward him with a smile. "I hope you enjoy London."

"Is that possible?" he rejoined laughing. "I think I shall be anxious to get back to Wales."

They shook hands then Steven hastened back to the kitchen.

Florilyn watched him go with a curious expression.

Later that afternoon, as she wandered through the stables and outside, she found herself thinking about the young man whom she had always regarded as little more than a shepherd but in whom her mother had placed so much trust. More and more he carried himself as a young man of breeding, even education, as did Steven's mother Adela. Besides being thoughtful and considerate, Steven was well spoken and genteel. She wondered if there had been more education in his background than she was aware of.

She and her mother were alone at lunch several hours later.

"Do you and Adela Muir still talk about MacDonald?" Florilyn asked. "Does she still read his books?"

"As avidly as ever," answered Katherine with a light laugh. "Whenever I get a new one, she usually finishes it before I do."

"You let her read them first?"

"She is a much faster reader than I. Even with her work, she breezes through them in three or four days. It only makes sense for her to read them first rather than having to wait several weeks for me to finish what is often a five-hundred-page book."

"Then you discuss them?"

Katherine nodded. "Usually she sees more in the characters and in the spiritual truths MacDonald has woven into their life stories than I do. She is a very perceptive reader."

"That seems unusual for a domestic."

"Adela was never a domestic until she came here. She is more educated than most people realize."

"How do you mean?"

"Her father was a schoolteacher on the peninsula. She grew up in an environment of learning and education, with books everywhere she says."

"I had no idea. Did you know that when you hired her?"

"Not exactly, though I had an idea there must have been something in her background to account for her love of books and her fluency with the world of ideas after she began to work here. Finally I asked her about it, and she told me the whole story."

"Which is. . .?"

"Just what I told you, that she is the daughter of a teacher who was the son of a curate. They were relatively poor, and she was the youngest of five. She had no opportunity to further her education beyond what her father and mother gave her. Her brother, Gwyneth's father, came to Llanfryniog to work in the slates at a young age, staying with their great-aunt, Mrs. Myfanawy, who was a native of Llanfryniog."

"That's Grannie?" said Florilyn.

Katherine nodded. "After the parents died," she went on, "Adela had no place to go. She followed Codnor here and also stayed with Mrs. Myfanawy awhile until she fell in love with Glythvyr Muir and became a shepherd's wife. But their father and grandfather—the teacher and the curate—were gentlemen and well educated."

"That would account for Steven, too."

"*Account* for him. . .? What do you mean?"

"He seems so much more than just a shepherd boy, as if he had more education and gentlemanly training than he would have received at the village school."

"Adela tried to do as much for his education as she could. She says he was always a great reader and devoured whatever books they could get their hands on. I must say, I have never regretted making him factor. He has as much business sense and skill in managing things as Tilman Heygate ever had."

"And now he's off to London on your business. I saw him all dressed up before he left. He looked like a dandy!"

"That was a shock, I have to admit!" laughed Katherine.

It grew silent for a few moments as mother and daughter each finished her soup.

"Will the new house be finished when Courtenay turns twenty-five?" asked Florilyn at length.

"There is little chance of that, I'm afraid," replied Katherine. "The work will slow considerably once winter sets in."

"What will we do? Do you really think he will kick us out of the manor?"

Katherine sighed. "I have long since stopped trying to predict what your brother will do. I doubt he will be quite so brazen as that. But he has made abundantly clear that I will not be welcome here. Until the new house is completed, I have assumed that we will go to Edward and Mary's in Glasgow. They would make us more than welcome. I am going down to the site this afternoon. There are two or three points Steven wanted me to look at. Care to join me?"

"I would like that."

Later that evening, alone in her room, the conversation with her mother and visit to Mochras Head and the construction site of the new house left Florilyn in an agitated state about the future. Months before, she would have written to Percy and poured out her heart and frustrations and uncertainties. As she sat down at her writing desk to attempt to do so now, however, she suddenly realized that she didn't even know where he was.

Almost the same moment, the image of Steven, handsome in his suit and with the top hat in his hand, rose into her mind. With the image came a smile, and she found herself wishing that, in Percy's absence, Steven were here and that she could talk to him. Whenever they chanced to talk, whether about the weather or horses or sometimes when Florilyn had mentioned something she had read, his responses always surprised her. They were calm, deliberate, well thought out. It seemed that whatever she found herself thinking about, Steven had thought about it already himself. Now that she had learned that he was not merely a talented peasant-shepherd but was of educated, even gentlemanly lineage, she would value his responses even more.

Forty-One

Laragh

Midway through his second day on the ancient Emerald Isle, Percy rode into the village of Laragh in the single-horse buggy he had rented in Wicklow. He had no idea what he would do here. But Laragh was his only lead. The addresses on the letters confirmed this as the home of his uncle's first wife.

What he hoped to find so many years later, Percy had no idea. If his uncle had not been able to find his daughter after an absence of only eight years, what could he hope to do after thirty? But perhaps the O'Sullivans had returned. He would try to find the addresses, perhaps inquire at the post for the people his uncle had written to. He would see what he could learn about the names on the envelopes. Surely there was someone here who knew them.

He found the town's only inn. After seeing to his horse's lodgings, he was soon comfortably laying out his few things in what would be his own accommodation until his next steps were shown him.

Again his grandfather's words returned to him.

"Listen to the heavenly nudges. As they grow within you, move one step at a time into the light of their leading."

Percy sat down at the small writing table in the room, took out his uncle's letters from his satchel, and set them before him. Now that he was here, he needed to read them again, slowly, quietly. He had to see what missing pieces they could provide of his uncle's story.

He withdrew the first and unfolded the yellowed sheet.

April 17, 1842
Pine Cottage
Laragh, County Wicklow

Dear Mrs. O'Sullivan,

I must first offer my profoundest apologies for being out of contact with you for so long. I have been attempting to set things in order in my life that will make it possible for me to be a responsible father and give young Morvern the life she deserves. She would be eight now, and my negligence in waiting so long to see her again weighs heavily upon my conscience. However, at last it is my hope to change that. I have not remarried, and the memory of dear Avonmara remains precious in my heart. My father died two years ago, and I have now come into his title in my own right. I did not fully divulge my position before. I wanted Avonmara to know me and love me as I was, not for any future title that might come to me. I am, however, now a viscount. I am not a wealthy man, but I can assure you that Morvern will have all the advantages of her position that I am able to give her.

I hope you and she and all your family are well. After hearing from you, I will make plans to come to Ireland personally so that Morvern might begin her life with me as her father.

I am,
Sincerely yours,
Your son-in-law,
Roderick Westbrooke, Viscount Lord Snowdon
Llanfryniog, Gwynedd, Wales

Percy refolded the letter and replaced it in the envelope then withdrew the next.

May 10, 1842
Pine Cottage
Laragh, County Wicklow

Dear Mrs. O'Sullivan,

I write again in hopes that my letter of last month, which came back to me unopened, was perhaps waylaid in the post and returned by mistake. I pray this letter will reach you. In it I expressed my sincere apologies for being out of contact with you so many years. In attempting to set things in order in my life, I believe that it is now possible for me to be a responsible father and give my daughter the life she deserves. My tardiness in being so long to contact you weighs heavily upon my conscience. However, my father died two years ago, and I have now come into a viscountcy in my own right. I am not wealthy, but I can assure you that I can give Morvern all the advantages of her position as the daughter of a viscount.

I pray you and she and your family are well. I would like to make plans to come to Ireland personally as soon as possible so that Morvern might begin her new life with me.

I am,
Sincerely yours,
Your son-in-law,
Roderick Westbrooke, Viscount Lord Snowdon
Llanfryniog, Gwynedd, Wales

Next he read the third, which followed yet a month later.

June 15, 1842
Pine Cottage
Laragh, County Wicklow

Dear Mrs. O'Sullivan,

This is my third attempt to establish contact with you. My previous two letters have been returned unopened. If you by any chance receive this, please forgive me for neglecting my duty for so long. It would be perfectly understandable if you never wanted to see me again; however, I hope you will find it in your heart to allow me to make up for the past by providing Morvern a future with the opportunities I can provide her as the daughter of a viscount.

I hope you and Morvern are well. Please reply. I am longing to see my daughter again.

I am, yet again,
Sincerely yours,
Your son-in-law,
Roderick Westbrooke, Viscount Lord Snowdon
Llanfryniog, Gwynedd, Wales

Finally Percy's uncle had written to his wife's sister.

July 21, 1842
Vanora Maloney
Dell Bank
Laragh, County Wicklow

Dear Vanora,

I have written to your mother three times, attempting to establish contact again with you all, and especially with Morvern. I realize it has been a long time, and my silence is inexcusable. I can only beg the forgiveness of you all and say that I am at last in a position to give my daughter every advantage I can afford her. I would very much appreciate your speaking to your mother on my behalf and assuring her of my good intentions. My letters are returned labeled "Moved Without Forward." If your mother and Morvern have indeed moved, perhaps you could put me in touch with them.

I would like to come to Ireland as soon as possible so that

Morvern might begin her life with me as her father.

I hope you and Daibheid and your family are well.

I am,
Sincerely yours,
Your brother-in-law,
Roderick Westbrooke, Viscount Lord Snowdon
Llanfryniog, Gwynedd, Wales

Then had followed another half dozen letters to both Pine Cottage and Dell Bank in the same vein throughout the fall of 1842, after which, Percy assumed, had come his uncle's ill-fated return to Ireland.

Forty-Two

Market Day

Market day in Llanfryniog in the year 1873 had been planned a week earlier than usual. Thus it was that on the Saturday of the last week of June, wagons and carts and carriages began to roll into the small coastal village of North Wales while the morning was early and a chill still hung in the air.

By midmorning, dozens of tables and booths and stands were spread out between the Methodist chapel and the village, displaying a great variety of homegrown and homemade wares. Of the former, because they were in season, strawberries and new potatoes were among the most prominent. They were supplemented by turnips, carrots, floral bouquets, bottles of elderberry and hedgerow wines, cheeses and jams, as well as small trinkets and sweeties for the children. Handcrafts made through the winter and spring months by the women of Llanfryniog rounded out the inventory of stock in trade. And of course all the fisher wives arrived with baskets full of the previous day's or night's catch.

Indeed, describing their goods as for *trade* was not far from the truth. As hard as they worked to prepare for it, few actually expected to go home that evening with more money in their pockets than they came with. Everyone saved up their pennies and shillings for market day. But though the collection did not amount to much, spending was as greatly anticipated as selling. Money *circulated* between the villagers, but there was little *accumulation*. This was a day not for profit but for fun. What one received from selling goods was happily spent or traded at a neighbor's table. All the women knitted wool caps and socks and sweaters and scarves, and everyone grew potatoes and made cheese. They did not *need* to buy from one another—it was simply the accepted means of lubricating commerce in a small farming and fishing community. Where cash was in short supply, barter was as common as coin. It was not the economic profitability of the exercise that everyone looked forward to but the social tradition in the life of the community. If visitors from inland or along the coast north and south added to the general flow of commerce with an influx of cash, perhaps all would go home feeling that the day had been well spent.

By noon the town was full with bustle and activity. Singing could be heard and would continue all afternoon. All three churches boasted choirs that practiced months for this day. The children from the school came together to alternate their own choral numbers with the adult choirs from the three churches. Fiddlers and accordionists and dancers filled in at every opportunity. There was not a minute throughout the day when some music was not drifting through the air over the numerous activities. Aromas from fires and kettles tempted the hungry to part with a few coins for their lunch. A variety of games and amusements kept children scurrying about excitedly from one to another to another.

Nor would any market day be complete without a suitable offering of animal flesh for sale or trade. At one end of the field was tied an assortment of pigs, sheep, horses, and several bulls to see what offers might be made. By noon, Chandos and Kyvwlch Gwarthegydd, Padrig Gwlwlwyd, Holin Radnor from the manor, and a handful of men were clustered about examining teeth and legs, hooves and flanks, and talking of all things equine, bovine, and porcine.

It was not the sort of gathering that Colville Burrenchobay would normally have given a tuppence for now that he was a sophisticated young man of twenty-four. But his sixteen-year-old brother Ainsworth had arrived at that age where young ladies and mischief in general exercised great fascination. When their sister Davina and her fiancé,

William Rasmussen, son of Baronet Rasmussen of Blaenau Ffestiniog, decided to join him, Colville was hardly inclined to stay home alone.

The brothers Burrenchobay led the way into Llanfryniog about one o'clock. Colville was not expecting much from the afternoon. Ainsworth, however, recently returned from a first year at Cambridge as undistinguished as that of his brother several years before, was hungry for amusement and sport. He was also eager to survey what pretty new faces the new summer might have turned up. Behind them, though she was engaged to the handsome young man at her side, Davina glanced about with as lively an eye as her younger brother. She was still a month shy of her nineteenth birthday and not quite yet cured of the flirtatious demon that had so successfully enchanted young Rasmussen.

Heads turned as the young people rode slowly up the road on their horses from the harbor to the chapel then made their way toward the town and site of the day's festivities. The three Burrenchobays were used to commanding attention wherever they went. Their father being the parliamentary representative for coastal Gwynedd was enough in itself to draw looks from men and women alike. They were not aristocrats by birth, though their father had been knighted and was now known as Sir Armond. With Lord Snowdon dead and Courtenay, his presumptive heir, out of the country, the MP's two sons and daughter were as close to aristocracy as anyone living along the coast was likely to claim on this day. That rumors had followed the two Burrenchobay sons for years added curiosity and a hint of terrified excitement on the part of the young ladies whenever the two were present. Colville's amorous escapades had been a subject of local gossip for years. Ainsworth was anxious to follow in his brother's tradition. Both were known to be good with their fists and even better with their guns. They were handsome, hot tempered, and enjoyed being in the limelight—an irresistible, if dangerous, combination.

As for young Willy Rasmussen, some might have questioned whether a mere baronet's son from the inland regions of Snowdonia would qualify as an aristocrat at all. It was universally accepted that Willy, never known for his intellectual prowess, had made the best of the match. The moment Davina's engagement was announced, there had been great disappointment in Llanfryniog. Though Davina was five years younger than Courtenay Westbrooke, many had hoped to see the important families of the region joined by two marriages. Colville's with Florilyn had been accepted for years as a *fait accompli.* Now, with Lady Florilyn involved with her Scots cousin—though no one quite knew where the thing stood—neither of the Westbrooke-Burrenchobay marriages seemed likely to materialize.

By the time the foursome split apart, the sheep-shearing contest was about ready to get under way. Ainsworth quickly disappeared with three or four girls in tow hanging on his every exaggerated tale of life at the great English university. Willy Rasmussen followed Davina about like a well-trained puppy as she visited with the village girls too old to wilt from Ainsworth's smiles. The envious glances went curiously in both directions. With the foolishness of youth that judged by looks rather than character, every girl in the place hoped someday to be so lucky as Davina in landing a squire as handsome as young Willy Rasmussen. On her part, however, pangs of envy also stole unbidden into Davina's heart to realize that for her the game of fascination and conquest was done. In her quieter moments, she wondered if she had perhaps acted too hastily in accepting Willy's proposal. The result was an occasional wistful glance about the crowd to see what young men were in attendance. If Willy noticed her roving eyes, he remained oblivious to its cause.

Colville, meanwhile, seeing no eligible young women near his own age—by their midtwenties, the young women of rural North Wales were either married or such as to be of no interest to him—had wandered toward the gathering of men looking over several horses that Padrig Gwlwlwyd, one of those who *did* hope to profit from the day's sales, had brought in for the occasion.

"Looking for a new addition to your father's stable, young Burrenchobay?" said Gwlwlwyd as Colville approached the gathering. "I have two or three that would do him proud."

"My father does not buy his horseflesh from village fairs," rejoined

Colville with obvious condescension.

"For yourself, then?"

"Horses are not my game, Gwlwlwyd," said Colville. He glanced about with humorous disdain. "Neither are cows or pigs. I will leave the animals to you."

At the far end of the field, shouts and cheers rose from the first shearing contestant—a burly young fifteen-year-old cousin of Chandos Gwarthegydd who displayed every indication of being a future champion. He was followed by Eardley White, Chandos's best friend of childhood who had filled out in direct opposite proportion to the blacksmith's son. Chandos could now claim to top sixteen stone, every pebble of it muscle and mostly concentrated in his chest, arms, and shoulders. One look at Eardley, on the other hand, at barely ten stone and over six feet tall, would have greatly interested the mathematician Euclid when devising his theory of what comprised a straight line.

But deft, coordination, and an innate skill in keeping a sheep relaxed under the knife were more necessary to shearing speed than brawn, and Eardley trimmed eleven seconds from Kethtrwm Gwarthegydd's time. After several more local shepherds had their go, the crowd became frenzied as it cheered on its favorites. That a good deal of modest betting had taken place on the outcome always added to the keen interest in the competition.

Six more contestants came and went. Still Eardley's time of forty-seven seconds held, though now the margin to second place had dropped to a mere three seconds.

Finally a late entrant who had just arrived stepped forward. A cheer rose, for he was a great favorite with everyone for miles. He had shown great promise as a youth in being the likely heir apparent to his father's unmatched skill with the razor-sharp shearing scissors. However, he had not entered the contest for two years. His current occupation was one that had not kept him in practice. Yet discussion and new bets were feverish as he readied himself for the contest. The predictions of his chances were mixed.

The new contestant's dress, indeed his entire bearing, might have led a newcomer to the village to conclude that he was of aristocratic blood, for he carried himself with a stature and authority that belied his humble roots in the foothills of the Snowdonian mountains. But the moment Steven Muir pulled off his shirt, for the day was hot, and turned toward the throng with a grin, they all knew the manor's young factor to whom they now paid their rent was still their own beloved Stevie.

Few noticed the young woman who had gradually worked her way closer to the front of the noisy commotion. Slowly she squeezed through until she was standing near the front, staring at the sight of his bare chest and rippling shoulders.

"We'll see what the work of a dandy's made of you now, Stevie!" shouted a man from amid the crowd.

"I can outshear you with my eyes closed, Dirmyg!" laughed Steven.

"But can you best young White?" said another above the din.

"There's only one way to find out, Fflergant," rejoined Steven. "I'm ready," he added, turning toward the judges. "Bring me the wiggliest one of the batch!"

The crowd quieted as Steven took hold of the sheep between his knees, gripped a fistful of thick wool with his left hand and held the scissors at the ready in his right, and awaited the command from Ehangwen Pugh who held the watch.

"Ready yourself, Stevie!" he shouted. "Five seconds. . .four. . .three. . . two. . .one. . .go!"

With lightning agility, Steven's hand tore into the mass of wool with the scissors with such speed that it seemed impossible to prevent its two sharp points from puncturing the animal's skin. Instantly the yelling and shouts resumed at a frantic pitch. Within seconds the back was bare. Steven flopped the sheep onto its back, keeping tight hold of the writhing legs.

Amid the din, a young woman's voice rose above the rest. It was not just who she was that suddenly turned all eyes toward her. She was also the only one in the crowd cheering Stevie on with his formal name. Most of the gathering had never heard it used of Glythvyr Muir's son in his life. "Go, Steven!" cried Florilyn. "Faster. . .you can do it—come on, Steven. . .Steven. Go. . .go!"

Caught up in the excitement of the moment, Florilyn did not notice that everyone's eyes were resting on her. That the viscount's daughter would take such interest in sheepshearing was unusual in itself. That she was so excitedly cheering on her mother's young factor was enough to spark more than idle curiosity.

With a last great effort, Steven flung the coat of wool in a single piece away from the tiny white body that emerged from beneath. Not a scratch of blood was showing. He turned expectantly toward Ehangwen Pugh.

"Forty-seven seconds!" called out the timekeeper. "It's a tie with Eardley."

Another rousing cheer rose, Florilyn's voice as loud as the rest. As she glanced about with a great smile on her face, Florilyn suddenly realized that everyone was staring at her. Her mouth hung open a moment longer. Her face reddened as she realized what she had done. Unaccountably embarrassed, quickly she turned and ran through the crowd and away from the scene.

Steven, who had heard her cheering voice, saw her go. He had no time to think about it further.

Lanky Eardley White now stepped forward and shook Steven's hand vigorously. "Well done, Stevie!" he said. "The factoring seems to agree with you. You've lost nothing of your touch."

The two turned together toward the crowd, which applauded them as the apparent victors. After five more contestants, the tie between the two young men still held.

Meanwhile, Florilyn hurried away, doing her best to avoid the stares that followed her. She ran between booths and tables and children and dogs and merrymakers to where she had tied her mount. Unaware from where he had been milling about the horse selling that Colville Burrenchobay had heard the commotion at the sheepshearing and had observed her strange flight, Florilyn mounted Red Rhud and made for the road.

The crowd thinned as she approached the harbor. The tide was low. Reaching the wide expanse of hard-packed wet sand, she encouraged her mount to a brief gallop. Once she was well alone, she reined back and continued on more slowly to the end of the beach.

She was thinking about many new and unexpected things.

Forty-Three

Aspirations Personal and Political

Colville Burrenchobay had been tempted to accompany Courtenay to the continent six weeks earlier. But what was to be gained by forever acting the part of a rich ne'er-do-well son? He was a university graduate with nothing else to show for his life. He had little interest in gallivanting about Europe with Courtenay Westbrooke, pretending they were still eighteen-year-olds.

As much as friendship, the relationship between the two best friends had always been one of competition and rivalry. Either would go to any length to best the other. That rivalry now took an unexpected turn in the brain of the MP's son.

In the year since the tragic accident, the viscount's death had exercised a strange and subtle effect on Colville Burrenchobay. The knowledge that his friend, younger by a year, was soon to become Viscount Lord Snowdon, occupant of a seat in the House of Lords, and overnight regarded as the most important man in the region, turned Colville's thoughts toward his own future. He did not like the idea of being suddenly forced to walk in the shadow of one to whom he had always felt superior.

If his reflections did not actually begin to revolve around the thought of "settling down," as was the custom for young men in their twenties, something akin to such motions of his brain became more active than before. He had rarely given much thought to his future. He assumed that his inheritance would be more than adequate for whatever life he chose for himself. A better entrée into the world of politics, however, could hardly be imagined than his father's reputation as a member of the House of Commons of long standing. It was like handing him an engraved invitation to Westminster on a plate with watercress around it. And in this modern age, Commons trumped the Lords in prestige by a mile. A viscount was nothing alongside a member of Commons.

The idea of a stand for parliament himself, whenever his father decided to step aside, thus began to take root in his thoughts. And with these slow-building reflections and shifting priorities, thoughts of marriage also began to intrude into the gray cells of his mind. As they did, the face of the most beautiful and eligible young lady in Snowdonia rose out of the mists of the past. That she would one day be rich besides, for her mother was known to be of independent wealth, was also a fact that did not escape Colville Burrenchobay's notice. Sight of her in the village during market day a week or two earlier had not left him. He had to admit. . .the little vixen was more beautiful than he remembered her. She would make heads turn in Westminster. He would be noticed instantly with a woman like that on his arm!

Thus it was, one warm day in mid-July, that Colville Burrenchobay presented himself at the door of Westbrooke Manor. He had come, he said to Broakes, to pay his respects to Lady Florilyn.

Florilyn's first thought was to turn around and retreat to the safety of her room. But it was a grand day, and Colville's smile and invitation for a ride seemed genuine enough. She accepted.

By day's end, she was delightfully surprised at the change that had come over him. He had behaved as a perfect gentleman.

"I must say, Colville," said Florilyn as they parted, "you have changed since we last rode together."

"I am a reformed young man," he said. "My foolish ways are behind me. I may even resume my studies and secure an advanced degree."

"My, oh my!" exclaimed Florilyn laughing. "Colville Burrenchobay, the scholar and academic."

"I doubt I would go that far."

"In any case—I enjoyed myself today. Thank you."

"The summer appears a fine one. Perhaps we could see one another again."

Florilyn nodded with a smile, and Colville left her.

Elsewhere on the grounds of Westbrooke Manor, Steven Muir continued his supervision of the construction of Katherine's new home on the promontory. Stone masons and carpenters had all been employed, some from Chester, others from Shrewsbury, still others from as far away as Cardiff. Their presence was straining the limits of Mistress Chattan's inn, though some of the workers were also put up in the servants' quarters at the manor. Huge wagons of stone and mortar and other supplies rumbled past Llanfryniog almost daily from all over England and Wales. The outer walls of granite had begun not merely to rise but to significantly alter the landscape. Slowly but surely the formidable outline of the house moved from drawings to reality.

Steven was at the site every day and reported progress to Katherine. Mistress and factor consulted together almost daily about whatever situations happened to arise. Katherine rode or walked down to the site, sometimes several times a day, as her enthusiasm mounted daily to see her house taking shape before her eyes. Her enthusiasm, however, was bittersweet. She loved the manor, and thoughts of the new house could not fail to be accompanied by reminders of the reason for its necessity.

Thinking little more about the ride with Colville than that two childhood friends had renewed their acquaintance for a day, and certainly anticipating nothing more coming of it, Florilyn was altogether unprepared for the invitation to Burrenchobay Hall for dinner that arrived several days later. Her own reaction surprised her almost as much as the invitation itself.

She showed her mother the letter that had come in the post. "It sounds like fun," said Florilyn.

"I have never cared for Colville Burrenchobay," rejoined Katherine. "I don't like your seeing him, Florilyn, especially after a young man as nice as Percy."

"Percy's not here, Mother," rejoined Florilyn a little testily. "What do you expect me to do, sit around and become a spinster?"

"I thought you and Percy—"

"It's over between Percy and me, Mother," said Florilyn. The frustration that had been fermenting in her subconscious that even she was unaware of at last bubbled to the surface. "He stayed all of three days and didn't even tell me where he was going," she went on. "That ought to show well enough what he thinks of me."

"His leaving had nothing to do with you."

"Maybe, but even when he was here, we hardly saw one another. I'm sure it is a relief to him to be away from me."

"Florilyn—goodness! What has put such thoughts in your head? You know better than that."

"Do I, Mother? Do I *really* know what Percy thinks of me? Sometimes I wonder if I ever did." She turned and walked away.

Katherine stared perplexed after her.

Alone later, Florilyn regretted her words. She knew well enough that she had broken it off with Percy, not him with her. Why had she taken her own uneasiness over what *she* had done out on her mother? She had been agitated ever since market day, for reasons she could not identify. For some peculiar reason, Colville's invitation came almost as a relief. It gave her an excuse to recall the childish attraction she once thought she had for him. Maybe he *had* changed. At any rate, it gave her something else to think about.

There was no denying that Florilyn had begun to worry about her future. The invitation sent a tingle of renewed hope through her. She would not think for an instant of actually marrying Colville Burrenchobay. But it was nice to have someone show some interest in her.

In the days following, Florilyn anticipated the evening more than she dared let on. When the day came, Colville presented himself in his father's finest buggy.

Steven watched them go with mixed thoughts of his own. Neither did he, any more than Katherine, like this new trend events were taking.

"So, Florilyn, my dear," said Sir Armond Burrenchobay as they sat at the exquisitely appointed table in the formal dining room two hours later, "tell me about this cousin of yours. You were engaged for a time, I understand, but now it is off?"

"That's pretty much it," replied Florilyn.

"What happened? Did the two of you come to blows?"

"Nothing like that. We just decided, after Daddy's accident, that perhaps we had rushed into it."

"Who is the fellow, anyway?"

"You met him right here, at Davina's birthday party—Percy Drummond."

"Ah yes, the Scottish chap. Your father seemed inordinately fond of him."

"Percy and my father were very close."

"Struck me as a trifle too religious for my blood. Wasn't his father a priest or some such? A twenty-year-old going about preaching. . .a bit much, what? Ah well, no harm done. Now you and Colville can get to know one another again, now that you're no longer children. See what comes of it, eh, Colville, my boy?" he added with a wink to his son. "Someone's got to start giving us some grandchildren before long, what? Young Davina's hopeless."

An awkward silence followed Sir Armond's candid rambling. Florilyn hoped no one noticed the redness she felt in her neck and face as she glanced down at her plate.

Forty-Four

Dead Ends in Laragh

For more than a week, Percy had been trying to locate the mysterious names to whom his uncle had written in 1842. He had discovered, however, that the name O'Sullivan in eastern Ireland was as common as MacDonald or Gordon or Campbell in his native Scotland. He met several O'Sullivans but none who had heard of Avonmara or Vanora O'Sullivan or their parents who might have lived at Pine Cottage or Dell Bank in the 1830s or 1840s.

Learning the locations of the two homes from the postmistress, he paid visits to both houses. The current residents knew nothing. The lady at the post told him to expect as much. At least six different families had lived in both places in the last twenty years, she said. To find anyone from three decades or more before was like the proverbial needle in a haystack.

Everyone said the same thing. The potato famine of 1845–48 had altered everything. Most had left. Few remained from the old times. Those who stayed saw faces and families come and go in a blur. All Ireland had been turned upside down. Thousands packed up and left without telling anyone where they were going. Most of the time they didn't know themselves. . .for England, for the United States if they were lucky enough to scrape together money for the passage. . .*anywhere* they might find work. . .anywhere there was someone who might take them in.

But 1842. . .wasn't that *before* the famine, Percy asked several times. Where had these people gone? Why had these letters not been delivered?

The postmistress, a woman in her forties, was too young to remember. She gave Percy the name of her predecessor, one Danny McNeil. Percy paid him a visit.

Yes, he remembered the O'Sullivans, he said. They had a lass who married an Englishman, he thought, or some foreigner.

"Do you remember her marriage?" Percy asked enthusiastically.

"Now that you mention it, I recollect something about it. She was too young to be marrying, folks said, a mere child herself, they said. But the laddie from England, or wherever it was, swept her off her feet, folks said. Then she had a child but died giving birth."

"After that, they left Laragh? And the baby with them?"

"Must have, now that you bring my mind back to it. Wasn't long after—can't remember exactly—that they were gone."

"Do you remember these?" said Percy, showing him the envelopes of his uncle's letters.

McNeil looked them over and shook his head. "Can't say as I do. But aye, that's my stamp."

"You have no idea where they went?"

"I wouldn't have stamped it 'Unknown' if I'd known where they were, would I now, laddie?"

"I suppose not. Do you remember who lived in these two cottages after Mrs. O'Sullivan and Avonmara's sister Vanora left?"

"Can't say I do. People come and people go. Even a postmaster can't keep track of them all, laddie. They were terrible times. They lasted three years. . .five years, in some places eight or ten. The potato crops gradually came back and life went on. But by then all Ireland had been changed, decimated some would say—so many people gone and dead. The whole country had to start over."

"Was there work to be had?"

"Aye, in time. There was always the shipbuilding down in Arklow if a man was willing to work hard. Decent pay in the shipyards, too, they say, though I was happy enough in the post and never did that kind of work myself."

McNeil paused a moment. "Now that you get my mind thinking on those times," he went on, "seems I recall that some of the men from here went down to the shipyards when the famine hit. It was a way to keep their families alive. Men would do anything for that."

FORTY-FIVE

Dubious Scion

Ever since Percy had seen the men in the mountains northeast of the manor, Katherine had been silently pondering the matter. Her disquiet had grown. Lord Litchfield's visit to Wales also preyed upon her mind. She could not prevent the foreboding sense that somehow the two events were related. She had done some investigating of her own since Percy's departure and had discovered more about Lord Litchfield than that he had been her husband's colleague in the House of Lords. He was also one of England's leading mining magnates. It was no secret that Wales contained some of the richest mineral deposits in all Britain—not slate merely, but also coal and gold.

She had retrieved the letters from Litchfield to her husband that Percy had discovered in the files in the study and perused them several times. But without seeing her husband's half of the correspondence, she could tell nothing definite. Yet more importantly, how had Courtenay's recent contact with the man begun. . .and for what purpose? One thing was clear—there had been discussions about the sale of estate lands.

As if materializing out of her thoughts, Courtenay Westbrooke returned from the continent no worse for wear and with less than £500 left in his account at Porthmadog. The dramatic shrinkage of his funds was in part explained by the fact that he was leading two one-year-old thoroughbreds and a two-year-old for which he had paid at least twice what they were worth. He had transported them by train across France, by ship across the channel, and by train the rest of the way, then led them himself overland for the final ten miles of their journey. He was in high spirits and well confident that the three speedsters would make him rich within five years.

His optimism over the future was short lived. As he passed along the main road south of Llanfryniog on his way to the manor, he observed more to alarm him than mere surveying on his land—a full-fledged building project of massive scale was under way on Mochras Head! Walls of stone had grown ten feet high. He had no idea his mother was planning anything so preposterously enormous. And there was the imbecile Muir walking about with papers in his hand as if he was in charge of the thing.

Courtenay reached home in a white fury and saw his prize new purchases into their new quarters. Though his father's aging groom knew more about horses than anyone in Gwynedd other than Padrig Gwlwlwyd, Courtenay would never trust his expensive new acquisitions with one like Hollin Radnor.

The moment the three horses were safely in their new stalls and provided with oats and water, he went angrily in search of his mother. He burst into the ground-floor sitting room like an enraged bull. "What is the meaning of this, Mother?" he demanded without word of greeting.

"It is nice to see you again, too, Courtenay," she said, not without a little bite in her tone.

"I want to know what is going on over on Mochras Head!"

"You told me that I would no longer be welcome at the manor after you inherit. You left me no alternative but to build a new home for myself."

"But it is on my land!"

"Not yet yours, Courtenay."

"It will be soon enough. I can evict you from there just as well as from the manor."

"I fear not, Courtenay. The parcel where my home is being

constructed is no longer part of the estate."

"What are you talking about? Of course it is."

"That portion of land has been sold."

"Sold! To whom?"

"To me. I purchased it from the estate in my own name. You can be assured that it is perfectly legal. Hamilton Murray has seen to that."

"I will stop you. I will have the sale invalidated."

"I'm afraid there is nothing you can do, Courtenay. It has been finalized for months. Before you complain too highly, I paid the estate more than market value for the land. Those funds will be yours once you are viscount. The whole thing will actually prove profitable to you. And while we are on the subject of land sales, I want to know what is going on between you and Lord Litchfield."

"That is none of your affair," answered Courtenay testily.

"It is my affair until you are twenty-five. Some men I suspect as being in his employ were seen in the mountains at the northeast of the estate. I want to know what they were doing there."

"As you have your secrets, Mother, perhaps I have mine."

"Are you planning to sell land to Lord Litchfield?"

"If I were, what business would it be of yours?"

"It is my business until next March. I do not like the idea of men trespassing on the estate. I want to know what business you have with Lord Litchfield."

"It is for the good of the estate that I invited Lord Litchfield to come," replied Courtenay, not directly addressing his mother's question. "I will not spend my life as a landed pauper like Father did. My means are none of your concern."

"I am trustee of the estate. All estate business is my concern."

"Nothing will be finalized until I am twenty-five. My business affairs at that point will be of no interest to you."

"Are you planning to sell him estate lands?" asked Katherine bluntly.

"I am considering it."

"I will not allow it. I will not allow you to tear up this land for coal, if that is the nature of whatever scheme you are hatching."

"Coal has nothing to do with it, Mother."

"I don't know whether to believe you or not."

"Believe what you like, Mother."

"Then why was Lord Litchfield here? Certainly not merely to welcome you to the House of Lords. Come, Courtenay, he is well known for his mining investments."

Able to contain himself no longer, Courtenay burst out in a laugh of derision. "There is really nothing so pitiful as a woman trying to exert power when she has none. You are pathetic, Mother. There is nothing you can do to prevent me doing whatever I like. All this will be mine in March. If I choose to sell a portion of land to Litchfield, I will do so. You can do nothing to stop me."

Courtenay turned and walked from the room, leaving his mother in tears.

Forty-Six

The Parish Church

All Percy's attempts to locate the apparent relations of his uncle's first wife had turned up nothing. Whether Mrs. O'Sullivan was even still alive was doubtful. She would probably be in her seventies or eighties by now. His uncle's affidavit stated that Avonmara had been eighteen at the time of their marriage. Forty years had passed since.

Besides the old postmaster, Percy knew that the person he most needed to speak with was the parish priest, and if possible examine the parish record books. Visiting the ancient Catholic church was not an easy task, however. Day after day he found it locked up like a drum, and the rectory behind it dark and to all appearances uninhabited.

On his fifth day to visit the place, an elderly woman saw him turning to leave, yet again, unsuccessfully. She ambled across the street. "Is it something you'll be wanting in the church, laddie?" she said to him.

"Yes, actually—I had hoped to speak with the priest," replied Percy. "But every day it is locked, and the place seems vacant."

"Aye, Father Halliday is down in Cork, you see. Won't be back till next week."

"He is coming back, then?"

"Oh, aye. But if it's mass you're wanting, the priest from Wicklow will be here tomorrow."

"No, I need to see your own priest. What was his name you said?"

"Father Halliday."

"Father Halliday—right. When do you think he will be back?"

"Tuesday or Wednesday is likely."

"Good—thank you very much."

"Where are you from, laddie?"

"Scotland."

"Oh, aye," said the woman, nodding knowingly, then walked off toward the center of the village.

The following Tuesday afternoon, at last Percy found the church and rectory occupied. His knock on the rectory door was answered by a man wearing a priest's robe who appeared in his midforties. Percy explained that he had been trying to see him and told him the reason for his visit. Father Halliday, like many Percy had spoken with, was too young to remember the events of the 1830s and 1840s. But he agreed to give Percy access to the record books of the church.

He led Percy from the rectory into the church and to the vestry. "Here we are," he said at length, opening the record of marriages. What was the year you said you were interested in?"

"The early 1830s, I believe," replied Percy. "My uncle was nineteen at the time. He died last year. I believe he was fifty-seven or fifty-eight. So that would be thirty-nine or forty years ago."

"I see," replied the priest. "Here are the listings for 1832. There were apparently nine marriages performed that year. What did you say was your uncle's name?"

"Westbrooke. . .Roderick Westbrooke."

Father Halliday scanned down the list of entries. "None here by that name." He turned over the large leaf of the book to the following year. "1833. . ." he said, tracing down the list with his finger. "Ah, yes. . . It would appear that you are right. Here is a marriage listed on April 11 between one Roderick Westbrook and Avonmara O'Sullivan."

"That's it!" exclaimed Percy. "So my uncle *was* married here, just like he said. Right here in this church. Is there any further information?"

"Only that the marriage was performed by my predecessor, Father O'Leary."

"Is he still living?"

"Yes, but he is very old."

"Is he still in Laragh?"

"He is. He lives in a small cottage provided him by the church."

"I would like to talk to him. What about the record of births?"

"That would be in another book. It should be over here. . ." said Father Halliday, closing the marriage book and taking down another from the shelf.

"What year?"

"A year later. . .1834."

"I see. . .all right," he said, laying the large book open on the desk and flipping through the pages. "There would seem to have been quite a number of births that year. . .scanning down. . .it would have to have been after, let me see. . .sometime after January. . . Here we are, January. . .February. . .March. . .ah yes, March 18—the birth of a daughter, Morvern, to Roderick and Avonmara Westbrooke. She was baptized one week later. Oh, but this is odd—the father does not appear to have been present."

"She is the woman I am looking for!" said Percy excitedly. "Morvern Westbrooke. . .although it is likely that she might be known as Morvern O'Sullivan. . .and of course, she would no doubt be married now. That would make her now, let me see, thirty-nine years old."

"Why would she be called O'Sullivan?"

"I don't know that," replied Percy. "But she was raised by her grandmother, Mrs. O'Sullivan. My uncle returned to Wales. When he came back for her, Mrs. O'Sullivan and his daughter were gone. He never saw them again."

"As you say, she would probably be married now."

"Do you think I would be able to speak with the priest who married them?" asked Percy. "You say he is still in the village?"

"Yes, but how much help he will be, I cannot say. He is elderly, and the past is fading from his mind. But I will take you to him. We can ask if he has the information you seek."

They left the church. After a five-minute walk through the village,

Percy found himself following the priest toward the rear of a small stone cottage into a small but obviously well-kept garden.

"If the sun is shining," said Father Halliday, "we will be sure to find Father O'Leary in his garden. . .and indeed, there he is. Father Bernard!" he said approaching with outstretched hand. "I have a young man here who would like to meet you."

An aging man, still wearing the black robe of his profession, turned from the rosebush that had been commanding his attention, clippers in hand, to meet them.

"This is Percival Drummond, Father Bernard," said the priest. "He has come from Wales searching for a long-lost relation."

"Not exactly a relation of mine—not directly at least," said Percy, shaking the older man's hand. "I am looking for a daughter of my uncle. I am his nephew by his second marriage. My uncle died last year. He lost track of his daughter shortly after her birth. I promised him I would try to find her."

The old priest appeared confused as Percy related his brief story. "I see. How may I help you then?" said Father O'Leary.

"We managed to locate the marriage and the girl's birth in the parish books," said Father Halliday. "The girl was born Morvern Westbrooke in 1834. It is likely, however, that she was raised by her maternal grandmother, Mrs. O'Sullivan."

"O'Sullivan. . .O'Sullivan. . .yes, I remember—the mother died in childbirth. Not altogether uncommon, yet a tragedy nevertheless."

"Do you remember what happened to the family. . .especially to the baby?" asked Percy.

"O'Sullivan you say the name was?"

Percy nodded.

"I cannot say. I lost track of them, I think. I believe they left some time later. Times became hard when the blight hit. It was impossible to remember them all."

"What about the relatives? Avonmara had a sister?"

"Avonmara. . . Who is Avonmara?"

"Avonmara O'Sullivan. . .my uncle's wife, the mother of the child."

"A sister, you say? What was her name?"

"Vanora. Her married name was Maloney, I believe."

"I really could not say. Hmm, Maloney. . .Maloney. . . It does seem that I remember. . .but no, it's gone now. Everyone was leaving, you see. They had to follow the work as best they could. Not that there was much work to be found. Some went to Arklow, as I recall."

"Is that where they went, do you think?"

"I am sorry, young man—I really cannot say. My memory, you see. . . it is not what it once was."

Forty-Seven

A Promise Kept and a Promise Scorned

During Percy's absence, Colville Burrenchobay was busy. For the next few weeks of the summer, he and Florilyn were nearly inseparable.

Katherine was beside herself over where it might lead. She saw the look in Colville's eye. It was not an expression she liked.

Suddenly Florilyn was reverting to her old ways. But what could a mother do? Daily she prayed for Percy's return. He had always had a good influence on Florilyn.

Meanwhile, Colville had so skillfully worked his magic that Florilyn was completely seduced by his charms. They rode together nearly every day—at the shore, in the mountains, to the nearby towns and villages for lunch or tea. Florilyn spent as much time at Burrenchobay Hall as at the manor. Sir Armond and Lady Burrenchobay had gone so far as to make up a special room for her use to stay over when she and Colville were together late in the evenings.

The changes in Florilyn had not gone unnoticed by Steven Muir. He saw his mistress's concern and shared it.

Hoping to revive something of the former friendship that had blossomed between them, one day he seized the opportunity he had been waiting for. Seeing Florilyn walking toward the stables, he hurried after her. "Good morning, Florilyn," he said.

She glanced toward him, seemingly affronted now by the familiar address that had once passed between them as easily as if they were brother and sister. She kept on without a reply.

"Little Nugget misses you," said Steven. "You spend little time with him now, unlike you did after he was born. I have been thinking of training him with the saddle. Would you like to help? You might like to ride him and teach him to know your seat and the commands of your voice."

"I don't think so, Steven," replied Florilyn. "Colville says I need a powerful mount beneath me."

"I do not like to see you spending so much time with him, Florilyn."

She spun around and shot him a piercing look.

"You may address me as *Lady* Florilyn, if you please!" she said.

"Forgive me, Lady Florilyn," said Steven calmly. "I still do not like to see you so much with Colville Burrenchobay."

"And why not, pray tell?" she shot back haughtily.

"Because he is not worthy of you. I have known him all my life."

"So have I."

"I do not trust him."

"He has changed."

"I doubt that, my lady. The expression in his eye when he looks at you is one of opportunism, not love."

"You presume to know the difference?" said Florilyn with disdain.

"I believe I do."

"And what gives you the right to interfere in my affairs?" she retorted angrily.

"The right of one who cares about you, my lady, who wants only the best for you, and who promised to protect you from harm."

"*Promised*... What makes you think I need your protection? Whom did you promise?"

"In a manner of speaking, your father."

"My father is dead. I do not recall his placing me in *your* charge."

"I promised one to whom he did entrust your well-being."

"Ah, my mother you mean. And you somehow assume that being her factor gives you the right—"

"I meant Percy, Lady Florilyn," said Steven.

"*Percy!* What does he have to do with me now?"

"I promised him that I would look after you, for his sake as well as my own."

"Percy can keep his nose out of my business! If he doesn't want to marry me, then he has nothing to say about it. He never liked Colville. He is just jealous."

"Percy knows nothing about Colville. I am merely telling you what I think he would say if he were here, that Colville Burrenchobay is not worthy of you."

"Well, you can tell Percy, when you happen to see him again, that I care not a straw for what he may think, and that if Colville proposes to me, I intend to accept him."

She turned and walked away, leaving Steven staring after her, heartbroken at how quickly her former teenage conceit had returned in the form of aristocratic womanly hauteur.

Forty-Eight

A Delicate Communiqué

By early August, Percy realized there was nothing left for him to do in Ireland.

He had confirmed his uncle's marriage to Avonmara O'Sullivan and the birth of their daughter, Morvern, and that the O'Sullivans were gone by the time of the viscount's return to Wales. Beyond those sketchy facts, he had come to a dead end. What point was there in trying to continue? He hadn't learned anything that his uncle didn't know. He shrank from returning to Westbrooke Manor just now, with nothing definite to tell anyone, nothing to account for his absence, no resolution to his future with Florilyn. Knowing nothing of the danger in which Florilyn stood, nor did he feel any urgency to do so. It would be best now to begin thinking through his own prospects in Glasgow.

Leaving the address of his parents with Father Halliday, he returned to Dublin, from where he set sail for Glasgow. Perhaps it was time to make plans for law school.

When he arrived home, Percy had a long talk with his mother and father. Then followed prayer between the three about Percy's future and especially about Florilyn.

"As you are weighing your options," said Edward as the evening drew to a close, "I have something I think you might like to read. Whether it will help focus your thoughts and prayers, I cannot say. But it is truly one of the most remarkable expositions of Scripture I have ever read. It has had a profound impact on me."

"Don't tell me," laughed Percy, "a new book by George MacDonald."

Edward joined him in laughter. "A good guess. But I'm afraid not. My friends at Henry King publishers, however, tell me that one of his best novels yet is in the works but won't be out for a couple of years."

"What's it about?"

"A fisherman," they say. "It's set in a fishing village up in your neck of the woods northwest of Aberdeen."

"Where's that?" asked Percy.

"Cullen."

"I've heard of it. One of my classmates was from there. As I recall also, some of the students went up there on holiday. So MacDonald's next novel takes place there?"

"The next one they will be publishing. MacDonald was there a year ago researching for it. But then a lecture tour in America set the schedule back. Apparently the MacDonalds are planning another visit to Cullen next month. In any event, it sounds like something to look forward to."

"But that's not what you were telling me about?"

"No. Actually I was referring to the manuscript young cousin Henry gave me to look at when he and his father came to Aberdeen for your graduation. I know he's a young man, but it is truly remarkable. I believe our cousin may have quite a future ahead of him. He may become the most famous Drummond of all."

"Then I would definitely like to read it," said Percy. "Have you spoken with him about it? Didn't he ask for your thoughts?"

"I wrote him a letter of lavish praise for his insights," replied Edward. "I told him it was the greatest thing in the world I have ever read on First Corinthians 13. I said he ought to publish it."

"What did Henry say?"

"He was flattered and appreciative. He said his father had also encouraged him to have it published but that he was not completely satisfied with it yet. He liked my phrase though. He said, if I had no objection, he might use that for the title."

"What phrase?"

"The greatest thing in the world. It is an exposition of love, as set forth by Paul in First Corinthians 13. What could be a greater thing in the world than love?"

"I will definitely look forward to reading it. Have you heard more about his hope to be involved with the Moody mission?"

"As far as I know he is still planning to join as a student volunteer."

"Now that I am more or less at loose ends," mused Percy, "perhaps I should join him after all."

Later in his room, it was not his cousin Henry Drummond's treatise on 1 Corinthians 13 that first drew Percy's attention, however, but rather the beginning of a long overdue letter to his aunt. Somehow he had to try to explain himself and, to the degree he was able, put the matter to rest in both his mind and hers. He would have to walk a tightrope to do so. Now that he had told his father a little more, he would let him read his words first, to avoid saying either too much or too little.

He set aside the manuscript of his cousin's that his father had given him and took out a fresh sheet of writing paper and pen.

Dear Aunt Katherine, he began.

My greetings both to you and Florilyn and everyone at Westbrooke Manor. I am back in Glasgow with my parents. I felt I needed to see them and talk some things over with my father. I have just arrived.

I know I left Wales hastily, and I apologize for that, also for not being able to explain more about my sudden departure and subsequent silence. I hope that you will understand my reasons for leaving abruptly when I tell you that the request Uncle Roderick made of me involved more than merely sorting through the papers and files in his study. There were certain delicate matters on his mind that he had too long neglected and which he felt might be of consequence to Courtenay, and indeed his entire family, concerning his legacy and the inheritance of his title and the estate should they come out.

I don't know how much of his life before your marriage you are familiar with, no doubt far more than me. You surely know that he spent time in Ireland during the latter years of his youth. He told me few details other than that while there he had been consumed by the lust for gold in that region of Ireland, which had experienced a gold rush in the early years of the century. During that time, he said, there were several associations with certain individuals he had not seen since and with whom he had lost touch. He asked me to see if I could locate among his papers any connections to those persons by which—

Percy paused, struggling desperately to find the right words. His position would be much easier had he never said a word to his aunt about his promise to his uncle. But it had come out, and now he must make the best of it.

He read over what he had just written then continued.

He asked me to see if I could locate among his papers any connections to those persons by which. . .they could be located, or that would give me reason to believe that they might one day jeopardize his or Courtenay's position as viscount, or make demands upon Courtenay that he would be unable to accede to.

I realize my words are dreadfully vague. I am sorry again. It was vague to me also when Uncle Roderick spoke to me of these things. He asked me specifically not to burden you with it if nothing came of it. Simply know that all his thoughts as he spoke to me were of you and the family he loved so dearly. He wanted no hurt or anxiety to come to any of you. He asked me to take care of this last request specifically for that reason, so that you would not be unnecessarily burdened with it.

Having found among his papers what I thought might lead me to the individuals involved, I went to Ireland to attempt to carry out this final request. However, all my attempts were unsuccessful. I discovered nothing untoward. Actually, I discovered nothing at all. There is no record that I was able to find of anyone who knew Uncle Roderick when he was there. I believe I can safely say that no associations or obligations from the past need be of concern to yourself or to Courtenay.

If there is anything that I can do for you, I hope you will not hesitate to call on me.

Percy paused, then added:

Please give my loving best to Florilyn. Tell her I will write soon.
All the best, and with deep affection,

Percy

He set down the pen and exhaled deeply, then undressed, blew out his candle, and fell sleepily onto his bed.

The following morning Percy found his father in his office preparing to leave for his office at the church. "Dad," said Percy, "I have a favor to ask."

"Anything, Percy."

"I wrote a letter to Aunt Katherine last night after I talked with you and Mom. Would you read it and tell me what you think?"

"Sure. . .absolutely."

"I need to know if you think I have said too much or too little, or have been too ambiguous or not ambiguous enough. I know you don't know what Uncle Roderick asked me to do any more than Aunt Katherine does. But I need to know what you think she will think. She is your sister. No one would know better than you." He handed his father the paper.

Edward read it slowly then set the letter aside.

"Knowing Roderick as I did," he began after a moment, "I would conclude from this that he was involved in something perhaps not altogether aboveboard—a scheme perhaps, probably with wealth at the bottom of it, that did not turn out as he had hoped. What that would possibly have to do with Courtenay's inheritance, I have no idea. Perhaps

Roderick still had debts from years before, and he was afraid of it coming back to haunt Courtenay. Perhaps he pledged Westbrooke Manor against the scheme. He was always a schemer. This rings true to what I knew of him. I could see any of a number of options. He might have bought into an old gold mine, for all I know. When he and Katherine first became involved, he was veiled about his past. We knew he had been in Ireland, but nothing more. Financial trouble would certainly explain it."

Percy nodded as he listened. He was both satisfied and dissatisfied with his father's answer. How could he know if he was doing the right thing, leading his aunt to believe, as his father had, something that *wasn't* true? It was either that or say nothing at all. He must *somehow* account for his actions. If only he had said nothing about his pledge to his uncle.

Forty-Nine

Subtle Innuendos

That same afternoon Percy sat down to write an equally difficult letter to his cousin.

Dear Florilyn, he began.

As I am sure your mother has told you, I am back in Glasgow with my parents after a generally uneventful time in Ireland.

I realize that the future is unsettled for us both. If my handling of my own uncertainties has contributed to your anxieties, I sincerely apologize. My focus was so entirely occupied last term with completion of my studies. Then our plans were turned upside down by the MacDonald novel we read and what you felt we were to do in consequence. As time went on, my promise to your father weighed more and more heavily upon me.

With all that at last behind me, I feel as if I am breathing a great sigh of relief!

He set aside the pen for a moment and drew in a breath. Ever since his father's mention the previous evening of his cousin Henry, an idea had been floating about in his subconscious. As he wrote, it began to take more definite form.

Naturally, Percy resumed, *my thoughts turn often to you and to the predicament, it might be called, of our situation. We were both agreed, as I am certain we still are, that what we want above all is God's will. We want to do what He wants us to do. I continue to ask Him to reveal that will. I know you are praying that prayer with me. It is hard at times, as I know it must be for you, that our plans remain nebulous. But I am confident that God will show us what we are to do in His time. We will both be stronger for it. As I think I once told you, my father says that God is never in a hurry. That is a difficult lesson for we who are young, but I realize the wisdom of such a truth.*

As we continue waiting for Him to reveal His will, and as I contemplate my own future and the possibility of law school, an exciting idea has come to me. I am certain you have heard of the American evangelist D. L. Moody. The newspapers are full of him and news of so many giving their lives to the Lord as a result of his powerful preaching. He is scheduling his first mission to Scotland in a few months. As one of Glasgow's leading ministers, my father will be involved to the extent he is able. In all his missions, Rev. Moody calls upon local Christian volunteers, many of them students, to help in his missions—with crowd control, organization, ushering, counseling, and distribution of literature and material, follow-up, and so on. If I decide to apply to law school, it will be a year or more before I would begin.

Therefore, I am seriously considering joining my cousin Henry, who shares my family name of Drummond, in becoming a volunteer for the Scotland Moody mission. He is about our age, and I know you would like him. They need women volunteers as well as men. It has occurred to me that it would provide a good opportunity for you and me to grow together in our spiritual lives, while participating in a worthy endeavor for the kingdom of God. By working side by side in such an environment, we would strengthen our spiritual bonds and perhaps be in a stronger position to discern His will for our future together.

As I went to the home of my aunt and uncle at a time of uncertainty in my life, what would you think of coming to Glasgow, where you would be welcome with my parents for as long as you liked, and joining me in working in the Moody mission? I think it would be...

Florilyn set the letter aside without reading further. She had read the whole thing once. But now on her second time through, she had had enough.

The day was a warm one. She had come outside to read the letter on one of the garden benches. She glanced up from where she sat to see Colville Burrenchobay riding up the drive. She had been expecting him.

He dismounted, tied his mount, and walked forward and sat down beside her. "A serious expression," he said, glancing at the handwritten sheets in her hand. "Bad news?"

"No," answered Florilyn with a light laugh. Her tone carried a hint of lingering annoyance from what she had been reading. "Just a letter from Percy."

"Ah, right...your Scottish cousin. So how goes the engagement?" probed Colville.

"It's off. You knew that. Why else would I be seeing you?"

"I thought...his writing you a letter...that perhaps the two of you had kissed and made up."

Something resembling a snort sounded from Florilyn's lips. "Hardly," she said without trying to hide her sarcasm. "I don't think Percy is interested in making up." She handed Colville the letter then rose and walked about the garden to work off her agitation.

Colville could hardly believe his good fortune. He had been subtly trying for weeks to learn how things stood between Florilyn and her erstwhile fiancé in order to more shrewdly plan his own strategy. All at once a letter from the young Scot had unexpectedly fallen into his lap. He read in haste lest she change her mind about wanting him to see it. "Sounds like a bit of a religious fanatic, what?" said Colville after two or three minutes, tentatively feeling which way the wind of Florilyn's reaction might be blowing.

Florilyn did not reply.

"Is that true," he added, "what he says about you and he trying to find, what did he call it. . .God's will?"

"That was the idea," replied Florilyn noncommittedly.

"About what?"

"Whether He wanted us to get married."

"What about what *you* want?" asked Colville.

"We're supposed to want what God wants."

"Well, I don't!" laughed Colville. "I want what I want. Life would be no fun if everyone went around trying to think what God wanted them to do."

Florilyn shrugged.

"You don't really go along with all that, do you?" he asked.

"I thought I did," sighed Florilyn.

"Where does your cousin get those ideas anyway?"

"His father's a minister."

"I guess I heard something about that. Still, he seems pretty young to be so religious. You don't really want to marry a fellow who's going to be a gray-haired old church mouse by the time he's forty. What if after you were married he decided to become a minister?"

"Actually he was thinking about that very thing."

"There, you see. I would keep clear of a bloke like that."

"Not to worry. He's decided to study law instead."

"Hmm. . .a lawyer with religion—an interesting combination. Still, what's this mission thing all about? Who's the fellow Moody?"

"Just what he says—an American evangelist."

"A hellfire preacher?"

"I suppose."

"And he wants you to join him in helping get people saved. Ha, ha, ha!" laughed Colville. "That's priceless. Florilyn Westbrooke, evangelist. Ha, ha!"

Colville's laughter grated on Florilyn and made her uncomfortable. But she said nothing further and quickly changed the subject.

Fifty

The Announcement

When Percy had not heard from Florilyn for two weeks, he began to grow concerned. Several more letters followed from Glasgow to Llanfryniog with the same result.

In north Wales, Percy's letter to her sent Katherine into a fresh round of anxiety. She realized that in all likelihood Percy would not be returning to Westbrooke Manor anytime soon. Everything in her cried out to write him to implore him to come. But how could she? As things stood between Percy and Florilyn, Percy was hardly the one to tell Florilyn to stop seeing Colville unless he planned to marry her himself. She had not even told Edward and Mary about the change in Florilyn. From two or three comments Florilyn had made, she knew that at present Percy's stock had dropped considerably in her daughter's estimation. She more than half suspected the cause.

Meanwhile, events moved inexorably toward their inevitable conclusion. Katherine Westbrooke's house continued to rise on the plateau overlooking Mochras Head. Colville Burrenchobay and Florilyn Westbrooke continued to spend most days together. It was only a matter of time before their engagement would be announced.

Christmas was approaching. Edward and Mary invited Katherine and Florilyn north for the holidays. Florilyn said she was not interested in seeing Percy, or any of them for that matter. Katherine did not want to leave her alone to spend Christmas at Burrenchobay Hall. She silently feared she would come back to discover that her daughter was engaged or, worse, had married Colville hastily in her absence.

Christmas was a strained affair at Westbrooke Manor, certainly nothing like the gay celebration of giving of a year before. Courtenay was gone. Florilyn was moody and anxious to be off to Burrenchobay Hall. Colville called for her shortly after eleven. Christmas dinner at the manor began quietly. Katherine's immediate family had now dwindled to one—herself. The thanksgiving in her heart, however, though tinged with sadness, was genuine. She had around her a staff that loved her, and Adela and Steven now seemed truly like her own family. She asked Steven to pray.

Florilyn spent the rest of Christmas day with Colville's family. A great feast was held at the hall in honor of the occasion. As she did frequently these days, Florilyn stayed over in what the whole family now called "Florilyn's room."

On the following morning, even before Florilyn had returned to Westbrooke Manor to tell her mother in person, the great Boxing Day news was all over Llanfryniog that on the previous evening at Burrenchobay Hall, the engagement had been announced of Florilyn Westbrooke to Colville Burrenchobay.

Part Three

Treasure of the Celtic Triangle

1874

Fifty-One

News from Ireland

D. L. Moody had arrived in England in June of 1873. He was unable to generate much interest in his evangelistic method by the local clergy. In his first meeting in York, he spoke to a congregation of eight. Over the following weeks, gradually attendance increased. However, the numbers remained small. The ministers of York continued cool and unsupportive toward the American.

From York, at the invitation of two interested ministers, Moody and his musical partner, Ira Sankey, traveled to Sunderland then to Newcastle. Though criticism continued from the English clergy, in Newcastle five ministers offered their chapels for meetings. Gradually a groundswell of interest began to grow.

But it was not until Moody and Sankey crossed into Scotland that Moody's evangelistic messages exploded upon the public. Scotland's centuries-old spiritual vitality immediately responded to Moody's challenge. From the first meetings held in Edinburgh in November, no building in the city was sufficient to hold the enormous crowds. The watch-night service on the last day of the year continued for five hours. Moody's farewell address to Edinburgh was held in early January of 1874 on the slopes of Arthur's Seat. From Edinburgh, Moody traveled to Dundee then to Glasgow where the story was much the same. Hundreds of local volunteers were kept busy with the thousands who responded to Moody's evangelistic call.

After working for a Glasgow law firm through the winter, Percy joined his cousin Henry to participate with the Moody mission when the evangelist arrived in Glasgow.

From Glasgow, Moody's meetings continued in Scotland as he traveled to Perth, Montrose, Aberdeen, Inverness, and finally all the way north to John o' Groats. In Aberdeen, it was estimated that up to twenty thousand attended the meetings.

Though Percy volunteered only for the Glasgow meetings, his cousin traveled with Moody for several months, during which time a lifelong friendship between young Drummond and the American was formed. During all this time, Percy did not visit Wales again.

A day at length came when Katherine could keep silent no longer. She finally asked Florilyn when she intended to tell Percy of her engagement to Colville Burrenchobay.

"I don't know, Mother," replied Florilyn testily. "Why would Percy care? He had the chance to marry me, didn't he? I'm twenty-three. I need to get on with my life and stop waiting for him to figure out what God wants him to do. What about what I want? I probably won't tell him at all."

"I was twenty-five when your father and I were married," rejoined Katherine. "It's not such a bad thing to wait a few years."

"I've waited long enough, Mother. I intend to marry Colville and maybe be the wife of a parliamentarian one day. That's what he says. It's better than being the wife of a roving evangelist. I can't think of anything worse! Percy's so changed from the man I thought I was in love with."

Katherine knew further expostulation was useless. It pained her to hear Florilyn speak so. Percy was not the only one who had changed. Colville's influence on Florilyn had been anything but healthy. Katherine shrank from telling Percy of the engagement herself. If only he were in Wales. Yet with Florilyn's attitude toward him so soured, what could even Percy do now? She only hoped something happened to intervene between now and the lavish summer wedding being planned for Burrenchobay Hall.

Steven was no less concerned than Katherine. He had considered writing Percy in Glasgow so that he would at least know how far Florilyn had sunk. His conclusion, however, was that his interference would probably only make the situation worse. Whatever change was to come had to come from within Florilyn herself.

What a grief it was to these two who loved her—the viscountess and her young factor—to see what the evil influence of one who did not love the truth had been able to work within Florilyn's heart and mind.

And thus as the weeks lengthened into months, the Drummond household in Glasgow had no inkling of the developments in North Wales. While uncertainty reigned at Westbrooke Manor, a letter arrived at the vicarage in Glasgow in late February with Percy's name on the envelope. Percy did not recognize the hand. The postmark was from Ireland. Motivated as much from curiosity concerning his failed quest as from the knowledge that Courtenay Westbrooke's twenty-fifth birthday was only three weeks away, he tore at the envelope with fumbling fingers, pulled out two blue sheets, and read:

My dear Mr. Drummond,

Though we have not spoken since you were in Laragh last summer inquiring after the O'Sullivan and Maloney families in your search for your uncle's antecedents in Ireland, I hope you will forgive my presumption in writing you and, for lack of a better phrase, taking matters into my own hands.

Your plight remained on my mind after you left me. Perhaps it was the earnestness of your desire to find the truth and do the right thing. It has been my experience that there are many who claim to love truth but are not quite so committed to doing the right thing—to following truth even when to do so becomes uncomfortable. Truth can be but an intellectual exercise if it is not empowered by an obedient heart determined to do the right thing. I knew that your heart hungered not only for truth, but also for right.

At length I took it upon myself to send out a brief letter through the priestly grapevine of eastern Ireland to inquire whether my brothers of nearby parishes were acquainted in their congregations with the names O'Sullivan or Maloney, or even Westbrooke, the other name you mentioned. That was before Christmas. I heard nothing until recently. Then I received a reply from a priest in Arklow who has a woman named Vanora Maloney in his church whose husband works in the shipyards. I told him briefly the reason for my inquiry and asked him to make discreet inquiries. It turns out that these Maloneys indeed at one time lived in Laragh and relocated with his family and mother-in-law, one Maighdlin O'Sullivan who is no longer living.

The names would hardly seem to be coincidental. Perhaps these are indeed the people you are looking for.

Hurriedly Percy scanned the remainder of the second sheet.

I wonder if you are following the work in your country of Rev. Moody. I believe he is planning to visit Ireland after leaving Scotland. The "Camp Meeting Revival" style is not what most Catholics are drawn to. I must admit, however, that I admire the man, and he is certainly a positive force for the kingdom of God in the world. Perhaps it would not be an altogether bad thing if more Catholics took their faith with the same personal ardor that evangelicals do. I have considered writing a book, trying to urge my fellow Catholics in that direction. The title Catholicism Renewed *continues to reverberate in my brain.*

But all that is a matter left for another discussion in the event we have the opportunity to meet again. But if we do not meet again in this world, perhaps we shall have that discussion in the next!

I am,
Sincerely yours,
Father Robert James Halliday,
Laragh Parish, Wicklow
Ireland

Excitedly Percy ran into the breakfast room where his parents were enjoying a last cup of tea together. "Mom. . .Dad," he said still holding the letter, "I have to go back to Ireland!"

"I take it there have been developments?" said his father.

"Possibly huge ones! I will tell you everything when I am able. But for now, as I told you before, I can say no more than you already know." He turned to leave the room.

"Where are you. . . You're not leaving now?" said his mother after him.

"I'll go down to the P & O office to see when there is a sailing for Dublin," replied Percy. "But yes, I will be on the first available ship. I'll stop by the law firm. They won't have a problem doing without me for a week."

Fifty-Two

Arklow

Percy did not write to tell Father Halliday of his plans. A letter would in all probability reach him no sooner than he would in person. When he walked into the small, dimly lit church, however, the priest did not seem surprised to see him.

"Ah, Mr. Drummond," he said with a warm smile. He strode toward Percy with outstretched hand. The two shook hands affectionately. "I had a feeling I would see you again! You must have left the instant you received my letter."

"I sailed a day later," said Percy. "It was the first ship I could make."

"I take it you think it possible the people I mentioned are the ones you are looking for?"

"There is no way to know for certain. I hope it will be possible to speak with them."

"I was so sure that you would want to investigate further that I wrote to Father Abban to expect us."

"*Us?*"

"I thought I would take you down, and we could both meet him together. I asked him if he might be able to discover whether there was a young girl in the family of his parish. Where are you staying?"

"Nowhere," laughed Percy. "I just arrived."

"Then you shall stay here with me tonight," said Father Halliday.

"I have a small guest room next to my quarters. We shall ride down to Arklow tomorrow."

The ride of fifteen miles south through the hills from Laragh in Father Halliday's one-horse buggy took most of the following morning. They arrived in the shipbuilding port of Arklow about midday. Even had Father Halliday not been familiar with the town, the church would not have been difficult to find. Its spire rose prominently over the stone buildings of the place. They found Father Abban in the rectory behind the church eating lunch.

"Robert!" he exclaimed when he opened the door to their knock. "How good to see you again!"

"And you, John," replied Father Halliday as the two priests embraced. "It has been too long. We must keep closer in touch. But may I introduce you to Mr. Drummond," he said, turning and drawing Percy forward. "He is the young man who has been looking for the people I mentioned."

"I am happy to meet you, Mr. Drummond," said the priest, who was himself a young man not more than six or eight years older than Percy.

"Thank you. The pleasure is mine," said Percy, shaking his hand.

"Come in, please. . . You must have had a long ride. I just sat down to lunch, and my housekeeper prepared enough for an army. You can join me. The teapot is still steaming."

The three went inside and were soon sitting at the table.

"After your letter, Robert," said Father Abban, "last Sunday I tentatively spoke to Mrs. Maloney. I broached the subject of whether a girl had accompanied them from Laragh when they left with Mrs. O'Sullivan. She nodded and said that it was her sister's daughter. They had helped her mother care for the girl after her sister's unexpected death."

"Then she must be the girl I am looking for!" said Percy with obvious enthusiasm.

"You are assuming that they are the same people."

"The coincidences seem too remarkable to be otherwise. What else did you learn?"

"Nothing really. Daibheid walked up then, the woman's husband. He told her to say nothing more. He seemed agitated. I probed a bit and asked if my sermon had somehow upset him. He is a tempestuous man. I have had to confront him about his temper on several occasions. He said he did not want people asking about a past they were trying to forget. I glanced at Vanora. She gave me a helpless look that said she would tell me more if she could."

"What is it all about, John?" now asked Father Halliday.

"I really don't know," replied Father Abban. "There are things from the past he does not want talked about. I think they must concern their niece."

"Do you think Mrs. Maloney would talk to me?" asked Percy.

"If she was alone. . .perhaps. If her husband found out, he could be furious. I would have to think long and hard before I allowed myself to be party to going behind his back. Is the matter truly of such importance?"

"I believe that the girl, the Maloneys' niece, may be the rightful heir to a sizeable estate, as well as a title, in North Wales," replied Percy. "The task of finding his daughter was entrusted to me by the late viscount, Lord Snowdon, shortly before his death."

"What is your personal interest?"

"Lord Snowdon was my uncle. For reasons of his own, he entrusted to me the facts of his first marriage, and the birth of a daughter, to one Avonmara O'Sullivan of Laragh, who died in childbirth. He told no one else of these things before he died. He asked me to do what I could to find his daughter."

"And if progeny could be proven, she would inherit. . .as a woman?"

"As far as I understand it, yes," replied Percy. "The terms of the original viscountcy were established such that the eldest, or his or her offspring or their issue, would inherit both estate and title irrespective of gender."

Both priests pondered his words a moment.

"I see," nodded Father Abban at length. "Your quest is based on no idle curiosity. Much indeed is at stake." He paused and drew in a thoughtful breath. "Under the circumstances," he nodded after a moment, "it would seem that we have no alternative but to see what we can learn further. I will arrange a visit with Vanora Maloney when her husband is at work. If the facts seem to warrant it, we will of course have to confide the nature of our inquiry to him as well."

Fifty-Three

A Family Grief

Percy and Father Halliday waited at the church while Father Abban paid a visit to the Maloney home. He returned within the hour to say that his request had been crowned with success—Vanora Maloney agreed to meet with Percy. Only they must be gone well before evening when her husband returned from work.

"What are we waiting for!" said Percy, jumping to his feet.

"After your long journey, I thought you might find it best to wait a day and rest?"

"I need to find the girl as soon as possible."

The two priests and their new young Welsh friend left the rectory by foot a short time later. Ten minutes later they approached a stone house set in the middle of a long row of attached dwellings. Father Abban led the way to the door. The other two stepped back as he knocked.

Moments later the door opened, revealing a woman who appeared in her middle to late fifties. Percy's eyes immediately went to her head of bright orange hair in which was mingled evidence of the approach of white.

"Hello again, Vanora," said Father Abban. "As you can see, we decided to come soon. We thought it best to get this behind us."

The woman smiled, though nervously as she glanced behind her own priest toward Percy and Father Halliday, then opened the door and gestured for them to enter. She led them inside. They sat down in a small but comfortable sitting room.

"Thank you for agreeing to speak with us, Vanora," began Father Abban. "I realize this is awkward as long as Daibheid does not want these things talked about. But Mr. Drummond here has convinced me that the matter is of great importance. When the time comes, I will speak with Daibheid. He will know that you only agreed upon my urging."

Mrs. Maloney nodded, again glancing uneasily toward the other two.

"So let me introduce my two friends," he said. "This is Father Halliday, priest in Laragh, where you were born I believe, isn't that correct?"

She nodded.

"Father, this is Vanora Maloney."

"I am pleased to meet you, Mrs. Maloney," said Father Halliday.

"Is Father O'Leary still living?" she asked.

"Yes, he is," replied Father Halliday.

"If you see him," said Mrs. Maloney, attempting another smile, "would you give him my greeting. We should have told him where we were going and why we were leaving."

"I will indeed. I am certain it will make him happy to know that you remember him."

"And this young man is Mr. Percival Drummond," Father Abban added, now turning toward Percy. "He is from Wales and came to Ireland last year hoping to locate your sister's daughter. At last finding where you are living, with Father Halliday's help, he hopes that you will not mind answering his questions. Mr. Drummond believes that he is the nephew of your sister's husband."

"Hello, Mrs. Maloney," said Percy, rising from his chair and extending his hand. "I very much appreciate your agreeing to see me."

She nodded, again forcing a nervous smile.

Percy resumed his seat.

"I don't know what I can tell you," said Mrs. Maloney. "It's been years since we left Laragh."

"The first thing is simply to confirm that your sister was indeed Avonmara O'Sullivan?" asked Percy.

Mrs. Maloney nodded.

"The same Avonmara O'Sullivan who married Roderick Westbrooke?"

"I believe that was the man's name."

"And they had a daughter?"

Again she nodded. "Her name was Morvern," she said. "But whatever happiness there might have been at her birth was short lived. My mother and I both knew, for we were at her side through the birthing, that Avonmara was weak. She had never been strong, you see. All her life she was not sickly exactly, but not strong. Though she was two years older, I was bigger and taller and stronger and faster from the time we were wee lassies. We both had bright carroty hair just like our mum, though mine's starting to fade, you see," she added, running a hand over her head. "All the O'Sullivan women had bright red crops, you see. But Avonmara was a beauty. Even frail like she was, there was a mystery about her. She was a quiet girl. When she looked at you, and smiled her mysterious smile, her eyes went straight through you. When the young Welshman came, he was smitten with her. And she was taken with his good looks and flair. She was too young to marry. Mother warned her. But Avonmara was in love, and she said that when love comes, you couldn't wait. You couldn't think that love would come again if you didn't take it when you had the chance.

"Those were hard times in Ireland. Our family wasn't poor, you see. We weren't of peasant stock, but times were hard for everyone. I don't know what the man told her about himself or if he thought he would take her away somewhere, but we all thought he had money and he told her that she would never want for a thing. So she didn't listen to anyone's cautions. She married the man, though she was but eighteen. He didn't take her away, and we were happy about that. They stayed there in Laragh, though I don't know what he did. He never seemed to work, but they had all they needed. When Avonmara knew that she was to be a mother, she was so happy. For a year she was happier than we'd ever seen her. Mother and Father began to think perhaps they had misjudged the man. He seemed to be a good enough husband. But then as her time drew near, I knew she was weakening. Her face was pale, and she did not put on the weight she should. Her face and cheeks were thin. I knew Mother was worried, too. She never spoke about it, but I could see it in her face. Then little Morvern was born, with a healthy crop of O'Sullivan orange hair, but within a day poor Avonmara was gone." Mrs. Maloney took a deep breath and looked down. She blinked hard, and her hand went to her eyes.

The three men waited.

"It didn't take long for us to know that Mum had been right about her husband," she went on after a moment. "For all his dash and good looks and all the rest, he fell apart. He hardly kept control of himself at the funeral. Maybe it showed how much he loved her, but he wasn't much of a man about it. Naturally Mum and I took care of the baby. That went without saying. She was Mum's granddaughter and my own niece, and Avonmara's husband was just a boy of twenty himself. What could *he* do to take care of a child? He didn't even give her her name, didn't attend the christening at the church. We would not see him for days at a time. Then came a day when he came to the house and told my mum that he was leaving Ireland, that he had to go home to see about his father. He promised to return when he was able to take care of the baby. But we never saw him again. That was the last time any of us ever saw him." Again she stopped, her hands folded and her eyes in her lap. Reliving the grief from the past had clearly not been easy.

"I am very sorry for the pain you and your family suffered," said Percy after a moment. "As Father Abban told you, Roderick Westbrooke was my uncle. He died a year ago. Among his last thoughts were reminders of your sister, his first wife, Avonmara—"

"So he remarried, did he?"

"Yes, ma'am," nodded Percy. "I am his nephew by his second marriage."

"What is his wife's name. . .his second wife?"

"Katherine, Mrs. Maloney. She is my aunt. But as I say, he was thinking, too, of your sister, for she was the love of his youth. He asked me to try to find her family—you and your mother, though I understand she is now gone, and of course his daughter. He hoped I would be able to convey something of his sorrow at having deserted you all after Avonmara's death. He was full of remorse for leaving as he did. I realize that is small consolation, but he wanted you to know. He also wanted you to know that he eventually returned to Laragh and made considerable effort to locate his daughter. But he could not find where you had gone." Percy pulled from his pocket the envelopes addressed in his uncle's hand both to her mother, Mrs. O'Sullivan, as well as to herself. He handed them to her.

Slowly she looked at them one by one then smiled sadly. "So he came back after all, did he?" she said. "I am surprised. . .but maybe not altogether surprised. He *did* love her—that much was plain. But it came too late to do his daughter much good. She never saw her father in her life."

"I know, Mrs. Maloney," said Percy. "I feel the sadness with you. But perhaps it is not completely too late for him to be a father to her. . .in a manner of speaking. I don't know how much of my uncle's background your family knew. I don't know what he told Avonmara and your parents. But my uncle was an important man. There is not a great deal of money involved. But more than money is at stake. Your niece Morvern, if we can prove that she was indeed his daughter, would be my uncle's firstborn. The terms of the inheritance are independent of gender. A daughter can inherit as well as a son. That is why I must find her. She is in all likelihood the heir of my uncle's estate."

Mrs. Maloney stared back at Percy with a blank expression.

"That is why I urged Father Abban to ask you to allow me to speak with you. So where is the girl now?" asked Percy. "I realize by now that she is a grown woman. Does she live around here?"

"Mr. Drummond. . . I thought you knew."

"Knew what?"

"I am afraid Morvern is dead."

Fifty-Four

A Bargain Struck

Early that same morning, Courtenay Westbrooke saddled his mount and set off on the northern road to meet his future colleague and business associate at a small hotel in Bronaber on the north-south inland road through the region of Gwynedd. It was a ride of fifteen to eighteen miles. Though Bronaber was a small and out-of-the-way village, Litchfield had wanted to stay in close proximity to his upcoming acquisition.

In two weeks, thought Courtenay with satisfaction, he would finally and officially be known as the Viscount Lord Snowdon. There was no need to pretend any longer or play what petty games had been necessary to keep his plans from his mother. His sale of the land to Lord Litchfield would be finalized the day following his birthday. He had therefore given Litchfield leave to begin moving equipment into the area in order to begin constructing the road into his new property. His mother could do nothing to stop them now.

Thus it was, as Percy Drummond sat in the home of Vanora Maloney in the shipbuilding center of Arklow on the eastern coast of Ireland, that on a remote corner of his late uncle's estate in North Wales, his cousin and the mining entrepreneur, Lord Coleraine Litchfield, along with several assembled experts from near London, made their way through the remote hills of Snowdonia. Courtenay still had no idea of Litchfield's ultimate ambitions. Litchfield merely identified his colleagues as construction consultants.

It was the prior-arranged responsibility of Litchfield's assistant, Palmer Sutcliffe, to engage Courtenay sufficiently in conversation, drawing him away from the rest, that Litchfield and his "consultants" might confer more easily with the scruffy man beside him, most of whose teeth were gone and who had apparently made no acquaintance with a razor or a bar of soap in a good while. As they went, Litchfield made pretext of looking about as though with nostalgic thoughts of his boyhood while considering the best potential location for a home in the Snowdonian mountains. He was not, however, thinking of the scenery but rather about the fortune that lay beneath it.

As yet, young Westbrooke had no idea of the exact location where his surveyors had been seen several months before. He preferred to keep it that way. The less the young fool knew, the better.

Coming into the grassy valley that lay in the hollows of the ridge adjacent to the lake, which was his object of interest, Litchfield reined in and dismounted. The others of the party followed his lead.

"Ah, yes," he exclaimed, "it is just as I remember it!" He began walking about, to all appearances considering the most suitable options for a building site.

In the distance, the sudden sound of many hooves interrupted the tranquility of the scene. They turned to see a dozen or fifteen horses galloping up the far ridge and out of sight.

"What are those?" exclaimed Litchfield.

"There are wild horses all throughout Snowdonia," replied Courtenay.

"Who do they belong to? They were magnificent!"

"Don't get any ideas," rejoined Courtenay. "The horses on any of this land are mine. They roam everywhere, but that gives you no rights if they come onto your thousand acres."

"Whatever you say," laughed Litchfield. "Horses are not my business."

"Mr. Westbrooke," said Sutcliffe, walking up to Courtenay's side, "I realize you were interested in seeing the proposed site for Lord Litchfield's mountain retreat. However, might I propose that you and

I now return to the hotel and go over the final documents together?"

"I thought the documents were finalized," said Courtenay.

"To be sure. . .yes, mostly they are. There remain just one or two details to be ironed out."

"Can't they wait until the final transfer is to take effect?"

"I fear not, Mr. Westbrooke," said Sutcliffe. "Everything must be in perfect order so that the transfer occurs the day after your assumption of the title. There is also," he added, "the matter of an additional payment."

"What additional payment?" asked Courtenay.

"Since we are so close to the final date of closing the transaction, Lord Litchfield thought that he might advance you an additional payment toward the agreed-upon sum. I have a check for one thousand pounds made out to you at the hotel."

"I see. . . Well, in that case," said Courtenay enthusiastically, "I suggest we get back and iron out those details you mentioned. . .and perhaps add a clause that excludes rights of horseflesh."

Litchfield smiled to himself as the two returned to their mounts. There were times, he mused, when Palmer Sutcliffe was worth every penny he paid him!

The moment they were out of sight, he walked back to his own horse. "All right," he shouted. "Let's get on with it."

Twenty minutes later, the party of four men arrived at the high overlook. Below them the waters of a small green mountain lake glistened in the sunlight.

"All right, Bagge," said Litchfield, inching his mount beside his scruffy crony, "it's time for you to keep up your half of the bargain. I want to know exactly where that gold came from that you showed us in Cardiff."

"There was some mention in our recent negotiations," said Bagge in a gravelly voice, "of two hundred pounds."

Litchfield smiled. "You are a sly one, Bagge. What? Don't you trust me?"

"I trust nobody. *Would* you pay me if you knew what I know without needing me no more?"

"Of course, Bagge. I am a man of my word."

"That may be, or not—I don't really care. But you get nothing more from me until I see the two hundred pounds."

Litchfield nodded, smiled again with condescending humor, then reached inside his coat. He pulled out ten crisp new twenty-pound notes—more money than Foulis Bagge had ever laid eyes on in one place in his life. He handed it to him.

With wide, greedy eyes, Bagge clutched the notes in his fist then held them to his leathery, hairy lips and kissed them. "You'll get what you paid for all right," he said. "It's down there, under the lake."

"What do you mean *under* it?"

"There's a cave. Nobody knows the entrance but me. It's where the gold came from. It was the year of the big draught, in '57. I used to know these hills like the back of my own hand. I found the cave when the water was low and the lake was nearly empty. That's when I found the gold. When I came back for more, the rains had begun again, and the lake had filled the cave. I've been coming back for years. But it's no use for the likes of me—I'm no fish. The gold's there, but the lower parts of the cave are filled with water."

Litchfield nodded and glanced at the two men who had been listening behind him.

"It's plausible enough," said one of them to his expression of question. "Of course it means we'll have to drain the lake or stop up its entry into the cave. But it's possible."

"All right then, Bagge," said Litchfield. "Lead the way. I want to see the entrance to this cave of gold. Once I am satisfied, you can keep the two hundred pounds and go to the devil for all I care."

Fifty-Five

End of the Quest. . .or Perhaps Not

Percy stared back dumbstruck at the sister of his uncle's first wife. "*Dead?*" he repeated, hoping he had not heard her correctly.

Mrs. Maloney nodded.

Slowly Percy shook his head dejectedly. "I guess that's it then," he said. He let out a long sigh then glanced at the two priests. "I suppose my search has suddenly come to an end," he said. "I had hoped that I was about to find my uncle's daughter. At least now I know. . .and I can put my uncle's past to rest once and for all."

Again he turned to Mrs. Maloney. "I hope you won't mind telling me what happened," he said. "After that I promise I will pester you with no more questions. You have been most kind, but I would like to know what happened."

"I see no reason not to tell you," she replied. "You have come a long way. Even if we had no use for your uncle, that is not your fault. I suppose you deserve to know."

She took a breath, again remembering the past, and resumed her story. "As I told you, we never saw Morvern's father, your uncle, again. Morvern grew up. Eventually I married my husband Daibheid. My father died, but my mother continued to keep Morvern with her, though we lived nearby and I helped with her on most days when she was young. But my Daibheid, you see, he wanted children of his own.

He said it was no business of ours to take her in. So she remained with my mum. We had a son. He was born when Morvern was five. Then the famine hit, and my husband was out of work. My papa was gone by then, and my mother had nothing. Daibheid had worked in the shipyards for a time, before we were married, you see. So we all left Laragh, Mum and Morvern and Daibheid and me and our little Nigel, and we came here to Arklow. We had to do something to keep from starving. Daibheid found good work again, and we've been here ever since."

Again she paused. "It wasn't until Morvern was eighteen that the trouble started again."

"Trouble? How do you mean. . .*again*?"

"She seemed fated to go the same way as her own mother. She was beautiful, you see, just like her mother, only tall and with the same bright red hair. But then she met a Welshman just like Avonmara. He was a good man, I suppose, and a hard worker, but we all hated to see our Morvern involved with a man when she was still so young. Morvern was all my mother had by then, you see, and she was just like Mum's own daughter. Mum never let her use your uncle's name. She was just Morvern O'Sullivan. My poor mum, God rest her soul, she cursed your uncle for deserting his daughter, though maybe that wasn't right now that you tell me he tried to find her. But she died hating him, which is a sad thing to say about any two people in this world."

She glanced again at the letters she still held in her hand, again smiling sadly to see her name and her mother's name on the envelopes. "We never knew, you see—never knew he was trying to find us. . .that he wanted to be a good father to her after all. How could we know? We were gone by then, you see. It might have been different had we known. But we didn't know. Then Morvern met the other Welshman, you see, come over for the work in the shipyards, just like my Daibheid. They met at work, you see, and were friends for a time. But when he took a fancy to young Morvern, my mum said it boded no good. But young Morvern was determined to marry him, just like her mother had been to marry your uncle. The mother and daughter were just alike, you see, young and beautiful and swept off their feet, you might say. So Morvern married the man, and my mum was terrified for what would happen. My mum was always one for premonitions, you might say. By then Mum's red hair had turned as white as snow, as mine's doing now, you see. And when Morvern came to be with child just like her own mother, Mum was dreadfully afraid the same fate would befall her as had poor Avonmara. There was a midwife in Arklow at that time. She was a strange woman, too acquainted with evil some said. Mrs. Faoiltiarna was her name. Whether that was her real name or not, no one knew, but it could not have suited her more perfectly."

"Why do you say that?" asked Percy.

"The name means Wolf Lady, and that's what she was. She made it her business to know other people's secrets, and she parlayed them into power over them, and she listened to such folk that other people would have nothing to do with. My mum was one, as she got older, who was too much taken with the peculiarities of life, you might say. My Daibheid said no good would come of it, but Mum insisted that the midwife attend the birth of Morvern's baby. She thought maybe the woman's strange powers would be able to fight off the power of death she was convinced was hovering over our family, trying to destroy us. My Daibheid and Mum argued fiercely over it and yelled at one another like mortal enemies, though one was my own mother and the other was my husband. Daibheid insisted the woman was evil. He said that to bring her into the house would portend no good. And Morvern's young husband, he agreed with Daibheid. But in the end, Morvern let her grandmother decide the matter, for she was the only mother she had ever known, you see, and she could do no other than to trust her. So the midwife was called in, and Morvern gave birth to a daughter."

"A daughter!" exclaimed Percy, his hopes suddenly revived.

"Aye, but not one you'll be wanting to find, I'm thinking."

"Why do you say that?"

"The instant Daibheid laid eyes on her, the first words out of his mouth were that the curse of the Wolf Lady's evil had come to the family. He was more furious at my mother than ever. After that he wouldn't let me or our Nigel see Morvern or her baby or her husband or my mother.

He was a devout man, you see, my Daibheid. He was certain there was evil afoot. He wanted nothing to do with the little girl or any of them anymore. As the weeks passed, then months, his words seemed to be confirmed."

"In what way?" asked Percy.

"The baby was strange from the start. In her eyes was a look from another world. Daibheid didn't want me to have anything to do with any of them. He called the midwife a witch. He said she had passed her evil into the family. But when he was at work, I couldn't help myself, you see, for I am a woman, and they were my family, you see—my mum and Morvern and her child. But Daibheid told people about her otherworldly look and her strange ways, and before long, you see, there was talk and dreadful things began being said about us. All at once Morvern's husband told my mum he was taking his wife and child and they were leaving Arklow. My mum was both heartbroken and furious at once, but she had brought it on herself with all the talk of evil forebodings and bringing in the midwife to the birth. The little man was a good man, you see, and he knew the evil such rumors about his child could work. He didn't want our family hurt by them either. So he took Morvern and the child away, and we never saw Morvern again. A year later, my mum received a letter from him telling her that Morvern was dead. Mum never recovered. It was a family curse, Daibheid said. Mum lived no more than a year after that. It was the midwife, Daibheid said. She was the cause of it. She was an evil that would mean the death of us all."

"Why did people call on her services?"

"She knew every birthing that was coming and wormed her way into their homes. People were afraid of her, that she would put a curse on them or work some other devilry. But eventually her evil ways caught up with her."

"What happened?"

"There was a man whose wife was about to give birth—you remember, Father," she said, glancing toward Father Abban, "Mr. Keefe, from the shipyards."

The priest nodded.

"When the woman came oiling around, he would have none of it," Mrs. Maloney went on. "He told her never to show her face around his house. There were threats and high words. She was enraged. No one had dared refuse her so publicly. He was an important man, you see, and everyone knew that he had rebuked her to her face. She shouted some incantation back at him then said that a gruesome and premature death would come to him. He laughed back in her face. No fat purple witch could tell the future, he said."

"She claimed to be able to see into the future?"

"It was one of the ways she made people fear her."

"Why did he call her a *purple* witch?"

"She always wore purple, and with horrid earrings of snakes and ugly creatures. But their argument, you see, took place outside the man's home. She shrieked terrible curses at him as she stormed off. The whole neighborhood heard her. Within days, what had happened was all over town, that he had called her a witch. Rumors began to circulate that her strange ways had all along been rooted in close connections to the dark forces of the underworld. And when poor Mr. Keefe died suddenly a year later, the charge of witch confirmed for all to see, some of the men of the community began devising a way to get rid of her."

"You mean kill her?"

"That may have been what they intended. Daibheid would never tell me. But she got wind of it and suddenly disappeared, fled for her life. Nobody ever saw her again, and no one was sorry. Morvern's daughter was the last child she delivered in Ireland. Daibheid said a curse was on the girl because of it. Even when she came back, though she was our own kin and my own sister's granddaughter, he wouldn't let us have anything to do with her."

"What do you mean, when she came back? Who came back?"

"Morvern's baby, my own niece—though she's grown into a woman now, of course. I haven't laid eyes on her myself, but I've spoken with them who have."

"She is back in Arklow?" said Percy.

"Not in the town. In the hills to the west, I believe. I don't know her exact whereabouts."

"I need to find her."

"She is not of this world. She is not one your uncle would want to claim as his own."

"But if she is his heir, as Morvern's daughter, then I must find her. She must know it."

"They say she is one of strange ways. There is truth to what Daibheid has always said, that evil has followed her because a witch brought her into the world. But when she is married, I hope to see her again. She is to be married soon, you see. There are those who know, and they tell me about her because I am her aunt."

"Do you know when the marriage is to take place?"

"In a week, I believe, though her husband-to-be is an older man in his thirties and she is still young."

"I must talk to this girl."

"I can't tell you where to find her even if I dared. All I can tell you is what I hear, that every Sunday morning, rain or shine, her habit is to climb to the top of Lugnaquilla, unless it is covered in snow. No one knows why."

"Lugnaquilla—what is that?"

"It is the highest mountain in County Wicklow. It is inland and north, about fifteen miles from here. It is easily visible on a clear day. As she goes, they say the girl plucks wildflowers along the path. They say she gathers them into a bouquet and leaves them at the top."

"There would not be many flowers at this time of the year."

"They say if there are no flowers, she makes her bouquets of weeds and grasses."

"What is the name of the mountain again?"

"Lugnaquilla. It is most often known by the name given to its peak."

"What is that?"

"It is called Percy's Table."

Percy smiled. *An interesting coincidence,* he thought. He had not known that he had a mountain named after him in Ireland!

The room fell silent.

"It seems that perhaps it is time for us to take our leave, Vanora," said Father Abban. "We do not want to presume on your kindness. I know you are concerned for the time."

Mrs. Maloney smiled, again nervously, and nodded.

"Thank you very much, Mrs. Maloney," said Percy as they rose. "I appreciate everything you have told me. You have been most helpful."

"And have no worries, Vanora," added Father Abban. "When the time comes, I will speak with Daibheid."

"Thank you, Father."

The three men walked toward the door.

"Oh," said Percy, pausing and turning back to Mrs. Maloney, "I meant to ask about this before when you mentioned it, but it slipped my mind. What did you mean when you said that the instant your husband laid eyes on Morvern's baby, his first words were that the curse of the woman's evil had come upon the family? Was it because of what you said about the look in her eyes?"

"No, not her eyes. That couldn't be seen until later, until she began to look about and you had the uncanny feeling she was seeing into you."

"What was it then?"

"It was her hair, you see."

"What about it?"

"All the O'Sullivan girls that anyone can remember had red hair, the girl's mother and grandmother, my sister and myself, and her great-grandmother."

"But Morvern's baby did not?"

"That's why the sight of it struck fear into my Daibheid's very soul. The moment she was born, the child's hair was white as my Mum's, you see."

Fifty-Six

The Heart of the Factor

Steven Muir was beside himself.

The primary source of his anxiety was not Courtenay's imminent assumption to the viscountcy and the loss of his job. He was worried neither for himself nor his mother. The house on Mochras Head, Katherine had already assured him, would contain quarters for them both, and their employment was assured. If Lady Katherine went to her brother's in Glasgow until its completion, a dozen or more homes in Llanfryniog or the surrounding hills would happily take him in, and his mother, until that time.

His anxiety was rather for Lady Florilyn. The thought of her marrying Colville Burrenchobay was so odious in his mind as to have rendered him physically sick for two weeks.

Steven's feelings were born in no petty human jealousy but rather in a lifelong acquaintance with the eldest son of Gwynedd's parliamentarian. He knew something of what Burrenchobay was. He had also gained more than a passing glimpse of what Florilyn *could be* and was on her way to becoming. That *was* and that *becoming* could not be united without one of the two destroying the other.

Light and darkness cannot coexist. One must be extinguished in the triumph of its opposite. God will triumph. Sin will be extinguished from the universe.

But the light that had been newly growing in Florilyn was not strong enough to illuminate a soul so consumed with itself as that of Colville Burrenchobay. A tender growing human plant can too easily wither in the overpowering presence of one who is far too pleased with himself. Nothing is so lethal to the need to "become" as self-satisfaction. Falling under the spell of his alluring blandishments, Florilyn was not even aware of the thousand subtleties by which he encouraged her to nourish the self rather than kill it. Like her ancient Mother of Life, she had eaten of the fruit, so pleasing to the eye. And it had done its work.

Though he had not been an intellectual standout at Cambridge, Colville Burrenchobay was bright enough instinctively to know that to control her he must divide Florilyn from her past. Nothing accomplishes that end so readily as feeding pride, while offering tantalizing innuendos of derogation against any and all who were part of that past.

Steven hoped, however, that what he thought of as the "new Florilyn" was not altogether dead yet.

But what could *he* do to reawaken her? He had again become as nothing in her eyes. What had seemed a genuine friendship blossoming between them had evaporated as if it had never been. To all appearances, she despised him. Whether this was due to Colville's whispered lies into her willing ear or from a deeper change in her own heart. . .he had not inquired too deeply. Indeed, perhaps the two were not so very different. That her ear had proved willing to listen to his subtle disseverations and gradually accept them as her own, perhaps revealed as much about her own insecurity as it did Colville's motives to lure her away from all former affections.

The evening was late as Steven stood at his window. The countryside of Wales glowed in the pale light of a full moon coming in and out from behind turbulent clouds in the night sky. It had rained most of the afternoon. Though the storm had passed inland toward England, its windy retreat was still evident overhead. The tumultuous sky mirrored the turmoil in Steven's own soul.

He had never paused to analyze his feelings for Florilyn to their depths. As a youth he had merely noticed her from afar and felt a strange sense of protectiveness over her. Hired by her father, then her mother, and brought into sudden and daily proximity to the family, his devotion had been as a servant who desired her best and sought to serve. That deeper feelings occasionally stirred within him, he took as merely a natural response of the human animal. He attached no great significance to them. That she had begun to reciprocate his friendship, that they had been able to laugh and talk together, these moments he treasured as among the manifold privileges of his job, but little more.

All the feelings—had he been another sort of young man, or from a higher social standing, that he might have looked at more closely and questioned where they might possibly lead—were subserved in his consciousness to the love that Florilyn had once carried toward his friend, Percy Drummond. Even the suspension of their engagement he assumed was but temporary. He considered nothing to be gained by it for himself other than the continued opportunity to serve his young mistress.

From the very day Florilyn began seeing Colville Burrenchobay, however, something new awoke in the heart of Steven Muir. A giant was born in the gentle young man. He knew what it was. He loved her more deeply than he had allowed himself to admit. But with the realization came the horrifying thought that his love might be born in jealousy toward Colville. If such were true, he would give Lady Katherine his notice and leave this place and never lay eyes on Florilyn again. Nothing was more hateful to him than even the merest possibility that he might succumb to such an evil emotion as jealousy.

And yet. . .was his concern for her future only for *himself*?

No, he knew it was not. He cared for *her* and desired her *best*. For her best, he would turn and walk away. Likewise. . .for her best he would come against any threat to her well-being. Not to possess her, but that the true Florilyn might emerge victorious over the Florilyn that Colville would attempt to control. Though she never laid eyes on him again, though she might hate him, he must still do his *best* for her and try to prevent her making a terrible mistake.

But how? What was his responsibility? How was he to do right for her, to do his best for her? How could things be set right again in Florilyn's life? Could *he*, such as he was in her eyes, assist in such a setting-right? What was he to *do*?

For several more minutes he stood gazing out upon the windy night. He was too agitated to sleep. At length he turned, lit a small candle, and left his room. With quiet step he crept through the darkened corridors of the great house. A few minutes later, he found himself at the doors of the library. However strange it may seem for the hired servants in a house of ancient title and property to have full access to such regions, it was Lady Katherine's will that everyone connected with Westbrooke Manor, from lowest to highest, consider the library his or her own personal region of dreams, rest, escape, retreat, learning, study, and imagination. Anyone might borrow any book or use the library at any time a schedule permitted.

As quietly as he could, he opened the double doors and swung them back wide enough to enter. His mother and Lady Katherine were forever talking about the author MacDonald. He was an avid reader himself, but his tastes in recent years had tended to run in different currents than were found in fiction. He knew what they all said, that MacDonald's fiction was unlike any other. The only thing of MacDonald's he had yet read himself was his volume of *Unspoken Sermons.*

He went to the shelf and stood before it. Everyone in the house by now knew where the MacDonald books were located. It was the most frequently used part of the library, and its contents grew yearly. Randomly he pulled out one volume after another, flipping through each, allowing his eyes to rest on one passage or another, hoping perhaps to discover some nugget of written gold buried within the pages between the decorated boards. . .something that would illuminate his way in this dark hour of his soul.

For half an hour he tried one book, then another, then another, returning to several a second, even a third time, also flipping slowly through his own favorite book of MacDonald's sermons.

He had nearly begun to despair when suddenly his eyes fell on a passage whose words seemed to compel him, even as they spoke of the compulsion of God's love toward the setting right of wrong in human life.

> " '*He will set it right, my lord,*' " he read, " '*but probably in a way your lordship will not like. He is compelled to do terrible things sometimes.*' "

The words arrested Steven's attention as if he had been struck in the face. That God would be *compelled* to do terrible things toward those he loves was a concept altogether new. He continued on.

> *" 'Compelled!—what should compel him?'*
> *'The love that is in him, the love that he is. He cannot let us have our own way to the ruin of everything in us he cares for!' "*

The words perfectly described exactly what he had been thinking about Florilyn—that she must not be allowed to have her own way to the ruin of everything good that had been growing in her.

Steven's eyes continued down the page.

> *"Then the spirit awoke in Donal—or came upon him—and he spoke.*
> *'My lord,' he said, 'anything I can do, watching with you night and day, giving myself to help you, I am ready for. It will be very hard, I know. I will do all that lies in me to deliver you. I will give my life to strengthen yours, and count it well spent and myself honoured. I shall have lived a life worth living! Resolve, my lord—in God's name resolve at once to be free. But one thing you may not have, my lord, is your own will. You will never be free by seeking your own will, until you make your will his.' "*

With a finger between the pages, Steven took the book and candle to one of the library's reading chairs and sat down. He turned to the beginning of the chapter and read it in its entirety in order to gain more of the context of the passage that had drawn his attention. Before he retired for the night two hours later, the book lay on the table in his own room. He had completed its first fifty pages before sleep overtook him.

The single word *compel* remained with him in sleep. By the time he awoke the following morning, his way had begun to become clear. If love required *compulsion* to do what was best for the beloved and set things right, then he would not shy away from it.

Fifty-Seven

Lugnaquilla

Percy was at the base of the mountain called Lugnaquilla shortly after daybreak on the following Sunday morning. He had been given directions and a map by Father Abban, along with precautions of the mountain treacheries if a thick morning fog or afternoon mist off the sea obscured his way.

The priest invited Percy to remain with him in Arklow as his guest for as long as his business made it necessary. He had been with him for three days, during which time the two young men had had many lively and informative discussions on matters of faith—discovering more points of commonality and brotherhood than either would have anticipated. In the meantime, Father Halliday returned to Laragh.

According to Father Abban, any of a half dozen sheep tracks and walking paths led to the summit of Lugnaquilla. Bogs and boulders and cliffs and ravines, however, were everywhere, and one must be attentive and vigilant. Having not the remotest idea from which direction the mystery girl he had heard about from Vanora Maloney came up the mountain on her weekly trek or when, Percy resolved to be at the top as early in the day as possible. He would remain until sunset if need be so as not to miss her.

He dressed warm and, at Father Abban's insistence, had packed food and water. Father Abban took him to the base of the mountain by buggy shortly after sunrise then returned to town for his weekly priestly duties presiding over Sunday's scheduled masses. As he began the assent, in his right hand Percy clutched one of his new friend's stout walking staffs.

The way gradually steepened as he went. He made his way across boggy fields and meadows, through light woodlands bordered by a few thickly forested glades and hillsides, up and down dells and valleys, jumping a dozen small brooks and watercourses, and sloshing through several chilly, frothing streams whose waters plunged down to meet the Avonbeg River where it flowed around the base of the mountain toward the sea.

Next to one of these, his step was arrested by an unexpected sight. It reminded him that death was slowly relinquishing the earth from its temporary prison, and that the Son of liberating spring was on its way to set the captives free. So near his foot that his step nearly crushed it, in the shadow of a large stone, the tiny yellow face of a new spring primrose peeped up at him from amid its rough cabbage-like leaves.

The sight of the simple blossom stung him with nostalgic reminders of many things—both conscious and subconscious. . .of Hugh Sutherland and Margaret Elginbrod and the fir wood of their story, of Florilyn and Snowdonia's green hills, of sunrises and sunsets and high overlooks above the sea, of angels and mysteries and floral bouquets. He paused, set down his staff, and stooped to pluck it. He stood again, drew in a deep breath of satisfaction, and slowly continued on his way.

It was not an especially steep or arduous climb. As he had been forewarned, however, he found his way long and circuitous and filled with many tracks and paths that appeared promising but that led nowhere or ended abruptly at the edge of some ravine or cliff. Thankfully, though the ground was wet, the day was relatively clear. No thick fog topped the mountain, though clusters of mist clung here and there to some of its low-lying valleys. Thus, it was after many retracings of his steps, as the spring sun rose high in the sky and began to send down what warmth it possessed in this first week of March, perspiring freely in spite of the chilly morning air, that Percy at last approached

Lugnaquilla's expansive flat summit that had been given his own name, "Percy's Table."

What he had expected, Percy himself could not have said. Reaching the top of the three-thousand-foot hill and finding it desolate and empty, without hint that another human being was within miles, filled him with a vague sense of disappointment.

He stopped and gazed about. Slowly he turned in every direction until he had peered into the distance toward all the 360 degrees of the compass. A few clouds of mists obscured visibility here and there. But the sea, east toward Wicklow fifteen miles distant, was easily visible stretching out to his right and left.

He strolled aimlessly about for a few minutes then found a dry bit of grass and sat down. He began his wait with an apple, a hunk of cheese, a piece of bread, and water from the canvas bag of provisions provided him by Father Abban. For the first time he now regretted that he had not thought to bring a book from the well-stocked library at the rectory.

He had arisen for his day's quest while it was yet dark. The walk had been easy enough, but the cumulative effect had fatigued him. After his brief breakfast, with the sun beating down and warming earth and humanity as one, it was not long before sleepiness began to overtake him.

Percy stretched out on the grass and began to doze.

Fifty-Eight

Percy's Table

The walker whose weekly habit for two years had been to make this solitary trek did not often encounter fellow sojourners at this time of year. Heart and mind were free to wander where they would without distraction or interruption.

Her thoughts on this day, as always, were of the one she came here to remember with the tiny bouquets that would be meaningless to any other. Her mind was filled, too, with the great change that was soon to come upon her. She would not long be able to continue this weekly habit. She had set out this morning knowing that today's journey would likely be her last. She would be married in two weeks. As another man's wife, she could not continue paying tribute to one from her past whom she would never see again.

The one to whom she had been pledged was a good man, and she must be a good wife to him. Love found easy reception in her heart toward all of God's creation. She could love, and therefore she *would* love. Her father had chosen him for her, in spite of the difference in their ages, because he knew he would be a caring husband for his daughter. She honored her father. And thus she would learn to love.

But on this day, one last time, her love would look back, not forward. . .and she would remember.

There came a breath of something in the west.

Percy stirred from where he lay, half rose, and looked about.

What had awakened him? No hint of wind caressed his face, unusual on such a peak as this. But some rustling, some far-off sound, some *presence* had intruded into his brain.

He sat. . .listening intently. It seemed that all the world was waiting in stillness for something at hand.

It came again.

Percy froze. A chill swept through his body.

A faint, far-off tune came floating up the mountain from somewhere. Someone was singing, but in no voice of this world. The sound was of some melancholy lament. . .haunting, mysterious, as from some ancient Celtic love ballad whose ethereal melody remained forever unresolved.

Slowly he rose to his feet, searching to detect from which direction it came.

As she softly sang, the walker stooped to grasp a handful of spring grasses and added them to the earthy bouquet clutched in her other hand. If this was indeed the last bouquet she would leave in memory of the one who lived in her heart, she was sorry it contained no flowers. But spring was still early, and she had seen none today.

She rose again to continue to the summit. As she did, she saw a figure ahead. The sight startled her.

A man stood in the distance staring at her.

Abruptly her singing stopped. It must be a vision, born in her imagination. She gazed at the figure in disbelief then slowly walked toward it.

A gasp escaped Percy's lips.

The rays of the sun, falling on the girl's head from behind, gave it a radiant golden hue. But as she came nearer, he saw that the wild crop of luxuriant hair was of purest white.

He stood transfixed. He could not move. He could only stare in wonder.

Closer she moved, gliding noiseless over the ground. Every line of her countenance came into focus, and he knew he was gazing at no mirage.

The *eyes*. . .deep blue-green. . .eyes that spoke of the sea! Changeable . . .depthless. . .radiant. . .liquid. . .alive with the light of life.

The *face*. . .the same, yet new. . .older, wiser, if possible more beautiful, full of mystery. . .and at peace.

The angel of his dreams had materialized as from out of Lugnaquilla's mists. Was she indeed, as he once said, an angel from on high? Had she always been an angel?

As he beheld her features, seeing them for the first time in more than three and a half years and now contained in a woman's face, suddenly all the eyes from the portraits on the landing at Westbrooke Manor leaped out at him. The truth had been in plain view all along. How could they not have seen it!

She slowed then stood before him.

"Gwyneth!" he breathed in a reverent whisper. "Is it. . .can it be. . .is it really *you* I have been searching for?"

For answer, she merely took another step forward, the smile on her face saying that somehow she did not find it incredible that the weekly vision she cherished in her heart had become real.

Percy opened his arms and swallowed her into his embrace. "I cannot believe that you are here," he whispered.

"I am always here, Percy," Gwyneth said. "In my heart, I am always with you."

They stood long minutes in silence. Or perhaps it was an hour. On the top of Percy's Table, for these two, time would nevermore have meaning. They were swallowed up in eternity.

"Until you spoke, I did not know if you were real," said Gwyneth at length. "I always see you when I come here. But the real you is older than the you of my imagination."

The spell was undone. She was the same Gwyneth of old!

Percy stepped back and broke into the laughter of pure joy. The sound of his happiness ringing out over the hilltop was as enchanting to Gwyneth as her mysterious voice of song was to him. She broke out in a giggle of delighted girlish pleasure.

"Here, Percy," she said, handing him the bouquet of weeds and grasses. "I picked these for you."

"Surely you meant them for someone else?" said Percy with a humorous smile.

"I come here every week and leave you a bouquet, Percy."

"Surely you don't give flowers to every stranger you meet."

"Only those who are going to become my friends," rejoined Gwyneth with a smile of her own.

"You knew that about me?"

"Of course."

"How did you know?"

"I saw on your face the look of a friend."

Again Percy laughed with delight to be reminded of their first meeting on the hills of Snowdonia. He turned and stooped to find the faded primrose where it had slipped from between his fingers when he had fallen asleep. "And I have something for you," he said, handing it to her.

"A new spring primrose! Oh, thank you, Percy!"

"Gwyneth, Gwyneth. . . I cannot believe it! But it really *is* you, isn't it?"

"I think so, Percy. I think I am me. Have you been in Wales?"

"Several times since you left. I visited your cottage. No one is living in it now. You will never guess who I saw—Bunny White Tail!"

Gwyneth smiled. "It was hard to leave the animals. I still do not understand why we had to leave. But my father said there was no other way. I know there was something he did not tell me. But I trust him to know best."

She glanced away. An expression crossed her face that Percy had never seen before. Then she looked earnestly back into his face. "Are you and Florilyn. . ." she began then hesitated.

"No, we are not married, if that's what you were about to ask," said Percy. "But I hear *you* are to be."

Gwyneth smiled and nodded. She had tried to hide it, but Percy saw that her heart was filled with complex emotions at the prospect. "My father thinks it best," she said. "He wants me well taken care of when he is gone. Oh, my father!" Gwyneth exclaimed as if suddenly remembering. "He will be so happy to see you!"

"Yes, and there are things I must talk over with him as well," nodded Percy. "Where do you live?"

"Just down the slope, in one of the dells along the side of the mountain. My father raises sheep now. We have a fine house, and he has a large flock. I think he is happier now than when he worked in the slates. Come, Percy," she said excitedly, taking his hand and beginning to run off down the mountain, "I will take you to him!"

"Wait, let me get my things!" laughed Percy. He quickly returned a few steps for the knapsack and staff then hurried after her.

Fifty-Nine

Factor and Son

As Gwyneth skipped merrily down the slope with Percy chasing after her, back at Westbrooke Manor, Steven Muir had sent through one of the housemaids in his mother's charge the request to Courtenay in his apartment, where he knew him to be at present, that he would be grateful to see him in his office at his earliest convenience.

Steven knew it would rankle Courtenay thus to be summoned as if *he* were the servant and Steven his master. In all likelihood it would ensure that the ensuing interview began in a combative tone. But he had done so intentionally. It was necessary to establish his authority, even if but briefly, to demand from Courtenay what the viscount's son would never condescend to give him by simple request—a straight and honest answer to a direct question. In other words, the truth.

Courtenay walked through the open door of the factor's office without benefit of knocking or announcing himself. He was breathing fire. "What is the meaning of this, Muir!" he demanded, striding angrily across the floor where he stood glaring down at Steven behind his desk. "Let us get one thing clear—you do not summon *me*! If you have business with me, then you come find me. I am not your lackey. I had been considering keeping you on after I am viscount. But if there are more incidents of this kind, I will turn you out on your ear without notice, and your mother with you. Do I make myself clear?"

Steven sat calmly staring into Courtenay's eyes until he had finished his rant. Slowly he rose, walked from behind the desk and across the floor, closed the door of the office, then returned where he stopped and faced Courtenay. "Please sit down, Courtenay," he said in a soft voice, gesturing toward one of two chairs.

"Did I not make myself understood?" rejoined Courtenay. "I will not have you telling me what to do!"

"Courtenay, please," repeated Steven. "Just sit down. I would like to speak with you about a serious matter."

"I have no intention of speaking to you about anything, Muir!" Courtenay shot back. "Now get out of my way before I dismiss you on the spot."

He took two steps toward the door. But he did not take a third. With a swiftness and strength of which he scarcely guessed the other capable, he found his shoulders clasped helplessly between Steven's two huge hands. As if he were a rag doll, he was unceremoniously thrown back and shoved down into the chair he had a moment earlier been invited to take under his own power.

Courtenay's face glowed crimson. "How dare you lay a hand on me, Muir!" he cried, his eyes flashing fire as he leaped to his feet. "You will pay for that!"

Even as a clenched fist shot toward Steven's face, his arm was arrested in mid-flight by the vice-grip of Steven's right hand. Courtenay stood glowering, though obviously powerless. Steven squeezed his arm then slowly twisted it and pushed backward until, with a cry of pain, Courtenay fell back again into the chair.

"You could have broken my arm!"

"I would have been sorry had you forced matters that far," said Steven. "I told you I wanted to talk to you. You and I *will* talk, with or without your cooperation. You took the whip to me once, and I did not defend myself. I had my reasons. But do not mistake me, Courtenay. I know something of your strength, for I have been watching you for years. I also know my own. I could put you on the ground without raising so much as a bead of sweat. You fancy yourself a powerful man, but I fear you no more than I would a ten-year-old. So I suggest we have our talk, that you answer my question, and that you go your way. It will be simpler for us both if you cooperate."

"What do you want, Muir?" said Courtenay in sulking fury.

"I have a simple question to ask, and I want a simple answer. Are you the father of Rhawn Lorimer's child?"

"Go to the devil, Muir."

"I will have to ask you for directions. Now I put you the question again—are you the father?"

"And I give you the same answer I gave you before. I will tell you nothing."

Standing before him, Steven drew in a breath then turned and paced about a few moments.

Courtenay's eyes darted toward the door. For a brief instant he considered trying to end this humiliation by making a dash for it. But he did not relish the consequences if he failed. Nor was his pride fond of the notion of running away like a frightened child.

"You will be viscount in what, nine or ten days," said Steven, turning again toward him. "Not that you may care about your reputation either in the community or the House of Lords, but there may come a time when what is said of you will be of some consequence. If you do not tell me, I will let it be known that you refused to answer me. You know what people will assume."

"I will tell them that *you* are the father of the Lorimer brat."

A smile spread across Steven's face. "Do you seriously think anyone would believe that?" he said. "To make such a charge would only convince everyone all the more that you are the guilty party. On the other hand, if you deny it and I learn you are lying, and if that is the case I *will* find out. . .I promise you that it will go worse for you than had you confessed honorably to the truth from the beginning. You have only one choice, Courtenay. That is to tell me the truth. If you are the father, and you tell me plainly, I will respect your honesty and pursue the matter no further."

Even in his fury at finding himself powerless before this clod-hopping interloper of a factor, Courtenay was yet in sufficient awe of his calm demeanor and measured tone that he did not for a moment doubt that he would do exactly as he said. He knew something of the esteem in which Steven was held throughout the community. He was practical enough to realize the consequences of crossing him. "I am not the father," he answered after a moment.

Steven nodded then walked back behind his desk and sat down.

"I presume that is all, Muir?"

"Yes. Thank you, Courtenay."

Courtenay rose and stood a moment. "You may consider this your notice, Muir," he said. "You are hereby terminated. I want you and your mother gone from the manor by six o'clock on the morning of the seventeenth, which is my birthday. Is that understood?"

"Very clearly."

Steven watched Courtenay go, more sad than angry, then took out a sheet of writing paper, set it before him, and took pen in hand.

Dear Percy, he began,

We are only days from Courtenay's birthday and his assumption of the viscountcy. However, that is not the reason I am writing, but rather about a crisis concerning Florilyn. I do not know if you have been apprised of recent events—her engagement to Colville Burrenchobay. My own concern for her well-being and future mounts daily. She is much changed—and I am heartbroken to have to say, not for the better. The spiritual being that had begun to blossom, under Burrenchobay's influence, is fast becoming a withered flower and a mere memory of happier times. I am writing to implore you to return for the purpose of speaking to her and warning her of the danger of being joined for life with such a one.

We are two men who love her. We cannot allow this to happen without speaking forthrightly to her. I do not want to act without you, but I fear time is critical. Every day that passes she seems to slip deeper into what I am convinced is a deceptive attempt to woo her affections and distance her from her mother and the rest of us.

Please consider my request seriously. The matter is urgent. Please come.

Your friend and servant,
Steven Muir

Sixty

The Viscount, the Miner, and the Scot

As they approached down one of Lugnaquilla's projecting ridges, Percy saw that the new Barrie home was indeed a fine one, easily twice the size of their former cottage in Wales. In the distance, the diminutive figure of Codnor Barrie was surrounded by several sheepdogs and a huge, moving mass of white.

They walked toward the shepherd and his flock. He saw them coming and turned to meet them.

"Look who I found on the mountain, Papa!" exclaimed Gwyneth, as they made their way into the midst of the flock.

Barrie's face held its perplexed expression but a moment then brightened into a huge smile as recognition dawned.

"Mr. Drummond!" he cried. "How do you come to be here?"

"It's a miracle, Papa," said Gwyneth simply. "I think an angel led him to us."

"Gwyneth may not be far wrong, Mr. Barrie," said Percy as the two shook hands. "I would rather say that God led my steps, and I *found* an angel."

Gwyneth glanced away shyly.

Barrie looked back and forth between the two and understood. "Do you and I need to have a talk, Mr. Drummond?" he said.

"We do indeed, sir," replied Percy.

Beside herself with curiosity about what the two were saying, Gwyneth's sense of the propriety of things kept her from intruding. She walked quietly toward the house, pausing once at the door to glance back.

The two men, the younger towering over the older, walked slowly away across the field, heads as close as their difference in height would allow. They were obviously engaged in earnest conversation.

Her heart full of many things she dared not think, she watched them a few moments more then went inside.

An hour later, from where she stood at the window, Gwyneth saw the two returning.

Her father's face wore a serious expression. He nodded occasionally as Percy spoke.

She stepped back from the window.

As they came nearer the house, Percy noticed above the door a beam of oak into which were carved two words in Gaelic—the house name, he presumed. Though he could not read them, they seemed somehow familiar. He had no leisure to think about it, for a moment later Barrie led him through the door and into the spacious sitting room.

"Grannie!" Percy exclaimed as he saw the old woman sitting across the room in a positive fever of anticipation for whom Gwyneth had told her was coming.

She scarcely had time to pull herself up before finding her aging frame nearly crushed by Percy's embrace. "Aye, laddie," she said, "you're as big and strong and handsome as I knew you must be!" she said. She pulled his head down toward her and kissed him on the cheek.

"And you, Grannie!" said Percy exuberantly. "You look well indeed."

"For an old woman of eighty-eight years, I'm just grateful enough to the Lord for keeping me here long enough to feast my eyes on your face one more time."

"Oh, but Grannie," said Percy excitedly as he released her, "I just remembered. I have something of yours!" He reached into his pocket and pulled from it the gold coin she had been given on the sands of Llanfryniog more than eighty years before. He held it toward her.

"No, no, laddie!" she said. "That night when I told you how I came by it, and the evil that had stalked me because of it, I said I wanted it no more. I gave it to another to keep. But I'm thinking it wasn't you."

"You're right," smiled Percy. "Perhaps it is time I returned it to her." He turned toward Gwyneth where she stood watching. "You gave me this for safekeeping," said Percy. "I told you at the time that I would always consider it yours. I have carried it with me every day since. Not a day went by that I did not think of you. It remained with me as an unspoken pledge of our. . .of a friendship that I treasured. You are a grown woman now. It is time I returned it." He held the coin to Gwyneth.

Her hand reached out, and he placed it in her palm. His fingers lingered briefly upon hers. She felt a sudden heat rising in her cheeks. She pulled her hand away as it closed over the coin and glanced away.

"But why have you come, laddie?" said Grannie as she eased back into her chair. "How did you find us?"

"It is a long and intricate story, Grannie," replied Percy as he and Codnor also took seats.

Gwyneth moved toward the kitchen at the far end of the room and put a kettle on the stove for tea.

"It concerns my uncle, the viscount," began Percy. "He had a riding accident a year ago, and his injuries were mortal. He died a week later."

"God bless the man—I am sorry to hear it."

"On his deathbed he asked me to do something," Percy continued. "He asked me to find someone that no one else in his family, not even my Aunt Katherine or Florilyn or Courtenay, knew about. Then he told me a story he had told no other living person in more than thirty years." Percy paused and drew in a breath.

By now Gwyneth was seated with the rest of them. She and Grannie listened intently as Percy told them what he had already told Gwyneth's father—of his uncle's sojourn in Ireland as a young man, of his marriage to Avonmara O'Sullivan, and of the tragic circumstances that had followed in which he lost track of the daughter that had been born to him. "It was this daughter, whom he had never seen again," said

Percy, "whom I thought he wanted me to find."

"But if he was dying," said Gwyneth, "why would it matter so much to him?"

"Because according to the terms of his viscountcy, she would be his legal heir, not Courtenay."

"But she was a girl, laddie," said Grannie. "How could that be?"

"Every peerage is unique," explained Percy. "They are established according to terms that must be legally followed in perpetuity unless the peerage is abolished. The particular viscountcy my uncle inherited from his father must originally have been established by a progressive and far-seeing man who determined that a firstborn daughter, and her own children who followed, was equally deserving of the rights and privileges of the title as a son. I have been studying law, you see, Grannie, and I looked into it as much as I was able. It is extremely unusual, but those are the terms. No doubt it will ultimately have to be decided in court. But my uncle was certain enough of the legality of the terms to commission me, as I thought, to find his daughter. He knew she was the rightful heir by his first marriage."

"Did you find her, laddie?"

"I am afraid not, Grannie," replied Percy. He turned toward Codnor Barrie. "Perhaps you should explain the rest of it, Codnor," he said.

Barrie nodded. The others waited as he collected his thoughts then turned toward Gwyneth. "I always told you, lassie," he began, "that you were born across the water from where we lived—that you were born here in Ireland. But you never knew why I was here. There came a time, you see, when the mine in Wales had to close. Parliament was trying to improve on safety everywhere, and the labor movement was gaining strength. So they closed the mine to make changes and make working conditions safer than before. I was a young man at the time, not as adventurous as some but with my own share of the adventurous spirit. There was talk of work in the shipyards of Arklow on Ireland's east coast. So I came here for the work. In the shipyards, I met an Irishman who had come south to the town for the same reason when his family fell on hard times in the years before the famine. He had brought his family with him, though that was years before I met him, which included his mother-in-law and her granddaughter. The girl was the man's niece. She was a beauty, with bright red hair and white skin that looked like an angel's face, tall and slender. She stood five inches above me, and I fell in love with her. She was your mother, lassie, and she was the best woman in the world. Her name was Morvern." He paused and smiled sadly as he remembered. Slowly he sighed as he allowed his thoughts to linger fondly over the memory. Then he continued. "But Morvern's grandmother didn't like me," he said. "She did not want us to marry."

"Why, Papa?" said Gwyneth with the simplicity of a devoted daughter. "Who would not like you?"

"It was because I was a Welshman," Codnor replied. "Morvern's father, you see, was also a Welshman, and he had deserted them after she was born. That's why Morvern lived with her grandmother, because her own mother died when giving birth, and her father promised to come back to provide for her and take care of her but never did. Then they fell on desperate times, and she became yet more bitter at the father for leaving them in such straits."

"What did you do, Papa, if Mama's mother didn't like you?"

"Morvern and I married in spite of her," Barrie replied. "Maybe it was wrong. Perhaps we should have waited. I was young, and sometimes the young are not as wise as they think. But I determined to be the best husband and father a man could be and to win Morvern's grandmother over. I would prove to her that I was a good man and wasn't like the man who had married her daughter. I would provide for her granddaughter, and for her, too, if she would let me. A year later you were born, Gwyneth. But your white hair frightened people. They thought a curse was on you. It was only the curse of goodness, though that was the last thing they could understand. They began to say cruel things about you and about me. Even my friend, Morvern's own uncle, said that I had brought evil to their family. I couldn't let my wife and daughter be spoken of in that way. By then the mines were operating again in Wales. Morvern and I made plans to sail from Ireland and begin a new life in my own country where we would be free from people thinking evil of us. So you and I and your mother sailed for Wales. But a terrible storm came up in the Celtic triangle on the day of our sailing, and your mother was swept overboard—"

He drew in a shaky breath and looked away, wiping at his eyes. "I never forgave myself for sailing that night." He struggled to go on. "I was only twenty-five at the time, heartbroken with grief and left alone with an infant daughter. When we arrived in Wales, there was nothing I could do but try to make the best of it for you. If I had gone back to your Irish kinfolk, they would have hated me all the more for bringing Morvern's death upon her. The poor family—they lost two daughters who married Welshmen. What else could they do but hate the Welsh? So I stayed where we were. I tried to be a good father—"

"You were the best father a girl ever had, Papa," said Gwyneth, rising and going to him. She knelt beside him and took his hands in hers.

He gazed down upon her, his eyes full of tears. "That's all I knew of it, lassie," said Barrie after a moment. "I tried to be a faithful man, and I sent what money I could to Mrs. O'Sullivan, who was your great-grandmother, until I was sent word that she had died. But I never heard anything from her or the rest of the family after that. You grew up into a fine girl. The other children were cruel to you, but you made the best of it, with Grannie's help. I doubt it's done you any harm. For the sticks and stones of hurtful words injure us no more than we let them. And like Grannie always told you, they make us into better people if we use them to learn to forgive."

"They did not hurt me, Papa."

"Then came a day," Barrie continued, "when I received a surprise visitor at the cottage. It was the viscount, Lord Snowdon himself. He asked if he could speak with me privately."

"I think I remember it," said Gwyneth. "I was with my animals behind the cottage. I thought he had come for his rent."

"The rent was the last thing on his mind that day," her father went on. "I invited him inside, and we had a long talk. He was curious, he said, about my past. I didn't know why. He asked if I had ever been in

Ireland. I told him about my time there, that I had gone looking for work and had married there. He asked about you, Gwyneth. I told him you were born in Ireland. He asked my wife's name. I replied that it was Morvern O'Sullivan. He seemed taken aback but then asked me where she was now. I told him she was dead. He was silent for a time, then rose, thanked me, and left.

"I thought the thing strange but could make nothing of it. Then came another visit, three or four years later. Gwyneth, by then you were growing into a beautiful young woman and you were working at the manor for his wife and daughter. That's when the viscount came to me again when you were away from the cottage. He was more serious now. He spoke to me like we were old friends. He told me he had been thinking much about our earlier conversation. He now had something to confide in me that I must never tell another soul. I replied that I would agree so long as my conscience allowed. He nodded and added that he did not think what he had to say would place a constraint on my conscience. Then he proceeded to tell me about his own past, how he, too, like me, had gone to Ireland as a young man and had fallen in love with a red-haired Irish beauty. Her name was Avonmara O'Sullivan."

Now for the first time, both Gwyneth and Grannie recognized the name O'Sullivan. Their eyes widened as Barrie continued.

He saw their reaction and smiled. "I see that you remember the name," he said, nodding. "I was shocked as well. In what seems a remarkable coincidence, the child that was born to the viscount and Avonmara O'Sullivan was a girl called Morvern. She was, in fact, the very same Morvern O'Sullivan I had fallen in love with and married... my own wife...and your mother, Gwyneth."

The room was silent as Gwyneth sat absorbing the stunning fact.

"You cannot be saying...but does that mean," she said slowly, "that Avonmara O'Sullivan was *my* grandmother. . ." She paused, hardly able to bring herself to complete the thought. Unable to believe she was saying the words, she slowly added, "And Lord Snowdon was my grandfather?"

"That is exactly what it means, my child," said Barrie tenderly.

Again the room was silent as Gwyneth struggled to take in what he had just said. "I always thought he looked at me strangely," she said after a moment. "There were times I saw him in the village, and he simply stared at me."

"It was one of those occasions," rejoined her father, "that prompted his first visit to me. He suddenly recognized in your face the very face of his young love. It was after that he came to talk to me. As you grew older, and after you were at the manor and he saw more of you, the conviction grew on him all the more that her eyes, the eyes of Avonmara O'Sullivan, had been passed on to you."

"What happened to her?" asked Gwyneth seriously.

"She died when your mother was born. After her death, the viscount returned to Wales. He planned to come back for his daughter. But by the time he returned, she was gone from the village where her family had lived, and he never saw his daughter again. He was devastated over the guilt he felt at having waited too long. And then, when you were older, as I say, he came to me again. He had reason to believe, he said, that you were his granddaughter. That had been the reason for his curiosity about my past. Now he realized that he wanted to do something for you. But he could not openly acknowledge that he had had a child before meeting his wife, Lady Snowdon. He did not want to hurt her or jeopardize her standing in the community. He saw no need for his past to come out. If he was to do something for you, provide for you, in acknowledgment of his love for your grandmother and mother, he must do so in secret. He was not a wealthy man, he said, but he would give us what money he could. Only I must agree to leave Llanfryniog in secret, telling not a soul the reason or where we were going. He did not even want to know himself, he said. We must simply disappear. If I would agree, then he would provide the means for us to have a good life."

He paused briefly. "Some might say that he was trying to cover up a youthful indiscretion. There would even be some who would say that he was trying to blackmail me into silence about something he had kept hushed up for over thirty years. But I honestly felt the man to be sincere. He had no reason to confess all this to me otherwise. His heart was genuine. He wanted to do good for you."

He drew in a breath. "For better or worse," he sighed, "I agreed. I knew that he was offering what I could never give you. I knew also that none of us would outlive the occasional persecutions that came to us in Llanfryniog, though they had lessened over the years. I felt it my responsibility to give you both—you, Grannie, as well," he added, glancing at his great-aunt, "a life free of that if I could. And I had to think of your future when I was gone, Gwyneth," he continued, turning again toward his daughter. "Before he was through, the poor viscount was in tears. His grief was more than he could bear not to have seen his daughter again. By then the poignant reality was borne in upon me that I was in the presence of my own father-in-law. I was watching him weep at the memory of his first love and the daughter they had together. . .the very woman I had loved myself. He told me how he had gone back and tried to find his daughter. So I agreed to the terms of his offer. That's when I told the two of you that we were leaving Llanfryniog, but that we must do so without telling a soul. If I was wrong, may God forgive me, and may you forgive me, Grannie, and you, Gwyneth dear. I did what I thought was best for us all. So we set sail and returned to the land of my former happiness. It was the only place outside north Wales I had ever lived, the only other place where I felt I could make a home."

Barrie let out a long emotional sigh.

Sixty-One

Unexpected Weight of Duty

At length, unable to say more, Codnor Barrie glanced toward Percy.

"But then," said Percy, picking up the story again from the viscount's side, "when my uncle knew he was dying, apparently he changed his mind about keeping his connection with you secret." He paused as he looked at Gwyneth. "He wanted me to find you," said Percy. "If I could, he wanted the truth to come out at last and for right to be done."

"Find *me*?" said Gwyneth. "You said before that he asked you to find his daughter."

"I said I *thought* he wanted me to find his daughter," rejoined Percy. "His mind was wandering by then. He was occasionally confused. He seemed to have forgotten what your father told him, that your mother was dead. He confused you with your mother. All this time, I thought he wanted me to find his daughter, when actually it was you he wanted me to find, Gwyneth. It was *you* he was thinking of on his deathbed."

"Why would Lord Snowdon care about me?"

"For the same reason he came to talk to your father about you. For the same reason he wanted to provide for you."

"But he had already done so, and we were gone. Why did he want you to find me then?"

"Because when he spoke to your father, he did not tell him

everything," answered Percy. "There was one vital bit of information he kept from him."

"What was that?"

"He did not tell his daughter's *real* name," answered Percy.

"It wasn't O'Sullivan?"

"Avonmara's *maiden* name was O'Sullivan. But when she married, she became Avonmara Westbrooke. Your mother's real name was Morvern Westbrooke."

Grannie had been intently following the conversation. "They were married!" she now exclaimed.

Percy nodded. "In Laragh, north of here. The marriage is listed in the parish record book for 1833. . .between Roderick Westbrooke, the future Lord Snowdon, and Avonmara O'Sullivan. Their marriage made your mother my uncle's rightful heir."

"The Lord be praised!" exclaimed Grannie.

Gwyneth glanced back and forth in bewilderment between Percy and her father.

"Gwyneth, lassie," said Barrie, "that's why young Percy came looking for you. You are not only Lord Snowdon's granddaughter. . .you are also his heir."

"Your father is right," nodded Percy. "Your mother, Morvern, whom your father married as Morvern O'Sullivan but who was really Morvern Westbrooke, was the daughter of Avonmara O'Sullivan and Roderick Westbrooke. You are the daughter of his firstborn and his heir. So we have to get back to Wales without delay."

"Back to Wales. . .why?"

"Courtenay's birthday is in a matter of days. He is about to inherit the title and the entire estate. Once he does, it will be too late. It may have been to prevent Courtenay from becoming viscount, seeing what sort of man he was becoming, that prompted my uncle to tell me of his past and send me on a quest to find his rightful heir. Having found you, I must complete that quest."

"But I have no desire to take it from Courtenay," said Gwyneth hesitantly. "I am happy where I am."

"Of course you are," said Percy. "But there is your duty to consider. If this is indeed the fate that has fallen to you, can you neglect it? You little know to what Courtenay has sunk. He has threatened to turn my Aunt Katherine out of the manor. I believe you have a responsibility to your grandfather's wish. That was simply that you as his true heir, if you could be found, should inherit in place of Courtenay. I think he knew that you would do right for everyone, for the village, and especially for his wife. I do not think he believed that would be true if Courtenay became viscount."

Gwyneth was quiet several long minutes. At length she rose, walked slowly across the room, and left the house.

"The lassie's suddenly got much for her mind to weigh," said Grannie when she was gone. "She was always a thoughtful lassie. But she's never had a worry or care in her life. Now there's a great burden on her shoulders. She's got to be a grown-up woman. It's likely a fearsome thing for her innocent heart."

"What should I do, Grannie?" said Codnor, still not pausing to reflect what change Percy's revelation might bring to his own life.

"Let her be, laddie. She's been building strength into her soul for twenty years. It strikes me as likely that it's all been preparing her for this moment. She's a strong lassie and getting stronger, I'll warrant, even as we speak. She'll see her way through to what the Lord would have of her. When that time comes, nothing will stop her from the doing of it."

Though the water in the kettle had been boiling for twenty minutes, tea had long been forgotten in the rush of the conversation and Percy's startling words about the viscount's first marriage. As it now grew quiet, the practicalities of the corporeal man began to make themselves felt. The man of the house realized that for some time he had been aware of the aroma of mutton roasting in the oven. Grannie, too, seemed to notice it. Slowly she rose and walked to the stove. From the bin she took two handfuls of potatoes and plopped them into a steaming kettle of water.

"Where are you staying, Percy, lad?" asked Barrie.

"With the young Catholic priest in Arklow, Father Abban."

"When were you to return to him?"

"I made no arrangements. I said I would walk back into town."

"It is a long way. You have come down on the far side of the mountain. I will take you back when the time comes. So you must join us for Sunday dinner and the afternoon."

"Nothing could delight me more."

"Then come," said Barrie rising, "I will introduce you to my sheep and dogs while the potatoes are boiling."

They left the cottage. In the distance, Percy saw Gwyneth walking away from the house. She entered a small wood near their home and disappeared from sight. The two men continued toward the sheep.

Thirty minutes later, Codnor Barrie began a walk down the hill on an unexpected mission. As he did, Percy made his way toward the wood.

It was with a mingling of strange emotions that he felt himself closed up in the shadows of the tall firs and pines a few minutes later. He hardly considered the significance of the moment, for it was not at all by accident that Percival Drummond now sought Gwyneth Barrie in the fir wood. Deeper into its depths he went.

She seemed to sense his presence behind her, even before she heard his footsteps behind her. She stopped and turned.

Her heart leaped at the sight. But she was not surprised. For how could she wonder to see before her eyes the form of which her soul was full? She stood watching. . .and waiting.

Percy approached slowly. "Gwyneth!" he whispered then held out his hand to her.

She took it. They walked on amid the tall trees in silence.

"Are you in love with him?" Percy asked at length.

"He is the man my father chose for me to marry," replied Gwyneth.

"But are you in love with him?"

"I will learn to love him."

"But. . .if there was someone else. . ."

She dared not glance at him.

"Gwyneth," he persisted, "*if* there was someone else. . .someone who loved you with all his heart. . ."

Tears began to rise in her eyes.

"Gwyneth. . .*must* you marry him?"

"It is what my father—"

"I *do* love you, Gwyneth," said Percy. "I think perhaps I always loved you, though it took me some years to know it. I have spoken with your father," he added. "He is on his way now to your betrothed with a request to relinquish you. . .if such is your wish. He has given me permission to ask. . .if you would be *my* wife instead."

Sixty-Two

New Friends

Having written his urgent request to Percy, Steven Muir's anxiety was only temporarily relieved.

An unintentionally overheard argument between Florilyn and Lady Katherine, during which he heard the words, in a rude and angry voice, "old enough to marry without your permission. . .Colville says. . . perhaps not even wait until summer," was enough to convince him that he must delay no longer. To act was imperative. He might not hear back from Percy for a week, maybe two. It could be months before he was actually in a position to return to Wales. By then it would be too late.

After two more days, therefore, Steven sought his mistress in her quarters. "Lady Katherine," he said, "I have what might seem a strange request. Before I make it, I must ask you a question."

"Of course, Steven," said Katherine.

"I apologize if I am interfering in your personal affairs, but I would very much like to know if you are in favor of Lady Florilyn's marriage to Colville Burrenchobay."

"Need you ask, Steven?"

"I have some idea how you feel, Lady Katherine, but I must be certain nothing has changed."

"Nothing has changed. I abhor the very idea. As much as it is possible for a Christian to say such a thing, I fear I loathe that young man. The thought of Florilyn marrying him is disgusting to me."

Steven listened somberly. It was as he suspected.

"Sadly, she no longer listens to me," Katherine went on. "She cares not a feather what I think. There was a time when young people sought their parents' wisdom and counsel in the matter of marriage. Apparently that time, at least in this family, is long past. I cannot prevent the sense that Colville has been subtly prejudicing her against me."

"I think it is entirely likely," nodded Steven.

"Why do you ask?" said Katherine.

"Because with your permission, I would like to speak with Lady Florilyn."

"Do you think it would do any good?"

"Perhaps not. She is entirely changed toward me as well. But I must try. I am considering speaking to her with another whom she was also once close to. I would rather not divulge more."

"You have my blessing, Steven," said Katherine. "I will be deeply grateful for anything you are able to do."

Steven left his mistress and walked briskly to the stables. Within minutes he was on his way in the two-seater buggy into Llanfryniog. Fifteen minutes after that, the buggy sat on the street in front of the Lorimer home, and Steven was walking toward the door. Ten minutes after that, Steven was guiding the horse out of town with Rhawn Lorimer seated at his side, her son in the care of her mother. The question he must put to Florilyn's onetime friend required quiet and solitude.

He led about a mile inland, on the dirt track that led in the direction of his former home in the hills, then reined in. They sat a few moments in silence, taking in the view of the sea in the distance.

"I realize you do not know me well, Rhawn," Steven began. "There have been few occasions through the years where our paths have crossed. But it is my sincere hope that you will consider me a friend and will be able to trust me."

"Everyone thinks well of you, Stevie," said Rhawn. "If I did not know better, I would think you were the viscount now."

Steven laughed. "Hardly that! It is merely my wish to serve Lady

Katherine faithfully. I hope you will know that it is from that same heart of service that I requested to speak with you."

"I know that, Stevie. Even though you and I have never been close friends, I know there is not a selfish bone in your body. What do you want to talk to me about?"

"Your son, Rhawn," replied Steven. "I need to know who the father is."

The bluntness of his statement took Rhawn off guard. She sat for a moment in silence. "I trust you enough to know that you would not ask unless you had a good reason," she said at length. "But I made a vow to myself three years ago that I would not divulge his name. I would rather my son have no father at all than to have a reluctant father who is unwilling to acknowledge him."

"I understand, and I respect you for that," said Steven. "But there are others involved. It may now be that you have to consider your silence in light of wider considerations than your son alone. I am thinking of Florilyn and our responsibility to her."

They continued to talk. Steven explained the burden that had been growing on his heart and what had come into his mind to do about it. His request coincided with a great longing that had arisen in Rhawn's heart in recent weeks for the father of her son to acknowledge the boy—even if it should be only to herself. By now she had all but given up hope that there would ever be more.

It was not long before Rhawn was in tears. Soon Steven knew the whole story. Steven's great arm around her as she wept quietly gave Rhawn a comfort she had never experienced in her life—the comfort of a caring, loving brother.

Steven pulled up in front of the Lorimer home an hour later.

Rhawn turned to look at him and smiled through eyes still moist and glistening. "It feels good to have told someone," she said.

"I hope it was not too hard for you."

"Good things are sometimes hard. No, it was not too hard."

Steven jumped out of the buggy and helped Rhawn to the ground. "Be ready at a moment's notice," he said. "I will look for an opportunity. When it comes, we may have to act quickly."

Sixty-Three

Confrontation

It was a rare day that Florilyn Westbrooke and Colville Burrenchobay did not see one another, if not spend most of the day together. Colville had been so successful in subtly creating division between Florilyn and her mother that Florilyn no longer apprised Katherine of her movements or plans. She came and went as she pleased, ordered the servants about with the same hauteur that had been characteristic of her young teen years, and in general carried herself as if *she* rather than her brother were about to come into the title and property.

It is hardly surprising under these circumstances that she and Courtenay resumed their former bonds. There was no more talk of Florilyn leaving the manor after Courtenay's birthday. They openly laughed about their mother building a grand new home and living in it by herself. They were equally mocking of Steven Muir, Courtenay counting the days when he could order him to pack his bags and they would never see him again.

Though both Katherine and Steven shrank from small stratagems, they were nonetheless enough convinced of the rightness of what must be done that they were watching and waiting together. Without divulging the secret he had learned, Steven had taken Katherine into his confidence sufficiently to gain her approval a second time. Thus it was that she came to him about one o'clock one day upon learning from

Mrs. Drynwydd that Florilyn had ordered afternoon tea to be served for herself and a guest at four o'clock in the sunroom. None had any doubt who that guest would be.

Steven was on his way into town within a quarter hour.

Their tea, with cakes and scones and biscuits, was well under way, Mrs. Drynwydd having departed a few minutes earlier, when the sunroom door opened. Florilyn and Colville glanced toward it, and the laughter died on their lips.

Rhawn Lorimer and Katherine walked in with a young boy between them who had just turned three.

Not having seen Rhawn for months and constrained by her presence from flying off the handle at her mother, for a few seconds Florilyn was merely flustered at the unexpected interruption. "Rhawn!" she said, "What are you. . .I mean, it is nice to see you, but. . .you can see that I am—"

Struggling to regain her poise, Florilyn's eyes darted back and forth between the two. Rhawn and her mother had not accidentally barged in upon her tête-à-tête with Colville. Something sinister was afoot.

The next moment, Katherine took the youngster by the hand and led him from the room. Florilyn's eyes flashed with suspicion. Rhawn's lips quivered then flitted toward Colville with an expression of silent entreaty.

He had been so thoroughly taken by surprise that nervousness overcame him. Hardly knowing what he said, he fell back on trying to make light of the awkward encounter. "So. . .Rhawn"—he half laughed, affecting cheerfulness—"I don't recall that we sent for a child. Nice-looking fellow, though."

Rhawn turned white at the rebuff.

Not one to lose her equanimity for long, Florilyn drew herself up to her full height. "What is going on here, Rhawn?" she said in a demanding tone. "Something tells me this is no coincidence. You came in here knowing full well that Colville and I were having tea. Did my mother—"

"Your mother had nothing to do with it," said Rhawn.

"Then what is she doing with. . .with—"

"He is my son, Florilyn," said Rhawn, recovering herself a little. "I told her I wanted to speak with you in private."

"Then come back another time. As you can see," added Florilyn haughtily, "I have a previous engagement."

The words seemed to wake Rhawn again to the business at hand. "Florilyn," she said, "I *want* to talk to you, and I want to talk to you now."

"What you have to say, then, you can say in front of Colville."

"What I have to say is for your ears alone. *Mister* Burrenchobay," she added, turning to Colville, "perhaps you would be so kind as to excuse us."

Seeing that Florilyn was taking his part, Colville had also recovered himself and was in no temper to be ordered about. "I believe that Lady Florilyn has made it clear enough," he replied coolly, "that she wishes me to stay."

Rhawn stood helplessly silent as the two stared daggers into her eyes.

The next moment, from where he had been listening outside on the terrace, Steven Muir opened the french doors and strode into the room.

SIXTY-FOUR

Return of the Heiress

About the time Colville Burrenchobay had set out from his home for afternoon tea at the manor, the southbound coach from Blaenau Ffestiniog left the main road, turned toward the sea, and bounced along toward its next stop in front of Mistress Chattan's inn on the main street of the coastal village of Llanfryniog.

As much as her calm demeanor was capable of yielding to girlish excitement, Gwyneth Barrie was looking out through the window with an exuberant smile on her face, taking in with eager anticipation the sights she had not known whether she would ever see again. Even the muddy main street of a town that had never extended its kindness to her was a sight imbued with nostalgic happiness.

At her side, having no idea that Steven's urgent letter to him was just arriving at his parents' home in Glasgow, Percival Drummond was filled with far different emotions than he had ever felt when returning to this beloved coastline of North Wales. Momentous changes were coming. One of them had already come. When he stepped onto the street a few minutes later and reached back up into the coach, it was to help to the ground his new fiancée.

It was the twelfth of March in the year 1874, five days before Courtenay Westbrooke's twenty-fifth birthday. Percy and Gwyneth had said good-bye to Gwyneth's father two days earlier in Dublin, promising to get word to him and Grannie the moment there were any developments to report.

Whenever Percy came to Llanfryniog, word quickly spread that "young Mr. Drummond" was back in town. On this occasion, however, the rumors surrounding his arrival quickly filled with additional fodder for gossip. A few eyes turned as the two waited for their bags, a few more as Percy left Gwyneth on the walkway and took their bags inside for a brief talk with Mistress Chattan. Gradually more eyes were drawn to the scene the moment they set out along the street together. Whereas the town's curious women had been following developments between himself and young Lady Florilyn for two years or more, within minutes of his arrival on this day, startled speculation began circulating like a brushfire from house to house.

As Percy and Gwyneth walked out of the village, more eyes than either had any idea were following them from behind curtained windows. Everyone was asking the same thing: Who was the light-haired beauty on Mr. Percy's arm?

"Would you like to visit your old cottage?" said Percy as they went. "That is if it is still unoccupied."

Gwyneth thought a moment. "Perhaps not immediately," she replied. "I may want to do so alone. I hope you don't mind. I think to see it again will make my heart too full for words."

"I don't mind," rejoined Percy. "You will always have places within you that are yours alone."

"All I want to do today is sit and look at the sea," said Gwyneth with a smile. "From this side again."

They left the road, crossed the grassy expanse in the direction of the rising headland, and continued up the slope toward the promontory of Mochras Head. Percy had as yet said nothing about the great change that Gwyneth would find there.

If such was possible, at the sight of Steven walking into the sunroom unannounced, Florilyn drew herself up yet higher. Her face flushed red, and her heart filled with indignation. "Now I see who is the author of this subterfuge!" she cried. "Get out of here, Steven! Leave this room immediately!"

"Happily, Lady Florilyn," replied Steven. "Colville and I will leave together. Miss Lorimer, I believe, requested to have a word with you."

"I will have no words with her or anyone else! I told you to get out. Who is mistress of this house—me or you?"

"Neither, Lady Florilyn. Your mother is my mistress. I take my orders from her." Steven turned to Colville. "Would you please come with me, Colville?" he said. "We will leave the ladies to themselves."

"I take no orders from *you*, Stevie Muir," said Colville with a sneer. "I believe Lady Florilyn ordered you out. I suggest you obey her, or I will throw you back outside myself. If you force me to do so, I will not be gentle about it."

A peculiar smile crossed Steven's lips. It was clear he was not cowed.

The expression enraged Colville, for he took it as mocking his threat. He stepped forward and laid a rude hand on Steven's arm.

Now Colville Burrenchobay was himself a powerful young man and stood some three inches above Steven. But the fact that he had all his life looked down on Stevie Muir as a weakling on this day proved his undoing. His overbearing confidence was not well founded.

Steven allowed himself to be shoved unceremoniously back toward the french doors, which stood still open. At the last instant, he spun suddenly and away from Colville's grasp. Before Colville knew what had happened, Steven placed two hands on Colville's shoulders and pushed him through to the outside with a force that nearly sent Colville to the ground. By the time he recovered himself, the doors were locked in front of him and the curtains pulled.

In impotent fury, he tried the handle then stood a moment, not relishing the idea of shouting and demanding entrance like a spurned schoolgirl. At length, imagining himself a squire who must defend the honor of a woman whom he had convinced himself he loved, he turned and sprinted for the front door of the house.

Sixty-Five

The Compulsion of Love

"I think at last I know why my father loved the sea," said Gwyneth as she and Percy sat on the overlook at Mochras Head, "but also why it made him sad. My mother is somewhere out there. I know he thinks of that every time he looks upon it. I think the sea will always make me sad when I gaze upon it, too, though perhaps in a quietly happy way. For now I know who she was."

As they had approached along the promontory, Percy explained about Lady Katherine's new home, which now loomed before them. Gwyneth was quiet for several minutes as they drew closer. Percy knew that her initial reaction was likely the same as his had been—disappointment that a house now stood on what had all her life been one of her "special places" of solitude.

It was a relatively small structure, for a manor house, especially by the standards of Westbrooke Manor or Burrenchobay Hall. Its design was simple, yet ornate, giving the impression of a miniature castle that had grown horizontally rather than in height, emerging out of the plateau of itself. In every respect Katherine had instructed the designers to make its every detail merge and blend in with its surroundings, so as to appear a natural part of the headland and coastline. This they had achieved admirably. It added to rather than detracted from the landscape surrounding it.

Its aspect was neither imposing nor high. She had not wanted to break the view of the sea from further up the plateau. The gray stone structure, therefore, rose but one floor above the ground and was shaped roughly as a horseshoe opening to the sea. The courtyard in the center of the three wings had been left in its natural habitat of coastal grasses liberally scattered with stones and small boulders. The outer walls and roof of the house were by now nearly complete where it sat back about three hundred yards from the edge of the cliff.

They sat quietly talking for thirty or forty minutes. Finally Percy remembered the question he had been waiting so long to ask. "By the way," he said, "why did you not come to meet me here that day when we agreed to meet before I left Wales?"

"You were waiting for me?" said Gwyneth in surprise.

"Yes, I waited for hours. You never came."

"I was waiting for you at the beach by the harbor."

"On the beach! But I thought—" He paused as the light dawned on his memory. Slowly he nodded. " 'At our special place, where land meets sea. . .' " he said reflectively. "I thought it was here. You thought I meant there. Were you really waiting for me all that time?"

"Finally I walked up from the harbor," she replied. "Then I heard the coach, and I saw you at the inn with Florilyn. She kissed you before you left, and I ran home in tears."

"Oh, Gwyneth. . .I *am* sorry!"

They both sat musing in silence.

"Who would have thought that it would be nearly four years before we would see one another again," said Percy, "or that, when we sat here again together looking out over the sea, we would be engaged." He paused a moment. "But when you left Llanfryniog, at least *you* didn't leave without saying good-bye like I did on that day."

"What do you mean?" asked Gwyneth. "I *didn't* say good-bye. You weren't even here."

"But still, you said good-bye to me in your own way." Percy pulled from his pocket the dried bouquet and note he had discovered at the cottage.

"You found it!" exclaimed Gwyneth with delight.

"I've been waiting until we were here again to show it to you."

"Oh Percy, do you really want to marry me?" asked Gwyneth simply.

"Gwyneth, how can you ask? I love you!"

"It seems that I have stepped into a dream too good to be true. But I love you, too, with all my heart."

At length Percy climbed to his feet. He offered his hand and pulled Gwyneth up beside him. "It is probably time that we see what destiny awaits us," he said.

They turned, and he led the way across the plateau, Gwyneth's hand in his, past Katherine's new house and toward the road and through the entry to the estate.

"Are you certain Lady Katherine will want us to stay at the manor?" asked Gwyneth.

"She will be delighted to see us both. Don't forget, I'm family. I have my own room." Percy paused and began laughing. "What am I saying? You are family, too, though no one knows it yet. We're *both* family!"

"What are you planning to tell them about me. . .about what I am doing here?"

Gwyneth's question reminded Percy of his uncle's earnest desire that his aunt be spared as much pain as possible. "They have to be told," he said seriously. "I haven't decided on a course of action yet. First of all, we must see how things stand when we arrive. I will have to speak with my aunt. The matter is delicate, yet I have no alternative but to tell her everything. But that can wait. For now I will simply say that I ran into you and encouraged you to come for a visit. That is entirely the truth. Then I will seek the best means to talk to her in private."

Finding herself suddenly alone in the sunroom, without an ally and with Rhawn Lorimer on one side of her and Steven Muir approaching from the french doors through which he had just deposited Colville Burrenchobay on the other, Florilyn did the only thing she could think to do under the circumstances. She made for the door on the opposite side of the room.

"Florilyn!" said Steven in a tone of command, calling her by her name.

She spun around. If wrath could burn, he would have been reduced to ashes on the spot. "How dare you address me in such a tone!"

"I have done what I could to serve you—"

"And I want no more of such service!"

"But you drive me to extremeties," he said, ignoring her interruption. "I am telling you now, as a friend and brother who loves you and cares more for you than you have any idea. . .you must not marry that man. At present he is a scoundrel, though I hope he may in time become something better. But as things stand, I will do all that is in my power to prevent you—"

"You. . .prevent *me*!" shrieked Florilyn in a paroxysm of rage. "What gives you the right to presume to know what is best for me?"

"The right of love, Florilyn. Even if it should cause you suffering, I *will* do my best for you, until you put it out of my power completely. I will do all that I am able to deliver you from the lies that man has told you. I will commit to whatever it takes to help the true self that was growing in you to waken again. I will give my life to strengthen yours. But one thing I will *not* do is stand by and watch you destroy your future."

Florilyn could hardly speak for the fury within her. Her lips quivered as she struggled to find her voice. The next words she heard, however, at last jolted her awake.

"Florilyn!" said Rhawn in a loud but measured voice.

Florilyn turned.

"Colville Burrenchobay is the father of my son," Rhawn added. "If you can marry him after the way you have seen him treat me for three years, while ignoring his own son, then perhaps you deserve each other. But he is a heartless man who will, I have no doubt, cast you adrift if such should suit his purpose just as he did me."

Florilyn stood staring like a statue, her face white as a sheet.

Sixty-Six

Surprise Reunion

As Colville raced around the corner of the manor toward its front entrance, he scarcely noticed the young man and woman walking toward it from the entryway drive. He cast a brief glance toward them but did not slow his step.

Knowing well enough who it was, and liking neither the look on his face nor the fact that he burst through the door without slowing, Percy merely cast Gwyneth a brief look then bolted after Colville. Some mischief was afoot. He feared a dangerous situation was brewing. Gwyneth hurried after him.

From the moment Percy ran into the darkened entryway, it did not take long to descry where the trouble was coming from. High words and shouts echoed through the corridor. He listened a moment then darted toward them.

It was in hopes of forcing an acknowledgment from the father that Rhawn had insisted that Colville be present when they confront Florilyn. Fearing it could too easily turn ugly, Steven had reluctantly agreed, for he could do nothing without Rhawn. His concerns were about to be realized. Colville had been taken by surprise once. It would not happen again.

He had just run into the room and issued a warning threat to Steven to leave at once or pay the price when Percy shot in after him.

It took Percy but a second to size up the situation. The next instant he heard the shriek of his name.

"Percy!" cried Rhawn and flew to his arms as if he were a knight in shining armor come to set everything right.

Again, events conspired to throw off Colville's designs. But this time he tried to use it to his advantage. "There, Florilyn," he said with a smile of patronizing humor, "it is just as I told you. He is the father himself."

At the words, a sob escaped Rhawn's lips. Ignoring the charge and continuing to clasp her to him with one arm, Percy looked toward Steven for enlightenment.

"Hello, Percy. It is very good to see you," said Steven. "Rhawn and I have been having a private conversation with Florilyn. Colville seems intent upon intruding where he is not wanted."

"Then perhaps, Colville," said Percy, "you and I should leave them."

"I will not leave Florilyn alone with this madman," said Colville. "I was about to throw him out, Drummond, and take Florilyn away from this charade when you barged in. I don't know what you are doing here, but you might as well leave. This is between Muir and me. I will settle it in my own way."

Just then Gwyneth walked through the open door. She saw Percy with his arm around Rhawn Lorimer. Unlike many young women confronted with such a sight, her first thoughts were not jealous ones. She trusted Percy entirely. Though Rhawn had never spoken a civil word to her in her life, and in fact during her younger years had spoken many a cruel one, Gwyneth intuitively recognized pain on her face. She knew that Percy's embrace was that of a comforting brother. As the helpmeet she was already preparing to be, she moved toward Rhawn and slid her arm around her from the other side.

For several seconds no one recognized her. At last truth dawned.

"*Gwyneth!*" said Florilyn in surprise.

Gwyneth smiled sweetly. "Hello, Florilyn," she said.

In Florilyn's mind, however, the former friendship between them was but a distant memory. The poison of division had spread throughout her being. Recovering her initial surprise, her next thought was that

Gwyneth and Percy were somehow involved in this plot against Colville.
"What are you doing here?" she said. Her tone was not friendly. "And what are *you* doing here, Percy? This is none of your concern."

"Steven?" said Percy, as he stepped into the middle of the room.

"Rhawn and I have been explaining to Florilyn," said Steven, "why she cannot marry Colville Burrenchobay."

"Marry him!" exclaimed Percy. "Is this true, Florilyn?"

"It is," Florilyn answered imperiously. "Colville and I are engaged."

"And you saw no reason to inform me?"

"I did not. You were no longer interested in me."

"That is not true."

"Percy!" now sobbed Rhawn, "he is the father of my son. Florilyn, he only wants to marry you for your money."

"That's a lie!" shouted Colville.

The volatile exchange momentarily silenced the room.

"He was always talking about how rich you would be one day," said Rhawn.

"I don't believe a word of it," said Florilyn.

"Yes, where is your proof?" said Colville, recovering himself with cool aplomb. "It's all lies. Come, Florilyn. They are all mad together. Let's get out of here."

"Gladly!"

They moved toward the door.

"A moment, Florilyn," said Percy, moving to block their way. "Would you indulge me with a brief word in private?"

"I will not! I am leaving with Colville."

"I would rather not insist, Florilyn. Please." Percy turned to Colville. "As you are a guest in this home, Colville, I believe I can safely speak on behalf of Lady Katherine in requesting you to take your leave."

"I will not take a step without Florilyn."

"Do you want me to summon the manservants to escort you forcibly from the premises?"

"What—two or three men twice my age?" laughed Colville.

"You are right," rejoined Percy. "They will hardly be necessary. Steven and I are well up to the task. Now, Florilyn," he said, taking his cousin's arm and leading her through the door and into the corridor, "come with me."

Unrepentant but powerless to argue, Florilyn squirmed to get free. Instead she found herself closeted a moment later with Percy in the adjacent sitting room. Steven, meanwhile, not relishing a further hostile encounter, reopened the curtains and slipped through the french doors and outside. Gwyneth led Rhawn after him. Colville found himself standing in an empty room.

Closing the door of the sitting room behind them, Percy turned to Florilyn. "You are much changed, Florilyn," he said. "I am sorry to say it does not become you. What happened?"

Florilyn looked away. She had not completely forgotten the feelings she had had for Percy and how much she had once desired to please him. Even in her present state, his words stung.

"You asked what Gwyneth and I are doing here," he went on. "What I am about to tell you, I implore you to breathe no word of until I make a full disclosure."

Florilyn's vanity flared up again. "You would place a muzzle on me?" she said.

"I think you will hold your tongue. The only person who will be hurt is your mother. I cannot believe, even now, that you would intentionally hurt her. So I have no choice but to hope you will comply with my request."

"What is it, then?" said Florilyn peevishly.

"Knowing something of what kind of man Colville Burrenchobay is, I cannot but imagine that his motives for wanting to marry you are mixed. What do you think he will say when he learns that you will inherit nothing from your father's estate and that you will no longer be known as the *Honorable* Florilyn Westbrooke?"

"What are you talking about? Courtenay inherits the title, not me."

"As sister of the viscount, you would still be deserving of the address of a viscount's daughter until he is married. That would obviously make a husband look good, especially one who might have political aspirations. What do you think he would say to know that you will not inherit one pound from your father's estate and to know that Courtenay will never be viscount?"

"That's absurd!" said Florilyn. "He is right—you are mad!"

"Listen to me, cousin," said Percy sternly. "Then make your choice—whether to send Colville away yourself or find him breaking your engagement when he learns that you have no claim to rights, privileges, title, or money and are not the prize in society's eyes he thought you. You may hate me for saying such a thing. All I ask is whether you know Colville Burrenchobay well enough to be absolutely *sure* of him."

The question jolted Florilyn. A glimmer of the "new Florilyn" flickered like a nearly extinguished candle coming back to life. It was a powerful and disturbing question. In her heart of hearts, she knew that she was *not* sure of Colville. One thing she did know, however, was that Percy Drummond would *never* lie. As she continued to listen, Florilyn's expression turned from anger to stunned disbelief. Slowly her pride began to wilt.

When Percy led her back into the sunroom a few minutes later, Colville had left the house through the front door. Through the window, Steven saw Percy and Florilyn come back into the room. He saw from Florilyn's countenance that her self-will had been defeated at last. The demon of division had been exorcised by the light of loving truth. The two disclosures concerning Rhawn and Gwyneth, coming one after the other, had finally penetrated the hard shell of Colville's deception, shattering the last vestige of pride she had allowed to reassert itself.

Percy led her to Steven. He took her gently and led her to a couch, then sat down beside her. Percy walked outside where he found Gwyneth and Rhawn talking quietly together. Rhawn was softly weeping in emotional exhaustion.

Sixty-Seven

Disclosure

Courtenay Westbrooke sat at the desk in his apartment on the third floor of Westbrooke Manor deep in thought. Before him was the most recent statement of his account in the Porthmadog Union Bank, which reflected the deposit of the check from Lord Litchfield's assistant of £1,000 he had received a week and a half earlier. The balance would be forthcoming within days.

Courtenay's brain was alive with the staggering possibilities presented by a cash balance of over £8,000. He had been perusing several flyers and brochures with the current offerings in the midlands horse market, thinking to himself that perhaps now he could afford to go after a major prize from one of the most distinguished stables. His was the mentality of one who assumed that money had been invented for one thing alone—to spend, and that as quickly as possible. He was still not fully appreciative of the fact that bank balances required regular supplementation to maintain themselves, nor that his forthcoming viscountcy came with a cash income that would be considered dubious by London's leading financiers. *Saving* for the proverbial rainy day was not an intrinsic element of his economic creed.

He had been hearing voices for some time. But as the feminine figured most prominently, his subconscious had ignored them. As things heated up two floors below him, however, the sounds intruded into his waking brain. He set down the flyer in his hand and listened. As by some primal instinct of the fighting male animal, men young and old, or it might be said, *boys* of all ages, are drawn even to the potential of conflict with a wide-eyed lust for violence. After a few more shouts, Courtenay rose to his feet and listened. Now it grew deathly quiet. He strained to hear more. A minute later he was out of his room and on his way for the stairs to investigate.

He flew down the stairs two at a time. The front door stood open. Outside Courtenay saw Colville with a look of angry consternation on his face. Perceiving no opportunity to get Florilyn alone, and having his own reasons for desiring to avoid Rhawn Lorimer in the company of so many allies, he was debating with himself whether he ought to simply get on his horse and beat a hasty retreat. "Colville," said Courtenay, running outside, "what's all the ruckus I hear?"

"That fool Stevie Muir hauled Rhawn Lorimer up here with her accusations. He's trying to discredit me in front of Florilyn."

"Why didn't you throw him out, or come find me and I would have?"

"The blackguard took me by surprise. They cornered Florilyn with their lies. Then that devil of a cousin of yours showed up and stuck his nose in."

"*Percy*. . .he's here?" exclaimed Courtenay. An expletive exploded from his mouth. "We'll see about this! Where are they?"

"I left Florilyn with him in the sunroom."

Courtenay turned and sprinted back inside and along the corridor. Colville followed, his eyes aflame. His fists were itching to redress the recent grievances against his pride, and these were odds he liked much better.

The two burst into the sunroom, ready to take out their anger on anyone who crossed them. They were, however, completely unprepared for the scene that met their eyes.

Percy had gone to find Katherine. After a brief and affectionate greeting, he had led his aunt and the boy back to join the others.

Katherine, Rhawn, Percy, and Gwyneth were speaking in low tones, with Rhawn's son in their midst. Gwyneth was telling Katherine where they had gone after leaving Llanfryniog and about Grannie and her father, though without divulging the reason for their sudden departure to Ireland.

On the couch across the room, Florilyn sat quietly weeping beside Steven Muir. One of her hands rested between his. A pulse of rage surged through Colville's frame.

At the sight of the two young men rushing into their midst, faces flushed and hands eager for a fight, Percy stepped away from the women and moved to intercept them.

Nothing could have been more to Courtenay's liking. An involuntary smirk passed over his lips.

Steven, too, rose and stepped protectively in front of Florilyn. Courtenay saw the movement and hesitated briefly. After the incident several days earlier, he was a little afraid of Steven. Not so, Colville Burrenchobay. Determined to be neither surprised nor foiled a second time, he charged like an angry bear.

"Defend yourself, Steven!" shouted Percy. "Don't stand on ceremony—he's dangerous!"

Florilyn and Rhawn screamed in a single voice. Percy shot a quick glance toward Gwyneth. She understood and hurried Rhawn, her son, and Katherine from the room.

Emboldened by Colville's aggression, Courtenay rushed Percy with a fierce series of blows. He had been waiting for this opportunity for a long time. He was not about to let it pass without giving full vent to his frustrated resentment against his goody-goody cousin.

Meanwhile, Colville landed several severe blows alongside Steven's head, one of which drew blood behind the ear. Steven was doing his best to evade or stop them, but with difficulty. Florilyn was yelling at them all to stop. Neither her brother nor Colville was inclined to back off from what they misperceived as a delicious advantage.

"Steven!" cried Percy again, not fearing Courtenay so much as he feared for Steven. "It's the whip the moneychangers need, not the gentle word. Defend yourself, man!"

Willing enough under the circumstances to bow to Percy's wisdom, ten seconds later Colville Burrenchobay was measuring the six-foot-two-inch length of his frame along the floor. Florilyn's shrieks stopped abruptly to see with what lightning speed Steven had rendered the threat to himself unconscious in front of her.

"Courtenay. . .Courtenay, please!" implored Percy. "I need to speak with you."

"Say it with your fists!' shouted Courtenay. "Take your own advice and defend yourself! Are you a coward?"

"I have no desire to fight you, Courtenay."

"It is too late for that!"

"Courtenay. . .*stop*!" It was now his sister's voice he heard.

"I will stop when this bounder has learned that we need no more of his interference."

"*Courtenay!*" cried Florilyn. "You've got to hear what Percy has to say."

For answer, several more wicked blows came battering toward Percy's head and body. But they did not continue much longer. Suddenly from behind, two huge arms clasped him round the chest. Finding himself caught in a straightjacket and held firmly against Steven Muir's massive chest, he writhed to free himself, but to no avail.

"You big lout!" he cried. "Unhand me, Muir! You will pay for this, I tell you! Release me, and I may not bring charges against you."

"Courtenay," said Florilyn, her voice softer now. "You *must* listen."

His audience at last a captive one, and by now his own righteous anger aroused, Percy walked close to Courtenay until he stood a foot in front of his face. "Courtenay," he said in a passionate and indignant voice, "you will be twenty-five in a matter of days. It is time you grew up and stopped behaving like a spoiled child who thinks he can do and have anything he wants. While I am loathe to call anyone a fool for fear of the fires of hell, you have acted the part of the fool of Proverbs. You are a foolish and self-centered young man. It is time to be a man. A *man*, Courtenay, not a boy. I have done the best I could to be a friend and faithful cousin to you. Before he died, I promised your father that I would do all that was in my power to help take care of your sister. With that vow came an equal commitment to you. I would have striven to do my best for you and Florilyn even without that promise. But you have foiled all my efforts to be your friend. You despised me since my first visit here. You have not loved or followed the truth. You have been selfish and conceited toward me and toward others. You have made no effort to follow the right. You have been rude toward the young woman I love. All her life you treated her pure heart and forgiving spirit with shameful disdain."

He paused, sensing Florilyn's unspoken question at his words. He turned toward her. "Yes, Florilyn," he said, nodding with a smile of acknowledgment, "I found Gwyneth in my own fir wood, as I think you knew I would. I have asked her to marry me."

"Oh, Percy," said Florilyn, rising and walking to him. "I am so happy for you."

He turned to meet her.

She embraced him as Courtenay, still powerless in Steven's grasp, looked on. Florilyn stepped back and now stood to face her brother. "Courtenay," she said, "Percy is our friend, not our enemy." Her voice was soft. The spell of lies at last was broken. "He has always been our friend. I don't know how I could have forgotten. Now you *need* to listen to him."

Slowly Steven relaxed his hold and stepped back.

"All right, then," spat Courtenay belligerently, "what is it?"

"You may prefer to sit down," said Percy.

"I will stand. I will submit to this childish show of power because you have me at a disadvantage," spat Courtenay. "But know this, *cousin*, in five days I will take great pleasure in throwing you out of this house—you and all your accomplices in whatever game you are playing."

"I do not think you will, Courtenay. I will not leave except by the word of the viscountess."

"In five days the manor will be mine. If you refuse my order, I will have you removed by force."

"Again, I think not, Courtenay. In five days the manor will *not* be yours."

"Don't talk bloody nonsense!"

"I speak the truth. You are not your father's rightful heir."

A stunned silence filled the room. Courtenay stared back speechless then broke into a laugh. "You are mad as a March hare! Who else would be his heir?"

Out of the corner of his eye, Percy saw Steven staring at him with an equally dumbfounded expression. "She whom your father commissioned me on his deathbed to find," he replied to Courtenay's question. "She who was his rightful heir by his first marriage, before he knew your mother."

"An outrageous claim!" cried Courtenay. "If my father had been married twice, I would know of it. Who is this mystery heir?" For the first time a hint of nervousness was evident in his tone.

"The very one whom you so long despised as too far beneath you even to deserve your contempt—she whom you know as Gwyneth Barrie."

Again a blank stare of incredulity met Percy's words. Steven's expression of disbelief drifted toward his own cousin. "She is but a peasant and guttersnipe!" he said. As he spoke, he laughed scornfully.

"Careful, Courtenay—she is the young woman who is to be my wife. I will let it pass this once. But do not insult her again, or I will give you cause to regret it. She is also your father's granddaughter."

The evident seriousness on his sister's face and the confidence with which Percy spoke at last succeeded in sobering Courtenay to the reality that there might be more to the claim than could so easily be laughed off. He believed not a word of it. But the mirth slowly died from his lips.

"I presume you have some sort of proof you intend to put forward in support of this preposterous notion," he said coolly.

As he spoke, on the floor Colville was returning to consciousness. His confused brain struggled to make sense of where he was. The only word that registered from out of the fog he now repeated in defense of the charge that had been brought against him.

"*Proof*. . ." he repeated in a slurred tongue, climbing groggily to his feet. "Proof. . .all lies. . .where's the proof?"

"I believe all the proof needed for the truth of Rhawn's words, Colville," said Florilyn, "may be seen clearly enough in the face of that little boy who just left with his mother. Steven," she said to Steven, "would you please escort Mr. Burrenchobay from the house. Our afternoon tea is over."

With one hand on his arm, Steven gently ushered Colville through the french doors. A pronounced stinging in the region of his right cheekbone was all the persuasion Colville needed to go quietly. Steven saw him safely to the front of the house, helped him mount his horse, and returned inside through the main front door. By the time he reached home, Colville's head was splitting, and he called for cold compresses.

Meanwhile, the three cousins were left alone in the sunroom.

"You spoke of proof," said Percy. "All the proof you may require shall be provided in due course."

"No doubt," rejoined Courtenay sullenly. "But my solicitor shall make inquiries."

"Florilyn," said Percy, "would you mind going to your mother? Tell her I need to speak with her in private. I will join her momentarily. You may return and tell me where to meet her."

Florilyn turned to go then hesitated. She gazed at Percy full in the face. "Percy. . .I am sorry," she said. "Can you ever forgive me for the dreadful things I said?"

Percy smiled. "You were forgiven without needing to ask."

She returned his smile, hugged him warmly, and left the room.

Percy and Courtenay exchanged a few more words in private.

Sixty-Eight

Ladies of the Manor

The moment they were alone, Katherine gave Gwyneth a warm hug.

"Gwyneth, my dear!" she exclaimed. "How you have grown. You are beautiful!"

Gwyneth smiled with peaceful embarrassment.

"But what are you doing here? No one knew where you had disappeared to."

"I will leave that for Percy to explain, Lady Katherine," replied Gwyneth. "I apologize that we came unannounced."

"Think nothing of it. You are both more welcome than I can say."

As they were talking, Florilyn walked through the door. She glanced about. There were her mother, Gwyneth, and Rhawn. All three turned toward her as the door opened. Her eyes filled with tears at the sight. She walked to her mother. Katherine received her into her embrace, and Florilyn broke into great cleansing sobs. "Mother," she cried. "I am so sorry! I'm sorry I didn't trust you or come to you."

Katherine stroked her hair and held her as she had not done in years.

Florilyn wept until the storm gradually subsided. She sniffed and wiped at her eyes, then turned to Gwyneth. The two embraced. No words were needed.

Florilyn now approached Rhawn, whose tears were not yet altogether spent either. The two friends embraced, with mutual words of renewed affection. "Thank you, Rhawn," said Florilyn. "It took courage to do what you did and tell me the truth. I know you didn't want to. But you did it for me. I am sorry for all you have been through and for the terrible things I said. You are a true friend. I will never forget what you did for me today."

Just then Steven returned from outside after seeing Colville on his way and walked into the room. Florilyn turned and saw him, then came toward him with a peaceful, humble, embarrassed smile. He opened his arms, and she walked into them without hesitation.

"I'm sorry, Steven," she said softly. "I treated you terribly. I have no excuse. I forgot who you were—that you were my friend. . .and more than a friend."

"It is over now," he said tenderly. "It will be as if it never was."

Florilyn now turned again to Katherine. "Mother," she said, "Percy wants to see you alone. He asked me to tell him where you would like to meet him."

Katherine nodded. She and Florilyn spoke further for a few moments, and then she left the room.

Percy entered Katherine's private sitting room on the second floor a few minutes later.

His aunt was waiting for him.

"Hello, Aunt Katherine," he said with a smile. "At last I can give you a proper greeting!"

She rose and embraced him. "You seem to have come just in time."

"I had no idea about Florilyn's engagement."

"I told her she needed to write you. But she has been very different since your last visit."

"I noticed."

"I should have told you and your parents, but. . .I was embarrassed. I suppose I kept hoping Florilyn would come to her senses. How I prayed you would come!"

"I hope all that is over now. I am sorry I gave you no advance warning. Our trip was very sudden."

"You are always welcome, Percy—with or without warning. Though I will not be at the manor much longer, as you know. This may be your final visit."

"We shall see about that," replied Percy. "Though I must say this wasn't exactly the peaceful homecoming I envisioned," he added with a light laugh. "It appears Gwyneth and I walked into a hornets' nest!"

"It is as much my fault as anyone's," replied Katherine. "Steven asked my permission to confront Florilyn about her engagement to Colville. I had no idea it would turn so heated and violent."

"Colville has a terrible temper. But if it is any consolation, I think she will soon be breaking her engagement."

"Yes, she told me. She already seems her old self again. Colville had cast such a spell over her. I am very relieved. And Gwyneth—she is looking wonderful! Who could have imagined she would turn into such a beautiful young lady."

"Did either she or Florilyn tell you?"

"About what?"

"Gwyneth and I are engaged."

"Oh, Percy—that's wonderful! Although," she said pausing momentarily, "I had been holding out hope that one day I would be able to call you my son-in-law as well as my nephew."

"I am hoping that it won't be long before you will be able to call one your son-in-law who is every bit the man I am. . .if not more!" Percy paused and drew in a deep breath. "But time for all that later," he said. "Aunt Katherine," he added quietly, "I need to talk to you very seriously. I think we should sit down. What I have to say may be painful for you. This is not how I envisioned it. I did not want to tell you like this. But events today seem rather to have overtaken us. It is imperative you know the truth without delay."

"The truth about what, Percy?"

Percy went on to tell her the whole story.

She listened quietly, with occasional tears. "I think I knew it all along," she said when he had concluded. "A woman knows when she is not the only one living in a man's heart, even if the other is but a memory. When you wrote me after returning from Ireland, I knew you were trying to protect my feelings. You probably hoped I would think Roderick was involved in some business deal that he wanted you to look into. I appreciate what you tried to do. But when you were so evasive, I had the feeling even then that there must have been a child."

"I am sorry, Aunt Katherine. If there had been a gentler way, or any other way. . ."

"I know, Percy. You had to do what you felt was right. Under the circumstances, this may prove to be for everyone's good in the end."

"Even Courtenay's?"

"If it serves to humble him and make a true man of him, then of course. What is a title and property alongside character? I would rather see my children paupers, and me along with them, if that is what it takes to build the character of godliness into us all."

"Hopefully it will not require quite such extreme measures," said Percy. He drew in a deep breath then rose. "I asked the others to wait for us downstairs in the sitting room," he said. "I told them I would explain more after talking to you."

"Then let us keep them waiting no longer."

"There is one thing, Aunt Katherine. . . I don't know how much you want me to say, or—"

"I would have no more secrets, Percy," said his aunt. "Tell them everything. Perhaps you should simply read the affidavit Roderick asked you to write out then tell about the letters and your going to Ireland and everything Mr. Barrie told you. After all these years, I would have light shed on it all. Please, you mustn't worry about my feelings. We must have the full truth."

Percy nodded seriously. "Perhaps Steven should take Rhawn home," he suggested. "Then the five of us can talk among ourselves."

Katherine thought a moment. "She has been through an emotional ordeal," she said. "She should not be alone right now. I think it would be good for her to remain here awhile, with her friends, perhaps for evening tea."

"And Steven?"

"Steven is as much a part of our family as anyone. He is Gwyneth's cousin. However. . .it may be that we should keep Roderick's disclosure among ourselves, at least for now. It will all come out soon enough, but. . .I shall talk to Steven. He will understand. He can keep Rhawn company while the five of us talk."

She rose, and they left the room and walked down one flight of stairs where the others were awaiting them in the east parlor. She walked straight to Gwyneth and folded her a second time into a loving embrace. "You dear, beautiful, mysterious young woman," she whispered into her ear, "Percy has told me everything. Welcome to the family!"

Sixty-Nine

The Affidavit

An hour later, after a break for tea and walk outside settling into old friendships, Katherine, Courtenay, Florilyn, Percy, and Gwyneth gathered upstairs in the sitting room of Katherine's apartment. Steven and Rhawn were outside in the stables where Steven was introducing Rhawn's son to the manor's horses.

"By now we all know why Percy and Gwyneth have returned," Katherine began. "There are pains to be borne, probably most severely by you, Courtenay, and myself. But the truth must come out. So I asked Percy to tell us everything." She turned toward Percy.

"Before Uncle Roderick died," Percy began, "he asked me to take down a statement he wanted to make. I know it may occur to you, Courtenay, to wonder why he made his confession to me rather than you or his solicitor or anyone else. I asked him that as well. His chief reason was simply that, should I prove unsuccessful in finding Gwyneth, whom he believed to be his granddaughter, then he saw no reason for any of this to come out at all. Telling me was his way of preserving confidentiality. I think he may have had some mistaken notion that my being a student of law gave the affidavit added veracity. It doesn't, of course. Nothing I took down from him carries the weight of a legal document. However, I think that may have influenced his thinking."

"If it is not a legal document," said Courtenay, "then what possible grounds do you have for thinking I intend to sit idly by and be deprived of my title and inheritance?"

"You asked for proof earlier," replied Percy. "Though it is not legally binding, I will give you what proof I am able for the moment in your father's own words. What additional proof there is will have to wait for another day, except to say that I have seen the parish records, both attesting to your father's first marriage and to the birth of Gwyneth's mother. Proving Gwyneth's maternity may be more difficult, but I am confident that proof will come in time."

"Go on, Percy," said Katherine. "Read Roderick's statement."

Percy nodded then unfolded the papers he had in his hand.

> *"To whom it may concern,"* Percy began aloud, *"especially to my dear wife Katherine, my family, and to Hamilton Murray, our faithful solicitor of many years:*
>
> *I make this affidavit on the 27th day of June in the year 1872 in the presence of my nephew, Percival Drummond, son of Edward and Mary Drummond of Glasgow. I am of sound mind, but failing body. . .*
>
> *At sixteen years of age,"* Percy continued, *"as a spoiled son of what I thought was wealth, I left Wales on a youthful grand tour, as we called it in those days—to see the world and spend money and generally squander my youth on the altar of irresponsibility. It turned out that my father was not the wealthy man I took him for. Before my travels were over, I was nearly out of money. I found myself in Ireland chasing the fleeting dream of riches in the rivers of Wicklow, though what remained to be found was doubtful. There my heart was smitten with a young Irish lass of working, though not peasant stock. Her name was Avonmara O'Sullivan. . ."*

Percy continued, not without many pauses and breaks, as Florilyn and Katherine listened with handkerchiefs in hand and eyes wet. At length he came to his uncle's final words.

"To you, Courtenay, if Percy is successful, you may hate me as well as him for what I have done and his part in it. I can only pray that it will make a man of you and that you will awaken to the claim of character sooner in your life than I did. You have the makings of goodness within you, my son. Heed their call and do not ignore them until it is too late."

Courtenay sat listening with a sullen scowl. As if it wasn't enough to be deprived of his inheritance in full view of this parcel of urchins, women, and cousins, he had to endure the further humiliation of being lectured at by his father from the grave!

"To you, my Flory, I have treasured our friendship of recent years. You have become a beautiful daughter to make a man proud—and I am assuredly proud of the young woman you have become. You will make your new husband a worthy and loving wife, and I am happy for you both."

Florilyn could contain herself no longer. She burst into sobs at her father's words. Percy waited.

"To you, my dear Katherine," he concluded at length, *"there are no words to tell you how sorry I am. You were the best wife a man could have—certainly far better than I deserved. Whatever happened before I met you, I only pray it will not cause you more pain than you can bear. But from the moment I met you, I loved you with all my heart. I love you now, and I will miss you until the day we meet again. Good-bye, my love."*

Percy glanced up, himself also blinking hard. Katherine was quietly weeping. Florilyn rose and went to her on the couch. Courtenay stood, his face stoic, and left the room. Percy and Gwyneth followed a moment later, leaving mother and daughter alone.

Seventy

Encounter in the Hills

In that mysterious process by which *news* spreads of itself, word had circulated through the Westbrooke Manor staff that something was up, that some great change was at hand, and that Gwyneth was at the center of it. They had been told nothing as yet, but whispered speculation ran rampant.

Gwyneth noticed curious looks coming her way from Mrs. Drynwydd and Mrs. Llewellyn and others of her former fellow servants. Percy knew her well enough to know that Gwyneth felt that her place ought to be with them, *serving* the family rather than pretending to be part of it. During that evening's tea, during which Courtenay was conspicuously absent, Percy noticed her embarrassment as she glanced about occasionally, smiling awkwardly and almost apologetically as Mrs. Drynwydd poured tea into her cup.

He knew she felt out of place. Though Steven was her cousin, and had grown up no more an aristocrat than she, he had been part of the manor family and treated as such by Katherine for more than a year. Everything was suddenly new to her.

When Katherine showed Gwyneth to one of the available guest rooms on the second floor where she and Florilyn and Courtenay and Percy all had their rooms, she asked Katherine if it wouldn't be better for her to stay in the servants' quarters. For answer, Katherine merely gave her another hug. The seeming luxury of her new surroundings would take time for Gwyneth to become accustomed to.

At Steven's suggestion and after he had hitched the manor's large carriage to two horses, the four young people loaded into it and together accompanied Rhawn and her son home to Llanfryniog. It was well past nine o'clock and dark before Percy, Gwyneth, Steven, and Florilyn returned.

Of the four, notwithstanding her discomfort at being waited on by her former fellow servants, only Gwyneth was asleep by ten. The other three, in their rooms and alone with their thoughts and the gamut of emotions and reactions the day had produced, lay awake past midnight.

The day had not gone as Percy had anticipated. His chief concern had been for his aunt. However, she had absorbed the news of her husband's past with all the poise and equanimity he should have known to expect. Instead, his thoughts alternated between the two girls who had been at the center of the day's fray—Rhawn and Florilyn. He knew the next days would be hard for them, adjusting to the sudden rush of events that had come upon them like a flood. Rhawn, especially, would probably feel alone and easily despondent. They needed to get together again and allow time for the emotion of change to settle and dissipate amid conversation, laughter, and friendship.

He spoke to Steven early the next morning. Thus it was that shortly before noon, with a great lunch packed behind two of the horses, Steven, Rhawn, Florilyn, Percy, and Gwyneth set off for a long ride north and east into the hills of Snowdonia. The five were older now, quieter, full of many thoughts. New times were coming to them all. A good deal of laughter was interspersed with serious talk, but there were no races on this day. Profound changes had overtaken them in recent days. The future now spreading out before them contained many unknowns but also new opportunities. They were subdued yet also alive to those possibilities.

As they went, Percy gradually drew back and allowed the others to ride ahead. He watched them with a smile, reminded of the rides he had taken during his first summer here. Now Florilyn was riding at Steven's side, talking together as they hadn't for months. Gwyneth and Rhawn followed as if they were old friends. How different this was from the day when Rhawn had tried to use her wiles on him and they had encountered young Gwyneth watching from the treetops. *She* would now be the one giving orders, not Courtenay as he had that day... for this would be *her* land. It was a peaceful day. Many bonds had been renewed and strengthened, and new and deeper ones formed. These five, henceforth, would always be friends.

"Would you three mind continuing on without us?" said Percy as they made their way back toward the coast several hours later. "There is someplace I want to go with Gwyneth."

They parted ten minutes later, Steven riding between Rhawn and Florilyn down the descending slopes westward, while Percy and Gwyneth veered north and again into the hills.

"Where are we going?" asked Gwyneth.

"Can't you guess?" rejoined Percy.

"To my special lake?"

"I went there after you were gone," said Percy. "I had no idea whether I would ever see you again. I suppose I went to be close to you. I've wanted to be there again *with* you ever since."

"Did you see the horses?" asked Gwyneth.

"I've been there twice but saw the horses neither time. They have probably been waiting for you."

Gwyneth smiled, and they continued on.

They reached the overlook above the crystal green waters forty minutes later. They dismounted, tied the horses, and sat for a few minutes gazing down upon the peaceful scene.

"Is this really happening to me, Percy?" said Gwyneth softly. "Or am I dreaming back in our cottage down near the village...or in our home in Ireland?"

"If you are dreaming, how do you account for the fact that we are both having the same dream?"

"Maybe I am dreaming you into my dream, and whatever you say is part of my dream."

Percy laughed lightly. "I have the feeling you will realize that you are awake soon enough. If I know you, you will very soon find yourself thinking of the good your position will allow you to do."

"I hope so, Percy. If it is true. . .oh, I *do* want to do good. I want to do good for *people*."

"You will, Gwyneth. Maybe this is God's way of allowing you to spread your bouquets of goodness to many, and with more than flowers."

"When will. . . I cannot say it, Percy," began Gwyneth. "But when will, you know. . ."

"When will you inherit?"

"*If* I do."

"It will be as it has been for Courtenay—when you are twenty-five."

"That will not be for five years," said Gwyneth in a tone of relief. "I am glad of that. What will happen until then?"

"Aunt Katherine—and now we may both call her that. . .although, no. . .she is actually your. . .hmm, let me see. . .yes, she would be your step-grandmother. In any event, she will continue to be viscountess and trustee of the estate."

Gwyneth drew in a breath and let it out slowly. "That means I don't really have to do anything now," she said then thought a moment. "I would like to do something, though, for Rhawn," she said. "She is sad. I know it is from the consequences of what she used to be. But I still hurt for her."

"Being a friend is what she needs most of all. I think now Florilyn will be a friend to her again, too."

"What is Florilyn to *me* now, Percy? Is she my aunt, or my half aunt? It is very confusing."

Percy smiled. "I hadn't thought of it," he said. "But I think a half-aunt qualifies as an aunt."

"It would be hard to call her Aunt Florilyn."

Percy laughed. "Just promise that I am present when you spring an *Uncle* Courtenay on Courtenay!"

Gwyneth drew in a deep breath as she peered down toward the lake.

"I see no movement down there at all," she said. "I don't even see deer. They are always there. Something is wrong, Percy."

"Shall we walk down and see? Maybe the rabbits are there."

They rose. Again Gwyneth hesitated. A puzzled expression came over her face.

"What is it?" asked Percy.

"I hear something," replied Gwyneth softly.

Gradually intruded faintly into Percy's hearing what sounded like the far-off sounds of machinery, the dull thudding of wood, an occasional clank of metal. . .even, though he could not quite be sure, shouts of men's voices. "I hear it, too," he said. "What can it be? We are miles from any farm."

They hurried to their horses and rode toward the sounds. The terrain was steep, and the hills and peaks surrounding the lake were rocky and jagged. Gwyneth led the way for she knew these hills far better than Percy. In fifteen minutes, they crested the north-south ridge east of the lake. Below them at a distance of about half a mile, a crew of perhaps a dozen men, surrounded by at least twice that many horses, some pulling wagons, others hitched to strange-looking machines, were hard at work. Some of the men appeared to be removing large rocks from a wagon track or roadbed stretching out behind them, while others, ahead of the wagons and machinery, were cutting trees and removing brush and clearing out a way forward. Where the road came from, they had no idea. But they were obviously moving up the ridge in the direction of the lake.

"What are they doing, Percy?" asked Gwyneth.

"I have no idea. But I don't like the look of it."

"I thought all this land was Lord Snowdon's. . .or Lady Katherine's now."

"As did I. Perhaps they are on someone else's land. I don't know where the boundary is. I saw several surveyors out here once before. When I told Aunt Katherine about it, she wasn't completely sure where the boundary was."

"Should we tell Lady Katherine?"

"Without a doubt—and immediately. Gwyneth, you know these hills better than I. You lead the way back to the manor. . .and with as much speed as you think is safe!"

Seventy-One

The Lady and the Lord

Gwyneth and Percy arrived at Westbrooke Manor an hour later, breathing hard and their two mounts lathered from the exertion.

By then Rhawn had returned to town. Steven and Florilyn, who were walking together back from the stables, saw them ride in.

Percy dismounted and ran for the house. "Tell them what we saw, Gwyneth," he said. "Maybe Steven knows something. I'll try to find Aunt Katherine!"

When Percy and Katherine emerged from the house two minutes later, Steven, Florilyn, and Gwyneth were standing beside the two sweating horses talking.

"Steven?" said Katherine as they approached.

"I know nothing about it," replied Steven, shaking his head.

"Do you know the place where Percy and Gwyneth saw the men? Do you know the lake?"

"I know it well."

"Is it near the boundary of the estate? Could it be someone else's land? Sir Armond's property borders ours to the northeast, I believe."

"There is no chance of that, Lady Katherine," said Steven. "The estate boundary lies two ridges east from that lake, not one. It is at least a half mile from where, if I have my bearings correct, Percy and Gwyneth describe seeing the men."

"How can you be sure?"

"After he hired me as a groom, your husband took me about to show me the extent of the estate. He was especially concerned that I knew where the boundaries were between his land and that of Mr. Burrenchobay. Whatever is going on. . .it is on *your* land, Lady Katherine."

Half an hour later, on fresh mounts, Katherine, Florilyn, Steven, Gwyneth, and Percy rode away from Westbrooke Manor northeast into the hills. As anxious as they were to make haste, they allowed Steven to set a pace that would not overly tax the horses. By the time they reached the final ridge and began the descent down the slope where the work was still in progress, the afternoon was well advanced.

Shadows from one of its two surrounding parallel ridges had nearly consumed the valley where the men were working, and their thoughts were turning to the dinner and beer that awaited them back at the inn in Bronaber. It happened that the mastermind of the project had ridden out at day's end to assess progress.

As they made their way down through the thickly wooded slope, Katherine nodded to Steven. The others slowed, and he rode on ahead. He made his way into the clearing and toward the scene. A few heads turned as he approached and reined in.

"Who's in charge here?" said Steven.

Other heads turned. A few comments filtered back through the ranks.

After a moment, a well-dressed man came forward from among them. He was obviously not one of the laborers. "I am Lord Coleraine Litchfield," he said. "And who might you be?"

"I am Steven Muir, factor of the Westbrooke Manor estate."

"Ah. . .Mr. Muir. Well, it is nice to meet my new neighbor."

"How do you mean, your neighbor?"

"I am the owner of this land."

Steven took in the statement calmly. "What are you doing here?" he asked.

"As you can see, my men are building a road."

"And this, you say, is your land?"

"It is."

"As of when?"

"Very recently."

"From whom did you purchase it?"

"From the Westbrooke estate."

"I see. That will come as a surprise to the trustee of the estate, who knows nothing about it." Still seated on his horse, Steven turned and signaled for Katherine to join him.

As she rode toward them, Lord Litchfield recognized the late viscount's widow. An indulgent smile came to his lips. "Lady Westbrooke," he said, "it seems we meet again."

"This man tells me that he is the owner of this land," said Steven.

Katherine had not liked Lord Litchfield from the first. It was with great difficulty that she now kept her anger in check. "That is a curious claim," she said, "in that I control the affairs of the estate and have heard nothing about it."

"The purchase was carried out through the new viscount," said Litchfield. "Your son, I believe."

"Courtenay sold you this land!"

"That is true."

"It is not his land. He has not inherited yet. None of this is his to sell."

"It will be in a matter of days."

"Do you mean to tell me that you are doing. . .whatever all this is. . . on my husband's land when it is not even yet legally yours?"

"Your son allowed me to commence my plans though the transaction will not be formally finalized for a few more days."

"But I do not give you permission. This is not his land."

"Three days. . .four days. . .what difference do a few hours make? He will be viscount, and this will be my land. Why should I not get under way?"

"Because at the moment you are trespassing, Lord Litchfield."

"Tut, tut, Lady Westbrooke. A mere technicality."

"Hardly a technicality, Lord Litchfield, when you consider the fact that although my son will indeed turn twenty-five in four days, he will not become viscount. . .not then, not ever. Whatever papers you may have signed are not legally binding."

"What are you talking about? He will become viscount in four days."

"I fear not, Lord Litchfield. Gwyneth dear," said Katherine, turning in her saddle and beckoning her forward.

Gwyneth urged her mount up to Katherine's side.

"Lord Litchfield," said Katherine, "may I introduce you to my husband's granddaughter and heir, the future viscountess and Lady Snowdon."

"Don't be absurd!" laughed Litchfield, sending his eyes in Gwyneth's direction. "She is a girl. . .and a young one at that."

"My son will not inherit, Lord Litchfield," said Katherine. "I will not trouble you with the legalities. However, I *will* trouble you to remove your men and equipment from our land. I will send Mr. Muir out tomorrow to make sure all activities have ceased and all equipment is gone."

At last Lord Litchfield found himself without words. But only briefly. "If what you say is true, Lady Westbrooke," he said. "Then there will be a lawsuit. I have paid your son a good deal of money."

"That is between you and him," rejoined Katherine. "He was not negotiating on behalf of the estate. Furthermore, I may be forced to bring a suit against you for trespassing and for the damage you have done to our land. Good day, Lord Litchfield. You will be hearing from my solicitor."

Speaking more boldly than she had ever spoken in her life, nearly trembling in righteous anger both toward Courtenay and Lord Litchfield for what they had tried to do behind her back, Katherine turned her mount around and galloped back to where Percy and Florilyn were waiting, followed by Steven and Gwyneth. She did not slow when she reached them but continued as fast as she was able up the ridge, into the trees, and back to the manor.

Somewhat calmed by the time she arrived home, Katherine was still infuriated at what Courtenay had tried to do. She went straight to her office and immediately drafted a letter to Hamilton Murray, informing him of what had taken place and requesting that he call at the manor as soon as possible. He must be made aware of Gwyneth's presence without delay.

Steven was on his way to Porthmadog with the letter shortly after breakfast the following morning.

Seventy-Two

The Solicitor

In Steven's absence, Katherine asked Percy to ride again into the hills to make sure Litchfield's men and equipment were nowhere to be seen. Gwyneth and Florilyn accompanied him. They set out after lunch. They found the site vacant except for the scar through the land that Litchfield had intended as the new road to the lake.

They returned through Llanfryniog. It was the first time Gwyneth had been in the village again since the day of their arrival on the coach.

"I would like to see Grannie's cottage," said Gwyneth as they rode. "Do you know if it is still vacant?"

"I don't know," replied Percy. "Do you, Florilyn?"

Florilyn shook her head.

"There is one way to find out," said Percy, turning and leading down a narrow side street between the close-built stone houses. As they went, he caught what seemed to be a brief glimpse of purple, which almost the same instant disappeared down one of the narrow lanes leading away from Grannie's cottage.

Gwyneth was quiet as they went. She had scampered among all these streets and lanes as a child, as most of the villagers considered her the peculiar stuttering "witch child" of Llanfryniog. The nostalgia of the sights, sounds, and smells brought mingled pains and joys to her heart. Riding down the town's main street, and now through its narrow lanes, the eyes that followed the three young people all knew Florilyn and Percy. Not a soul recognized the light-haired girl between them nor would have guessed that she was the very one they had feared to speak to fifteen years before. Rumors about the sudden change in her fortunes would begin soon enough, as rumors always do. As yet no whisper had reached them that the urchin who had once left forgiveness bouquets on Llanfryniog's doors would soon wed their beloved young Scot and then, five years from now, would become the viscountess and mistress of the manor to whom they would pay their rents.

Percy and Gwyneth dismounted in front of Grannie's door. Percy tried the latch. The door opened on creaky hinges. He poked his head inside. "There's nobody here, Gwyneth," he said.

Slowly Gwyneth walked inside the poor cottage that had been a second home to her.

Sensing that it was time to let her ponder the past and future quietly and alone, Percy stepped back into the street. While Gwyneth renewed her memories, Percy helped Florilyn dismount. The two led their horses as they strolled up the lane.

"Remember the day we visited that creepy lady?" said Florilyn, pointing to the strange and weirdly appointed house at the end of the street.

"I do indeed. In fact, I thought I saw her a minute ago. It looked like she was scurrying away from Grannie's cottage."

Slowly they wandered toward the house. It was of wood, unusual in this place where stone predominated, painted in white and purple and of an architecture more reminiscent of Germany's Black Forest than north Wales. The roof was steep slanted, boasting atop it an occultish weathervane. Gargoyles and statues of fairies, trolls, goblins, and other strange figures sat round the small yard. The mere look of the place sent a shiver up Florilyn's spine.

A sign above the door, ornate with Celtic symbolism, read: MADAME FLEMING, PSYCHIC—FORTUNES AND FUTURES FORETOLD.

No one knew why the enigmatic "Madame Fleming" had come to this coastal village with her fortune-telling boutique or where she had come from. On the few occasions she chanced to be seen—in dresses and scarves of reds, pinks, and purples and with gaudy jewelry dangling from ears and neck and wrists—there was no mistaking her.

When they returned back along the street a few minutes later, Grannie's former neighbor was talking over a low fence with Gwyneth. None of them had any idea that they were being watched through one of Madame Fleming's curtained windows. Neither could they have divined what thoughts were racing through the devilish woman's cunning brain. Nor why, hearing rumors of a young, white-haired beauty newly arrived in the village, she had grown newly fearful of what clues to her own identity might have been left behind in Grannie's cottage.

". . .just left without a word," Grannie's neighbor was saying. "No one knew where she had gone."

"She is happy and well, Mrs. Hueil," said Gwyneth.

"She is alive! But how do you know, lassie?"

"I am Gwyneth, Mrs. Hueil."

The woman stared back at her speechless.

"The saints preserve us!" she said in disbelief. "*Gwyneth*. . .is it really you, lassie?"

Gwyneth smiled. "My father and Grannie are in Ireland, Mrs. Hueil. It is a long story. I came back with Percy for a visit."

Mrs. Hueil glanced toward Percy and Florilyn as they walked up the lane toward them.

"Mr. Drummond. . .you're back again, I see," she said then nodded with a timid smile toward Florilyn. She was dying to know whether any significance might be attached to Florilyn's being with Percy on this day, for the whole town knew of their broken engagement and her subsequent engagement to Colville Burrenchobay.

But the rumor mills would have no more grist to add to their grinding wheels on this day. When the three remounted their horses and rode the rest of the way through the village and out of town, they appeared no more nor less than what they were—three friends who had known each other a long time and had been seen together numerous times.

Steven returned in midafternoon to say that Hamilton Murray would call at the manor on the following day.

By eleven thirty the next morning, Katherine was seated with the solicitor in the manor's formal sitting room with Florilyn, Percy, Gwyneth, and Steven, whom she had asked to be present, also. She had just given Mr. Murray a brief account of the turn of events and introduced him to Gwyneth.

"Well, I must say these are unexpected developments indeed," said Murray as he and Gwyneth and Katherine resumed their seats. "However, I must confess that I knew something of it before I came. Your son has been busy, Lady Katherine. After you left me yesterday, Mr. Muir," he said, nodding toward Steven, "I received a telegram from one of London's noted barristers informing me that he was filing a suit on behalf of one Courtenay Westbrooke, son of the late Viscount Lord Snowdon, in substantiation of his claim as the rightful and legal heir to his father's title and property."

A few comments went round the room. No one was surprised at what Courtenay had done, though having managed it so quickly took them off guard.

"Obviously I need to research the legal background of the viscountcy and its unique stipulations of inheritance," said Murray. "I should also read the affidavit you told me about."

"I have it here," said Percy. He rose and handed Murray the folded papers.

Murray took them and read it in silence, nodding a few times as he did so. "Very interesting," he said when he had completed it. "Of course, it might have been advantageous had Roderick shared this with me. But I think we all understand his reasons for handling it as he did. A document such as this, in and of itself, would have little standing in a court of law. However, as supplemental evidence, especially if its facts can be confirmed elsewhere, by parish records of the marriage and births in question, there would be a strong case to be made to substantiate Miss Barrie as the viscount's heir—that is, of course, if her maternity and her mother's paternity can be likewise substantiated."

"Tell him what you found in Ireland, Percy," said Katherine.

Percy recounted the details of his two visits to Ireland, what he had seen in the parish record books, and his talk with Mrs. Maloney, Gwyneth's aunt, along with the details both of Morvern's birth and Gwyneth's.

Murray listened attentively, taking notes and occasionally asking questions. "Even with all his," he said when Percy was through, "I fear that in the hands of a capable, and perhaps unscrupulous, barrister, the case could be troublesome in court. Without the mother—I'm sorry, Miss Barrie," he added, turning to Gwyneth, "without *your* mother. . . or some substantiating record or testimony, we really have no absolute *proof* that you are Morvern Westbrooke's. . .a.k.a. Morvern O'Sullivan's daughter. And according to what you say, Mr. Drummond, about the nature of the birth and the superstitions voiced by the aunt's husband, it is probable that the birth was never entered in the parish register. At least you never saw it, isn't that correct?"

Percy nodded. "What do you mean by a substantiating testimony?" he asked.

"An eyewitness who could absolutely establish that Miss Barrie is in fact Lord Snowdon's granddaughter by his daughter Morvern, known as Morvern O'Sullivan—someone other than Miss Barrie's father or aunt."

"There was a midwife who attended the birth," said Percy. "They were all afraid of her, but she—" He stopped in midsentence as his eyes shot open.

Suddenly Mrs. Maloney's words came back into his brain with forceful clarity—*"She claimed to be able to see into the future. . .always wore purple. . .horrid earrings of snakes and ugly creatures. . .purple, purple, purple!"*

The next moment he was out of his chair and rushing toward the door. "This may mean nothing," he said, "but there is someone in town I must see immediately. Steven, would you mind helping me hitch up the small buggy?"

The two young men ran from the room, leaving the others staring after them in bewilderment.

Seventy-Three

The Fleming

On this day Percy did not care who saw him or knew whom he had come into Llanfryniog to visit. He tied the horse to the iron post on the street. Moments later he was jingling the brass bell on Madame Fleming's front door.

Several seconds later the door opened. The face that appeared was older and more wrinkled even than Percy had expected. She did not seem surprised as she cast a brief glance behind him. "So you're alone this time, are you, Mr. Drummond," said Madame Fleming.

"That's right," said Percy abruptly. "I want to talk to you."

"Come in, come in. How can Madame Fleming be of service to you?" said the woman, leading Percy into her lair and closing the door behind him. Several candles burned inside, casting shadows upon the shelves and chairs and statues and tapestries and paintings with which the place was furnished. The bookshelf still stood against the far wall. The air was stifling with incense mingled with unpleasant odors of a more personal nature. The woman was dressed in several layers of thin, flowing purple material, her head wrapped in an orange scarf wound several times around a head mostly of gray that fell loosely over her shoulders. From her ears dangled two silver snakes. "You've had some reversals in love, I understand," she said as she waddled into the interior. "Come to see what your future holds, have you?"

"It's not my future I'm here to talk about," said Percy, "but yours. . . and your past." He stopped and stood in the middle of the crowded, dimly lit room.

The words jolted Madame Fleming, though she did not allow her reaction to show. She continued toward the small anteroom where she conducted her fortune-telling art until she realized Percy was not following her. She stopped and turned. "Come, young Drummond—come into my den where we may sit. I will look at your hand with the aid of my crystals and—"

"I have no intention of letting you look at my hand or any other part of me," said Percy. "I shall stay right here, and you shall answer my questions. I want to know where you came from before you arrived in Llanfryniog."

"Madame Fleming divulges nothing of her—"

"I want to know," interrupted Percy. "And you can stop the fake accent. You are no more Bulgarian than I am. Perhaps I should be more direct and simply ask if you came from Ireland. . .*Mrs. Faoiltiarna*?"

Even in the dim light, Percy saw the word hit her like a physical blow. Slowly she tottered on wobbly knees like a tree about to fall then staggered to a chair and sat down. "Where did you hear that name?" she said.

"It is my business where I heard it," replied Percy. "I see that you know it. You must know, too, that if those who know what you are and have cause against you. . .if they were to discover where you have been hiding all these years, it might not bode well for you."

Quickly Madame Fleming recovered herself. Her eyes flashed with anger. "It was all lies!" she spat. "What do my affairs have to do with you, young Drummond? Take care that you do not anger me, or evil may come to you when you least—"

"Don't threaten me with your mumbo jumbo," interrupted Percy. "You may be able to pull off your charade as a psychic with superstitious old men and women, but it will not work with me. Your threats mean nothing. I know that you practiced as a midwife in eastern Ireland before escaping with your life under threat of witchcraft. Unless you tell me what I want to know, I will expose you as a deceiver and fraud. I will contact the authorities in Arklow, informing them of your whereabouts. I think you know that the religious climate in Wales would not be friendly to the knowledge that witchcraft was being practiced in its midst."

A vile string of imprecations exploded from Madame Fleming's mouth.

"Guard your tongue!" shouted Percy. "Threaten or curse me again, and I will walk out of here and broadcast what I know. Now calm yourself. I have questions to ask, and I want answers. If you cooperate, I will promise to keep your secrets."

Thirty minutes later, Percy and Madame Fleming left the latter's house together. If either had qualms about being seen with the other, they did not show it. The proprietress of Madame Fleming, Ltd. was notably subdued from the interview recently concluded. But inside her dark soul, the fires of fury still burned hot.

They climbed into the buggy where it stood on the street. The springs groaned and tipped under the bulk of Llanfryniog's colorful seer. Percy sat down beside her, flipped the reins, and they bounded off. What those curious eyes who saw them might have thought would have been interesting to inquire.

It would have made an even more interesting inquiry to know what the erstwhile Mrs. Faoiltiarna, alias the Wolf Lady, alias Madame Fleming, thought to find herself gazing up at the stone walls of Westbrooke Manor as they rode toward it and, a few minutes later, being led toward its front door. What the manor residents and staff thought as word gradually spread concerning whom Percy had brought into their midst might have been yet more interesting to know.

Percy led her through the front doors. "Wait here," he said when they were inside. He disappeared up the main staircase, taking the steps two at a time.

The others were still gathered in the sitting room, having tea and waiting for him.

"Mr. Murray, I have with me," he began as all eyes turned toward him, "a woman who can, I believe, provide you the testimony you speak of. She is waiting downstairs."

"Who can that be?" asked Katherine.

"It is a long story, Aunt Katherine," replied Percy. "I heard about her when I was in Ireland. All the pieces did not fit together until we were talking a short while ago. Suddenly the light dawned, and I realized that the very woman who might hold the clues to prove Gwyneth's identity had left Ireland, changed her identity, and had been in Llanfryniog all along. She is not someone I would normally trust. However, Mr. Murray, that I know her former identity, I believe, gives us sufficient power over her that she will tell the truth. If you question her and take down her statement, along with Uncle Roderick's affidavit and the parish records. . .hopefully you will have enough documentation to meet Courtenay's challenge."

"Then let us see what the woman has to say," said Murray. "Lady Katherine, if you would provide me a room where I can interview the woman in private, I shall see what I can learn."

"I want to hear everything, too!" said Florilyn.

"I promised her confidentiality," said Percy. "She has a past she is anxious not be known. That I figured it out makes her hate me. But I promised not to tell her secrets if she would give Mr. Murray a full statement of the facts of Gwyneth's birth. We must let her speak with him alone."

"I will need a third party to witness to the attestation to insure its legality," said Murray. "You are of age, Mr. Drummond, and not directly related by blood to any of the principles involved. It would seem that you are the likely candidate."

Percy hesitated a moment. "Yes, I see what you mean," he said. "But I would prefer that Steven also be present, either as the primary witness or you can use both of us if you prefer. He has nothing to gain, and it could be argued that I do."

"A wise observation, Mr. Drummond," nodded Murray. "Two witnesses will be better than one."

Five minutes later, Percy showed Madame Fleming into a small office on the first floor that had several chairs and a writing table. He introduced her to Hamilton Murray then himself took a chair beside where Steven already sat across the room.

Madame Fleming sat down in one of the chairs while Murray took his place at the desk. With pen in hand, he wrote down a few preliminary remarks of time, date, place, and the names of Steven and Percy and himself as witnesses. Then he looked up at Madame Fleming. "Please tell me your name, for the record," he said.

The name she gave was neither of the names by which Percy knew her.

"Now tell me, please, in as much detail as possible, what you know of the parentage and birth of the young woman known as Gwyneth Barrie."

Madame Fleming cast a brief glance of wrath in Percy's direction, still incensed that another was capable of exerting power over her. "I was for many years a midwife in Arklow, on the eastern coast of Ireland," she began, almost as through clenched teeth. "A time came when I was called upon by a certain lady of the name Maighdlin O'Sullivan. Her granddaughter had been raised by her and had recently married and was with child. She employed me for the birthing."

"What was the granddaughter's name?" asked Murray.

"Morvern. . .Morvern O'Sullivan. That was the name Mrs. O'Sullivan gave me."

"Do you know the names of her parents?"

"No. They were either dead or gone, I don't know. She was raised by Mrs. O'Sullivan."

"And she was now married and expecting?"

"Yes."

"What was her husband's name?"

"Barrie. . .Codnor Barrie."

"So the expectant mother's married name was actually Morvern Barrie?"

"I suppose so."

"And then?"

"The time for the birthing came. I delivered the baby—a girl."

"Did they name the child immediately?"

"They did."

"What name did they give her?"

"Gwyneth."

"Was there anything unique or distinctive about the birth?"

"Nothing. The child was healthy, the mother was healthy. Only, the baby was born with pure white hair, not the red hair of the mother and, as I understand it, the grandmother as well. The mother's uncle—an irrational man of violent temper—threatened me on account of it. He said that I had brought a curse on the family and the white hair proved it. After that, because of him, my life was in danger. I left Ireland and came to Wales and changed my name."

Murray nodded and looked over his transcription of the conversation.

"Did you ever see any of them again?" he asked.

"The man Barrie and his daughter, of course," replied Madame Fleming. "It wasn't long after I arrived in Llanfryniog that he came here himself. I had had no idea that he was Welsh. One day I saw him in the village, and I knew in an instant who he was. I had my own reasons for not wanting him to recognize me. But I soon learned that he had come to Wales with the child. When I saw her for myself, even though it was from a distance when Mrs. Myfanawy was caring for her, I recognized her in an instant. There was no mistaking that hair. What the man and his girl were doing in Llanfryniog, I hadn't an idea. I later heard that the mother, the girl called Morvern, had died and that he was a widower alone with his baby. But there's no mistake that the child called Gwyneth Barrie was the same baby I delivered in Arklow."

Again Murray paused and looked over the transcript. "All right then," he said, rising from the desk. "I believe that is all I need for now. If I should need to question you further, Mr. Drummond, I believe, knows how to contact you."

Again Madame Fleming shot Percy a hateful glance then lifted her ponderous bulk from the chair.

"If you would just sign here," said Murray, handing her the pen.

She did so, with obvious displeasure.

"And you as well, Mr. Muir. . .and Mr. Drummond."

Steven walked across the room, still stunned by the amazing turn of events, and also signed the paper, as did Percy.

Finally Murray added his own signature. "With the parish records you located," he said to Percy, "along with the viscount's affidavit, and now this. . .I believe Miss Barrie's claim to be virtually unassailable. No court will overturn it."

Percy escorted Madame Fleming, whose curiosity was heightened by Murray's final words, out of the office and to the front door. They again climbed into the buggy, and he returned her to her home.

Not a word was spoken between them.

Seventy-Four

The Grandparents

Courtenay's twenty-fifth birthday came and went without fanfare. He had not been seen since Percy's and Gwyneth's arrival.

It was a great relief, for the present at least, for Katherine to know that she would not be forced to depart for Glasgow in the immediate future. Several letters were dispatched to Percy's parents, informing them of developments.

Percy and Gwyneth planned to leave Llanfryniog for Scotland as soon as they were certain that Katherine and Florilyn would find no unexpected notices of eviction slid under their doors during the night. In thoroughly reviewing the legalities of the case, Hamilton Murray assured them that Courtenay could make no move against them. In the extremely unlikely event that he should prevail in court, if the matter went that far, it would be months, if not years, before any change would be enforced. Gradually Katherine began to breathe more easily.

Two days after Courtenay's birthday, Palmer Sutcliffe appeared at the manor requesting an interview with Katherine. He presented her with a legal demand for a return of £5,400 that had been paid to Courtenay, in two payments, the most recent £1,000 only two weeks previously, by Lord Litchfield as down payment for sale of one thousand acres of Westbrooke land. Katherine confessed herself completely unaware of the transaction. Be that as it may, rejoined Sutcliffe coolly, papers had been signed on behalf of the estate and a large amount of money had changed hands. If that amount was not returned within a week, said Sutcliffe, interest at 4 percent would commence, to be added to the balance monthly, along with legal proceedings against the Westbrooke estate for fraud. Stunned by the charge, Katherine did her best to preserve her outward calm. She said that she was very sorry Lord Litchfield had not been more careful and had entered into a transaction with her son when he had no legal power to act on behalf of the estate. However, she hardly saw what she was able to do about it. She suggested he speak with the manor's solicitor. Another consultation between Katherine and Hamilton Murray followed almost immediately.

With their old friendship rekindled, drawn together on deeper spiritual levels by the blossoming maturity of their mutual womanhood, as well as by the fact that both had suffered at the hands of the same man, Florilyn and Rhawn saw one another nearly every day. The reciprocity of their friendship now sought more meaningful levels of communication and exchange than was possible when they were self-centered teens, for they now desired to become women of dignity and character. Gwyneth's presence at the manor, too, drew the best out of Florilyn. Their former friendship resumed, and Rhawn could not but be drawn into it. It was not long before the three young women were the best of friends. In spite of the fact that Gwyneth was several years younger than both, the two older girls sensed her calm, soft-spoken, and mystical union with God, made all the more profound as she now entered the fullness of her womanhood. It was only natural that Florilyn and Rhawn looked to Gwyneth as the unspoken spiritual head of their threefold cord of friendship. She had been attuning herself to the subtleties of the inner voice all her life. She had learned much that still lay years in the future for them. When they prayed together, however, Gwyneth remained curiously silent. Most of her prayers were prayers of listening. What she had to *say* to God, she said in her heart.

One day when Rhawn appeared at the manor to visit her friends, she wore a strange look on her face. "I have a favor to ask," she said.

Gwyneth and Florilyn waited.

"There is something I want to do. . .something I *need* to do. I am afraid of doing it alone. I have spoken with my parents, and they agree that it is time. I would like to ask the two of you to accompany me."

The three left the manor for town a short while later. They stopped at the Lorimer home where Mr. Lorimer had a buggy hitched and ready. He greeted Florilyn and Gwyneth and took charge of their horses while Rhawn went into the house for her son. A short while later the three girls and young boy, with Rhawn at the reins, set out northward.

By the time they reached their destination, Florilyn and Gwyneth knew what was in Rhawn's heart to do. At length Rhawn reined up in front of Burrenchobay Hall. With her friends at her side and her son's hand in hers, they walked to the front door. When it opened, she asked the butler to see Mr. and Mrs. Burrenchobay.

The wait of two minutes seemed like ten. When at last they heard footsteps approaching, Florilyn and Gwyneth stepped back. Florilyn had her own reasons for being apprehensive. She had not seen Colville's parents since breaking off the engagement. She had no idea what they might have been told.

What the butler had said, or whether they had suspected the truth before now, the expressions on the faces of the member of parliament and his wife were neither hostile nor unwelcoming. Lady Burrenchobay smiled, betraying slight nervousness. Her eyes flitted down to the boy at Rhawn's side. Instantly her eyes filled as the years fell away and she found herself looking at the very image of her son twenty-two years before.

"Hello, Sir Armond. . .Lady Burrenchobay," said Rhawn. "I know this is awkward, and I know you may hate me, and I won't blame you if you do, but you need to know. . .this has waited far too long. I would like to introduce you to your grandson, Amren. Amren, dear, this woman is your grandmother, and this man is your grandfather."

The boy smiled and nodded sheepishly, then held out his hand as he had obviously been told to do.

Swallowing hard and blinking a time or two, Sir Armond reached down and shook it. "A good firm handshake, my boy," he said in a husky voice. "That is a sign of character. Good for you."

Lady Burrenchobay, tears in her eyes, stooped down as her husband stood and stepped back. "Hello, Amren," she said, desperately trying to keep from breaking down altogether. "I am so happy to know you. Would you like to come in and see our house, and perhaps have some biscuits and milk?"

"Yes, ma'am," said Amren. "Thank you very much."

Lady Burrenchobay stood then turned to Rhawn and looked deep into her eyes. "Oh, my dear," she said, taking a step forward and embracing Rhawn affectionately. "I am so sorry for what you have been through. Thank you *so* much!" When she stepped back, she and Rhawn were both weeping.

Rhawn forced a smile then turned. "You both know Florilyn," she said.

"Yes. . .certainly, of course. Hello, Florilyn," said Sir Armond. Neither of Colville's parents knew the full details of what had transpired between Florilyn and their son. They only knew there had been some change. They did not yet know, however, that Florilyn had formally terminated the engagement.

"I would also like you to meet my friend, Gwyneth Barrie," said Rhawn. "You will be hearing more about her, I am certain, in the future. Gwyneth, please meet Sir Armond Burrenchobay and Lady Burrenchobay."

Gwyneth stepped forward, smiled, and shook hands with them both. "I am very pleased to meet you," she said simply. The man and woman returned her smile, disarmed by her penetrating expression and countenance.

Lady Burrenchobay turned again to Rhawn. "Come in, my dear," she said. "I think it is time you and I became better acquainted."

Rhawn looked back at her two friends. She smiled as if to say, *I will be okay now.*

"Shall we come back for you later?" said Florilyn.

"Don't worry about a thing," said Sir Armond. "I will take Rhawn and the little fellow back to Llanfryniog. Perhaps you will stay and have tea with us, Rhawn," he added to Rhawn. "Florilyn, if you would tell Styles that I will bring them home."

Seventy-Five

The Storm

As the train pulled into the Glasgow station, Gwyneth stared out the window with wide-eyed anticipation.

"Do you remember that first day we met?" asked Percy beside her. "You said you wanted to see Glasgow one day. That's why you asked my name...so you would know who to look for when you came to Glasgow. Well, here we are...and you know my name!"

Gwyneth laughed. "I remember," she said. "I also said I wanted to visit London. Will you take me to London someday?"

"Your wish is my command!"

Having never before had occasion to meet Gwyneth when visiting Wales, Edward and Mary Drummond could not have been more delighted with their future daughter-in-law. After a few days in Glasgow, however, Gwyneth was anxious to see her father again. They had written him, but she wanted to tell him about everything that had happened in person.

She and Percy sailed from Glasgow to Dublin, where Codnor was waiting for them. Though the great change in her life was only a few weeks old, already there was an obvious change in Gwyneth's countenance. What a reunion they had with him and Grannie! Grannie seemed about to die of happiness at the double blessing that had come to Gwyneth. Percy also took her to meet Father O'Leary. With him accompanying them, they paid a visit to Gwyneth's aunt, Vanora Maloney, telling her about Percy's climb up to Percy's Table and revealing Gwyneth's engagement to Percy but not the full details of her altered social status.

With Gwyneth now heir to Westbrooke Manor and its title, her future was obviously in Snowdonia. Her father and Grannie, too, were anxious to return to Wales. What to do with the house on the lower slopes of Lugnaquilla remained uncertain, though Codnor would sell his flock to neighboring sheep farmers at whatever price they could afford. He and Grannie, they said, would try to be ready to sail for Wales by summer. With their former cottages still vacant, both planned to return to life as it had been before. Learning of their plans, however, Katherine would hear nothing of it. They would come live at the manor, she insisted, where Grannie would be well cared for by loving hands and where Gwyneth's father could help Steven with his duties and gradually replace aging Holin Radnor as the manor's groom. Steven could not have been more excited at the prospect of working with his uncle. He had missed shepherding. And Adela was greatly anticipating sitting in the library with her brother and reminiscing about their grandfather's library.

As for Katherine's new house on Mochras Head, due to be completed within a year, it was obvious that Courtenay would not be displacing her from the manor, at least anytime soon. After wondering briefly if she had been too hasty in constructing a new home, Katherine realized that Gwyneth and Percy, as Master and Mistress of Westbrooke Manor, would one day want to have a family of their own and occupy the manor's family quarters on the second floor. Therefore, she would herself take up residence in her new home whenever it suited Gwyneth for her to do so. Notwithstanding that she herself would be legal trustee of the estate until Gwyneth herself turned twenty-five, Katherine quickly began to defer to Gwyneth regarding future plans.

The glaring uncertainty about the future remained to be Courtenay. He returned from London after a month, clearly aware that the prospects of his legal contestation of Gwyneth's position were not favorable. He was rarely seen. What his future held was anyone's guess. Thus far, only Katherine knew of the financial dilemma facing him. Whether she would have bailed him out and cleared off his debt to Litchfield had she been able, she could not have said. But as her every available pound had been sunk into the construction of the new house, it would be two or three years before her resources would sufficiently accumulate to keep Courtenay from serious legal problems. If Litchfield pressed the matter to the extreme and brought charges of fraud against Courtenay, the specter of jail was not out of the question. But she did not see what she could do. She had no intention of asking for Edward's help.

In late May, a month after Percy's and Gwyneth's return from Ireland, a tremendous storm blew in off the North Atlantic, consuming Ireland in wind and hurricane tides. The battering spread through the Irish Sea to the west coast of Scotland and Wales, threatening to flood their low-lying coastal villages. The fishermen of Llanfryniog secured their boats in the harbor as best they could and prepared to ride out the siege, hoping they would not find their boats in splinters when it was over.

The worst of the storm hit between three and five o'clock in the morning. Whether anyone in north Wales was still asleep was doubtful. Most lay awake in their beds, listening to the dreadful tempest doing its best to blow the roofs from their houses. Thankfully those roofs were of heavy Welsh slates!

Percy finally rose about six thirty, thinking himself likely the first in the great mansion to venture from his room. Instead, he found Florilyn and Katherine already in the breakfast room with tea. Mrs. Drynwydd had just put out a pot of fresh coffee.

Steven joined them a few minutes later. "Is the roof still on?" he laughed.

"I thought my window would burst," said Florilyn. "I kept thinking the glass was about to shatter and the rain come splashing in all over my bed!"

"When it is light, Steven," said Katherine, "we will have to check all the upper floors and the garret for leaks."

"I will see to it, as well as the windows on the west and north of the building."

"Where's Gwyneth?" asked Percy, glancing about at the others. "I would expect her to be up at the crack of dawn. She loves tempestuous weather!"

"I think I heard her door close and footsteps in the hall," said Florilyn.

"When?"

"Earlier. . .an hour or more ago."

"Oh, no—then she's out in it!" laughed Percy.

"Do you think she's in any danger?" said Katherine.

"Not for a second," answered Percy. "She could no more be in danger from the weather than Steven could from a sheep. She loves whatever face nature puts on and fears none of them, except snow in the mountains. She does have a healthy regard for the perils of winter."

Percy went to the window and gazed out. The dawn was still dark and gray. Fierce winds whipped at the trees as if it would uproot them with a single blast. In spite of his words to Katherine, the sight sent a momentary shudder up his spine. This wind was stronger than he had ever seen. It could sweep Gwyneth off her feet in an instant. If she stood too near the cliff edge or too close to the sea at the harbor. . . He shuddered to think what might be the result.

After a cup of coffee and a few minutes more conversation, he excused himself, hurried back to his room, bundled himself in what protection from the elements he could, grabbed a second rain slicker, and then left the house by the back stairs and side door.

A great blast of wind nearly knocked him over as he came round the side wall of the house and into the seaward brunt of the storm. Recovering himself, he set off down the drive toward the plateau, bending hard into the face of the tumult. There were only two places where he expected to find Gwyneth. This time he would check *both*.

The rain had let up since the worst of its drenching onslaught between midnight and three. Percy trudged across the spongy, soaked turf toward Katherine's new house. As he passed the house, he could see clearly to the point of the promontory of Mochras Head. It was obvious that Gwyneth was not there or had been blown into the sea!

Percy turned toward town but then paused. He glanced back up at the newly constructed stone walls of Katherine's proposed home. A dozen or more openings where the windows would be installed seemed to look out upon the coastline as if from dead, hollow eye sockets. One day this house would be full of life, Percy thought. Those window-eyes would gaze out upon the countryside with light from within. As yet, however, the edifice was an empty shell awaiting the life of human touch, in the same way that the human animal had been an empty shell until implanted with the soul-life of God's divine touch.

Moved by some impulse, he turned and walked toward the house. He entered through one of several openings where doors, like the windows, would eventually be installed. He had been inside the house with Steven a time or two since his arrival back in Wales but had paid little attention to the details of its interior. Now he stood gazing about in the darkness of a stormy morning. All around him were the signs of construction—piles of boards, half-finished walls and ceilings, and bare floors. The wind whistled and sang through its many openings, up and down staircases, around corners, and through vacant rooms.

Slowly Percy made his way to the stone staircase at the center of the ground floor and up to the landing above the first floor. Something seemed to guide his steps. Ahead of him, the centerpiece of the entire house, envisioned in Katherine's mind's eye from the beginning, was what would be the large central sitting room, facing due west toward the promontory, its seaward wall comprised nearly in its entirety of three enormous windows, giving the entire room a spectacular vantage point of the promontory. The coastline stretched away north and south as far as the eye could see. The view straight ahead looked out westward toward Ireland, whose own coastline, Katherine hoped, on a clear day, might faintly be seen.

As Percy entered, across the great room, he saw a figure seated on the bare stone floor six or eight feet away from the opening of the largest central window.

The early riser knew whose footsteps were approaching behind her without turning.

Percy sat down beside her and took her hand in his.

"There could not be a house with a more beautiful view than this," said Gwyneth quietly.

"How long have you been here?" asked Percy.

"I don't know," replied Gwyneth. "The storm drew me. I think I have changed my mind about Lady Katherine's new house. It is the perfect place to have built it. How did you know where to find me?"

"I didn't. This time, if you weren't here, I was planning to check the harbor next!"

They sat for a few minutes in silence, gazing out at the wild, windy, gray sky and sea blended in turbulent motion. The sea appeared angry, but Gwyneth found it no less mesmerizing than on a day when its radiant blues and greens stretched westward to the land of her birth.

"As I was looking up at the house, with the empty windows," said Percy, "it reminded me of the empty eyes of the skull you saw in the cave."

"Don't remind me. It frightened me to death!"

"If ever a storm were going to wash the sand away from that old pirate again, this would be the time."

"Do you really think what I saw was the skull of the old pirate from Grannie's tale, the same man who gave her the coin?"

"I thought she said they found the man dead on the beach the next morning."

"Oh, that's right. Then who did the skull belong to?"

"Maybe there were two pirates. What if one of them made it to the cave, but the man Grannie saw didn't? We'll go look at low tide as soon as the storm passes!"

"Not me, Percy!"

"Then I will go myself."

"Well. . .maybe I will go with you."

Seventy-Six

The Cave

The idea of exploring the cave again did not leave Percy all day. By late afternoon the storm showed signs of easing. When night fell, the moon was making sporadic appearances between the clouds, and the wind had nearly ceased. By then Gwyneth's enthusiasm for the project had mounted as well.

When Percy appeared in the breakfast room the next morning, she was eagerly waiting for him. "The tide is rising, Percy," she said excitedly. "It will be high sometime before noon."

"What—you've already been out!"

"Of course," she laughed.

"Don't we need a low tide?" he asked.

"Yes, and low tide will be late in the afternoon when the sun is going down. It will be perfect—the sun will shine off the water straight into the cave!"

"This afternoon it is, then. We have a date with a pirate's skull!"

They were at the beach by three, walking leisurely hand in hand along the shoreline at the water's edge of the outgoing tide. It was obvious to Gwyneth's eyes that the storm had wreaked havoc with the coastline she knew so well. She scampered about looking at everything excitedly.

By four o'clock, the water had retreated most of the way out of the cave's mouth, and they crept inside.

"The cave floor is lower," said Gwyneth as they made their way into the darkness. "I can tell that the roof is higher above me. The outgoing tide must have removed at least six inches of sand."

"Can you remember where you saw the skull?"

"I don't know—about halfway back to the end, I think."

As their eyes accustomed to the darkness, Percy went to his knees and began to crawl about on all fours, his eyes probing and his hands feeling the sand. Back and forth he crawled, feeling about, digging with his fingers all around the area where Gwyneth thought the skull might have been.

"Wait. . .there, I felt something hard," he said at length. He brushed his hands about the spot again. "Yes, there it is—look," he said, removing bit of wet sand from the spot.

"Look, yes . . .I think it's a bit of bone!"

Percy continued to rub away the sand then scooped more away with his hand until the rounded top of a human cranium was clearly visible. "It's the pirate!"

"Oh Percy, let's leave him where he is. I don't think I can bear to see those horrid empty eyes again."

"We've got to solve the mystery. What was he doing here? I'll go get a spade from Chandos."

"Wait for me. I don't want to be left alone. . .with *him*!"

They ran out of the cave. In the distance, in the direction of the harbor, they saw two horses. As Percy ran toward them, he saw Steven and Florilyn.

"Where are you off to in such a hurry?" laughed Steven.

"I think we found the old pirate in the cave!" he replied. "I'm going to find a spade."

"Pirate!" exclaimed Steven, but already Percy was running toward the village.

A minute later Gwyneth came hurrying up. They dismounted and tied their horses at the harbor.

"What's this about a pirate, Gwyneth?" asked Florilyn.

"Haven't I ever told you about the pirate's skull I found?"

"No. . .ugh—that sounds horrid!"

"It was in the cave back there, after a terrific storm when the tide was low—just like today. You know the cave, Steven. All the children played in it. I never saw it after that. It was covered over with sand. Percy thinks we've found it again. He wants to dig it up."

"But why?"

"Because when Grannie was a girl, she saw a pirate who had washed up on the beach from a shipwreck. He gave her a gold coin."

"Gold!"

"The pirate said there was more. But by the next morning he was dead. Look—I've got the coin right here. Grannie gave it to me." She dug in her pocket and pulled out the coin.

Steven and Florilyn looked at it with wide eyes. "I want to see this pirate!" said Steven.

He ran on ahead. By the time Gwyneth and Florilyn followed him into the darkness of the cave, Steven was on his hands and knees where he saw evidence of Percy's clawing about the cave floor, digging in the hard-packed sand with his fingers.

When Percy returned five minutes later with a spade, Steven had uncovered the eye sockets that had struck such fear into thirteen-year-old Gwyneth Barrie. Immediately, Percy set in with the spade.

"Careful. . .careful," said Steven. "If the old fellow's head is still attached to the rest of him, you don't want to behead him."

"Steven. . .ugh!" exclaimed Florilyn.

Slowly as they dug down, the skull came more into view. Percy gently loosened the sand while Steven scooped it away with his hands. The two girls gradually moved back out of the cave into the sunlight. This was man's work. They had seen enough!

By now the day was reaching its end. Most of the village men were either on their way to Mistress Chattan's inn for a pint of ale or were walking home from their day's labors for evening tea.

The sun continued to settle toward the western horizon. As it did, it sent longer and longer shafts of light into the mouth of the cave where Percy and Steven continued with what seemed to Gwyneth and

Florilyn a gruesome task.

It did not take much more excavation before the excited young men were convinced that it was no mere skull Gwyneth had discovered seven years before but the entire skeleton of a man laying his full length toward the mouth of the cave, buried a foot beneath the surface. A few shards of clothing remained, preserved in the salty, sandy grave.

"Come look!" yelled Percy, his voice echoing to the outside through the cave mouth. "We've found the pirate. . .all of him!"

"I don't want to look!" Florilyn shouted back. "I would have nightmares for weeks."

But Gwyneth ventured slowly back inside. She stood for a moment looking down at the trench Percy and Steven had dug in the growing light. A bony human frame lay at the bottom of it, still more than half embedded in the hard sand.

"It looks like he was trying to crawl out of the cave," she said. "If he was trying to get away from the other man—the pirate who gave Grannie the coin—or if he was trying to find shelter in the cave, he should be facing the other direction."

"You're right," said Steven. "I hadn't thought of that. Why is he facing toward the cave mouth?"

"Maybe he came in here for shelter," suggested Percy, "but then was trapped by the incoming tide and tried to get out but then drowned."

By then the rays of the setting sun were sending their light from the level of the sea directly into the mouth of the cave, illuminating its wet walls of rock and sandy floor that sloped up toward the back of the cave. As Percy glanced about, it seemed as though the violent waters of the storm had also cleared away a good amount of the sand from the back of the cave wall. Slowly he wandered deeper inside where the rock ceiling above him sloped down to meet the cave floor. He dropped to his hands and knees to examine the farthest end of the cave.

"What have you found?" asked Steven, following him.

"I don't know, maybe nothing," replied Percy. "I remember being curious about this before. Now that the sunlight is shining on the back of the cave. . .it looks different. Some of the sand is gone. And look, there is a trickle of water coming out from somewhere."

"What's this," said Steven, stooping and probing with his hand. "It looks like. . ." He dug about harder. "There is a small hole that extends through the rock. . .or under it."

Percy scrambled back for the spade. Within seconds, he was again at Steven's side, digging away furiously at the base of what appeared as the back wall of the cave. After a minute he stopped, stretched out on his belly, and reached his hand through the opening he had made under the rock, feeling about with his fingers. In another moment, his hand poked through into an opening behind it. Immediately a rush of cool air met his face.

"There's a cavity behind the rock," he said. He stretched his arm as far as he could through the hole. "I'm moving my hand about. I think the cave goes farther back. It's been blocked up by sand!"

He pulled his arm out, grabbed the spade again, and now began digging harder than ever.

"I can feel back in there. There's definitely an opening! And I'm feeling something. . . It feels like rope."

"Watch yourself," said Steven. "It might be alive!"

By now Gwyneth had come up behind them and was watching intently. Even Florilyn, hearing the conversation in the distance, crept a step or two into the cave mouth to listen.

Working together, Percy and Steven managed to excavate an opening a foot deep under the back wall of the cave. As it required digging out below the level of the cave floor, it would fill with sea water the moment the incoming tide reached it again. As soon as it did, their excavated tunnel would fill with sand.

"We've got to get a deeper opening," said Percy. "I need to squeeze in before the tide."

"You're not going to crawl back through there?" said Steven.

"I'm thinner than you. Somebody has to. We have to see what's there."

"And if the tide comes in, you'll be trapped inside! A hundred years from now someone will be digging up *your* skeleton."

"I have more faith in you than that," laughed Percy. "You won't let that happen to me."

"Then we need to dig a wider opening," said Steven. He took up the spade again.

Without looking too closely, Florilyn crept past the crypt where the silent skeleton lay. Both girls now watched the progress. They did not like the idea of Percy trying to crawl into what looked like an opening too small for a cat.

Fifteen minutes later, a tunnel through the cave floor under the sloping back wall appeared large enough for Percy to make an attempt.

"Percy, be careful!" said Florilyn.

"I don't know that I like this," said Gwyneth. "Once it turns, the tide rises quickly."

"Then you all keep an eye on it. The moment there is any danger, I promise I'll come right back out." Percy lay flat, the entire front of his body now wet, and began to wriggle and squeeze into the opening he and Steven had excavated. Inch by inch, he wormed his way into the darkness until his feet disappeared from sight.

"Percy!" wailed Florilyn.

As her voice echoed away, the cave fell silent.

The next sound they heard was Percy's voice. It sounded a mile away and echoed strangely off the stone walls of the cave.

"I'm inside a small chamber," he said. "It's nearly black. I can't see a thing. I'm feeling about. . .there's not room to stand. . .it's probably five feet by four feet. The larger cave must originally have included this little back part. There is definitely a rope and. . .now I'm feeling what I think are two or three cork floats. It must have washed in here when the cave was open. . .and. . .wait, there's something. . ."

The other three waited.

"There's some kind of box," Percy's voice echoed back again. "I can't see it, but. . .it's too heavy to lift. It's tangled up in the rope. Steven, hand your knife through. I'll try to cut away some of the rope."

Steven lay down and stretched his hand through the tunnel. A moment later, Percy's hand fumbled from the other side, grabbing for the knife. Again they waited.

"I've cut it away from this mess of rope," called Percy. "I can hardly move it... it feels like there's a lock...it must be made of metal, otherwise it would have rotted. Here, Steven, take your knife."

Again Steven reached through and retrieved his knife.

"I'll try to get the box into the opening. . .I'll shove it your way. . . you're stronger than I am, Steven—if you can pull it through. . ." Grunting and pushing sounds followed as Percy struggled with whatever he had discovered.

Still on his stomach looking through the tunnel with what light the sun sent in, Steven saw the black end of a box some eight or nine inches square being pushed toward him from the inner portion of the cave.

"That's as far as I can move it," Percy called to him. "It's so heavy it wants to sink into the sand. I can't budge it another inch."

Steven stretched his hand as far as he could reach. It took several minutes and a great effort, but inch by inch he managed to pull the box through toward the open side of the cave. As the girls waited anxiously, behind them a wave sounded on the shoreline outside.

"Percy. . .the tide!" cried Florilyn. "Whatever is in there isn't worth you getting trapped!"

Gwyneth turned and ran out to the beach, glanced to her right and left, then out to sea, then hurried back inside. "The tide has turned, Percy," she said into the darkened tunnel of the cave floor. "Probably fifteen minutes ago."

"She's right, old man," said Steven. "I didn't want to mention it, but the bottom of this little tunnel we dug is getting soggy. It will fill up with water anytime. I've got the box. It's time you got out of there before this cave becomes known for *two* graves."

"Just give me another minute or two. I want to make sure there's nothing else in here."

"Like another pirate!"

"I don't know. But we may not have this chance again."

"Percy!" cried Florilyn again.

By the time the fading light of the sun began to reflect off Percy's white face as he wriggled back into the front of the cave, his hair was matted and wet, and his shirt and trousers soaked and caked with sand. Both girls let out great sighs of relief when he was through and back on his hands and knees.

Nearly the same moment the sun began to sink below the horizon. The briefly lit cave again grew dark.

"I'm getting out of here while I can still see," said Florilyn. "I don't want to trip and fall on that old pirate!"

Gwyneth followed her out. Percy and Steven together lugged the small chest behind them into the open air.

"This thing weighs a ton!" said Percy. "It must be made of solid lead."

"Are you going to open it?" said Florilyn excitedly.

"The box must be of brass or silver not to have rusted," began Steven, "but that lock is definitely rusted shut."

Percy turned and ran back inside the cave. He returned with the spade. Two whacks was all it took to demolish latch and lock together.

The four knelt down around it.

"Well, Gwyneth," said Percy. "If you are the future owner of all this, which I assume includes the land all the way down to the water's edge, I suppose technically this box belongs to you. You should do the honors."

"You discovered it, Percy," said Gwyneth. "I would rather you open it."

Percy reached out his hand, took hold of the broken latch, and pulled hard on the lid. The two rusted hinges on the other side shattered. The lid swung free and flew back.

Four gasps of disbelief sounded simultaneously at the sight that met their eyes in the golden light of the setting sun.

Seventy-Seven

Rebuke and Forgiveness

It took some time for their stupefaction at what they had found, and their subsequent frenzied discussion of what it must be worth, to subside.

Steven at length sounded the practical note. "We need to get this back to the manor," he said. "We obviously can't carry it. I'll ride back and bring a buggy. Florilyn and I left our horses at the harbor."

"I'll go with you," said Florilyn, jumping to her feet.

"And we shall stand guard," added Percy.

"Do you really think all that gold is mine, Percy?" asked Gwyneth when they were again alone and dusk began to settle around them.

"It will be. I suppose it is Aunt Katherine's right now. Who else's would it be but yours?"

"You and Steven found it."

"All four of us found it. . .and on *your* land."

"What will be my land. Or *may* be. It's not mine yet. But this gold must belong to somebody."

"I doubt it. Look at these inscriptions," said Percy, removing one of the gold coins from the chest. I never paid much attention to the markings on Grannie's coin before. But these are all identical—and very old. Those pirates must have stumbled on some ancient site, maybe going back to King Alfred's time or earlier. I'm no expert, but I would guess these to be of Celtic origin from somewhere in Wales or Scotland or Ireland. Whatever the value of the gold, which is considerable, the historical value is probably greater."

"What should we do with it?"

"That will be up to you and Aunt Katherine."

After Steven and Percy had lugged the bog to the waiting buggy at the harbor, and once it was safely locked in the safe in the late viscount's office that evening, Katherine, Gwyneth, and Percy had a long discussion. They judged it best to say nothing to anyone for the present, even to Courtenay. They needed to consult with experts and seek legal advice without allowing rumors to begin circulating.

Meanwhile, Katherine told several of the leading men of the village about the skeleton that had been found. That would be fuel for rumor enough. She arranged for them to dig up the remains and bury them in the village cemetery beside the shipmate who had been found two generations before.

At first pass, Hamilton Murray agreed with Percy's assessment that the gold belonged to the Westbrooke estate where it had been found. He would look into the matter, he said. In the meantime, if they had need of any portion of it, he could arrange to sell some of the coins through confidential antiquarian sources.

A few weeks later, Percy and Gwyneth returned to Ireland to help Gwyneth's father with the return move to Wales. Codnor Barrie and Grannie arrived back in Llanfryniog in July. By now, all of north Wales knew that the former urchin and witch child of Llanfryniog had all along been the viscount's secret granddaughter and was now the future viscountess and Lady Snowdon. This raised Codnor Barrie and Grannie almost to the level of royalty in the eyes of their former neighbors. Their arrival was greeted with great fanfare.

One person who was not rejoicing at the many changes coming to Westbrooke Manor was Courtenay Westbrooke. In his opinion, the place was becoming a home for peasants and vagabonds. The sooner he could get away from it the better. But he had bigger problems than Gwyneth and her family. His mother did not have the money to clear off his debt to Litchfield. She had as good as told him she wouldn't do so even if she did. Pride prevented him going cap in hand to his religious uncle, Percy's father, for a handout.

It killed him, but he knew there was only one way to hope to raise a portion of the cash needed to keep him out of jail. He would have to sell his racehorses. He had floated an offer to Lord Litchfield, offering his four thoroughbreds in exchange for the full sum. Though the reply had been sent in writing, he could feel Litchfield laughing in his face at the absurdity of the suggestion, concluding with a summary of the current amount due, including interest, and a renewed threat of legal action if the matter was not resolved in a timely fashion.

He might be able to get £2,500 for the four animals, £3,000 *if* he was lucky. That would hardly raise half the cash he needed. And where would he find buyers out in this wasteland of north Wales? He was in trouble, and he knew it. Litchfield's were no idle threats. He knew the man would have no qualms seeing him sent to prison. If he could just get his fastest horse into a race or two during the summer, perhaps the winnings would get him out of this pickle.

He walked into the new stables in an irritable temper, piqued to think that he might soon have to say good-bye to these magnificent horses and angry at the rest of the world for putting him in this position. He was especially angry at his father for his ridiculous deathbed pangs of conscience, at Percy for interfering when he could have simply let the thing drop, at his mother for all her religious claptrap, and most of all at the little fool Gwyneth Barrie for. . .just for being alive at all. Blast his father for his youthful indiscretion! Why couldn't he have just died and let his secret be buried with him.

As his eyes accustomed to the dim light, he saw someone standing in front of the stall of the jewel of his stable, a three-year-old reddish-brown filly from the south of France. He had had such high hopes for this animal.

As he walked closer, his pent-up frustration finally exploded. "Gwyneth, what are you doing here?" he cried angrily. "Get away from that horse!"

"She won't hurt me, Courtenay," said Gwyneth calmly.

"It's not you I'm worried about. Get back, I tell you. That is an expensive racehorse. You've meddled enough in my affairs. I won't have you disturbing my animals."

"I'm sorry, Courtenay," said Gwyneth as she stepped back.

"These horses of mine are extremely valuable. I don't want you near them, is that clear? What do you know about horses anyway? Because of you, I am being forced to sell them to pay a debt that I would not have if it weren't for you. You have caused me enough trouble without meddling with my thoroughbreds."

"I didn't mean to meddle."

"No, no. . .of course you didn't *mean* to," said Courtenay sarcastically. "You never mean anything but sweetness and light, do you? But I know your conniving little game. You wormed your way into the manor with my sister and mother years ago. Then somehow you deceived my father into thinking you were his heir. But it won't work, you little vixen. You are a crafty one, and you've got them all blinded to the truth, especially my imbecilic cousin. He is nothing but a fool. The two of you deserve one another. But I know your game, and it won't work. I will fight you in court. When I become viscount, don't come to me for any handouts. Enjoy it while you can, because the moment I am able, I will throw you and your father out in the street and never think twice about it, and that idiot Percy with you. Now get out of here, you stuttering little white-haired shrew, before you make me angry!"

Gwyneth's eyes stung from the bitter rebuke. She turned and ran from the barn.

From one of the library windows, Percy saw the familiar figure running down the drive then onto the plateau and down the incline toward her former home. She was running too fast, he thought. Gwyneth's was a spirit whose deep currents ran as calm placid waters, not as turbulent rapids. The sight of her flying across the grass seemed wrong.

He turned from the window, set down the book in his hand, and made for the stairway. He had a feeling where he knew he would find her. He did not hurry as he left the house but walked purposefully in the direction he had last seen her.

About twenty minutes later, he approached the still-vacant cottage. Behind it, where the pens and fences and coops and shelters for her animals had once been, he saw Gwyneth seated on the grass with her back to the house. Slowly he walked forward and sat down beside her. She was gently stroking the back of a small rabbit in her lap. She did not turn toward him.

"Bunny White Tail remembers you," he said.

She nodded.

"I see you coming here nearly every day. Are the animals beginning to return?"

Again Gwyneth nodded but kept her face down. No words were spoken for a minute or two.

"Gwyneth?" said Percy at length. "What is it?"

At last she turned toward him. Her eyes were red. Her face wore the most miserable, forlorn expression he had ever seen. She tried to speak but only succeeded in breaking out in fresh sobs.

"Gwyneth. . .what happened?" said Percy, stretching his arm around her.

"Oh, Percy. . .I don't know what to do!" she wailed, laying her head against his shoulder.

"About what?"

"About Courtenay. I don't want to have people think I am an important person. I don't want to inherit all this and have a title. I don't want it, Percy! Why shouldn't I let Courtenay have it?"

Percy waited before replying. Gradually Gwyneth's tears spent themselves. They sat several minutes in silence. In the distance, a doe with two fawns wandered out of a thicket of woods and seemed to think about coming closer. Several other rabbits scampered about the meadow in front of them.

"You know what I would say in answer to your question?" said Percy at length.

"I think so—that it is my duty. . .that I would probably treat the people more fairly than Courtenay would. . .that my grandfather—it is still hard to think of him as that. . .Lord Snowdon, that he would want me to accept my rightful inheritance."

"Why do you feel you should not?"

"I don't know. . .I just. . .it is hard to have people think bad things of me."

"Who thinks ill of you, Gwyneth?"

Again Gwyneth did not answer.

"What happened, Gwyneth? Something happened. What was it?"

"Do I have to tell you?"

"I won't make you, if that is what you mean. But I would like for you to tell me."

Gwyneth was quiet then drew in a long breath. "Courtenay was rude to me," she said. "He said cruel things. I don't know if it is worth it. It seems easier to simply let him have what he wants. People have been cruel to me all my life. But that doesn't make it easy. It still hurts. It hurts deep, Percy." Again Gwyneth began to gently weep.

"Gwyneth," said Percy at length, "it is obvious that Courtenay is selfish and immature, even in what just happened. He is not qualified to be viscount. He would probably double rents just to pay for his silly scheme of racing horses. If he is cruel to you, imagine what he would be like to his tenants. Do you want to be responsible for the cruelty he might inflict on others?"

Gwyneth sighed and slowly shook her head.

"If by some chance Courtenay matures and reforms and somehow is able to conquer his self-centeredness," Percy went on, "maybe when he is thirty-five or forty or fifty, if you feel he would make a compassionate landlord and viscount and you still do not like being in the position you are in. . .nothing would stop you from stepping aside at that point. People relinquish titles. You could do so then, and Courtenay would inherit. By then he might be of a character that you could trust to do good for the people."

"That is wise, Percy," said Gwyneth after a moment. "That is *very* wise. I had not thought of that. I don't have to make a decision right now that will be binding forever. I am still young, too. In my own way I may be just as immature as Courtenay. I need to grow inside, just like he does. After all, I will not even inherit for several years. Everything does not have to be decided immediately."

They sat and watched the rabbits and deer, though none made closer approach.

"Don't worry about Courtenay," said Percy at length. "I will have a talk with him and tell him to stay away from you. If he is rude to you again, he will have to answer to me for it."

"I would rather you did not talk to him, Percy."

"Why?"

"I don't want the two of you arguing over me. This is time for another forgiveness bouquet. Then you and I will think of what Courtenay said to me no more."

Percy sighed then nodded.

"I would rather march back to the house and take it out of his hide," he said, then paused and nodded. "But you are right."

It was silent a moment.

"So will you pick a handful of wildflowers on the way back?" he asked.

"I don't know," replied Gwyneth thoughtfully. "That would only make Courtenay laugh at my childishness. I think I must find something that will get the forgiveness deep inside him—some other kind of forgiveness bouquet than wildflowers."

Percy rose. Gwyneth set Bunny White Tail on the grass, and Percy helped her to her feet. They walked slowly back in the direction of the cottage.

"What does that mean?" said Percy, pointing to the words in Gaelic carved into the stones near the front door.

"MOR BHAIRNE A INBHEAR DÉ" said Gwyneth. "That's what my father named the house."

"What does it mean?"

"It's my mother's name in Gaelic—MORVERN FROM ARKLOW. He never wanted to forget her."

"Of course. Now I remember—I saw it at your house in Ireland! This was the clue I needed to find you. It was right in front of me all along!"

"If you had known what the Gaelic meant..."

Seventy-Eight

An Equine Bouquet

Percy and Gwyneth left the cottage, walked toward the coastline, up the edge of the promontory, then turned toward Katherine's new home and slowly made their way back in the direction of the manor. They had been so preoccupied that they had not noticed the single horse and buggy coming up the main road that had turned into the manor drive some time before. When they arrived back at the manor, they found the rest of the family, along with Hamilton Murray, waiting for them. Courtenay had been apprised of the fact that the family solicitor had come with news of the disposition of the estate. He declined to be present. A written notice of the same news in the form of a letter was, in fact, awaiting him in town at the post.

"I have come," Murray began when Katherine, Florilyn, Percy, Gwyneth, Steven, and Codnor were all seated, "with good news to report. Just yesterday I received word from the barrister in London who has been representing your son, Lady Katherine, informing me that all legal objections have been dropped. He had, he said, extensively researched both the Snowdon viscountcy as well as the evidence I had presented him concerning Miss Barrie's claim. He reached the conclusion that it was no longer in his interest to pursue the contest against her inheritance. He was therefore dropping the suit. He could not predict what would be his client's response, he said. He was likely perhaps to engage other counsel, though he assured me that no suit, after what his research had made clear, would succeed. After receiving his letter, therefore, I immediately filed the necessary documents concerning title, as well as your continuing trusteeship, Lady Katherine, until such time as Miss Barrie's formal assumption of her title."

Murray paused then walked to the couch where Gwyneth sat at Percy's side. He reached out his hand.

Slowly Gwyneth rose.

"May I be the first to congratulate you, Miss Barrie," said Murray, "or, I should say, now as the recognized heir apparent to your grandfather's viscountcy, Mistress of Snowdon."

The others rose and gathered around her, with many hugs and kisses and warm congratulations. Still ambivilant and uncertain, Gwyneth accepted their attentions with embarrassed gratitude.

As the young people were talking among themselves, Gwyneth's father sidled up to Katherine. "I think I have nearly begun to understand how all the pieces of this puzzle fit together," he said in a tone of wry humor. "You will of course continue to be *Lady* Westbrooke. . .but I wonder what people will call *me*. Do you suppose I will have to get used to wearing a top hat?"

Katherine laughed. "Who would make you, Codnor?" she said. "Surely not the future viscountess."

"I don't know—custom, convention, tradition. Maybe my Gwyneth will turn hoity-toity and uppity when she inherits."

"You don't really believe that. . ."

"No," replied Codnor with a light chuckle.

"I cannot imagine a title having less power to go to anyone's head than Gwyneth's," added Katherine.

Already having had a long ride, and the afternoon drawing down upon them, Hamilton Murray willingly accepted Katherine's offer to spend the night at the manor. A brief conversation between Katherine and Gwyneth, largely bearing on the specifics of Courtenay's financial difficulties, resulted in a private meeting of some length between Murray and the two women after evening tea during which the disposition of a portion of the gold in the safe was discussed.

The result was, when he returned the next day to Porthmadog, that Hamilton Murray's briefcase carried one of the long-buried coins to have appraised. Gwyneth was desirous, with Katherine's blessing, of raising, she said, a sum of approximately £5,500.

Six weeks later, following the completion of the several aspects of her plan, Gwyneth set out alone one morning for a walk in the hills. Gathering this bouquet was something she needed to do alone, that the exercise might accomplish its full work within her. Forgiveness always comes with a price. It is a price whose payment deepens the wells of character within the human soul and draws both payer and payee closer to the heart of God. In the case of the latter, however, those results may not easily nor quickly be seen. As Gwyneth went, therefore, her prayers were full on behalf of Courtenay. It was not easy to find blooms at this time of year as autumn began, but she was determined to find them.

Later that afternoon, after watching for her opportunity, Gwyneth saw Courtenay approaching the stables. She hurried after him then paused at the door. "Courtenay," she called into the darkness.

A moment later his voice sounded from inside. "What do you want?" he said.

"May I see you for a moment?"

"No. Go away."

"Please, Courtenay. I know you do not want me going near your horses, but please. . .just for a moment."

Gwyneth heard a muttered oath, and then footsteps approached. Slowly Courtenay's scowling face came into view. "All right, here I am," he barked. "What do you want? I'm busy."

"I wanted to give you this," said Gwyneth. She handed him a small bouquet of wildflowers, tied with a short length of ribbon. She then turned and walked away.

Courtenay started to throw it to the ground, intending to grind the flowers in the dirt with his foot. At the last moment he noticed that among them was tied what appeared to be a tightly rolled slip of paper. Curious, he fumbled with it, letting the flowers drop to the ground as he did. He loosened it from the ribbon then unrolled the paper. He found that he was holding a three-inch by nine-inch parchment, along the top of which was imprinted the single word RECEIPT.

Below Courtenay read the words, *"Received of Gwyneth Barrie, on behalf of Courtenay Westbrooke, the sum of £5,379. All indebtedness, including interest, in repayment of earnest money deposit, paid in full."* It was signed, *"Lord Coleraine Litchfield."*

Thunderstruck, Courtenay stared at the paper in disbelief. He read over the words a second time then finally looked up.

Gwyneth was just disappearing into the house.

Quickly he stooped down, picked up the flowers she had spent three hours to find, and hurried after her. "Wait. . .Gwyneth, wait!" he called.

She turned and faced him.

"What is. . .I mean, is this. . .what does this mean—how did you. . ."

"I paid your bill," said Gwyneth simply.

"So. . .I don't understand. Do I now owe you the money?"

"No, Courtenay, you owe me nothing."

"But it was *my* debt."

"I know. But I took your debt on myself so that you would not have to pay it."

"Why would you do that?" he said, shaking his head in stunned disbelief.

"Because I care about you, Courtenay, and I want the best for you. After all, you are my half brother or my uncle or something—I still am a little confused about all that. I think you are my uncle. But most of all, you are a person God made and that makes you wonderful and special. I think I will even learn to love you in time. For now I wanted to do something for you to show you that I bear you no ill will despite that you are sometimes cruel to me. But I do not think you will be rude to me after this, because you will know that you are forgiven."

Speechless, Courtenay stared at her for another moment then turned, still holding both receipt and forgiveness bouquet, and walked slowly back in the direction of the stables.

Seventy-Nine

The Offer

Courtenay excitedly read for the third time the letter that had come that morning. He could hardly believe the words on the page in front of him.

Dear Mr. Westbrooke, he read.

A late scratch by one of the primary contenders in next month's Chester Open has left the field one entrant short. Because of the strong showing by your three-year-old Viscount's Pride in the Wales Handicap two months ago, the organizers would like to offer you this final slot in our field. Please reply as soon as possible. This year's entry fee is £225.

I am,
Sincerely yours,
Garfield Smythe,
Chairman of the Organizing Committee,
The Chester Open

Courtenay set the letter down, his mind racing. This was the opportunity he had been waiting for! But he had spent his account completely dry engaging that imbecile of a barrister in London who now said there was nothing more he could do. Where could he lay his hands on £225?

For the rest of the day, Courtenay hung about more than was generally his custom. Early in the afternoon, Percy, Steven, and Codnor rode into the hills to check on the new flock of sheep they had taken to one of the high meadows a month earlier. He happened to know that Florilyn was in town visiting Rhawn Lorimer. He also knew that Gwyneth never remained cooped up inside on a nice day for long.

He busied himself in and about the stables, checking on his horses, dreaming and scheming what he dared hope might be a chance to compete in a major race. After about twenty minutes, he saw Gwyneth walking from the kitchen garden behind the house. Though shorter than any of the young people of the manor, the grace and dignity of her bearing made her appear taller than she actually was. Even wearing a worker's frock and with her hands soiled with dirt, one look was enough to command an observer's attention. Her entire countenance said that here was a young woman somehow set apart from her peers. As yet, however, because they were focused on himself, Courtenay's eyes were unseeing of all this. He came out from the shadow of the barn and, with pretended nonchalance, intercepted her.

"Hello, Courtenay," said Gwyneth sweetly.

"What are you doing today?" he asked.

"I was helping Mrs. Drynwydd pick the beans for tonight's dinner."

"If you are going to be viscountess one day, don't you think you should let the servants do that kind of work?"

"I will never want anyone waiting on me. Why should someone else do for me what I can do well enough for myself. Besides, I like to work."

An awkward silence followed.

"I say, uh. . .Gwyneth," began Courtenay, "you know my, uh—the racehorses that you, well. . .that you helped me keep?"

"Of course, Courtenay."

"I have a chance. . .that is, I've been invited to enter a big race next month."

"Oh, that's wonderful, Courtenay. Congratulations."

"Thank you," he said, smiling awkwardly. "It wouldn't have been possible if you hadn't. . .you know, done what you did."

Gwyneth smiled.

"Are you, uh. . .interested in horses?"

"I thought you knew that. I love all kinds of animals, especially horses."

"Do you think I should enter the race?"

"Oh yes—it sounds like just what you have wanted."

"Yes, well. . .actually, yes it is. I would be very excited about it if. . . well, you see, there is one little problem. I need £225 to enter the race."

"Don't you have that much?"

"I'm afraid not."

"And you are trying to find a way to ask if you could borrow it from me," said Gwyneth with the hint of a playful smile.

"I suppose that is about the size of it," replied Courtenay, with an uncharacteristically sheepish expression on his own face.

"What would you say if I just *gave* you the money instead of loaned it to you?"

"I would be very appreciative."

"It would be my investment in your horses."

"I suppose that is only fair, since I wouldn't even have them if it weren't for you. So how big a cut of the action would you want for your investment?"

"I'm not sure what you mean. What is a cut of the action?"

"What percentage of my winnings would be yours, and what percentage would be mine?"

"I don't want anything in return, Courtenay!" laughed Gwyneth. "Whatever you win would be yours."

"What about the entry fee—you know, the two-twenty-five?"

"If I give it to you, Courtenay, I would not expect it back. Don't you know what Jesus said—to do good and lend and give to others and expect nothing in return? I try to do what Jesus said, that is all. The money would be yours, Courtenay."

"Hmm. . .yes, well. . .there is that, I suppose, though I never thought of anything *He* said having to do with finances or racehorses."

"But," Gwyneth added, "there would be one condition."

"A condition—what kind of condition?"

"Would you be riding in the race yourself?"

Courtenay nodded.

"Then if I am going to invest in this race, I would want to give you riding lessons."

"What!" Courtenay began in a blustering tone. "Do you think that you are actually—" He stopped abruptly and managed to control himself. This was a gift horse into whose mouth he didn't want to look too closely! He drew in a deep breath, trying to find the wherewithal to swallow his gigantic pride—no mean feat for one like Courtenay—and put up with whatever absurdities were being hatched in Gwyneth's brain.

"Yes, Courtenay," said Gwyneth. "I know what you are thinking, that you are a superior horseman to me. But you are not all you could be. If you gave me two weeks with any of your horses, I would beat you in a race with you riding any of the others. I know how to talk to horses in a way you don't, Courtenay. You are not that good in the saddle. I can teach you to race much faster."

Momentarily Courtenay's calm gave way.

"How dare you propose to—" he began. Again he caught himself. This was galling, but if he wanted to race, he had no choice. "What exactly did you have in mind?" he said.

"Just to teach you how to talk to your horses, how to sit in the saddle, and how to ride faster. It will take me a few days to get you the £225. I will have to speak to my father and some other people. Would you like to start your riding lessons tomorrow?"

"Whatever you say," replied Courtenay with a supreme effort at self-control.

"Then we will take two horses to the wide sand south of the harbor tomorrow at low tide," said Gwyneth. "You should ride the horse you plan to race, and I will show you how fast it might be."

"I will be sure to bring my whip," said Courtenay with a touch of sarcasm.

"You will not need your whip, Courtenay. The only use it might have would be to show you, if you tried to use it, how much faster than you I can ride without it. But I would rather you did not bring it. I don't think you will ever need your whip again."

"We shall see about that."

For the next week, every day at low tide, Courtenay and Gwyneth met at the beach for Courtenay's riding lessons. By the third day, Courtenay ceased his objections. Whether he had begun to *see* into Gwyneth as a person was doubtful, but he was a sufficient horseman to recognize that she knew what she was about.

From the promontory above the beach, Percy, Florilyn, and Steven watched the proceedings every day with amusement. What they would not have given to be able to hear the conversation taking place on the sand below them.

"I have to hand it to Courtenay," said Percy. "He seems to be taking his medicine like a man."

"You probably know everything Gwyneth is saying to him," said Florilyn. "This is how she taught you to beat me."

" 'High, forward, and loose in the saddle,' " nodded Percy. " 'Be one with your horse. . .feel the rhythm. . .relax and let him run.' You're right—I can imagine exactly what she is saying!"

"Are we witnessing the beginning of Courtenay's transformation?" said Steven.

"I don't think I would go *that* far!" laughed Florilyn. "Although," she added in a thoughtful tone, "Gwyneth does have the power to get under the skin. If I can change, though it took me awhile, I suppose maybe Courtenay can, too. But I'm not holding my breath."

Eighty

The Race

As the twelve entries in the Chester Derby entered the starting gate, few expected anything from the late entrant from the north coast of Wales, Viscount's Pride. At twenty-five to one, neither had the three-year-old garnered much activity with the punters and bookmakers, though a few late rumors that the filly's pedigree came from France and could surprise had aroused a mild flurry of interest. Most of the bets laid down, however, followed conventional wisdom and remained with the three favorites, the Empress, Red Heat, and Birdsong Meadow.

In the seats just above the rail about fifty yards from the finish line, however, sat a small cluster of visitors to the Cheshire city, some of whom, in the excitement of participation more than expectation of gain, held markers for the wagers they had placed on the long shot.

Katherine had invited any from the manor who desired to accompany them to watch the race. Mrs. Drynwydd and Mrs. Llewellyn, attired in their finest Sunday dresses, were beside themselves at the fun of such an adventure and behaving like two schoolgirls in the midst of the great crowd. This was the first horse race either had seen in their lives. They had speculated to the sum of ten shillings each and were now clutching their receipts as if the economy of the entire British Empire was at stake. Stuart Wyckham was more daring. He had invested a pound and now sat more nervous than excited, fearing the worst and regretting having been caught up in the prerace enthusiasm of the others. Florilyn had bet four pounds, Steven two. They had also invited Rhawn Lorimer to accompany them, and she had equaled Florilyn's bet. Adela Muir had declined to place a wager. Beside her, however, the mother whose son would carry the hopes of Snowdonia on his shoulders had invested five pounds. Only one of the company had sufficient personal prior experience with the techniques of Viscount's Pride's diminutive trainer to have reason for optimism. Percy was so convinced of Gwyneth's genius with animals that he had confidently placed a ten-pound note on the table in front of the skeptical bookie, who, he said, had no objection if the young Scotsman wanted to throw his money away, and he would be glad to take it. Gwyneth, most quietly confident of all, placed no bet. She had no desire to profit from the day's adventure. She was thinking more of the eternal consequences of her investment and what interest might be gained from it within Courtenay's heart.

Courtenay arranged to go ahead with the horse several days before. The contingent from the manor followed two days prior to the race, riding in two large carriages to Blaenau Ffestiniog, where they caught the train the rest of the way. A festive dinner at the hotel had capped off the adventure. Katherine and Adela treated the women to ice cream, and her housekeeper and cook thought they were in heaven. They invited Stuart Wyckham to accompany them. Glancing about at the four women, however, he declined and instead spent a boring evening in his room, wishing that Hollin Radnor had been up for the trip, or that Codnor Barrie did not possess such a keen sense of duty that compelled him to stay behind and keep watch over affairs at the manor.

Steven and Florilyn walked through the city with Percy, Gwyneth, and Rhawn. As they made their way back toward the hotel, Gwyneth and Florilyn were engaged in conversation with Steven and gradually moved ahead. Behind them Percy and Rhawn found themselves alone together.

"What is it like being without your little Amren for so long?" asked Percy.

"I miss him," replied Rhawn. "But it feels so good to be free of the duties of a mother for a few days. Sir Armond and Doris are like two little children in a candy store to have their grandson to themselves for three days. My parents are going to Burrenchobay Hall one evening as well. You don't know how much I appreciate your asking me along. I know I'm sort of the odd woman out—you and Gwyneth, Steven and Florilyn, you know—but I appreciate it."

"It was Gwyneth's idea."

Rhawn smiled. "Somehow, I am not surprised. She is an amazing girl," she said. "After how I treated her all those years when we were young, now she acts as if I am her best friend. You are a very lucky man."

"She cares for you, Rhawn. She *does* consider you a friend. I think she is proud of you, too, for not giving up, for growing, for becoming the person you are. I am proud of you, too."

"You have been so good to me, Percy. Whatever I may be growing into, I owe it to you."

"You have made your own choices, Rhawn. You've been strong and have grown through the adversity. Nobody's done that for you."

"But watching you helped me make good choices, Percy. I watched you making good choices. It had a profound impact on me. You were no saint either when you first came to Wales."

"Don't remind me!" laughed Percy.

"But you grew and changed. I know it seemed that I was just trying to get my hooks into you with all my flirting and conniving. . .but I was watching. It took awhile, but it began to get into me. I had never been around a boy who was unselfish and kind. Courtenay and Colville had no depth of character, yet all the girls for miles around swooned over them. Girls can be really stupid, Percy. They don't look for character. So they get into bad situations, just like I did. When I met you, I began to see that character mattered. Then I began to see that it mattered within my own heart most of all. Anyway, I am very grateful. You will always be special to me. I wish you and Gwyneth all the happiness in the world."

"Thank you, Rhawn," said Percy. "Is there. . . What is going on with Colville, now that you are seeing his parents regularly?"

"He was angry at first," answered Rhawn. "He always managed to be away when I went to visit. But we have exchanged some civil words since. I think he is getting used to the idea that Amren and I are in his life to stay."

"Has Amren been told that Colville is his father?"

"No, it's too soon for that."

"Do you think. . .I mean, is there any chance that you and Colville will marry one day?"

Rhawn smiled sadly. "I don't know, Percy. I suppose part of me does love him. Whether he loves me, or ever loved me—honestly, I don't know. He is the father of my son. Of course I wish we could be a family. His parents don't like things the way they are. But we all know that we have to give Colville time to adjust to it all. Whether he will decide he wants to become a man of character, much depends on that, too. I would not marry him unless I was convinced that I would be the only woman in his life. If by some chance he did ask me to marry him, he will have to show me that things have changed before I would accept him."

"Well, for all your sakes, I hope he is capable of that," said Percy. "It may be that your growth is having more of an effect on him than you realize."

It was after ten when the five young people returned to the hotel the night before the race.

"I hardly recognize Courtenay," said Katherine as she watched the horses lining up on the far side of the track. "I think he's lost nearly a stone in preparation for this race."

"He is still large for a jockey," said Steven from the other side of his mother. "But the loss of weight should help him be more competitive."

"Do you think he has a chance, Steven?" asked Florilyn beside him. "I just hope he isn't last. Can you imagine how impossible he would be to live with?"

Steven glanced past Florilyn and Rhawn to Gwyneth seated beside her. Her vision was fixed on Courtenay, her eyes glowing with a strange light.

"I'm not the one you should be asking," he replied after a moment.

Florilyn looked to her right.

Gwyneth sensed the movement and turned toward her. "Yes, he has a chance, Florilyn," she said calmly. "He will beat most of the others. I cannot say for certain that he will win. I can see that two of the others are very fast. But I *think* he may win."

Between them, Rhawn's thoughts were not on the race but on Colville Burrenchobay and the conversation she and Percy had had on the way back to the hotel the night before. *God,* she said silently, *I do pray that You would put within Colville's heart the desire to grow and to become a man of character.*

Her thoughts and prayers were interrupted by the starter's bugle. All eyes turned to the opposite side of the track. As if shot from a gun, the twelve horses exploded forward out of the gate. Instantly a great roar from the crowd went up. Along the back straight the twelve competitors quickly spread out almost in single file. The light, pinkish-gray Empress led the way into the first turn.

"Where's Courtenay!" shouted Katherine, glancing down toward Steven and Percy.

"I am afraid that's him bringing up the rear," said Steven. "But he has time to regroup."

Nothing more was said as they watched the field come round the curve and into the straight. Birdsong Meadow made a move out of the curve, passing the Empress on the outside and galloping out to half a length's lead. He was followed by the rest of the closely bunched field. Out of the curve, Courtenay swung wide and eased up on the rider in front of him.

As they came down the straight, slowly Gwyneth rose from her seat and leaned over the rail. She stared intently as they came on, as if trying to exert her will into Courtenay's brain and into the mighty frame of Viscount's Pride.

All around her the others were yelling frantically. "Courtenay. . .go, Courtenay!"

"Faster, Courtenay!"

"Courtenay, Courtenay!"

Stuart Wyckham was pounding his hat on his leg, yelling at the top of his lungs, "Move out around them, boy. No time to hold it back now!"

Mrs. Drynwydd and Mrs. Llewellyn had risen to their feet, all propriety abandoned, and were shouting in Welsh too thick for anyone around them to understand.

Only Gwyneth was silent as the field thundered past in front of them. Percy looked at her out of the corner of his eye. Her hands were together, as if clutching two imaginary reins, her elbows out, her upper body gently rocking, her lips moving with the silent words, *Be one. . .feel her rhythm.*

Percy smiled then turned his attention back to the race. "Go, Courtenay!" he cried. "Don't wait too long! Go!" He thought he detected Courtenay's head turn toward them for the briefest moment. Had he heard them calling his name? Or had he sensed Gwyneth's piercing stare?

As quickly as they flew down the straight, they were gone. Seconds later the field entered the far turn. Birdsong Meadow still led, followed by Red Heat and Empress neck and neck. Around the curve, none wanted to swing wide, and all held their positions. As the track again straightened, several swung out and flailed their whips as they flew down the backstretch. Courtenay alone among the twelve jockeys held no whip in his hand. He passed one more horse. Quickly the two behind him faded back. He swung out, drawing even with a cluster of four running side by side halfway down the far straight.

Gradually he inched ahead, pulled out half a length, then a length in front of the four, then swung back into the pole. Birdsong Meadow, Red Heat, and Empress led down the straight, no more than a half a length separating them, while two lengths back, a black stallion and a roan gelding tried desperately to hold the pace. In the gap between them and the cluster of four, rode Courtenay alone.

Into the final curve they came. The Empress appeared strong and gathering herself for another challenge. Red Heat began to fade. The roan drew even then passed him. Courtenay came alongside the stallion's rear and held position halfway through the curve. The black swung out to pass Red Heat, brushing Courtenay's left leg. He swung out but kept even. Red Heat faded behind them. The six who trailed fell back.

It was now a five-horse race.

They emerged into the final straight. A deafening roar from the crowd nearly drowned out the pounding hooves on the hard-packed dirt. The Empress came even with Birdsong Meadow. But the roan was gaining. Behind him the black stallion and Viscount's Pride were coming on strong less than a length back.

Suddenly Courtenay swung wide, too wide it seemed. An audible gasp sounded from the crowd. The sudden lurch appeared to have been caused by the stallion. But now Courtenay leaned far forward, elbows out, his entire frame moving in rhythm with the powerful beast beneath him. He appeared to be speaking into her ear. No one would ever know what was said.

As the two favorites and roan and stallion thundered toward the finish beside the pole, yards to their right, in the middle of the track and alone, Viscount's Pride came on at great speed.

Percy was on his feet and waving his hands wildly. "Courtenay. . .go, Courtenay!" he cried.

Steven and Florilyn and Katherine and Rhawn and Mrs. Drynwydd and Mrs. Llewellyn and Stuart Wyckham were yelling in a frenzy. "Courtenay, Courtenay! Go, Courtenay!"

Only Gwyneth stood calmly at the rail, saying nothing, a peaceful smile on her face as she watched the field thunder toward her.

As he passed them, Courtenay drew even with the Empress. He glanced briefly toward the stands. On his face was a great smile of exhilaration. Then he was gone, pounding toward the finish.

Courtenay flew across the line half a length ahead. Birdsong Meadow surged past the Empress by a nose at the line, followed by the black stallion in fourth.

The twenty-five-to-one long shot had triumphed in the Chester Derby!

Percy and Steven jumped out of their seats and ran through the tumultuous crowd for the winner's circle. They were followed by Florilyn and Rhawn. After all the excitement, Stuart Wyckham sat down in his seat thinking what he could do with his winnings, while beside him the housekeeper and cook were trying to compute what their winnings would be.

By the time they reached the winner's circle, Courtenay was being congratulated by the race organizers and presented with the first-place cup. Percy and Steven and Florilyn and Rhawn were swallowed in a great swarm. Courtenay saw them, finally dismounted, and made his way through the throng toward them.

"Magnificent race, Courtenay!" exclaimed Percy with a great smile, shaking his hand.

"Well done, man!" said Steven.

"Thanks," said Courtenay. "An amazing last two hundred yards. I don't know quite what happened myself."

Florilyn stepped forward and gave her brother a tight hug. There were tears in her eyes.

Rhawn hugged him, also. "I can't believe it, Courtenay," she said. "That was a fantastic ride."

"I don't know that I believe it myself!" laughed Courtenay.

Even as he was greeting the others, it was obvious that Courtenay's eyes were flitting about the sea of faces looking for someone else. But she stood a head shorter than everyone and was not easy to find in a crowd. At last he detected the head of white. He bumped and inched toward it.

A moment later, Gwyneth's face came into view.

Courtenay stopped and stood, his left hand holding the reins, staring down at her.

Gwyneth returned his gaze with an innocent and peaceful smile, as if she were not surprised in the least with the result. "Congratulations, Courtenay," she said. "That was masterful. I knew you could do it."

He smiled almost sheepishly then slowly began to shake his head in disbelief. "*You* did it, Gwyneth," he said. "Thank you. Thank you. . .for *everything*!"

Eighty-One

Mochras Head

Percy remained in Wales throughout the fall, working every day with Steven and Codnor about the manor and grounds and at the new house. Never had he enjoyed hard, honest labor so much. Even Courtenay occasionally joined them.

As the year 1874 drew to a close, Edward and Mary Drummond made plans again to spend the Christmas holidays at Westbrooke Manor. There was not only much to celebrate, there were plans to be made and much to discuss. Percy was eager to talk over the future with his father and arrive at some resolution regarding his plans for his law studies.

The season would be highlighted by a family reunion with Edward and Katherine's parents, the earl and his wife, returning at last from China to retire from the mission field. Their future plans were not yet firm. Before leaving for China, they had sold their home and parted with most of their worldly possessions. Son and daughter were doing their utmost to persuade them to spend their remaining years with one or the other of them—at the vicarage in Glasgow or with Katherine in north Wales.

Edward and Mary, with the senior Mr. and Mrs. Drummond, arrived several days before Christmas. Katherine had seen her parents but once since their departure for China twelve years earlier. They were now in their late seventies. Though in good health, they were clearly slower of step and more stooped since she had seen them. The gray atop her head, however, signaled as great a change in their eyes as their increasing frailty did in hers. They had laid eyes on their three grandchildren but briefly since they were children, during a furlough from the mission some years before. Tears flowed freely throughout the day of their arrival. Three fine young adults now greeted them warmly, with handshakes and hugs, and, at least in the case of Percy and Florilyn, countenances of character to make them proud. Even Courtenay, who had avoided such gatherings in recent years, was present. He seemed genuinely glad to be part of the family again. The earl and his wife fell in love instantly with Percy's young fiancée. They perceived in her eyes the light of truth and immediately took her to their hearts as had Edward and Mary earlier in the year.

"So, Katherine," said the earl the next evening as the extended family gathered in the large sitting room, "this is where you think we should retire and live out our days? Edward has been doing his best to convince us that he and Mary should take us in."

"I am aware of that!" laughed Katherine, glancing at her brother with a smile. "But can Glasgow compare with the beautiful coast of Snowdonia? Surely you would be happier in the country."

"You would certainly have room for us. I had forgotten how huge the manor is."

"Actually, you would not be living in the manor, Father," said Katherine. "I have been building a new house out toward the promontory, about three-quarters of a mile from here. You probably saw it when you came up the hill."

"Why a new house?" asked Mrs. Drummond.

"After Roderick died, there was some question about the inheritance and my future," replied Katherine vaguely. "It seemed best that I have a place of my own and leave the manor for the new. . .uh, the new owner when that time came."

"This place is big enough for ten families," rejoined the earl.

"You may be right, Father. But young families need a home of their own. I did not want to be underfoot."

"Yes, well. . .I see what you mean. Right—can't have too many old people around when youngsters are scurrying about. Although I must say, on the mission field children multiply like rabbits. Their energy is exhilarating. I have to say, I hope to go to my grave with tiny little hands and feet nearby that occasionally cease their play long enough to climb into an old man's lap."

A pause came in the conversation. Katherine, Adela, and Florilyn rose to refill tea cups.

As they resumed their seats, Steven took the opportunity afforded by the lull to stand and look about the room. "If I might be permitted a few words," he said. All eyes turned toward him, wondering what the normally reticent young man had on his mind. He drew in a deep breath. He appeared uncharacteristically nervous. Had the company not been looking at him, some would have noticed a sudden reddening of Florilyn's cheeks as she buried her hands and eyes in her lap.

"For many years," Steven continued when he had composed himself, "I have admired from afar a certain one of our number, trying to find ways to serve her in whatever humble capacity I might despite the vast gulf that existed between our stations. I was but the son of a poor sheep-herding crofter and certainly never dreamed of a more personal or intimate approach. When the late viscount was kind enough to employ me at the manor, and when Lady Katherine added to that kindness by showing such trust as to make me her factor, my opportunities for service toward the one I speak of, though occasionally frustrated by herself, were increased by closer proximity. Yet I remained what I was—but a poor crofter in the guise of a factor. However, when suddenly a few months ago my dear cousin was revealed to be Lord Snowdon's granddaughter, hope sprang up in me that perhaps I myself might claim to be a *little* more than a mere peasant, even if not directly so. If I am not quite an aristocrat, perhaps I might claim sufficient standing to look a young lady of noble birth and character in the eye and tell her I love her. Therefore, after speaking to her mother, this I have done. Unbelievably, she reciprocated my sentiments. The result of all this is that I have the following announcement to make—that this afternoon I asked Miss Florilyn Westbrooke to be my wife, and she accepted me."

Even before the words were out of his mouth, Florilyn was on her feet and hurrying toward him. As they embraced, the room erupted in surprised exclamations. The two were quickly surrounded by their family and friends and smothered in hugs and backslaps and handshakes and kisses of congratulations.

Steven's announcement at last prompted Percy to talk seriously with his father and mother. Gwyneth had a similar conference with her father. The five then met together, Percy and Gwyneth seeking the combined counsel and wisdom of their three parents concerning their future and its timetable. No resolution was reached regarding Percy's plans to attend law school, though his father recommended, and Mary and Codnor agreed, that he should travel to Aberdeen within the coming months to reassess possibilities. Now that it seemed clear that his future was in Wales, he needed to decide where his heart was leading him about his studies and future profession.

Out of these discussions and the prayer that followed, one decision was reached. The wedding that would join their two families would be held in Wales in eighteen months, a year from the following June. At Percy's request, Vicar Edward Drummond would be presiding.

Two days after a festive and joyous Christmas, following a great Boxing Day "open house" at the manor to which the entire village had been invited, on a bright, sunny, cold afternoon, Gwyneth found Percy in the garden with his father and grandfather.

"Come join us, my dear!" said the earl, rising from the stone garden bench and greeting his grandson's future wife with an embracing hug of affection.

"I don't want to interrupt," said Gwyneth, "but Percy, would you walk to the promontory with me later?"

"Sure—it is a perfect day for a walk."

"Sit down, Gwyneth," said Edward. "We were just talking about you. Percy was telling my father about his adventure in Ireland trying to find you, when he didn't even know it was you he was trying to find!"

"I certainly never dreamed I would see Percy again," said Gwyneth. "No, that's not quite right," she added. "I *dreamed* of seeing Percy again every day. But I did not see how I ever would."

"I have to tell you," Percy's father went on, "I have tremendously enjoyed becoming acquainted with your father these last few days. He is a remarkable man."

"I could not agree more," smiled Gwyneth. "I don't know that I have ever seen him happier. For my sake he was willing to make a new life for us in Ireland. But he is, after all, a Welshman at heart. He is so happy to be back home, as is Grannie."

"But she is not actually your grandmother?"

"No, my great-great-aunt."

"And Steven. . ."

"Is my cousin. His mother Adela is my father's sister."

"Ah. . .I think I have it straight at last!" laughed Edward.

An hour later Percy and Gwyneth walked to the edge of the promontory, bundled in several layers of clothes, and sat down on the damp grass. The winter sun was slowly dying into the sea in front of them.

"This is one of my favorite places," said Gwyneth softly.

"One of *our* favorite places," rejoined Percy, "as long as you're not waiting for me at the harbor!"

"I have been coming here and sitting looking out over the sea since before I can remember," Gwyneth went on. "I always associated the mystery of the sea with my mother. Now I know what happened. I have been to Ireland. I have seen the land where I was born. Yet I love it here no less that the mystery has been solved."

"The sea is mysterious of itself," said Percy. "And we still don't know how that chest of gold came to be buried in the cave down there. That mystery may always baffle us."

"But we found it. Imagine, Percy—we actually found a buried treasure! It's a fairy tale!"

Percy turned toward Gwyneth. The setting sun had grown bright red at the wintry horizon. Whenever the sun shone just right, its rays turned Gwyneth's light hair into a luminescent crown of gold.

"More a fairy tale for me than you," said Percy as a smile played on his lips.

Gwyneth returned his gaze with a puzzled expression.

"I discovered the *real* treasure," he said, "though it took me sailing back and forth across the Celtic triangle to find it. What is a chest of old coins compared to the gold I found? I found *you*!"

Gwyneth smiled and laid her head on Percy's shoulder. He stretched his arm around her and drew her close.

"I love you, Gwyneth Barrie," said Percy.

"And I you, Percival Drummond. I may be your gold, but you are every girl's dream come true."

They sat watching the sun slowly set. The moment the final speck of its red disappeared, the sky immediately seemed to explode in color. But the brilliant sunset was short lived. It was winter and the atmosphere was too thin to sustain the colors for long. Within fifteen minutes, dark blues and purples of approaching night began to engulf them in a descending blanket of darkness.

"Just think if we could live our lives with this view all the time," said Percy, "overlooking the sea, watching every sunset."

"Perhaps we can," said Gwyneth.

"What do you mean?"

"Stand up, Percy, and turn around."

Percy rose to his feet then pulled Gwyneth up to his side. They turned their backs to the sea. There stood the outline of Katherine's new house against the night sky three hundred yards inland from the promontory.

"Are you thinking what I think you might be thinking?" said Percy slowly.

"I don't think Lady Katherine really wants to move to the new house," said Gwyneth.

"She is planning to. I've heard her say so."

"Only because she thinks she ought to," said Gwyneth. "She probably thinks we will want her to after I inherit. But we would get lost in the manor by ourselves. I would feel very awkward. It will always be Lady Katherine's home to me. The new house is not half so big. Why should *we* not live in the new house, where we can see the sea every day and let Katherine and Florilyn and Steven and Adela all remain at the manor."

"Gwyneth, that is a fantastic idea!"

"I will speak with Lady Katherine. We will do whatever she wants. As long as I am with you, Percy, I will be happy anywhere. But I cannot think of anything I would love more than to wake up every morning beside you and go to bed every night with the sound of the sea in our ears."

Eighty-Two

Knotted Strands

Tears came to Katherine's eyes the next day when she realized what Gwyneth was suggesting.

"Oh, my dear girl!" she said, embracing Gwyneth with all the affection of true motherhood. "You would do that for me?"

"I would do whatever I could for you, Lady Katherine. Your happiness means more to me than anything."

"More than your own?"

"Of course."

Katherine shook her head in wonder. "I know you mean that with all your heart," she said, stepping away and smiling down at the girl who had become to her as an adopted daughter. "I would love to be able to remain at the manor. There would also be more room for my parents. I only decided to build the new house because I assumed I would have to find another place to live. Once we realized that Courtenay would not inherit, I must admit wondering if I had made a mistake. Still, the manor *will* be yours one day. Should it not be your home?"

"I would rather think of it as *yours*, Lady Katherine," replied Gwyneth. "The manor will be yours to live in and make use of as your own for as long as you wish it. If you would allow my family to live in your new house, I would be honored for you to remain at the manor."

"Then the new house shall be my wedding gift to you."

"To use, perhaps, but not to own," said Gwyneth. "The new house and land shall remain yours. In your name, I mean," said Gwyneth, "so that you will have them to pass on to Florilyn or Courtenay one day. You need to be mindful of your inheritance to them as well."

"Perhaps you are right. We do not need to decide all those particulars just now. But you have made me very happy, Gwyneth. Thank you!"

With the arrangement between the present and future viscountesses, work at the new house continued as rapidly as the winter weather would permit. Doors, windows, cabinetry, shelves, fixtures, fireplaces and other brick- and stonework, and paneling and trim, were all completed by early February. By that time Percy, Steven, Courtenay, and Codnor were in the process of painting those rooms whose walls had been plastered rather than paneled in wood. Carpet and drapes were ordered and in place by early April. By the end of the month, though sparse of furnishings, the new house was ready for Codnor, Gwyneth, and Grannie to take up residence within its new stone walls. What remained of their furniture in the two cottages in the village, as well as what had been shipped from Ireland, was carted to the new house. Katherine added many furnishings from the manor as well. For two weeks the entire company at the manor contributed to the move. Carts, buggies, and wagons moved back and forth between the two houses and the village bearing furniture, boxes, beds, crates, chairs, clothes, wardrobes, utensils, food, wall hangings, pictures, and tapestries. The men of the manor helped Codnor outfit the new stables with tack, tools, saddles, feed, and all things needful for the barn and workshop. Meanwhile, the women remained busy in Gwyneth's new kitchen and in making the bedrooms and other rooms of the house cozy and livable.

When at last the small Barrie family left the manor one evening after a great supper and prepared to spend their first night in their new home, it seemed as though some portion of the glory had departed. And indeed, life seemed dreary for a time in both houses. Even Gwyneth in the new house, notwithstanding her daily view of the sea, found it perhaps a little *too* quiet. But she saw Florilyn and Steven and Katherine and Adela daily. The path between the two houses was already well worn. Stuart Wyckham had planted a boxwood hedge and other shrubs alongside it. Gradually life returned to its old channels. Gwyneth ministered to Grannie and her father as she had in Ireland. Steven and Codnor continued to work on what interior details remained to be completed at the new house. Life between the two homes was soon flourishing as if they were one.

Percy spent much of the spring in Glasgow with his parents, taking up again his occasional legal work, and made a trip to Aberdeen to assess his options for resuming his law studies. Whenever he was in Wales, he took up residence in his former room at the manor.

Steven and Florilyn were married the following August. Percy stood beside Steven as best man, with Courtenay beside him. Gwyneth and Rhawn served as Florilyn's two maids of honor. Steven and Codnor, along with their work on the new house, and with the help of several able carpenters and joiners, had remodeled a portion of the wing of the manor that had been used in former times as servants' quarters. They had transformed it into an expansive apartment of seven rooms, occupying two floors, including a newly outfitted kitchen. It was ready by the day of the wedding. After a week's honeymoon by boat north through Scotland's western isles, the wedding couple took up residence in their new east-wing quarters.

Percy and Gwyneth were married a year later, in June of 1876. Percy would have chosen his father to be his best man had he not been officiating for the service. Those who stood before the proud vicar were the same six from the previous August. Edward's own son, however, was now the bridegroom. The ceremony was conducted on the flat plateau between the new house and the promontory of Mochras Head. The entire village was invited, and nearly every one of its number attended. Percy had always been a great favorite. And now, even if belatedly, those of the community embraced his new bride and their future viscountess as if they had always secretly known that she was something beyond the ordinary. A great feast and celebration was held afterward on the grounds of the new house. As the day was bright and warm, it lasted most of the day. The bride and groom did not depart in their honeymoon carriage—which would take them that night to Barmouth, thence to the Lincolnshire resort village of Cumberworth—until after six o'clock.

One of the surprise guests of the day was Colville Burrenchobay. He and Rhawn spent most of the afternoon together. He was even seen a time or two in the midst of the festivities engaged in what appeared to be cordial conversation with Styles Lorimer. Drawn together by their mutual grandson, the Lorimer and Burrenchobay families had been visiting with increasing frequency. How much the people of the community knew was doubtful. The truth was not long in coming out, however, when Colville began calling at the Lorimer home later that summer. A few buggy rides followed. After some time, these began to include young Amren. With unhurried wisdom, Rhawn allowed the two men in her life to become accustomed to one another slowly. By the time their engagement was announced the following year, Amren had begun calling Colville "Daddy." Colville and Rhawn were married and eventually had three more children. They took up residence in Burrenchobay Hall, which Colville inherited at the passing of his parents. As true as it is that most people do not change, anyone who *wants* to change is easily made capable of it by that desire. Influenced primarily by what he observed in Rhawn and Florilyn, a spark of that desire began to flicker to life within the heart of Colville Burrenchobay. He never stood for parliament, and though no one would have called him a saint, he turned out to be a surprisingly good father and was faithful to Rhawn for the rest of his life.

Grannie lived in the new house and was honored by the families and staff of both houses as matriarch of the extended clan of Westbrooke Manor and the new house. She lived to be ninety-seven and died in her own bed in the new house with Gwyneth and Adela at her side. Her passing was mourned by the entire village that had once scorned her.

Percy and Gwyneth spent three school terms in Aberdeen while Percy completed his law degree, returning with great joy to Wales every summer.

Gwyneth inherited the title of viscountess and all the property of the Westbrooke estate on her twenty-fifth birthday. The day-to-day affairs of the estate continued to function as they had. All the people of the village and manor addressed both she and Katherine either as "Viscountess" or "Lady Gwyneth" and "Lady Katherine."

Gwyneth's only order as the new first lady of Snowdonia was that someone from one of the two houses—she or Katherine or Percy or Steven or Florilyn or Courtenay or Codnor or Adela—should visit the village every day, whether for a pint of Mistress Chattan's ale or a visit to one of the shops or even simply a ride on horseback through the main street. She was determined that everyone should have easy and unrestricted access to the viscountess and her people and know that their concerns would always be listened to and their needs attended to.

Steven continued as factor for the entire estate and all the affairs concerning both houses. He attempted to make Codnor his co-factor and spoke to both Gwyneth and Katherine with the request to formalize the office and pay Gwyneth's father accordingly. But Codnor would have none of it. The humble man would happily serve as his nephew's assistant and his daughter's willing servant, he said, but would accept no title nor pay for his services.

Percy apprenticed for two years under Hamilton Murray, riding into Porthmadog weekly, then established his own law practice from an office in the new house on Mochras Head. More than half the local cases that came his way he performed *gratis*. The new viscountess was determined to *serve* her people, not profit from them. Percy's gradually expanding reputation throughout Snowdonia and north Wales, however, along with regular referrals from Hamilton Murray, kept his legal practice mostly in the black.

The earl and Mrs. Drummond moved to Westbrooke Manor and lived out their days with their daughter attending lovingly to their every need. They died within a year of one another, both aged eighty-eight.

Though an invitation was sent them, Vanora and Daibheid Maloney declined to attend Gwyneth's wedding. Now that Gwyneth knew the details of her own personal history and of the sufferings the O'Sullivan and Maloney side of her family had endured, she longed to know her Irish relatives and see the Welsh and Irish strains reconciled. She was conscious, however, that not all the suffering had been accidental. It was clear that Daibheid Maloney had inflicted his own share of grief upon others. Nor could she seek to win the man's favor on the basis of what she had become. True reconciliation must be based on a recognition of her father's character and a desire on the part of Maloney to make amends with the man he had scorned and rebuffed.

Gwyneth and her father, therefore, planned a trip to Ireland and a visit to the home of Vanora and Daibheid Maloney. Vanora was cordial but concerned about her husband's reaction. After humble apologies by Codnor for his contribution to the family rift, a gradual thaw began in the heart of Daibheid Maloney toward his former friend and coworker. Several more visits over three or four years culminated in Gwyneth at last revealing to Daibheid Maloney the full truth of her inheritance. Her aunt Vanora rejoiced, wept freely at last to have it out in the open, and embraced the daughter of her beloved sister. Gwyneth's desire was to help the family financially to the extent Daibheid Maloney's pride would allow. It was the least she could do for her mother's family. All she was able to accomplish, however, after consultation with her father, was to turn over the deed to the house and land on Lugnaquilla. As the purchase had originated as a gift from the late viscount, Daibheid Maloney accepted the gift more freely than would have been possible had he considered it charity from Gwyneth's hand. Friendship with several of Gwyneth's Irish cousins in future years, and their children with her children, followed.

Cousin Henry's treatise on love, which Edward and Percy had read in manuscript, was finally published in book form in 1880. It became one of the best-selling and most beloved books on the Christian life ever published, and in coming decades sold an astonishing twelve million copies.

Inspired by what he had read from his young cousin Henry, and under the continued influence of the pen of George MacDonald, Edward Drummond wrote a book simply called *The Commands of Jesus*, urging obedience as the central and only priority of Christianity.

D. L. Moody returned to Britain between 1882 and 1884. Kyvwlch

Gwarthegydd served as a volunteer for the evangelist's meetings in Wales. Henry Drummond was again involved in Moody's work.

Moody later recalled a memorable night during the tiring campaign.

> *"I was staying with a party of friends in a country house during my visit to England in 1884,"* he wrote. *"On Sunday evening as we sat around the fire, they asked me to read and expound some portion of Scripture. Being tired after the services of the day, I told them to ask Henry Drummond, who was one of the party. After some urging he drew a small Testament from his hip pocket, opened it at the thirteenth chapter of First Corinthians, and began to speak on the subject of Love.*
>
> *"It seemed to me that I had never heard anything so beautiful, and I determined not to rest until I brought Henry Drummond to America to deliver that address. Since then I have requested the principals of my schools to have it read before the students every year. The one great need in our Christian life is love, more love to God and to each other. Would that we could all move into that Love chapter, and live there."*

Gwyneth sold what remained of the chest of gold to the British Museum in London for an undisclosed sum. The research of the museum's historians had identified the gold as from a cache at the ancient Celtic site of Dolau Cothi that had disappeared shortly after its discovery in the previous century, thought to have been stolen by pirates and never heard of again.

The actual value of the gold was impossible to determine. Seeking the advice of Hamilton Murray, Katherine, Steven, her father, and her own husband-lawyer, Gwyneth received no more from the sale than sufficient to recoup most of the losses of previous generations and thus place the affairs of the estate on a permanently sound financial footing again. Beyond that, she did not feel it right to profit from the discovery in excess of need. Rather, she considered it her duty to allow the museum to determine whatever future the coins should have, whether to keep them or sell a portion of the find as artifacts to help support the museum and finance its future acquisitions.

When Madame Fleming, a.k.a the Wolf Lady, of dubious reputation in Arklow, Ireland, died of natural causes, Gwyneth ordered her house demolished and all its contents burned.

Courtenay continued to race his horses with somewhat regular success. He won several more events at various tracks in England, though never another at such long odds as at the Chester Derby. After great effort, he convinced Gwyneth to jockey for a few of these. Her success convinced Courtenay that he had indeed discovered the golden goose. She only laughed at his plea that she become his permanent jockey, saying that she had more important concerns on which to expend her energies. To please him, however, she agreed to ride in one race a year. Courtenay's racing activities at last made full use of his father's new stables at the manor. A reputation began to follow him as one of north Wales's leading owners and jockeys. He was often seen in close counsel with Gwyneth, the two walking side by side, Courtenay towering a foot above her, picking her brain about some aspect of horse training or race preparation and strategy. It was a sight none would have expected but which made Katherine's heart swell.

Courtenay met the daughter of a horse breeder from Barmouth at the annual Chester Derby of 1879. They were married two years later. After a year at the manor, an illness prevented his father-in-law being able to keep up with the work and oversight of his stables. Courtenay and his wife moved to the Barmouth estate, taking with them Courtenay's gradually growing stable of thoroughbreds. There Courtenay took over the daily operation of the farm and business. He and his wife visited Llanfryniog frequently, however, bringing their children to visit their cousins and grandmother, while Courtenay slipped away to hold counsel with Gwyneth and Steven, whose knowledge and wisdom about animals and racing he respected more and more with every passing year. He was never able to bring himself to draw close to Percy, and they never formed what would be called a warm relationship. As brothers-in-law, however, Courtenay and Steven became the best of friends.

By her choice, Adela Muir continued in the role of staff manager at the manor for the rest of her life. As Florilyn's mother-in-law and aunt of the viscountess, her status in the home was as a family member. But she had to work, she said. It was the natural order of things. She could never be happy living a life of leisure. She and Katherine read every new MacDonald book they could get their hands on. Indeed, the Scottish bard and seer from Huntly continued to produce best-selling books at such a rate that the MacDonald shelf in the manor library grew to encompass nearly three shelves full of many editions and several thumb-worn copies of each title.

Codnor Barrie never worked in the slate mine again. With his nephew Steven, he developed a breed of sheep especially suited to the climate of north Wales. Their flocks roamed the hills of Snowdonia, and their wool was highly prized throughout Britain.

Lord Coleraine Litchfield was censured by the House of Lords when it was discovered that he had entered into a contract to purchase a tract of land on the Lleyn Peninsula under false pretenses. The ensuing scandal made all the papers, sullying Litchfield's reputation with charges of embezzlement and fraud. Whether formal criminal charges would be brought remained in doubt. His secretarial assistant, Palmer Sutcliffe, fled the country and was last reported to be somewhere in France. Bagge, Litchfield, and Sutcliffe all went to their graves, in that order, never seeing the gold they had so lusted after, and the secret of what lay under the lake died with them.

No one ever knew about the gold under the emerald Snowdonian lake until years later. After a long and serious summer's draught, one of Percy's and Gwyneth's adventurous grandchildren was exploring in the hills and came across the long-hidden cave. Hurriedly he rode back excitedly to the new house to tell his grandmother, the viscountess, of his discovery.

Steven and Florilyn had four children—three boys and a girl. Only one of the boys took after Steven. He grew into a burly youngster who loved the out-of-doors. By the age of twelve, he was already being touted as a future sheepshearing champion.

An altogether unexpected visitor appeared one day at the new house on Mochras Head. The girl who answered the door was new to the area and did not recognize the plump figure standing before her in the finest dress and hat she owned.

"Begging your pardon, miss," said the woman, obviously nervous, "but would your mistress, the viscountess, I mean. . .is she at home, miss? If I could just have a word with her, you see."

The girl disappeared into the house. Gwyneth appeared a minute later dressed in a working frock, wiping her hands with a kitchen towel. Even on her usually placid countenance, the surprise was instantly visible.

"Hello, Mistress Chattan," she said. "It is nice to see you. Won't you come in?"

"No, Miss. . .I mean, begging your pardon—Lady Gwyneth, that is. I'll just stay here and say my piece."

"How can I be of service to you, Mistress Chattan?" asked Gwyneth.

From somewhere in the folds of her expansive dress, the innkeeper pulled a dry, faded cluster of what appeared to be dead wildflowers and grasses.

"Do you know this?" she asked, showing it to Gwyneth.

Gwyneth smiled. "Is it one of mine?" she said.

"You left it on my back door one day many years ago. I had been rude to you that day, you see. But like you always did, you returned me kindness for it. I'm sorry to say, I cursed you that day and threw this on the floor. But something made me pick it up the next day, and I can't say why, but I saved it all this time. I wanted you to know that I'm sorry for the times I was rude to you. You were a good girl, and you've become a fine lady, and I'm hoping you'll forgive me for whatever unkind words I spoke to you."

Gwyneth's eyes filled with tears. "Oh, Mistress Chattan, of course you are forgiven. You are a dear for saving one of my little forgiveness bouquets all this time!" She stepped forward and stretched her arms around the great bulk of the woman who was more than twice her size.

Mistress Chattan had not cried in years. Nor did she cry now. But she came dangerously close.

"Please. . ." said Gwyneth as she stepped back, "won't you come in and have tea with me. I would enjoy it very much. I would like to show you the beautiful view of the sea from our sitting room."

With a nervous but appreciative smile, feeling greatly lightened from the release of her long-carried burden of conscience, Mistress Chattan nodded then followed Gwyneth inside.

Chandos Gwarthegydd married Mistress Chattan's niece from Dolgellau. The innkeeper's personal life had always been so shrouded in mystery that no one really knew where she had come from or whether she had living relatives at all. The identity of Chandos's bride was greeted with many questions. Little was learned, however, beyond the fact that she was the daughter of Mistress Chattan's brother. A beautifully incongruous relationship developed between the hulking young blacksmith and the aging aunt of his wife. The two young people took care of her during her final years with the most tender kindness imaginable. When the Keeper of the Ale died at the age of seventy-three, a handwritten will was found in her cash box, which Percy confirmed as legal and binding. It left the inn and all its contents to Chandos's wife. The building that housed the inn and pub was one of the few in the village that was privately owned and not the property of the viscount or viscountess of Snowdon.

Chandos continued blacksmithing with his father. An increasing amount of his time, however, was spent on his wife's new enterprise. They upgraded, restored, and added several rooms, turning it into a seacoast hotel of some repute. Many of those bound for the village on the north- or southbound coaches got out at the hotel and remained in Llanfryniog for several days. The pub of the newly renamed *Chattan Arms* continued to serve the best ale in Snowdonia.

Percy and Gwyneth had five children, three boys and two girls.

As Katherine's hair gradually turned a silvery white, her countenance took on more and more the radiance of that quiet, humble, peaceful, wise daughterhood that only lifelong attentiveness to the commands of Christ can produce in God's women. She continued to read and reread the works of the Scotsman, along with her brother's writings. With every passing year, she became more deeply convinced that the answers to life's quandaries were to be found in uncomplicated, practical obedience to the words of Jesus. All her grandchildren adored her and took every opportunity to scamper into her lap, where they felt at home, content, and at peace.

One morning in early summer, bright and warm, as Percy sat at the breakfast table with his tea, a girl of six and a boy of three walked into the room, rubbing their eyes and looking about.

"Daddy, where's mummy?" asked the girl.

"I don't know, sweetheart," replied Percy. "I haven't seen her this morning. Would you like something to eat?"

"Yes, please, Daddy."

After Percy had the two situated at the table, with glasses of milk and a plate of oatcakes in front of them, he left the house. A glance north and south along the promontory revealed nothing. He continued around the north wing of the house until his gaze opened toward the hills of Snowdonia eastward from the coastline.

On a green hillside in the distance he saw a simply dressed figure walking through the grass as it sloped up toward the inland ridge that overlooked Tremadog Bay. The light hair bathed in sunlight was unmistakable.

He smiled as he saw her stoop to the ground. He knew what she was doing. She was plucking wildflowers.

Gwyneth would always be Gwyneth, thought Percy with a full heart. Deep inside, she would never *really* be a viscountess, whatever people might call her. She would always be the mysterious daughter of the Snowdonian hills whose childlike nature spread life and goodness wherever she went.

A Few Notes of Interest from Michael Phillips

The account of D. L. Moody's first British mission in 1873 and 1874, though brief, is recounted as accurately as possible from the historical records. In that mission, twenty-five-year-old Henry Drummond took leave from his divinity studies in order to join the mission as a volunteer. He formed a great friendship with Moody that lasted for the rest of their lives. The draft of the manuscript on love that he had begun working on that same year, 1873, was not finally published until 1880, seven years later. *The Greatest Thing in the World* became an international best seller and has been profoundly influencing Christians toward Christlikeness ever since.

After bidding farewell to Scotland in September of 1874, Moody sailed to Ireland. There for over three months he held meetings in Belfast and Ireland. When at length he returned to England, reports of the earlier revival in Scotland sparked greater interest than had been present earlier. At last the English were ready to listen enthusiastically to D. L. Moody. For the next ten months, huge crowds in Liverpool, Manchester, Birmingham, and London flocked to hear the evangelist. The number of converts was beyond counting. Moody's comments about Drummond's farmhouse talk on love during his visit to England a few years later is quoted directly from Moody's own reminiscences.

Henry Drummond died in 1897 at the young age of 47, but his vision of "the greatest thing" lives on through this work for which he continues to be revered in the annals of Christian writers.

The mountain Lugnaquilla is the thirteenth highest peak in Ireland at 925 meters and the country's highest mountain outside Kerry. There are a number of routes up to the flat peak, known as "Percy's Table," which is often shrouded in mist, though when clear it affords distant and spectacular views. However there are also several treacherous ridges, cliffs, bouldery outcroppings, and severe slopes, making good weather or expert navigation a necessity for the hiker unfamiliar with Lugnaquilla's many secrets.

Some may perhaps have found it unusual for one fiction book to play such a key role in another. I employed the works of George MacDonald in this way to highlight a point that most fiction readers know so well—the power of fictional characters, if they are truly drawn and real to life, by their struggles and failings and triumphs, to profoundly affect our lives. My desire was not merely to dedicate this volume to George MacDonald, but to convey something of the unique power of his writing. I am certain many of you are already well acquainted with his books. If you are not, you may learn more at the website www.FatherOfTheInklings.com, where you will also find ordering information for MacDonald's original titles as well as my own redacted editions of his work. The title that plays such a prominent role in *Treasure of the Celtic Triangle* is available in both formats, as *David Elginbrod* or *The Tutor's First Love*. These may be found through any online book service, or at www.FatherOfTheInklings.com/the-bookstore/sunrise-centenary-editions/.

For the MacDonald readers among you, I must confess to one stretching of historical verisimilitude. The quote in chapter 57 discovered by Steven in the library was taken from MacDonald's book *Donal Grant,* which was in actual fact not yet published at the time. It was published in 1882, eight years later. I hope purists will forgive my use of this one of MacDonald's central themes for the sake of the story. This quote, too, as well as several of the others, has been slightly paraphrased for brevity. All the other of MacDonald's books that are mentioned and quoted from were available at the times where they appeared in the story and were indeed being read avidly throughout England, Scotland, and Wales.

The gold rush in County Wicklow, Ireland, during the end of the eighteenth and early nineteenth centuries, took place substantially as described. There was also substantial gold mining in the Snowdonian region of North Wales.

If you enjoyed these two books set in Wales, you might also like my recent doublet set in the northernmost region of the Celtic Triangle, Scotland. They are entitled *Angel Harp* and *Heather Song*.

MICHAEL PHILLIPS (b. 1946) is one of the best-selling and most beloved Christian novelists of our generation, author of dozens of books of great diversity, both historical and contemporary.

Phillips began his distinguished writing career in 1977 with several nonfiction titles. Since that time, he has authored over twenty nonfiction books, most notably dealing with the nature and character of God and the fatherhood of God. His loyal readership through the years has come to depend on the signature tune running through all his writings—the personal call to what Phillips calls bold-thinking Christianity. After turning to the writing of novels in the mid-1980s, Phillips has penned some sixty fiction titles of wide-reaching scope and variety. The enormous breadth of his faithful audience is testimony that his writings are universal in their appeal.

He is also one of many in a rising generation of spiritual offspring of C. S. Lewis, George MacDonald, and the legacy of the Inklings. Phillips is widely known as George MacDonald's redactor, publisher, and biographer, whose vision and editorial expertise helped bring MacDonald back from obscurity when his realistic novels had been nearly forgotten. After discovering the writings of the Victorian Scotsman whose books were foundational in leading C. S. Lewis out of atheism into Christianity, Phillips made it his life's work to bring to public attention the literary and spiritual links between MacDonald and Lewis, and to promote the teachings of these giants of the past. If MacDonald is the "father of the Inklings," Phillips calls himself one of thousands of "sons of the Inklings." His multidimensional efforts helped ignite the MacDonald renaissance of recent years and have resulted in a new generation of readers having access to MacDonald's books again for themselves.

As one of those responsible for the widespread renewal of MacDonald's influence, Phillips is recognized as among the world's foremost purveyors of MacDonald's message, with particular insight into the Scotsman's heart and spiritual vision.

As his own volume of work reaches a stature of significance in its own right, Phillips is regarded as one of many successors to MacDonald's vision and spiritual legacy for a new generation.

For a complete listing of books by Michael Phillips,
see www.FatherOfTheInklings.com, or write to the author at:
P. O. Box 7003, Eureka, CA 95502.

Discussion Questions

1. Many readers of fiction agree with Thomas Jefferson (quoted at the beginning) that books of fiction and imagination are powerful to move us, and "contribute to fix us in the principles and practice of virtue." Discuss Jefferson's comment in light of people who downplay the power of fiction. What are some of the fiction books that have been most influential in your life to motivate you toward "the principles and practice of virtue"?

2. Did you like or dislike the literary device of using one fictional book within another—George MacDonald's *David Elginbrod* playing a pivotal role in *this* fictional story? Share from your experience when a book you have read—and the struggles, thoughts, and growth of its characters—has influenced you, perhaps even contributing toward some major decision in your life. Do you think it is realistic to base decisions on lessons learned from fictional characters? In what circumstances? How has fiction contributed to your spiritual life and your inner walk with God?

3. How do you respond when super-spiritual types say, "I don't have time for fiction. I only read what's real?" or "I only read the Bible." Do you want to remind them that Jesus used fiction more than any other technique to convey truth? Discuss Jesus' use of stories to communicate deep spiritual principles to His listeners.

4. What kinds of fiction are most able to "fix us in the principles and practice of virtue"? Edgy, dramatic, fast-paced, and sometimes morally explicit fiction is very much in vogue today—even in Christian fiction. How does "edgy" fiction move us toward living lives of virtue? Or does it? To be realistic, is a novelist required to explore life's dark side? George MacDonald (also quoted at the beginning) was clear in saying that he was *not* interested in writing

about "spoilt humanity," but rather wanted to point his readers toward goodness: "I will try to show what we might be, may be, must be, shall be—and something of the struggle to gain it." We could say that MacDonald, like Jesus, was not interested in "edgy" fiction but in stories where *goodness* was the true hero of the story and where his characters were striving to attain it. Do you agree or disagree with this motive for a novelist? Is it unrealistic to want to model our lives after good characters in stories?

5. In my novels, I always try to set up an array of characters—good, bad, and in between—and put them in situations that pull and tug on their motivations, challenging them with spiritual truth. Then I sit back and watch what each becomes. Fiction, in my opinion, is all about watching characters *grow*. Some characters grow toward God, toward truth, toward goodness, and toward maturity. . .others grow away from them. When this series began, what did you expect of the various characters? Which ones surprised you? Which were most realistic or unrealistic?

6. How did you respond to Florilyn and Percy calling off their engagement? When the first book ended, did you think their decision to marry was a little too hasty? Did you see trouble on their horizon? Discuss how marriages might be strengthened if more couples had the humility and courage to honestly assess whether they are moving too quickly.

7. On the other hand, how did you respond to Gwyneth's willingness to marry a man her father chose for her? Did you consider her willing attitude realistic? Is her perspective—"I will learn to love him"—an adequate foundation for a good marriage?

8. Percy was in an awkward position, caught between his promise to his uncle and his desire to protect his aunt from hurt. He was uncomfortable being what he felt was less than truthful, but he

saw no other way to achieve both ends than by being vague. Did you feel that he compromised truthfulness in what he told his aunt and his father? If so, how should he have handled it differently?

9. Discuss Florilyn's changeability. Did you feel it was realistic that she altered so dramatically from the selfish girl she was before to seemingly becoming a young woman of strength and character. . . only to then fall prey to Colville's deceptive charms? What do you consider was the chief cause of the "backsliding" of Florilyn's attitudes and outlook—Colville's working division in her mind between herself and those around her, or her own mixed and confused emotions about her relationship with Percy?

10. Who is the central character in *From Across the Ancient Waters* and *Treasure of the Celtic Triangle*? Whose influence is most pervasive in impacting the other characters? Whom do you want to know more about?

A final word: We realize most of you will be using these questions in discussion groups and book clubs. However, Judy and I would be most interested for you to share with us your responses to these questions, or any ideas raised by these or other books of mine. We would love to hear from you! We may be reached either through the website www.FatherOfTheInklings.com or at: P. O. Box 7003, Eureka, CA 95502.